CANOWIC

To my brother

CAN
OWI
C

A Novel

BEN BISHOP

BOOK I

...

Chapter One

HANKASI

. . .

In early spring of the Year of the Rat, Hankasi, self-styled Lord of Lords, led his war band into the woods above Aghuax to open the raiding season. As they slid through the shadow of Char Gate, the banners on their lances fluttered in the warm breeze coming off the bay. They skirted the wooded flanks of Merwa, traveling six days and six nights until they reached the edge of a vast steppe beyond which they knew of no other land save what legend surmised.

Hankasi's scouts reconnoitered the lush plain by starlight and returned with news of an encampment. At dawn, with a dusting of frost still white on the turf, the raiders rose up from the bottom of a long swale wherein they had lain hidden through the night and edged their ponies into a sinuous, cantering line. Tattered morning mist streamed from the horses' flanks as they surged forward.

The camp was a loose confederation of herders gathered for their annual festival to gods of grass and rain; small children and nursing mothers and the elderly swaddled alongside the men in tents of bone and stretched hide. A handful of women were already up, reviving dim coals in that predawn stillness when the world trembles softly. They looked up from the ashes of their fires at the sound of a great beast shaking the ground like a boar shakes fleas from its hide.

The first soul the line overtook was a young boy with a harelip. Caught out alone in the grass the boy stood transfixed by the wall of horseflesh thundering towards him, scattering his terrified stock. A warrior swung low from his saddle, face violet in the breaking sun, and struck the boy across his forehead with the heel of his hand. Moments later another rider, scarcely older than the boy himself, leaned down and ran him through with a lance. The boy's willow goad fell from his lifeless hands and disappeared into the thick grass.

The war band broke across the camp like a powerful surf, black hair flying, faces done up in midnight oils, the blood of their pre-battle offerings spilling down their chins. They screamed like birds of prey as they hacked at children and loosed flaming arrows at the tents. Riding in the van came Hankasi, son of Teshuwa, king of the Ancagua, his piebald pony's mane interwoven with fetishes and pieces of bone.

On his first pass through the camp he glimpsed a face peeking out of a tent. Moving at a dead gallop he sawed his reins mercilessly, bringing his mount up short and heeling it straight into the assortment of hides. As he burst through the flap the smoke of a cook fire temporarily blinded him. His horse shied from the coals, knocking against a support pole and threatening to bring down the entire tent. In the dimness and confusion a young woman ran past him clutching a bundle to her chest.

In one motion, Hankasi backed out of the collapsing tent and dropped to the ground. He caught up with the girl after only a few strides and grasped her wrist, but she wrenched free, clawing at his face while shielding what he could now see was a newborn baby with her other arm. Enraged, the king ripped the infant from her grasp and hurled it to the ground. She screamed and dove for the child, but it was too late.

As the girl lay wailing on the ground, cradling her baby's broken body, an old man crawled from the wreckage of the tent and began hobbling toward Hankasi. He was shouting in a foreign tongue, and his eyes were ablaze with sorrow and rage. It was a measure of the blackness of Hankasi's heart that he laughed to see the old man so distraught. He watched as his captain, Yengwa, stepped in front of the doddering fool and swung his war hammer at the man's temple, dropping him like a side of meat cut from a drying rack.

Dust hung in the air like chaff while the dirge of battle droned on; the crackle of fire, the screams of the dying, the chime of metal on metal, and the trampling of hooves all blending together. Hankasi looked down at the full figure of the girl where she was crumpled in the mud. He started to lift his loincloth. Suddenly a jet of white-hot fire bloomed in his side. He winced and doubled over. A few yards away stood a boy with an empty bow, staring incredulously at the feathered shaft protruding from the king's ribs.

The young archer trembled all over. He did not run when Hankasi began to weave unsteadily towards him, nor did he resist when the wound-drunk king grasped a thatch of his hair and stared into his bright green eyes, wide as a frightened calf's. When Hankasi slit his gosling throat, a bubble of red saliva rose to the boy's lips and burst. He dropped to his knees beside the young woman, gasping for breath, his life a thin stick snapped easily over the king's knee.

Yengwa rushed to Hankasi's side, the war bells on his ankles jangling softly.

"You are struck, lord."

"You worry like a woman," Hankasi said, breaking the arrow off with a grimace. "It is nothing."

But he was wrong.

Chapter Two

CANOWIC

. . .

C anowic ignored the fiery cold waters surging around her ankles and tugging her toward the bay, just as she disregarded the gulls wheeling through the fog overhead. The birds were sacred animals, severe messengers able to commune with the drowned. The fishermen threw them offerings on their way home each night in an attempt to appease the sea. Normally, Canowic would have heeded their cries and at least bowed to them. But today she paid them no mind. Her focus lay further down the beach, where the procession was drawing near. The magi were coming.

As she straddled the tideline, the between-place where land converged with sea and the membrane of the other world thinned, she thought of haughty Remerac dancing along the rim of a crater in the stories the magi told. Now the sorcerers reached the crowd. The people melted away before them, hurrying to open a path through their midst. The magi wound along in single file, completely covered by their vermilion robes, the heavy cowls hiding even their faces from view. Four of them bore a palanquin on their shoulders, a moving house with velvet curtains drawn about its inner chamber.

The line of hooded figures tailed the litter like the body of a snake, with the High Mage himself walking in the rear. When the palanquin's curtains were drawn back and the idol of Teulanic was removed and set upon the sand that it might observe the coming rite, Canowic felt a wave of power impinge on her mind. A throb started up behind her temples.

The widowed queen waited off to the side with her head held high. Even at this remove Canowic could detect her revulsion as the sorcerers passed by. Muttering in fell voices, they began to circle the funeral pyre.

Like everyone in Aghuax, Canowic knew Kulkas had been only a girl when she was taken captive. Dragged off to be an unwilling bride here amongst the People of Unruly Seas. Although it was covered by a mourning veil, Canowic could picture the queen's face perfectly. The gently hooked nose curving down toward her mouth like the tip of a warrior's blade; the fathomless eyes that seemed to change color depending on the light; the lush, severe brows; the hollow in her neck that sometimes flushed pink. Her skin, though unblemished and smooth as cream, was considered ugly by the Ancagua for its light color, but to Canowic she was beautiful.

The queen normally wore giant discs of jade in her ear lobes, traditional ornaments of the Odmarsim that Hankasi had allowed her to keep and wear despite the whisperings of his court. Some of the warriors and advisors who frequented the king's Council felt that his foreign wife weakened him. Though they never vocalized their disdain for the impurity Kulkas introduced to the royal line, their feelings were common knowledge.

Today the queen had traded her jade discs for black horn,

a symbol of the bereaved. Canowic was surprised. Hankasi had been a cruel man, and it was difficult to imagine Kulkas mourning him. On the queen's head there rested a diadem of six blood red stones; six stars for the six lords of the magi. Though flanked on either side by her daughters and handmaidens, Kulkas seemed utterly alone, waiting in the silent chamber of her heart for what the day would bring.

Canowic had seen the princesses before, on one of the rare occasions she had gone to the castle with the shaman. The eldest, Gikzil, had sat quietly on a calfskin stool next to her mother's white throne, taking everything in with the same steady gaze. Though still just a child, there was something indomitable about her. Ontec, the middle girl, was completely different. She had squirmed in the chief handmaiden's arms while the king discussed the upcoming harvest with his advisers. At one point she broke away and scurried over to the ornate sandalwood rack near the entrance to the throne room where visitors left their slippers. Grabbing a pair of kidskin boots, she ran to the nearest warrior and held them out, as if informing him it was time to go. Hankasi had been in a black mood, and the warrior's good-natured laugh had been all that saved Ontec from a beating. Now, Gikzil fixed the turning magi with the same unblinking stare Canowic remembered from court, while Ontec buried her head in her mother's skirts, her little legs trembling as she tried to hide herself.

For close to an hour the magi circumambulated the funeral bed in a slow shuffle, lifting their voices with increasing urgency as they called upon their gods to draw near. Their interminable chanting was finally cut off by the sudden doom of drums. The magi fell silent as the burial guard appeared. The warriors' faces were painted white as corpses. The muscles in their arms bulged as they struggled through the sand, carrying above them a brightly colored war canoe in which lay the body of their lord. They were led forth by the king's favored concubine, a lithe young woman with bangles on her arms. Her body was visible beneath a sheer garment dyed green as the life-giving sea. She came bearing a curved horn and singing the song of the Tombmaidens in a strange, lilting voice. Everything was still and quiet save for the scornful call of the gulls and the concubine's broken incantation as she led the warriors toward the pyre.

Beyond the pyre a teeming throng spread out across the beach, wrapped in blankets and hides against the unseasonable chill. All morning the people had murmured in their thousands, their breath steaming in the air. They waited on their king one final time while ghostly white tatters swirled down the beach, the fog tearing and reforming and insinuating itself into the spaces between them, chilling them to the roots of their hair.

Aghuax had begun to empty before dawn, starting with a few discreet figures winding their way toward Diamond Gate through streets still thick with the last of night's darkness. These forerunners had arrived at the beach to find the true early risers, the meat sellers, already waiting, their charcoal braziers crackling optimistically in anticipation of the crowds. As the sky began to lighten in the east, the ones and twos swelled to a steady stream, and by the time the sun dipped its first finger into the waters of the bay the strand was nearly full.

The excitement that might have accompanied such a large gathering was soured by an anxiety that hung thick as musk in the air. The members of the war band not involved with the burial guard stood watching, their faces like chiseled monoliths. Old men swayed in their heavy robes. Tentwives chewed pieces of doe fat and gossiped quietly while babes dozed on their backs. Some of these same women stared at Canowic where she stood separated from the crowd, their scornful eyes reminding her that she would never be one of them.

Early in the morning a group of raucous young men had drifted by. Mere boys really, their faces painted in dark oils like the warriors they longed to be. They hooted like owls, calling for her to expose herself. Canowic had taken up a rock and started walking toward them, eyebrows raised, inviting them to test her. One of the boys groped himself while his friends laughed, then doubled over as Canowic's stone struck him hard in the thigh. There had been a moment of stunned silence, quickly followed by an explosion of vile profanities. They called her the daughter of a prostituted horse. She picked up another rock.

Though they screamed their lungs out she knew they would not come near. Fear of magic kept them away. The deerskin hood on her head marked Canowic as an acolyte scryer, a searcher of hidden ways and a reader of stars and stones. She was also standing in front of the cave she dwelt in with her master. Some amongst the Ancagua feared being seen near the cave now that the shaman was at odds with the magi. Others feared the cave itself, believing the very rocks were infused with the powers of its inhabitants.

Then there were the wolves. They had watched the morning's proceedings with a fixed intensity from the mouth of the cave. When the heckling clutch of boys arrived they had risen as one. After Canowic picked up her second stone, three of the wolves trotted over to stand next to her, scattering the boys like doves.

That had been hours before. Now everyone in the city was focused on the funeral pageant, ignoring her for more important matters. Canowic felt a roiling in her stomach. She did not understand why, but the sight of the dead king being borne aloft brought on a feeling of longing. She knew the end of one thing often signaled the beginning of another—the blossoms of the world falling to the earth to bloom again.

Canowic loved her master and the wolves. They had always kept her safe and given her their full acceptance. It was not safety she found herself longing for, though, nor even love. The familiar pang lancing her heart had to do with something else. She wanted to know *who she was*, why she found herself here, an outcast amongst these cold people. She was not one of them, and she never would be.

When the shaman appeared beside her it was as though he had risen silently from the ground or materialized from thin air. His skin, dark from years of salt and sun, shone like burnished bronze, the muscles underneath taut despite his venerable age. His eyes were banded with charcoal, and about his shoulders he wore a cape of raven feathers that rustled softly in the breeze. Another wave came in. Like his acolyte, the shaman seemed not to notice the cold.

"The king draws near," he said, his smile both wry and wistful as he watched the warriors lower Hankasi onto the stacked wood. When he spoke again his voice was quiet, and he seemed to be remembering something long past.

"So this is the day of your final journey. How certain you were it would not end like this."

Chapter Three

SENECWO

. . .

K ulkas turned from the sight of her dead husband being borne down the beach to attend to her daughters. Her first-born was putting on a brave face, but failing to hide the tears swimming in her new-moon eyes. Kulkas ran her fingers through both girls' hair and leaned down to whisper in their ears.

"Peace, my daughters," she murmured. "Take heart. All is not lost."

As she stroked their hair she called them by their secret names, which she had bestowed upon each of them on the nights of their birth as they slept at her breast. Knowing that every child's foot began treading against the wheel of fate as soon as they came screaming into the world, and believing deeply in the power the magic of naming held to bless and to curse, she had wasted no time in covering her own brood with the shroud of a first name, sealing them against any sorcery to come.

At sunset on the fourth day following the birth of her first child, Hankasi and his magi had arrived in the queen's chambers without warning and pulled the child from her breast despite her screams. The guards locked her in, refusing to open the door though she cried herself hoarse and beat on it until her hands were bloody. She stayed up all night, pacing her chambers, pulling at her hair, kneeling in anguish. When a servant finally returned the baby in the morning the queen anxiously pored over her tiny body, searching for signs of harm but finding nothing until she came across scorch marks on the tender skin of her daughter's feet. She shuddered, picturing a ceremony in a dark cavern beneath the castle, and whispered the girl's name over and over as if to wash any evil away.

The feeling of helplessness she had felt on that night had thrown fresh fuel on the fire that burned in her soul. This same fire had raged unabated in her since the day she first laid eyes on Hankasi, a glowing flame that led her to seek any way in which to assert herself, reminding the king and his pack of curs that she was not weak, and would never submit like a dog.

The firstborn the magi had called Gikzil, which translates to "disappointment," for Hankasi had desired a son. They dedicated her to the handmaids of Ahurewa, the mistress of Teulanic, not knowing that her mother had already named her Leokita, Star of Light. The second girl they named Ontec, Bearer of Chains, but to the queen she was Mictanta, Rosy Lips. The third child, the infant currently lying in the arms of the chief handmaiden, was known to her father as Kulza, which means "agony" in the tongue of the magi, but her mother treasured her as Kisoko, the Harvester of Hearts.

Before he had torn any of her children away, the High Mage, Ixiltical, had renamed the queen herself. It had happened on the day she was wedded to Hankasi. The chief of the Tomic magi had taken her chin in his hand and pierced her nose with a piece of shark bone in front of all the people. Ignoring the blood running into her mouth and the tears in her eyes, he had looked at Hankasi as he proclaimed her Kulkas,

Empress of the Broken Moon. In that moment a memory of her father had come to her. The sound of his voice as he spoke her name on a summer night with the cicadas harrowing the trees.

"Senecwo."

Her name sounded like a rich dish on his lips. In the language of her people it meant, The Helper. It was this name—her own secret name— by which the queen would forever measure herself.

. . .

Mictanta turned her face up at the sound of her mother's voice, her tear-streaked cheeks ripping Senecwo's heart a little further open. But she couldn't let the girl see. Instead, she offered a comforting smile. She knew her daughters did not hide their faces because of sorrow. Their father had rarely showed them any kindness. He had paid his daughters little attention, parading them before the people on festival days but otherwise leaving them to the care of their mother, whom he increasingly disdained for her inability to produce a son. The girls hardly knew Hankasi. No, it was not sadness that set them on edge, but fear.

The warriors with their faces painted white as death and heads half shorn in mourning scared them. They were also frightened by the seething crowds assembled on the beach. Attuned with the prescience of children to the hidden motives of others, they sensed animosity in the twisted faces of the crones and the young men, seal traders and grizzled mothers, lesser warriors and deeply tanned fishermen all staring at them from the corners of their eyes.

Looking up from her girls, Senecwo noticed movement down the beach. At the far end of the strand the shaman's acolyte was looking back at her, the creamy hide of her hood standing out against the darkness of a huge boulder. The queen silently tongued the girl's name in her mind

—*Canowic*—a beautiful name for such a lonely-looking girl. Senecwo felt something familiar lapping against the shore of her heart. Then the sound of the concubine's disembodied laughter drew her attention back to the procession. It was the laughter of one whose spirit is far away, set adrift by the sacred wine in her horn. The warriors had reached the pyre and were lowering the king onto the wood.

Hankasi's corpse rested atop a thick bed of skins that lifted him up so his face and torso were visible above the edge of the canoe. One of the warriors leaned forward and placed a clay jar of wine in the dead king's hands, while another fitted his feet with fawn-skin boots that he might stalk his prey quietly on the long hunting journey ahead of him. A third removed his circlet of gold and fitted his brow with a ring of leaves. Their blades lisped gently in the wind. These tasks accomplished, the warriors moved off toward a green linen tent standing nearby.

The people of the city were arrayed across from Senecwo, held back by some invisible line. They had whispered all morning, an echo of the susurrating bay. The queen wondered what, if anything, they had been told about her that was true. Right and custom held that she would now ascend to the throne. But custom did not always hold with the Ancagua. She was a foreigner, and one who had produced only daughters. She knew they hated her, and Hankasi for having married her. In their minds she was the usurper of a great inheritance, however unwilling she had been. Now they began to whisper again. They knew what was going on in the tent.

The warriors waited patiently outside. One at a time they entered, each man laying down his lance before ducking under the horse mane fetishes and dried shark meat hung at the entrance. Inside, they found the concubine waiting on a bed of cushions, naked to the wind and drunk on the bloodwine that filled her horn. Each in their turn the warriors entered her, putting their life into her. Upon finishing, each man spoke the ritual words, "Tell my master I did this out of my love for him."

While the warriors discharged their final duty to their lord, the High Mage moved forward with a smoldering bundle and began to prowl around the canoe, his jerky, stork-like movements punctuated by the crack of breakers snapping across the bay's long reef. As he circled the king's feet with his burning herbs, preparing him for the long journey into sunset lands, Senecwo wondered where Hankasi had really gone upon death. Whether there was any god willing to take him in. The sight of the mage daubing his sacred oil in the dead man's sightless eyes made her blink. The breeze was picking up now, turning the lips of the waves to froth. Senecwo felt the gooseflesh rising on her arms.

Chapter Four

CANOWIC

. . .

D own at the end of the beach Canowic pulled her cloak tighter and imagined the Tombmaidens wheeling their smoldering chariots out of the gates of Usthil. She wondered if the pressure building inside her chest had to do with their arrival, which, though invisible, she felt as surely as the changing of the wind. She noticed the warriors entering the tent, but found it difficult to tear her eyes away from the queen. This was not only because of the woman's majestic bearing, which commanded the attention of all who encountered her; it was because she was one of the few people in Aghuax who looked like Canowic.

There were others in the city. Men and women with the same long necks, their light skin so starkly different from the burnished, cinnamon limbs of the Ancagua. Canowic would occasionally encounter them in the market. They always seemed cloaked in sadness, the corners of their eyes crinkled prematurely, the worry lines in their faces worn deep as spring gullies. Most of those who made up this harried minority were slaves dragged from the villages and mountain holds Hankasi had stormed. Whenever she saw them, Canowic's pity was interwoven with intense curiosity.

The queen was different. She comported herself with a self-possession that, along with her mesmerizing appearance, transfixed the young acolyte, pinning her attention like a butterfly to parchment. For now, the queen's eyes were focused on the soft green fabric of the funeral tent fluttering just beyond the pyre.

Upon exiting the tent, the warriors retrieved their lances and laid them at Hankasi's feet, more fuel to speed him home the faster. Yengwa exited last. Canowic's lips parted in a sneer as he emerged. The pure white clay he wore for the ceremony made his disfigured face that much more hideous, caking in the scarred ruts that devoured his cheek and neck. He assumed a position at the head of the canoe with his back to Canowic, but she could imagine his eyes, heavy-lidded as a basilisk's and void of sorrow or regret.

Yengwa was famous for his cruelty. Stories were told of his having tied the legs of pregnant women together in childbirth, and he was said to use the cured tongues of slaves as chew things for the king's hunting dogs. Canowic had her own reason for hating him.

The shaman's cloak of feathers rustled softly beside her. Canowic turned to find him craning his neck toward the sky. Axal, the Dark Star, bleakest of the evening portents, had appeared the night before. Despite the sun's rising, it still hung fat in the east like a dangling egg sack. Canowic followed her master's gaze for a moment, staring at the un-star's light-eating corona before letting her eyes drop back to the pyre where Ixiltical was advancing with hands upheld. His lips moved and green flames danced along the wood. Now the freezing water seemed like a ward, its cold tongues reassuring against her skin as she watched the flames trickle toward the king's flesh. Her master's presence beside her was a comfort. She wondered what was going through his mind.

. . .

There had been a time when the shaman was afforded great respect and a high seat at the tables of a succession of kings, up to and including Hankasi's father. No one amongst the Ancagua, including even the circle of elders, knew when he had come to live in the seaside cave. He had simply always been there, coming and going as he pleased. But times had changed. The shaman made no secret of his disdain for the magi. Indeed, he alone amongst the people seemed not to fear them. Now the citizens of Aghuax spurned him along with his gods, whispering in his shadow when he came to the city, heaping ignominy on his name and spreading rumors about his liaisons with his foreign acolyte.

Perhaps they hated him for not being cowed as they were, or for reminding them of their infidelities. He was possessed of powers and integrities they had forsaken. And though he could have dispatched them with a flick of his wrist, he did not, for he loved them.

There was much the people of the great city had forgotten about the shaman, but stories still abounded about him and his predecessors. Some of these held that the ancient shamans were able to take the shape of living beasts. It was rumored that Canowic's master could assume the form of a bear, though none had seen him do it and only a few believed he could. Of those few who yet believed, a handful still came to see him.

Most of these were old and frail; widowers, invalids, the unimportant and poor. The forgotten and the neglected. The shaman would make sacrifices on their behalf and listen to them. Sometimes, if the occasion called for it, he would read his stone and advise them regarding what he had seen in its mists. In secret, these motley rebels still referred to the shaman by his other, still more ancient name, Walks The Stars.

One day two old women came to the cave. Both were bent and hobbled with age, but one was nearly unable to walk. Her companion was helping her limp down the beach, supporting the weaker woman with an arm around the waist. The sufferer leaned heavily on a cane of gnarled wood. Her face was drawn and haggard and she listed to one side like a tree in a stiff wind. As they tottered up to the mouth of the cave, the shaman laid out several pelts and helped the weaker woman lay down, displaying a tenderness that might have surprised the people of the city.

"What troubles you, sister?"

"My back," the woman wheezed. "For months the pain has grown worse. I woke this morning barely able to walk."

"And you have come to me," the shaman murmured, holding her hand. "Some would not take kindly to knowing it."

This was an understatement. The magi had threatened any who denied the majesty of their Desert Lords with death. Perhaps the woman was too old to be frightened, Canowic thought. A gleam kindled in the old crone's eyes.

"Those worms who have bewitched the king," she said, her lips twisting into a disdainful smile. "They have threatened us, yes. But what can they do to me? I am already in agony."

She paused to catch her breath, as if even speaking was exhausting. Then she patted the shaman's hand, wincing with the effort. "I know you can help me."

Canowic wondered at the woman's belief. In all her years living with the shaman she had never seen him physically heal someone, yet this woman seemed confident. Maybe it was desperation, a lack of other options. Maybe she was senile.

Something passed across the shaman's face, brightening his features for a moment, as if the sun had lanced through a boiling cloud. Then the master was reaching for the woman's other hand, taking it in his own.

"It is time to dance."

. . .

That evening, as the sun distended and fell into the bloody sea, a tattered band descended on the cave. Dressed in the rags and skins of beggars, they shambled across the sand, shadows trailing behind them like oily streams of paint. Their faces were hidden by masks, some depicting birds or animals, others blank pieces of driftwood with only slits for eyes.

The shaman had set Canowic to building a bonfire, and as the stars began to appear she threw another pair of logs on, sending a shower of sparks kicking upward. The shaman moved the injured woman near the fire, close enough that beads of sweat stood out on her forehead. The masked ones gathered silently around them, forming a loose circle around the fire's perimeter. While they took up their places the shaman ducked into the cave. He returned wearing nothing but his white loincloth and his own mask in the likeness of a grimacing white bear.

The shaman gestured to Canowic and she moved back, joining the wolves where they sat watching from the shadows. The fire was hot on her face but the sand cold beneath her feet; another in-between place. She wondered what was about to happen and felt a thrill in her chest.

The shaman knelt by the old woman and rolled her onto her side. She gasped in pain, but the sound was lost in the roar of the fire. As he stood, the shaman reached into the flames and removed a burning brand. Holding this torch aloft he shouted, but it was not the voice of a man that issued from his throat. The sound that tore from his chest was the rough, throaty roar of a bear. At this signal the masked ones began to dance.

They moved slowly at first, dipping low to graze their fingers across the sand before rising again, shoulders hunched, feet tapping in front of them as they leaned back, then forward, now back again, reeling like drunks. The wheel of bodies turned around the fire, panthers and ravens and ghoulish misshapen creatures, their shadows hurled and distorted by the wild light. With each revolution their dance took on a greater urgency. The dancers began to sweat, and some shed their garments, exposing old and mottled skin to the moonlight, but they never removed their masks. Now they were dancing as if it was the last dance of their lives, limbs flailing, kicking the sand, and as they danced they began to sing.

Their voices were raw and keening, the disembodied voices of men and animals intermingling and piercing Canowic's heart like blades. Their song spiraled crazily, shattering and dissolving into itself before drawing back to cohere again and start anew. The dancers praised the shaman's god and accused Him in the next breath. They sang to the Ancient One, the Creator, and to his wife and all the old gods. Theirs was a song of both desperate supplication and fearless indignation, a wild vehicle of madness or purity. Canowic could not tell. She was not thinking about the words. She had been transported, caught up in the heart of the song itself. There were spirits in the dancers or spirits on the wind. A river opened in the air, and the moon leaned low to investigate the uproar, and the sea glittered like many jewels, and still the dancers whirled.

When it seemed they had been dancing forever and might continue into eternity, the dancers converged on the woman, skipping and leaping to form a tight circle around her where she lay on the ground. The shaman got down on his knees and put a hand on the small of the woman's back. Sweat dripped from the white bear's carved wooden teeth onto the woman's bony chest. Her eyes were screwed tight.

Into the silence the shaman spoke. Canowic had heard words of power being spoken before, but she still felt a thrill of terror at the visceral sound of magic being wrought. Her master's voice started out soft as a whisper, a tiny seed that grew and grew and somehow grew yet more, until it rang in the air like the peal of a golden horn. The old woman moaned, her eyes flying open in pain or illumination while her mouth formed a perfect circle, as if she were astonished by a vision only she could see. Then she screamed, and the menagerie of beasts hooted and shrieked with her. The wolves howled at the stars. Canowic shivered uncontrollably.

Afterwards, the shaman gently kept his hands on the woman's back until she was ready to sit up. When she finally did, clasping her friend's hands in her own, the woman's face conveyed what had happened. She stood, straightening, her back whole and restored. Tears were streaming down her face. She prostrated herself before the shaman only to have him help her to her feet again. When she finally departed in the company of her fearsome band of friends, who had never removed their masks, she left her cane leaning against the wall of the cave.

. . .

Sometimes the shaman decamped from his cave at the water's edge for weeks on end to seek the solitude of still lonelier places. On the day Hankasi set out from Aghuax at the head of his spring raiders, the shaman had taken Canowic and departed at dawn for the fastnesses of Merwa. For the first few miles Canowic kept looking behind her, wondering when she would see Yengwa galloping toward them, coming to settle his debt. But he never did, and all she saw were the wolves trailing behind them.

Just before sunset they came upon a mere. The water spread out like silver pooled at the bottom of a dish, motionless save for the occasional passing riffle. After making camp, the shaman led Canowic down to the shore. The stars had come out and were twinned in the surface of the glassy waters.

It was several years since the shaman had first begun instructing her in his ancient arts, chief amongst which was scrying.

"Clear your mind," he said, once they had settled themselves on the grass.

This was always the first step. Clearing her mind of the day's driftwood so she could be free to receive the shaman's instruction and whatever might follow. She conjured the image of a single point of light, as the shaman had taught her. She could smell the loamy waters, and feel the damp cold of the muddy grass. She set these aside and honed in on the light, drawing her mind down onto a white needle and then allowing that point to dissolve into nothingness. Thus unmoored, she drifted from the dock of the present world and floated out upon the inner sea.

At length she opened her eyes.

"Look into the waters," the shaman murmured. "What do you see?"

Canowic gazed out at the depths of the mere. At first she registered only the greater blue-blackness, but soon the stars reified and stood out. She began connecting their points into shapes and images. The Hawk. The Troubled Skiff. Yenhatalax. The Stagslayer. The Swan.

Afterwards, surrounded by the silence of the benighted forest, master and acolyte lay on their backs and looked up at the stars themselves, as if gazing up from the bottom of a well. Canowic recounted the associations she had made, the relative positions of the stars, her suppositions about how the scroll of the sky might be read that night. The shaman listened thoughtfully. He did not correct her in anything. Instead, he told her again the tales of the constellations she had listed, their images and the powerful names different peoples had given them. He reminded her of the centrality of certain stories, explaining how their throughlines re-emerged again and again across time in the vehicles of different heroes.

The shaman was constantly revisiting certain themes, repeating the same points in different ways so that she might fully understand their connections. Usually his stories kindled something deep inside of Canowic, a hunger to reach out and touch the numinous, invisible world and be known by the gods. On that night, however, she had been annoyed. She already knew everything the master was telling her. Or so she thought. Eventually though, as he continued speaking in his rich, sonorous voice, she realized there were things she had forgotten. The shaman made a few associations of his own. The Hawk was hovering next to the Vines, but would soon turn towards the bow of the Ship. She had forgotten to take into account the phase of the moon. She was glad it was dark out, and the shaman could not see her blushing. As always, she was the first to fall asleep.

Upon waking, she found the shaman already up and sitting by the fire. He was picking through the innards of a coney the wolves had brought back. The pack would feed them while they remained in the mountains, pulling down black-tailed deer or leaping into rushing streams to catch radiant trout that stood warping in the current. They were a rumor of lithe shapes flitting through the long brakes and quiet sheets of rain, slipping along the selvage at the rim of the world. They howled at sunrise and sunset, whether returning from the hunt or sitting limned by the setting stars on thrones of broken granite, taking up the primordial songs of their forebears.

The shaman offered Canowic a skewer of coney meat before returning to his study of the twistings in the animal's guts. They sat quietly by the fire, both of them wrapped in their thick blankets against the chill, their breath coming in shaggy bursts of steam. Canowic chewed her meat and tried to remember her dream.

For some time she had striven to learn how to foster her dreams, a skill intimately tied to interpretation. The shaman dreamed richly every night, and it was his practice to recount the contents of his reveries each morning at dawn, so as to snatch them from the ether of the mind's eye before they swirled away. Canowic was having trouble recalling what she had seen while asleep. There had been a dark, animal presence, then radiant light and deep waters.

"What is troubling you, my daughter?" the shaman asked at length.

Canowic confessed she could not remember her dream.

"It will come back," the shaman said. "That is the way of important dreams and of life itself. That which is vital tends to return."

Canowic finished chewing and wiped her lips on her arm. She nodded slowly.

"You have a question," the shaman said.

"We must be ready," Canowic said, her brow knitting in thought. "But what if I am not ready? I don't want to miss an opportunity to know that which I am called to know."

"Seriousness in training is essential," the shaman nodded. "Yet we are fragile vessels, and must remember we only ever receive the visions of the gods imperfectly."

"But we interpret the signs," Canowic said. "We must find the meaning in them."

"That is too simple a view," the shaman said.

Canowic frowned. "Surely we play some role in the seeing."

"Yes. The gods have seen fit to assign us a role in the story of heaven and earth. And you are correct in recognizing this is a profound honor and privilege." The shaman paused. "But it is also a terrible weight."

"Why trust us at all?" Canowic asked. "Why do the gods let us interpret anything? Why do they not speak to us directly, instead of through signs that may be mistaken or missed entirely?"

The shaman's eyes flickered as with mirth. "Now you begin to ask the right kind of questions."

Canowic shook her head, unsatisfied.

"No riddles today, master. Please. I want to know the answer. A real answer."

"As you should," the shaman said. "But I have none. At least not to the question you are asking. It is the gods' pleasure to dwell in mystery and reveal themselves as they desire."

"It seems cruel. If they know we need help and wisdom, how can they not give it more readily?"

"There was a time when I asked the same question," the shaman said.

"When did you stop asking it?"

The shaman closed his eyes and thought back to the time when he himself had been an acolyte disputing just such issues with his own master. This was so long ago the seas had known a different shape and the ancestors of the Ancagua were not yet a people. Yet in hearing Canowic's questions he knew some things had not changed. How remarkable, in light of all the years he had seen, to know his days were drawing to an end. He was finally approaching his rest. That much he had been given to know. What he did not see was what part his acolyte would play. Her presence in his life was an artful and mysterious gift. He looked at her across the fire.

"I never did."

Canowic cocked her head.

"Not all gods are the same," he continued. "Like men, they have their separate natures. And like men, they make their choices and walk their paths. This is why you must distinguish carefully between which gods you will serve and which you will defy."

Canowic poked the fire with a stick, causing a spent log to disintegrate in a flurry of ash.

"You still haven't answered my question."

"I am nothing if not fearful of the gods of my fathers," the shaman said. His voice was even and strong, neither berating her nor soft-ening his words. "They are the lords of all the worlds. If they do not deign to reveal themselves in the ways I desire, it is not because they are impo-tent. It is they who inflame our hearts to begin with. It is they who stir the waters of the other world."

Canowic remained silent.

"I will be dead and flown to the hall of my fathers before I judge the gods. And until they see fit to allow me to cross over to that bless-ed place I will beseech them on behalf of my people, who are currently possessed of madness and running crazily upon the earth like ants driven from their hill. As for you, you must decide for yourself how to contend with the gods. But make no mistake, they do not desire abjection alone. You must prostrate your heart, but you must also bring your fire. Only then, inhabiting the fullness of your being, will you truly have eyes to see."

Finished, he leaned back and looked up at the morning clouds listing overhead. Or that is how it seemed to Canowic. In truth, he looked away because he could not stand to see the longing in her eyes.

· · ·

On one of their last nights out, master and acolyte camped in the lee of an abandoned shepherd's hovel. The shaman brought out his shewstone and set it in Canowic's hands.

Of all the mediums used for interpretation, the most sacred were the shewstones. The shaman had explained to Canowic how his own crys-tal sphere was but one seeing stone among those come down out of antiq-uity. There were others; the Heart Stone with its raw, unworked shape and power to show only the past; the Pyramid of Ne'Marfud with its murmur-ing voices; the Martyr's Stone, which could only be used by the dead.

The fire was well stoked and the coals flickered brilliantly against the pooling blackness. The shaman's stone gleamed translucent red in the light of the flames. It was rare for Canowic to be allowed to use the stone, but the shaman was not one for unnecessary fanfare.

"Look into the stone," he said without ceremony. "Tell me what you see."

Canowic leaned forward and looked into the perfect quartz sphere. As she did, her hair fell across her eyes in a way that reminded the shaman of something, or someone, a memory he could not quite grasp. Focused on the crystal, Canowic did not see the look of concentration tightening her master's face. The stone danced orange in the firelight, its edges blurring as she slipped into a trance. The world disappeared.

As always, she was partially disoriented upon her return. The shaman waited patiently, letting her gather herself. She took a deep drink from the water skin and wiped her lips with the back of her hand.

"Tell me what you have seen, my child."

Canowic took a deep breath.

"I saw a vulture, molting and ragged as a beggar yet strong and hard of flesh. It was drifting in slow circles above a battlefield littered with corpses. Next I saw a human skull grinning at me with chipped and broken teeth. Lastly, I saw a doe looking back over her shoulder, frozen in panic."

Finished, she met the shaman's eyes and was frightened to see they had gone cold. He stared into the fire, watching the embers for such a long time that she was unsure whether he would speak at all.

"The vulture represents the king," he said at last. "A fell soul that circles above the people and preys upon them. The skull portends death or rebirth."

He said nothing of the doe. When Canowic asked, he only shook his head.

"I do not know."

The idea that there was something her master could not know was foreign to her. There was nothing beyond his ken. The lines and hollows of his face were accentuated by the dancing shadows, his eyes refracting the flames like tiny shewstones. When Canowic finally lay down to sleep he was still sitting by the fire, examining its many-hued depths. The following day as they descended from the mountain, the doom of mourning drums echoed up from the city.

• • •

Tongues of fire skipped across the kindling at the base of Hankasi's pyre.

"How certain you were it would not end like this."

Canowic considered her master's words. The king had been young and his reign short, yet there was not a single corner of her heart in which she felt any pity for him.

"They say he was shot by a little boy," she said, spitting on the sand. "He will not be remembered kindly. But they will say his name forever."

"No, they will not," the shaman said quietly. "But there is truth in what you say."

Canowic sighed inwardly. Sometimes her master was profound, and sometimes he was exhausting. No one else could scold and praise at the same time, making her feel such different emotions all at once. She didn't want to get into a debate. She just wanted to watch Hankasi burn.

"Wrong how?"

"They will not say his name forever."

Canowic frowned, drawing her cloak tighter against the breeze.

"Master, the great singers can recite the kings of a thousand years."

"Look closer," the shaman commanded.

By now the flames had ignited the main logs of the pyre. The edges of the ornate war canoe were beginning to steam. Canowic smelled wood smoke on the breeze.

"What is it to him that they will sing his name, in praise or in scorn?" her master asked.

Canowic looked at Hankasi's face. Eyes closed, his features slack and drawn as the husk of a beehive fallen in winter. She described what she saw.

"He knows nothing, sees nothing, feels nothing."

"Soon we will all join him."

She was surprised. It was a profane thing her master implied. "So the memory of the dead means nothing?"

He answered her with another question. "What of that time when those who do the remembering are gone?" He raised his chin towards the consuming fire. "People may speak this man's name for a thousand years, but what of the slaves in his kitchen? I do not know their names, though their mothers do. When the lowest slave in the king's household dies, her mother will mourn. But when her mother finally dies, and everyone who ever knew that slave and her name, what then? What of the coming time when the last spark of her memory is extinguished, and nothing remains to prove she ever existed?"

"But you hold all the memories of your ancestors."

"There are ancestors before those ancestors," the shaman shrugged. "No one's memory stretches back to the great dawn, when the Creator breathed upon the world and darkness fled like dew before the sun."

"What then?" She felt an unexpected despair lurking at the edges of her heart.

The shaman watched the flames.

"I will return to the earth, as one day you will too. Within a few years—and how many is not important—there will be no one left alive on the face of the earth who remembers you. The sound of your voice, the look of your face when you were young, what you cherished, the sound of your laughter, all of it will be gone."

"Extinguished," she said.

"No," the shaman shook his head, "not extinguished. But gone from the world of men. All that will matter is who you loved and were loved by. That and those things which are hidden in the secret places of the heart, stored up to be revealed in the other world."

Canowic tried to picture Hankasi rising from his pyre in the other world to face the Ride to Judgment. She pulled up the deerskin hood that hung against her back. The pelt was singing with energy. She closed her eyes and let herself sink into its pulse. There was a heavy buzzing in the air, inaudible but nonetheless clear. It emanated from within the circle of the godwood, up on the hill above the beach. Fell voices rode the wind, husky with power. The gods of the magi were awakening. Canowic listened for the voice of the Torchbearer, willing it to cut through the noise.

Long moments passed. The frigid heartbeat of the incoming tide pulsed against her shins while the dark gods whispered in their totem houses. Then another, fainter voice. If it could even be called that. It was more like an aroma, fleeting yet fresh and altogether different from the raw energies bloodying the ether. She tried to hold herself open like an outstretched hand as the waters of being flowed past, over, and through her. The shaman's gods were there, but she could not discern their thoughts.

When she opened her eyes the flames were skipping everywhere. The queen had not moved, though the heat now swarming from the pyre had driven her handmaidens back, pulling her daughters to safety with them. Hankasi's skin was beginning to slough off, his soul leaping towards the low-sweeping chariots of the Usthilim, the Tombmaidens who gather in the souls of the dead. After adding their lances to the pyre, the warriors helped the concubine onto Hankasi's war shield and raised her to their shoulders just as they had the king. As the crown of leaves on Hankasi's brow caught fire and turned to a circle of light, the warriors lifted the girl on high so she could see over the flames. She was nodding dumbly, heavy-lidded, her eyes glazed with ecstasy. This was the moment that the wine and the warriors' seed had prepared her for.

Once, the warriors lifted her towards the sky, and the girl saw a field of grasses where the waters of the ocean should be.

Twice, and she glimpsed her master beckoning to her.

Thrice, and she spied a way to the magic door that leads to the other world, the gate from beneath whose lintel all who pass need never return.

Sweat that had nothing to do with the heat of the distant flames ran down Canowic's breast as she watched the warriors helping the concubine down from the shield. Then Yengwa was leading her to the arms of the High Mage. The girl did not recoil, her face remaining slack even when Ixiltical swiveled the cowl of his cloak down toward her face and grasped her hair. He spoke to her, perhaps asking after the revelation she had just seen, seeking to draw from her some word of knowledge regarding the way to the secret door. Canowic wondered whether he even believed the door existed. The magi spurned the old ways, but that did not mean they ignored the ancient gods, for they were no fools. Power respects power even as it seeks to destroy all that would oppose it.

Finally it was time. Holding the concubine in one arm as if cradling a child, Ixiltical reached into his thick robe and removed a knife of white bone. When he drew the blade across the girl's throat she jerked and sank into him, covering him in her spurting life. Then the High Mage lifted her in his arms and carried her up onto the pyre, stepping into the midst of flames that would have proved too much for any mortal man. He bent amidst the roaring logs and laid the girl on Hankasi's chest.

As he stepped back onto the sand the High Mage looked straight down the beach at Canowic and the shaman. The distance between them evaporated, and Canowic saw straight into the shadows of his crimson hood, where tendrils of smoke curled around cracked lips. She closed her eyes and the sound of rushing wings filled her ears.

Chapter Five

HANKASI

. . .

Teshuwa the Blue-Eyed was carried off by an infection several days after his hand was crushed by a war club during a skirmish with Nalene outriders at the Ford of Hehek. He spoke his final words to his son while lying on a blanket beneath the spreading boughs of a willow upstream from the ford, his entire arm swollen and darkened to a venomous shade of purple. Hankasi dismissed the king's guards for this penultimate moment, and afterward there were those who thought this was so no one could hear what passed between the delirious ruler and his power-hungry son. In reality it was simply Hankasi's wish to have a final moment with the only person he had ever loved.

The prince walked the entire way back to Aghuax behind his father's warhorse. Normally the returning war band would have stopped short of the city to repaint themselves and their mounts before driving their captives down toward Char Gate in glory. But Hankasi did not stop, not even at the gate itself, where crowds had gathered to welcome the warriors home with garlands of flowers. The people stared at Hankasi as he passed by. His legs were still caked in mud and dirt, his hair matted with sweat. At the sight of his mourning a ripple passed through the crowd like wind through ripe grain.

A fortnight after Teshuwa's pyreday the magi arrived at the northern edge of the city, pulling their huge dromedaries up in front of Arrow Gate. The animals' flanks were chalked with strange and complex symbols. Their riders wore heavy crimson robes, cowls pulled up over their heads such that no part of their skin could be seen save for their tanned, jewel-bedecked hands holding their reigns. The shadows inside those hoods seemed to eat the light.

The guards atop the gate appraised them with narrowed eyes and arrows notched to their bows. The captain of the gate bid the strangers be gone, but they begged an audience with Hankasi, claiming to have read of his ascension in the stars. The captain cursed under his breath. It did not seem possible that anyone beyond the lands of the Ancagua could yet have heard of Teshuwa's death. He dispatched a runner to the castle, instructing his men to keep their bows trained on the suspicious riders and their snorting beasts in the meantime. To his surprise, the runner returned with word that the riders were to be escorted to the king.

When the guards threw open the heavy doors of the throne room, Hankasi was waiting surrounded by his advisers.

"Hail strangers," the herald called out in his booming voice. "State your business in the great city of Aghuax."

The visitors gave the impression of uniformity in height and size, though it was difficult to know what lay under their robes. At the herald's call one of them stepped forward. He carried a long staff, slender as a willow switch and white as bone. When he spoke his voice was like a river stone sliding off a silk pillow.

"We are searchers of stars," he said, "and have come from far away. While yet in our homeland, we scried your name in the heavens, o king. We have crossed the great desert to learn how we may serve him whose name is indelibly written in the firmament."

Hankasi stared into the darkness of the stranger's hood.

"No one has ever crossed the great desert."

The robed one inclined his head, as if to acknowledge that the king's skepticism was in line with common belief.

"It is no frequent feat."

"You yourself have said it," Hankasi said. The tension in the room was as thick as the moment before a spring thunderstorm. The king lifted a hand towards the visitors and turned to Yengwa, his captain. "Is it not strange that they hide themselves beneath these robes and go hooded even inside?"

Yengwa stared at the leader of the self-proclaimed stargazers.

"Strange is a kind word for it, my king. There are others that come to mind."

If this bothered the strangers they gave no indication. They stood patiently waiting, as if the king's words were utterly civil and they were not locked in a room of stone and surrounded by heavily armed warriors.

"I do not trust a man who goes about veiled like a woman," Hankasi continued, turning back to face the strangers. "Reveal yourself, or I will have my warriors relieve you of those hoods and the heads beneath them."

All about the chamber warriors tightened their grips on spears and the hafts of war hammers. Just as Yengwa's hand was starting to twitch and it seemed the room might burst into a conflagration of violence, the leader of the foreign star-gazers reached up with hands heavy with rings of amethyst and jade and slowly pulled back the hood of his robe. Hankasi had seen men spitted on young saplings and hung with their own intestines, and the face before him filled him with a fascination as morbid as any victim's final moment ever had.

The robed stranger's face was utterly hairless, his eyes having neither brows nor lashes. His skin was tanned a brown so deep as to be nearly red, and stretched tight over cheekbones fragile as the shank of a suckling kid. He had a mouth like a sea cave, sunken and treacherous, with broken teeth hidden behind twisted lips. His eyes were dominated by swirling gray pupils that shifted and flickered in the torchlight, communicating wordlessly, constantly reaching out, seeking ingress.

"I am Ixiltical," the gray-eyed mage said, his voice soft yet resonant. "High Mage of the Tomic remnant. My brethren and I have indeed traveled the sands of the great desert, and followed burning stars to your throne."

"You say that you would serve me," Hankasi said, smoothly masking his shock at the mage's unveiling. "But I have no want for servants. My people supply all that I need."

"We are the servants of the Desert Mysteries," Ixiltical said quietly, still staring at the king. "Fell lords of wondrous power. It is they who have led us to you. They have a purpose for you, and we are but instruments in their hands."

As he said this, Ixiltical held out his willow wand and let it drop to the floor. Before it hit the ground the wood turned to a rod of water that splashed across the stones. Each drop erupted into one of a hundred snakes, writhing and twisting and beginning instantly to devour one another.

"Behold their power," Ixiltical said, his voice emanating like waves from a heavy gong. One of the snakes was nearing Hankasi's bare foot. Yengwa raised his blade to strike, but then the mage held out a hand and the snakes vanished as suddenly as they had appeared. The wand reappeared in his hand, solid and wooden again. Hankasi's eyes were wide as coins. The advisers looked to the king while the warriors of the guard drew their blades and bent their bows, the strings groaning audibly.

If Hankasi had given the word, or made the slightest movement toward his own spear, the magi would instantly have been cut down by a dozen arrows. When the king finally found his voice he spoke slowly, his eyes already telling the story of all that was to come.

"Speak to me of your lords," said the king, "that I may know their power."

· · ·

Later that summer when the prescribed time of mourning had ended, Hankasi was formally enthroned in an oceanside coronation attended by all the people of Aghuax. Custom held that the eldest of the holy men would present him with a budding branch at this ceremony, signifying the perpetuation and renewal of the previous king's line. But Hankasi refused to allow the shaman to participate and prohibited the performance of any rites to the gods of his fathers. Instead it was the magi who presided.

"I will not have the tongues of soothsayers in my ears," Hankasi declared, daring any to oppose him. At the time, the people had not yet fallen completely from their adherence to the ways of the old gods, and there were some who let their dismay be known. Spurning the shaman on such a momentous day was the last affront for three members of the Council of Elders, who protested that Ixiltical and his minions were not holy men but a cabal ridden down out of the death stars. It was the magi who were the soothsayers, they claimed, not the shaman. When their bodies were found on the beach several days later, their throats cut and their eyes eaten by crows, it was clear the old order of things had passed away.

There had been a time when the whole city had held the shaman in esteem, revering him as a powerful searcher of ways. Not even the eldest amongst the Ancagua could remember when he had come amongst them, nor a story in which he was not already ancient. The shaman defied age. Weathered as a salt-pitted walrus hide, he could still crush a thick mug in his hand, and the eyes that peered out from beneath his craggy brow shone with a clarity that belied his primordial origins. Teshuwa had often come to him for counsel, and the shaman's judgments and interpretations had always proved canny and worthy of trust. Many was the night the old king had asked the seer to accompany him on a long walk down the crescent moon of the beach and up onto the cliff where the grove of papery birches huddled in their circle.

The shaman was chief amongst those who upheld the rites of the Self-Named God, whom Teshuwa feared as his fathers had before him. The Ancient One was an immutable deity, just yet never capricious. Teshuwa relied on the shaman as his intermediary, trusting him to convey his willingness to do the god's will and to submit his supplications.

On these nighttime visits to the godwood the king would stand in silence and watch as the shaman entered his seeing trance, keeping guard over his body until the seer returned from the other world and spoke of what he had seen. It was here, in the sacred grove of the Ancagua, that Ixiltical and his black magi had prevailed upon Hankasi to set up totems to the Lords of the Desert, the Great Mysteries whom they served, seeking through their colonization to usurp the place's undiluted power.

Six cedars from the slopes of Merwa had been cut down and hauled to the grove, where Hankasi's craftsmen were tasked with carving them into the images of the Desert Lords. These included Gaugazik, the razor-mouthed serpent with the eyes of a dead man and sweeping black wings, and Nceugacet the World-Spider, with his hundred eyes and gossamer webs that let him leave the land and ride upon the wind. They were fearsome gods all of them, and none as frightening as Teulanic, the giant lizard who roamed the blinding sands of the desert. The magi taught that he had flown to the moon and coursed among the stars. They said his teeth were like swords, and had been sharpened on the lathe of Ahurewa, the rock witch. They said he could take horses into his mouth four at a time and that he would come out of the desert at the last day to judge all men, consigning any who did not fear him to swim the rivers of fire that blossomed from the heart of the abyss.

Sinuous Gaugazik and leaping Nceugacet flanked Teulanic's massive totem on either side. Ahurewa, who had weeds for hair and sailed the desert in a ship fashioned from the limbs of the dead, stood further out. Beside her was Tebebet, god of sacrificial victims, whom the magi propitiated by dropping fawns into the roiling waters of a blowhole each full moon. Finally there was Remerac. The god of chance and fortune was rendered as a beautiful man with dark eyes, clean-shaven jaw, and a bright red cape.

The slaves had rolled the log that would become Remerac's totem up the hill last of all. Just before reaching the crown of the ridge, one of the men was momentarily distracted as a shadow from a passing bird crossed his eyes. He lost his footing and the guide rope slipped from his hands. Now unbalanced, the log swung to one side and opened the skull of a young boy who had been working another rope with his father, christening Remerac's idol in blood.

When it came time to dedicate the totems Hankasi decreed that everyone in the city must attend the ceremony. He summoned all the holy men and elders as well as the full complement of the war band. Senecwo was carried up to the grove on a litter of ivory. Hankasi had sent a runner to personally summon the shaman, bearing a message with the king's own seal. It was not enough for the shaman to be denied his place of honor. He would be humiliated too, forced to watch while the magi performed a ceremony he had previously presided over a dozen times. When he was late in arriving Hankasi sent warriors to bring him forth, bound if necessary, only to have them return confused and unable to describe what had happened when they reached the seaside cave.

Despite the young king's power and the ruthlessness with which he dispatched those who opposed him, the shaman did not fear him. This lack of fear only stoked Hankasi's hatred. The magi hated the shaman as well, for he defied them when all others had fled before them or been cowed by their awesome displays of power. From the day of Hankasi's coronation they began plotting in earnest how they might destroy him.

Years turned like leaves. Ixiltical took up residence in the highest of the king's towers, where he could be glimpsed on the roof late at night, haggling with the sky as he sought the will of the Divine Lizard whose unblinking eye roves ceaselessly throughout all the world, penetrating even to the hearts and minds of men.

The magi tended their idols slavishly, painting them afresh each summer at the time when the whales migrated off the coast, and bringing them sacrifices of fish heart, chicken feet, new wine, and finally human blood. They introduced the people of Aghuax to their rites of spring and half-moon. At first their progress was limited. The people resisted them, for though the Ancagua were not immune to the pleasures of ruthlessness, they had a fundamental respect for justice. Had they chosen the way of courage and laid hold of the willingness to suffer on its behalf, they might have risen up and thrown off the yoke of their new overlords, for they were many and the king and his magi were few.

But the people were frightened by the executions and the black omens the new priests wrought in the sky above the waters of the bay. The faithful few who came to the shaman's cave appeared less and less often. The magi fully infiltrated Hankasi's court through open appointment and hidden machination, spurring the king ever onward toward conquest and bloodshed, until his spirit was driven before them and the rumor of war hung constantly about the city.

Eventually the Ancagua assumed the worship of the totems. They may not have loved the new gods, but their hearts were apathetic, and they let the power of the magi's brimstone lords usurp the thrones of the old gods. The people desired powerful deities to guide them through challenging times. Or that is what some said in the markets and high streets of the city. Privately, they may have felt there was no choice to make. The Torchbearer, who once danced with the swan maids on the emerald grass of eternity, seemed to have forgotten them.

Chapter Six

CANOWIC

. . .

L ong after the pyre had burned to the ground, leaving behind a mountain range of ash, Canowic sat cross-legged in the sand waiting for something. She had watched the queen depart the beach flanked by the burial guard. The white-faced warriors were ostensibly there to protect her, but the way Kulkas stared straight ahead made it seem as though she was being marched off to a dungeon. The shaman left soon after with the wolves.

It had taken longer for the multitudes to disperse. Finally the meat sellers—first to arrive and last to leave—dragged their rickety carts away in a clanking herd, jibing one another as they went in voices hoarse from a day of shouting. As Canowic watched them shamble away, wearing threadbare clothes yet rich in one another's company, she experienced a sharp stab of the loneliness that was her constant companion.

Over the last few weeks she had increasingly felt like one of the islands shrouded in fog just offshore, encroached on by a lapping sea that hemmed her in but would never embrace her. She had the shaman and the wolves, but their comfort could not fully quiet the storms that troubled her soul with primal questions of origin.

Canowic had no recollection of anything prior to life with the shaman. Her earliest memories were of his weathered face dappled with the light playing across the wall of the cave, the smell of seaweed and saltwater infusing everything. When sorrow crept up on her, she drew these memories like arrows from a quiver.

The shaman had raised her in full knowledge of the fact that he was not her father, but she would have known even if he had not told her. Like the rest of the Ancagua, he had russet skin that deepened in the sun but never burned. Canowic's complexion was much lighter, like the meat of an almond. There was also her height. Though not yet fully grown, she was already taller than many women of the city. Her hands and fingers were long and slender, and her nose was narrow. Sometimes she pulled the corners of her eyes back with her fingers, wishing they could stay elongated and beautiful like the other girls'. But when she let go they always snapped back to their true shape, as round and ugly as turtle eggs. The first time she had asked the shaman about her mother she had been five winters old.

"Your mother is not here child," he had answered. "Nor will she ever be."

Something in her face must have shown him how final this sounded.

"You are mine," he went on, his gravel voice as calm and reassuring as his words were direct. "I love you as a daughter."

The words had comforted Canowic in the moment, but ultimately the sharp edge of her longing had returned. As she grew, she continued to wonder about her mother and father, and her questions became more complex. One night several years later, she asked the shaman about it all again. They were sitting in the mouth of the cave, cooking dinner.

"Where do I come from?"

The shaman was packing his pipe, a bit of horn carved in the shape of a flying swan. His cracked fingernails shone dully in the ember-light. Once he got his weed lit he took a few deep puffs and looked into the fire. The wolves were gathered around, some laying with their heads upon their paws, their ancient eyes refracting the fire like coals pulled from a forge.

"One evening in the summer of the fifteenth year of Teshuwa's reign, I was sitting here in the entrance to my cave when I heard the voice of an infant crying in the darkness beyond the light of my fire. When I went to investigate, I found Elil standing over a bundle lying in the sand. She was sniffing curiously at your face. I think she already loved you."

Canowic looked over at Elil where she lay in the sand across the fire and found the dappled wolf staring back at her.

"You were dressed in clean cloths and wrapped snugly against the cold," the shaman continued. "There was no one around, no letter of explanation secreted in your swaddling. Nothing to tell me where you had come from."

Canowic felt a prickling in her throat. A terrible pressure was building deep inside her, a weak seam ripping open. She craned her head toward the night sky to try and keep the tears from running out of her eyes.

"They just left me?" she said, the words coming out in a husky whisper.

The shaman drew on his pipe again and let out a stream of blue smoke. Canowic looked over at him and was surprised to see wetness spar-kling dully in the corners of his eyes too.

"I did not know what to think," he said, the firelight catching on the underside of his jaw. "You were so beautiful. Who could have abandoned a child, I wondered, let alone one as perfect as you?"

Canowic began shaking silently, sobs wracking her body as she leaned forward, nearly doubled over with her face in her hands. The shaman could have done many things in that moment. He could have tried to explain her mother's unknowable motives, or given an impassioned speech about how she was his and reiterated how much he loved her. Instead he got up, crossed the space between them, and sat down next to her. He put his strong, hoary arm around her shoulders and she cried into his chest with deep, rolling sobs that went on and on. When her shuddering finally subsided the shaman spoke again.

"It is time you learned the story of your name."

Canowic wiped her eyes on the edge of her cloak and blew her nose.

"There have not been many queens in the history of our people," the shaman said.

Canowic wasn't sure whether the Ancagua had ever been her people, but she let him continue.

"Tecanowic was the only child of the great king Selaway. Her mother the queen died giving birth to her, and Selaway believed something of his wife's spirit lived on in their daughter. He doted on her, and in the fullness of time she grew to be a beautiful maiden, fairer than any woman in the land. In addition to her beauty she was a seer of surpassing wisdom, and studied at the feet of Imre himself. When Selaway died at the Siege of Burzen, Tecanowic became queen. Her rule was long and filled with peace, and she was renowned for her love of justice."

"You named me," Canowic said.

The shaman looked at her, as if contemplating all she had ever been to him and ever might be.

"I did."

"Did it come to you in a dream?"

He shook his head. "No, I had no dream. I did not need a dream to know what to name you. The morning after Elil discovered you I looked at you lying in your wrappings and knew I must give you a name worthy of all that I already felt in my heart. I did not contemplate your name. It came to me and I immediately knew it was fitting."

Canowic was crying again, jagged pain and love's ache both throbbing within her.

"It was a name worthy of growing into," the shaman said, rubbing her back. "And you have. You have."

. . .

Canowic thought back on that night now as she looked out across the beach at the dying embers of Hankasi's funeral pyre. The intervening years had dulled the sting of that initial discovery regarding her origins, but her melancholy curiosity had never gone away. Some days it swelled inside of her like a tumor. On others she could barely feel it. But it was always there, nagging at her. Who was she? Where did she come from? Was she so unlovely as to deserve abandonment?

She stood, stretching her arms over her head and arching her stiff back. The surface of the bay was being burnished to a molten sheen by the setting sun. Ash from the pyre blew through the air like snow, adding a strange aspect to the nearly deserted beach. The only other people left on the strand were a pair of beggars dragging their spidery legs along behind them. They called out for alms as Canowic passed, but all she had for them was a smile.

Back at the cave she found her master in a trance. The wolves were arranged around him in a protective arrowhead. He sat draped in shadow against the back wall, his legs bound with cords of whale-gut and his glazed eyes fixed on something far off. Canowic smelled the thick incense of magic.

The wolves were beautiful animals, lithe and powerful and un-obliged by the constraints that governed their earthly brethren. Though capable of death, the Wolves of Hylene were ageless. They were creatures of myth, descended from the stars and one day destined to return to them. The shaman had told her the story of how they had come to live with him many times.

One day while journeying through the saltwater marshes south of the city he had come across a pack of hunting wolves. Recognizing the power that emanated from them, he had greeted them with honor, and they in turn had spoken to him of their purposes. Both parties had then submitted themselves, man and wolves, to become bound to one another for a period of time so as to accomplish all that was fated for them. Canowic had never asked what this fate was, nor how they had come to know it.

Canowic looked at the two identical males reclining near the shaman's feet. Asha and Syrxes were brothers. Not all the wolves looked young, but these two did, with their moist black noses and their swift, sure movements. Each had the same black coat and honey eyes, the same massive build. They were truly prodigious in size, half again as heavy as the smaller wolves. Despite their towering proportions and the feats of strength she had seen them perform, Canowic knew them to be among the gentlest animals in the pack. She could tell them apart but couldn't explain how.

The brothers had risen when she entered, and then settled again upon recognizing her. The rest of the pack scattered around the cave varied widely in their appearance. Their fur ranged from auburn to eider-down to midnight black, their coats solid or speckled or a motley patch-work. Some had thick and lustrous pelts while others were patchy and balding. Their diversity extended to their size as well. Some, including the brothers, were huge, while others, like little Buli, were small and lean. Most seemed healthy but a few were gaunt, their ribcages visible through their skin. One of the mangiest, Serouac, had only one ear and one eye, which glowed a reddish-orange by night.

The legend of Hylene held that each wolf would play a role in the doom fated for the entire pack, facing a moment of truth when the destiny of the collective would hinge upon his or her actions. Gentle, quiet Buli would be called upon no less than their leader, Gila, the pure white she-wolf who lay in the entrance to the cave looking out to sea.

As Gila turned to face Canowic, the acolyte was transfixed as if for the first time by the wolf's emerald eyes. They held a fiery sentience utterly different than what one saw in the eyes of the city dogs. Whenever the pack entered Aghuax, the mongrels populating the city's alleys and gutters took up with a baleful keening, stirred by some lost primal memory. Sometimes Canowic heard these same dogs crying at night, braying at the stars in frustrated longing as they called upon ancestors they did not know how to reach. The bitter empathy she felt in those moments hollowed her like few things could.

Wolves of the stars, the shaman had said, destined to return again. More than once Canowic had wondered what they were waiting for. Watching them patiently attending to the shaman, she wondered again.

"What are you waiting for?" she whispered, talking mostly to herself. "Why do you remain in the thresher of this world?"

She looked at her master. His lips were moving slowly but no sound emerged. She knew he was merely in preparation. When he came out of his trance he would be traveling far away to the place where the spirits dwell. To wake him now would be disastrous. Moving quietly, she blew on the coals of the previous night's fire and set a bowl of day-old stew to warm. Then she shrugged off her hooded cape, shook out her hair and sat down in the sand to watch the black sails of the fishing fleet tack-

ing back to shore at the end of the day. The fishermen called to one another as they came ashore, helping each other haul their boats up on the
sand. Canowic watched their camaraderie with envy until Buli came over
and nuzzled her face.

Sometimes when her feelings of loneliness were strongest, like
when she was trying to fall asleep and had nothing to distract herself
with, Canowic would try to empty herself. Now, feeling the rip inside tugging open again, she wrapped herself in her blanket, rolled over, and let
her eyes focus on the stars beginning to appear in the steadily darkening
vault above her. The sand was still warm and the fire crackled softly.
A memory came to her from the day the shaman had first begun teaching
her to see.

· · ·

She had been sitting in the very same spot. For months she had been asking him to show her how to use the shewstone, and for months he had
turned her away, telling her the life of a seer was a calling and not something to be entered into quickly.

"If you are truly called," he had said, "you will be compelled
beyond simple curiosity." These words were accompanied by a stern look.
"And I will be compelled to teach you."

She wasn't sure what it would be like to be called. Was she sup-
posed to be looking for a sign or listening for a voice? She knew only that
she burned to use the stone and enter its world of dreams and visions,
where she might learn something of her family. There was something else
too, an even deeper source that pulled at her, beckoning from the world of
spirit, but she had no words for it.

She told the shaman she *was* compelled (for surely this was what
he wanted to hear), insisted for months that turned to years, and still he

deflected her requests. She had almost given up hope that he would ever teach her, when one day he approached her as she sat mending a fishing spear. He held the stone in his hand. Before he said a word, she knew her time had come. The master looked down at her.

"Do you still desire to learn?"

She nodded, her heart racing.

"I have not kept you waiting out of spite," he said. "I had to wait until I was certain. Now I am."

Canowic wondered what had changed his mind, but she wasn't going to ask now, not when he'd finally agreed. Her hands shook in anticipation of handling the shewstone. Soon she would learn the secret words of power that would allow her to glimpse future and past in its gauzy depths. Or that is what she had expected.

"Your first lesson begins now," the shaman said. She waited for him to hand her the stone. "Sit here and think of nothing at all."

She raised her eyebrows, waiting for more. But nothing more was forthcoming.

"Think of nothing?"

The shaman just nodded and returned to where he had been patching an old wineskin, taking the stone with him. It seemed a cruel taunt. But he appeared to be serious, so Canowic obeyed. It was hot out, and he had left her sitting in the sand with no shewstone, no clear objective, and no shade. Despite all that, she thought it would be easy. After all, she didn't have to do anything. But as time went by she found herself unable to go more than a few moments without a random thought intruding on her consciousness, a colorful shred impinging on the silent void she was trying to cultivate. In the end she was consumed by annoyance and a sense of failure. It was all she could do to remain seated until he returned to check on her. The tide had come all the way in and receded again.

"Open your hands," the shaman said. She obeyed, placing them palm up on her knees.

"Now do the same with your mind. Thoughts will come. You cannot keep them from coming. Let them slide over your mind like water over a smooth stone. Become a rock at the bottom of the river, thoughts coming, thoughts going."

Then he left her again. All afternoon she sat in the sun, trying and failing to clear her mind. Thoughts came, relentlessly, but rather than sliding past they got stuck, as if she were not a rock but a branch, snagging every piece of grass floating downstream. The sound of a gull crying would bring to mind a picture of the bird and she would find herself imagining its pinioned spiral. From there she would carom to an image of the city, or a scrap of conversation, or a refrain from deeper in her mind, a feeling neither fully word nor fully image, yet real as any imagined landscape.

By sunset she was wrung out like a wet rag. But the shaman had not come to tell her to stop, and she was stubborn. She needed to void herself, but she fought her body along with her mind. She squirmed in the sand, trying and failing and trying and failing. The worst part was knowing she could not fight her way through the problem. She couldn't bear down and simply clear her mind through force of will, like pulling out a root or lifting a heavy stone. It was a test of her ability to let go, and she was failing miserably.

She passed through frustration into resentment and was nearing a state of rage when the master finally returned and sat down next to her. Without saying a word, he held out a piece of dried fruit. Canowic just stared at him. He shrugged and took a bite himself.

"I did not last nearly as long when my master gave me the same task," he mused. It was hard for Canowic to picture the shaman as having had a master. She was still mulling this over when he started laughing.

"I threw his shewstone into the creek he'd made me sit by. He hided me so badly I couldn't sit for a week."

The sun was setting in the west, purple streamers trailing out of sight over the waters of the bay. The shaman shook his head in remembrance and laid a reassuring hand on Canowic's shoulder. He let it rest there for a moment. Then he got up, went to his mat, and lay down to sleep. It was one of the only times in her life Canowic could remember the master falling asleep before her, and she took it as a message: *You have done all that is required for today. Now we rest.*

. . .

Red Wing let out a huge yawn from behind her, reeling Canowic back into the present. She looked at the auburn wolf, her fur almost golden in the light of sunset. The outgoing tide had stranded a piece of driftwood. At the back of the cave, the shaman stirred.

Chapter Seven

SENECWO

. . .

From the beginning, Hankasi had dispatched his personal physician to check on Senecwo each month. The man's name was Braug, and he seemed as miserable as the king was confident. He was not hard to read, being given to heavy sighs and fits of bad temper, and the young queen would eventually leverage her understanding of his situation into an act of resistance.

By the end of his third visit they had developed a routine. Braug would arrive, quickly complete a thorough if impatient examination of the queen's person, and then leave abruptly. It was unclear to Senecwo what other errands were so pressing that he did not have time for her. She did not labor under the delusion that anyone in the court respected her, but surely Braug feared the king.

For years little changed. Braug would arrive, perform his battery of tests, engage in a perfunctory discussion of any concerns she might have, and be gone before she had a chance to raise any real issues. When he strode into her apartments the week after harvest had begun, in the thirteenth year of her captivity, Senecwo was in her dressing room.

"Your majesty!" he called indignantly, "I have rounds to make!"

Senecwo rolled her eyes at the impatience in his voice. It was always the same; if she was doing anything other than sitting and waiting for Braug's arrival—and she was always doing something else, as he never gave any indication of when he would be dropping by—he would be frustrated. She was done accommodating him. *Let him wait.* She finished putting up her hair and took a sip of water from a golden cup before walking out to greet him.

Braug was short but solidly built, with firm calves and thick, muscled arms. His hairline was receding and his nose had been broken at some point. Unlike most of the Ancagua, he was capable of growing a beard, and was currently experimenting with a cone of white hair that extended from his chin like a ceremonial dagger. He raised both eyebrows at her appearance and threw up his hands. "At last."

"Noble Braug." Senecwo knew Hankasi only sent Braug along in order to keep an eye on her. It was because of this suspicion that she had tolerated the man for so long. As much as she had initially wanted to spurn anything Hankasi did, she had grasped that Braug could be useful. His volcanic temper was a sign of self-doubt. Beneath his bluster he was insecure.

Braug did not return her greeting. He set his leather bag on the table and began to rummage in it. Senecwo felt her long forbearance melting away at the sight of his sour expression. To think he saw *her* as a nuisance. She had been trying to win him over for years with her dignity, wry humor, and compliance. But she'd had it wrong. She held the power, not him.

"Your arm," Braug said, removing from his bag a string with a weight attached. He wrapped this string around her arm during each visit, to what end she did not know.

"We are going out to the people," she said, keeping her arm at her side.

Braug sighed and rolled his eyes toward the ceiling.

"Please, your majesty. I have only so much time."

He looked at her expectantly, and then realized she was serious. He thrust his lower jaw out.

"My orders are to care for her majesty here."

"I am healthy, Braug. You know this. Not all of the king's people are so fortunate. I have had Yakwe make an announcement in the market that the king's physician will be seeing the people today."

She had not actually told the steward to make such an announcement, but there was no way for Braug to know this. Still, he might check with the captain of the household guard. Over time Senecwo had come to have a certain kind of autonomy, but it was always clear to her—and, she was sure, to everyone in the city—that she was in many ways little more than a glorified prisoner. The guards merely tolerated her, and the court only made a show of respecting her out of a desire not to offend the king.

Braug stared at her.

"You did what?"

She turned the corners of her mouth up, but the smile did not reach her eyes.

"Does the king know of this *decree?*"

"The king is pleased to care for his people," Senecwo replied. She let the implication sink in before dropping her second hook. "He would not do well with the knowledge that you are defying me."

She wasn't sure what she was doing. It was a dangerous game, and she was making it up as she went along. The king knew nothing of her plan. She'd barely formulated it herself.

"First you will see to me," she said. "Then we shall proceed to the courtyard. But you are early. Wait here while I change."

Leaving him to contemplate her words, Senecwo retired to her dressing room where she quietly instructed her handmaidens to make their way to the marketplace and let it be known that the king's physician would attend to any sick person who could come to the castle yard immediately. Then she returned to her audience chamber, half expecting Braug to be gone. There was nothing to keep him from walking out and conferring with someone—a guard, the king himself—about what she wanted him to do. In which case the game would be up.

When she passed through the door into the chamber her heart caught in her throat. The door to the room was open and Braug was nowhere in sight. A moment later he stepped out from behind a curtain. He had been looking down into the courtyard.

"I see the people are already arriving." He turned and walked briskly back to his satchel. "Come. Let me attend to you before we go down."

When they arrived in the courtyard, several dozen people were waiting. Cripples, lepers, a young girl with a bloody rag in her hand that she used to stifle a wet cough. These hapless souls were surrounded by a dozen skeptical warriors. As they approached, one of the men called out to Braug.

"They claim the king's physician is going to treat the sick in the courtyard. We've heard nothing about that."

"By order of the queen," Braug said, mirthlessly holding out a hand toward Senecwo.

The guard looked at her, then leaned over and spat on the ground. He turned his gaze up toward the windows of the king's chamber. Senecwo held her breath. Then the girl with the rag coughed horribly and the warrior scowled at her, distracted.

Ignoring the warriors, Senecwo focused on the girl and felt a trickle of despair leaking into her heart. It was obvious there was little to be done for her or any of the other wretches, many of whom had been carried to the courtyard on litters, too sick even to stand. To her surprise, Braug opened his bag and began removing bundles of herbs. He approached the girl with the bloody cough and knelt beside her.

"Come," he said. "Tell me what is wrong."

. . .

Just after sunset that evening, Hankasi swept into Senecwo's rooms unannounced. Startled, she looked up from the dinner of venison she had been taking alone.

"My lord," she said coolly, before going back to her meal.

He walked slowly toward the stone table where she sat. He was wearing a half-cape of white calfskin. His long black hair gleamed magnificently in the orange light of dusk. Senecwo had seen the king enraged and the calm he was displaying now frightened her more than any screaming might have. When he spoke his voice was even and measured and gilded with violence.

"You have used my physician for your own whims."

Senecwo tightened her grip on the knife in her hand, but kept her eyes on the plate in front of her.

"The people are dying."

"The people are not dying," Hankasi said, biting the words off. "The weak are dying."

"The weak are the ones who need you most."

Before she could register what was happening the king had grabbed the plate and flung it across the room where it exploded into a thousand pieces. Hankasi's chest was heaving now, his nostrils flaring like a rutting stallion's. Yet when he spoke his voice was calm as the eye of a storm.

"If you ever defy me again," he said, his voice a deadly whisper, "you will learn what it means when I pour my wrath out."

She could feel the tears in her eyes, and for once didn't care if he saw her this way. It would be better to die than to be like him, with a heart of stone.

"I already do," she said.

For a moment she thought he was going to strike her. A part of her wanted him to. She stared at him in open defiance, willing him to do it. In the end he did nothing. Just turned and walked away.

The next week a larger crowd appeared at the courtyard gate. Old women, hobbling cripples, mothers with palsied children. The guards turned the butts of their spears on them, thrusting them viciously through the bars in an effort to drive the people away. But they clamored all the louder.

"Do you not have the kindness to at least end our misery?" one old woman cried. "Do you feel no shame? If not, come out and kill us, for we aren't going anywhere."

Two young men had brought drums. They started up with a slow, funereal beat. The drums brought Senecwo to her window and then quickly down to the courtyard.

As she ran across the stones toward the soldiers, not caring if she looked undignified, she glanced up at the window of the king's apartment. To her surprise, Hankasi was watching her. The king raised his arms and everyone fell silent.

"Let them enter," he called to the guards. "And see to it they are well-ordered and patient while they await their treatment."

The captain of the guard bowed in acknowledgment, but Hankasi ignored him. The king was looking at Senecwo. He nodded to her, the look on his face unreadable.

. . .

A month later there was a rap at the queen's door. Senecwo waited for Wiwoka to answer it, only realizing after another round of knocking that all her handmaidens were gone on various errands. She cracked the door. The man in the hallway was advanced in years. He seemed hale, but also had the look of one who knows he has gotten more than he had reason to expect from the gods and has not taken it for granted. A sober, inscrutable man. He wore a sky blue cape pinioned at the shoulder, a gray loincloth embroidered with shells, and boots of fine, creamy leather. His long hair was streaked with silver.

Senecwo did not recognize him, and wondered why the guards had allowed him to bother her. She nearly called out for them only to shut her mouth awkwardly, realizing they were not in the hall, which meant they had either abandoned their posts, been paid off, or were dead. The man read all of this in her eyes.

"You have nothing to fear," he rasped. His voice had a granular sound, like rough wood being planed. A memory swam back to her of a day in the king's court months earlier.

"You are one of the elders."

The Council of Elders advised the king, supposedly checking his powers while helping him rule the city. Ever since the three dissenters who had opposed the magi turned up dead, it had been clear that the Council was a puppet body, legitimizing nothing but the king's will.

"I am Iyaye," the man said. "Member of the Council of Elders since the time of Minkotep, Hankasi's father's father. I know what you have done."

Senecwo felt a tightening in her stomach. Iyaye's glacial blue eyes bore into her with penetrating intensity. She found some part of her wanted to trust him. This did not seem like the kind of visitation an accuser would make. She opened the door.

"Come in, honored Iyaye."

As he stepped inside she gestured to a chair.

"Please, sit."

Iyaye shook his head.

"There is little time. I have provided a few moments for us to talk, but the guards will soon return and then I must away."

So he had bribed them.

"Just what is it I have done?" Senecwo asked.

"You have attended to the needs of the people," Iyaye said in his gritty voice. "In the days of Minkotep and Teshuwa, the sick were not ignored. But Hankasi seems to feel the weakest and most vulnerable among us are a nuisance. Word has reached the Council of his decision to let old Braug treat the poor. Anyone can see this was not his idea. And it was certainly not Braug's."

Senecwo was dumbfounded. If this man had so easily inferred the chain of events, who else knew?

"The Council has discussed you," Iyaye said. "At length."

Now Senecwo was certain her fear was blossoming on her face. Fear not for herself, but for her children.

"You are right to be afraid," Iyaye said, his white eyebrows creasing in concern. "The Council is controlled by the king. They live in fear of him and the hooded snakes who whisper in his ear."

Senecwo shook her head. "Why are you here?"

In response, Iyaye gestured towards the window without taking his eyes from her face. "There is a garden in my home, with a pond and a path that curves through the willow trees. It is a tranquil place, o queen. If the city burns it will not hold." He let his words sink in. "I am here because the people deserve a ruler who will rule."

"And because you fear what will happen to your family should the city fall into chaos," Senecwo said. "But what makes you think this is a possibility?"

"The men who would strive for power in Hankasi's absence are violent and pitiless, even by the standards of the Ancagua."

"But Hankasi is young and strong."

"The wise make plans that look beyond the summer, for winter is dark and always arrives sooner than the songbirds think."

Senecwo searched the old man's face for signs of treachery but found she could not read him.

"There are rumors," he went on, "not openly discussed amongst the Council, but known to me. You are not safe. Certainly, you are only protected now because of Hankasi. Were anything to befall him your life would be forfeit, as would the lives of your daughters."

"You speak treason," Senecwo said.

Iyaye did not flinch. "These are treasonous times."

The icy light in his eyes hardened. When he spoke again his voice was lower, even rougher. "I despise the magi. I also fear what the king will do to the kingdom of which he is but a custodian."

Senecwo felt her heart racing in her breast. This man could be killed for far less than what he had already said.

"Are there others on the Council who share your view?"

"Few."

"It may come as little surprise to you to learn that I have little love for my husband or his kingdom. I saw the suffering of the poor and sick and I acted, perhaps foolishly. That is all."

"I am not here to offer support for your succession, should the king die," Iyaye said. "I am not asking you to rule in his stead."

"What are you here for then?"

"I am here to warn you," Iyaye said. "And to offer you encouragement."

"What are you planning?" Senecwo asked.

"That," Iyaye said, "is the question of the hour."

Senecwo said nothing. They stood in silence, the young queen and the old man, while tiny motes danced in the sun's last rays.

"We are born of dust, you and I," Iyaye said. "We shall surely die, be it tomorrow or many winters from now. The question is not how to run from death, but rather how we shall live between this day and our last." Before she could reply he bowed deeply at the waist.

"Be of good hope. When the time comes, you will hear from me."

Then he was gone.

Chapter Eight

GLIMMER

. . .

The monstrosity had been crouching in the mouth of the cliff-side cave since before sunrise, hidden behind a large stalagmite jutting up from the bed of the underground river that doubled as the city's sewer. Filthy water streamed around its feet before falling out over the lip of the cave in a long horsetail. The pool at the falls' terminus was scoured by high tides only intermittently, and the stench kept passersby away from its edge, making the opening above a perfect vantage from which to espy the day's events unobserved.

The creature watched as the puppet king was borne down onto the strand and set alight. From time to time it shifted slightly, adjusting massive limbs, but for the most part it remained motionless and silent, its black eyes tracking the proceedings with inhuman patience. Before the first meat sellers rolled their clattering carts onto the beach, it bore witness to the recession of the wheeling stars and the appearance of the first tendrils of gray in the east. Then the slow trickle of mourners building to a flood. When the boy with the red feathers in his hair walked out onto the beach sucking on a melon rind, just one piece of driftwood in a sea of thousands, the creature saw him too.

Few in Aghuax were aware of the creature's existence, though it had lived in the darkness beneath the tidal plain where the city would one day rise since long before the arrival of its founders, the people who would later come to call themselves the Ancagua. One night soon after the magi arrived in Aghuax, their leader had disappeared beneath the foundations of the castle, seeking in sunless caverns and amidst the roots of stone for a venue where he might practice his dark arts in utter secrecy. The king's tower was fine for stargazing, but there were things that even the stars could not be allowed to see.

As the mage made his way deeper and deeper into the earth, his path was lit by a cold luminescence, which emanated from the tip of his long staff. After walking for some time, he heard the sound of running water, and moments later sensed powerful emanations. He quickly doused his light. Just up ahead, a thin wash of blue flame cut the darkness. Stealing closer, he discovered the source of the blue glow, and thrilled with wonder.

There on the black shore of an underground river, Ixiltical came upon a giant creature crouching intently over the waters, its naked flesh pale as ivory. Even hunched over it was obviously a colossus. Muscles rippled like cables across its limbs and back. Though not a man, its limbs and proportions were man-like. Tusks like those of a boar protruded from the sides of its mouth.

The creature was feeding silently, a snakelike tongue flickering wetly into the belly of a dead fish it clutched in its massive hands. Those hands were what Ixiltical had seen from a distance. They were engulfed in tongues of blue fire that flickered and danced like actual flame, yet did not burn the beast. Here was a creature unlike anything Ixiltical had ever seen, and he had seen much.

For a long while Ixiltical watched the creature as it fed, in awe of its power and dark grace. Then he gripped his wand and flooded the cavern with red light. The beast flashed to its feet, allowing the mage to see its full height. It was half again as tall as the greatest champions of men. Its hands ignited with redoubled flame, throwing indigo sparks into the water with a hiss of steam. Waves of energy roiled from the creature's chest and hands, setting the air of the cave vibrating with a flavor of magic the sorcerer had never tasted. The beast and the High Mage stared at each other across the water for a long moment, both of them silent and still.

Without warning, the creature sprang forward in an impossible bound that ate half the distance between them, unleashing a bolt of white energy that nearly overwhelmed the mage. Ixiltical only just managed to throw up a protective screen and fire off a counter-spell. The rocks echoed with concussions. A great struggle ensued, in which there were moments when Ixiltical was certain he would die. Near what proved to be the end of their confrontation, the creature landed a curse that froze the left side of the mage's body. Ixiltical tumbled roughly to the rocks. Half paralyzed, he watched the beast walk toward him, jaws opening wide to reveal huge canines that matched its yellowed tusks.

At the last moment Ixiltical managed to scream a garbled word of power with the working half of his mouth, calling down an entire section of the cavern's granite ceiling and burying his attacker beneath a gigantic mound of rock and bat shit. The cave-in would have killed a whale, yet the pile began moving before the dust had even settled. Amazed, Ixiltical limped over toward the head already emerging from the debris. Blood was running from the beast's jet black eyes and there was a great wound on its forehead, but it managed to bare its teeth in rage. Here, thought the mage, was a worthy thing.

There on the shores of the black river, Ixiltical bound the vile and wondrous creature to a new name by means of an immense and painful spell that thereafter compelled it to do his bidding. Glimmer, the High Mage called it, or Cthon, *That Which Slithers in the Darkness.*

· · ·

Now the flags of night were unfurling, their great banners drawing down around the corners of the day. Smoke drifted up from a thousand cook fires, sooty fingers probing the sky as the citizens of Aghuax, hungry after the long day's ceremony, all began cooking at once. The city settled down to rest like a great predator in its den, ignoring the young boy as he flew through its smoky streets.

The boy's hair was grown out like a man's, though he could not have been more than ten summers old. It fluttered behind him, its long waves worked with two red feathers that danced as he sprinted through the coins of light tossed from open doorways. He ran silently, the balls of his bare feet barely touching the ground. Ahead of him, dark spires beckoned.

His journey had begun at a side entrance to the Lodge of the Elders, a long, low structure of burnished wood that lay like a beehive fallen on its side in the middle of Bitter Square, its gleaming curves standing out amidst the surrounding structures of stone and mud. The boy with the red feathers in his hair had watched the Council arrive at the lodge following Hankasi's cremation, the old men flapping in from the darkness like bats. As they trickled in by ones and twos the lodge's circular door opened to receive them, allowing firelight to spill out from within. Once the last elder had arrived the door was barred and the Council went into seclusion. They had much to deliberate.

It was impossible to spy on the elders. The wards set about the lodge—a necessary precaution against those who would eavesdrop through spiritwalking or other means—were far too strong. A fly could not have entered the place without being detected. But in many cases you didn't need to be inside. You just needed to catch the first runner sent out with a message. The elders guarded against this by sending multiple boys, some of whom unwittingly carried false papers, or by encoding their communications in ciphers for which the runners did not possess the key. Such precautions made the message itself more secure while doing little to protect the messengers. A month earlier, on a night the elders were rumored to be discussing the problem of the magi, two different runners had been found drowned in a sewer grate, tied back to back with their ears and noses cut off.

Despite the danger there was never a shortage of willing couriers. One could earn enough to feed a family for a week by successfully delivering a single important message, and there were always boys who were desperate, hungry, or bored enough to try their luck in the alleys and lonely places of the city. None among them was as swift or fearless as the boy with the red feathers in his hair.

Less than an hour after the Council had gone into seclusion, the lodge herald emerged from the ocular doorway holding an unlit torch. Several loiterers surged forward, but the boy with the red feathers in his hair drew back into the shadows, recognizing the pre-arranged sign. While the herald made a show of assigning one of the clamoring novices a scroll that was in fact a decoy, the boy with the red feathers in his hair took a circuitous loop through the alleys bordering the lodge, eventually emerging at a little-used side door where an old man waited in the shadows, draped in the thick ceremonial furs the elders wore in their meetings.

"My message is for the queen," the man said, wasting no time. His hoary voice was cast low, a match for the flickering shadows. When he lifted his arm to hold out a neatly rolled piece of silvery parchment, his heavy robe parted and the boy saw a flash of blue silk from beneath.

He had run messages for Iyaye many times. Over time he had become accustomed to the elder's matter-of-fact style. There was something about the old man's face that made the street-wise boy feel safe, although he would not have been able to articulate this. Part of it was Iyaye's appearance. The hair streaked with white. The chain of sunspots spread across his wide forehead. The eyes that had seen much of life yet not been deadened.

The boy took the scroll without a word.

"Kulkas and her daughters are in danger," Iyaye said. "Yengwa has designs on the throne. To move forward he must eradicate the queen and the Council is unwilling to stop him. She will have no protection and little time. I fear he comes this very night."

The boy glanced at the scroll. It was stamped with Iyaye's personal seal, a half-severed reed. The boy did not understand why a noble old man, one with a large family and a proud name, would risk his life to warn a foreign-born queen. Everyone knew she was a weak and unfit heir to Hankasi's throne. But it was not the boy's place to ask and he knew better than to seem curious. That was an easy way to get killed.

"My seal will gain you access to the castle," Iyaye went on. "Let no one open or take the scroll, but see that you set it in the queen's own hand, lest we both be put to death. If you are questioned, insist on the message's urgency."

The boy understood. If he were found carrying a message contradicting the will of the Council, both he and Iyaye would face a slow death on the city wall.

"You are assuming a great risk," Iyaye said. "If you successfully deliver this message I will pay you five times the standard wage."

The boy was shocked. The money would feed his mother and sisters for a year. He felt a momentary flash of shame for having already considered how much he could get for the message from the king's representatives. Now he bowed low.

"You can rely upon me."

There was nothing else to say. He took the scroll and began to run.

. . .

High in the shadows above, a hulking figure set out along with the boy. Flitting from rooftop to rooftop, it matched his pace with ease. The High Mage had journeyed to the sewers the night before and given his most fell servant instructions regarding a child who wore red feathers in his hair. Glimmer had tracked the boy all morning, watching as he wove through the crowd on the beach, picking the occasional pocket. Though he had arrived late, the boy still managed to end up with a perfect vantage point for the firing, atop a giant sandstone block discarded during a renovation of the city wall. When the moment came for Ixiltical to relieve the concubine of the burdens of life, Glimmer noted that the boy did not look away.

The boy left soon after the torches were set to Hankasi's pyre, causing Glimmer to retreat into the darkness. Tracing the boy's movements from lookout to lookout, the creature crawled through black passageways, swam fetid pools, and glided along slimed corridors until finally emerging from the sewers behind the Lodge of the Elders. It waited until a pair of passing fishwives rounded the corner before flashing across the street and silently scaling a wall. There, in the shadowed join where two buildings met, the beast hung like a lizard and waited.

The boy was currently out of sight around the corner, near the entrance to the lodge, but Glimmer knew he would soon approach the side door directly below. The creature had seen this as clearly as if it had already happened, for it had its own powers of foresight, and could draw on deep veins of magic not even the High Mage could understand or manipulate.

Before long, the boy appeared and engaged in conversation with one of the elders. The old man spoke quietly, but it made no difference. Glimmer heard every word as clearly as if they had been standing a yard away. Soon the boy was off, sprinting into the darkened streets with remarkable speed. He stuck to the city's dark hem, hurdling sleeping beggars and deftly dodging the rickety wheels of turnip carts being drawn home for the evening. He flew like the wind. But Glimmer flew faster.

The High Mage's servant considered making the kill in the last few alleys of the Meatsellers Quarter, but when it drew near the boy put on an extra burst of speed, looking over his shoulder as if sensing something. It would have been a small thing to catch him even then, but silence was more important. The boy might cry out. The scroll might be damaged or lost. The creature did not care about the machinations of men, but it was being carried along by an external will, a harsh whip cracking invisibly within the fibers of its being, compelling it to obey the merciless wizard in the blood red robe.

By the time the boy burst into the light of the guardhouse fire at the entrance to the castle courtyard, Glimmer was already clinging easily to the rampart's flank, waiting and watching. Startled by the boy's explosive entrance, the trio of guards standing around the flames instinctively cocked their spear arms. They nearly impaled him, only just restraining themselves after registering his tender age.

The boy slowed to a walk upon reaching the safety of the light. Chest heaving, he approached the guards with confidence, holding the scroll before him like a key. Two of the men kept their spears pointed at his chest while the third swiped the parchment roughly from his hand.

"What is this?" the guard snarled.

"My message is for the queen alone," the boy said calmly.

The guard laughed. The sound was like flint sparking in his chest. "The queen." He waved the scroll like a baton. "The elders have a message for the queen that we do not know about?"

"You know about it now," the boy said, wondering if Iyaye had been wise to seal the letter so prominently with his signet. The guard hadn't looked down at it yet, but when he did there would be no mistaking it, for better or worse. "Time is of the essence."

"Is it?" The guard said, turning to his companions. "The boy says he cannot wait for us."

The second guard, a man with a long scar running from his eye socket to his jaw, had not stopped staring at the boy since he arrived. For a moment it seemed there would be further questions. Or maybe they would just run the boy through and be done with it. If they took the paper Glimmer would have to kill them all. Messier than taking the boy alone, but still simple. The second guard took the scroll and examined the seal.

"Iyaye," he grunted. Then he shrugged. Better to err on the side of keeping the elders happy, what with the king dead and everything uncertain. Let the guards at the queen's door make the final decision on whether a little boy was a threat. The scarred one raised his spear. The boy held out an upturned palm, and the warrior slapped the parchment into his hand before turning back to face the courtyard.

As the boy crossed the pavement his head tilted up towards the ramparts. The walls of the fortress were lined with heads in various stages of decomposition, leering down from their horrible vantage with rictus smiles. Chieftains and their sons, taken captive in Hankasi's raids and brought back to Aghuax in chains, their eyes put out, their tongues cut off, their fiefdoms decapitated along with their bodies. The boy seemed particularly transfixed by the disembodied head of a woman. There was hardly any hair left on her head, the skin drawn and sunken like hide. A sharp wind had come up off the bay and the head creaked on its spit, the ruined eyes seeming to follow the boy as he walked.

Glimmer's powers of perception, already acute at the time of capture and further amplified by Ixiltical's brutal ministrations, allowed it to sense the additional guards posted in front of the queen's chamber without seeing them. The creature could hear their footsteps on the stone, the breath in their nostrils, the beating of their hearts. There were others stationed throughout the fortress, in the inner courtyard and along the walls. Avoiding them would be easy. Slinking through the brokemouth shadows, Glimmer slipped over the outer wall and crawled headfirst down the stones, dead eyes reflecting no light.

The boy with the red feathers in his hair walked briskly through the inner courtyard, eager to leave behind the accusatory gazes of the heads on the wall. At the far edge of the square he reached a lone guard warming his hands by a brazier.

"Which way to the queen's chamber?" Glimmer heard him ask.

The warrior nodded toward the shadowy mouth of an open archway. The boy entered and found himself in a hall that turned to the right. He slowed his steps as he padded along the cool flags, leaving behind both guards and ghosts. The parchment scroll in his hand whispered in the breeze. Light seeped around a bend in the hallway up ahead. He had made it.

Glimmer sensed the boy's sudden terror as long cold fingers clamped over his mouth. The beast gently probed the child's neck with razor nails, testing the skin. There was a scream trapped inside the boy's throat. The muscles of his neck had gone taut as tendons, but Glimmer's vice grip kept even the faintest whimper from escaping. The boy never saw his attacker's face, or the giant mouth opening in a strange approximation of a smile. As Glimmer eased the boy's body to the ground, the guard at the fire pulled his cloak tighter against the wind and began to whistle a lonely tune.

Chapter Nine

SENECWO

. . .

S enecwo looked up as Wiwoka entered the room. The queen noted how her chief handmaiden unconsciously rung her hands as she crossed the floor, sliding a thumb and forefinger around the opposite wrist in an agitated bracelet. When they had been brought to Aghuax both women had enjoyed thick heads of lustrous jet hair. Though subjected to cataclysmic trials, Senecwo's body had not yet begun to break down. She remained as beautiful as the day they had first arrived in the city, her skin clear and smooth, her hair the same perfect glossy black it had always been. Wiwoka had not been sustained by the same mysterious powers. The skin near her eyes was hatched with premature creases, and on the left side of her scalp a brilliant shock of pure white hair had appeared amidst the waves of black.

"The guards said it was nothing, my lady."

Senecwo gave a wan smile. "I will be an old woman before you stop calling me that."

To the queen's surprise, Wiwoka lowered her eyes and looked

as if she might cry.

"Forgive me, I did not mean to reprimand you," Senecwo said, pushing back from the dressing table. She patted the chair next to her. "Come. Sit with me."

The dressing room was painted the color of sea foam. A golden band of light from the setting sun slid down the eastern wall.

"They said it was nothing?"

Wiwoka nodded wearily as she sat down. Moments earlier they had heard raised voices out in the hall, and she had gone to investigate.

"They told me not to worry," Wiwoka sighed, putting her forehead in her hands. Senecwo reached up and began rubbing her friend's back. She caught herself thinking about how deeply strange and inappropriate it would seem to the people of Aghuax, a queen comforting her handmaiden.

Upon returning from the funeral she had been unsurprised to find the normal complement of two guards stationed outside her door doubled to four. Whether their orders were to keep her safe, or just keep her shut in, they would never say. She had her suspicions.

For thirteen years now she and her handmaidens had lived in exhausting, privileged captivity. Captured in a raid that left their village in flames, they had been spared the beheading and sudden oblivion of their families for reasons that became clear long before they arrived in the city of their conquerors. On the agonizing journey to Aghuax, Senecwo had been forced to ride behind Hankasi, her arms about his waist as if she were his young lover. At night she had agonized to the sound of her friends weeping as their captors toyed with them.

The queen poured a cup of water from the pitcher on her dressing table and passed it to Wiwoka.

"What comes with the night?" Wiwoka asked, raising the cup to her lips.

Senecwo wondered as much herself. In her heart she feared mutiny. Would naming the fear assuage it, or only serve to frighten them both? Her hand lingered on the handle of the pitcher, thumb rubbing absently.

"I fear a darkened road unwinds before us."

Wiwoka set the cup down, a far-off look in her eyes. Senecwo could see how tired her friend was. Stray hairs floated around her head, giving her the look of a child. Senecwo harbored little faith the elders would uphold her right to the throne. If left to fend for herself, flight would be the only option. Escaping into the wilderness with an infant and two young children was a prospect so grim she had previously banished it from her thoughts whenever it arose. Now it nagged at her again.

A cool breeze carried the salt tang of the ocean in through the open window. This rumor of the beach caused Senecwo to think again, as she already had several times that day, of the shaman. He kept his distance from the world of the castle, and as a result she had only seen him a handful of times. She knew the magi despised him. The people seemed to think he was a relic at best, an enemy at worst. To her he was something else entirely.

"At least we'll walk it together," Wiwoka said. She sounded resigned, but there was something else in her voice too. A fragile, loving note that made something inside of Senecwo quiver, something good and vulnerable she had been forced to shield all these years, only letting its fire warm her in fits and spurts. The queen put her head on her friend's shoulder.

"At least that," she murmured.

. . .

Earlier that year, on one of the sacred days the magi had proclaimed for the honoring of their gods, Senecwo had been in the godwood. The light was falling with perfect symmetry across the giant totems arrayed along the cliff. Ixiltical and his hooded cabal stood in a ring beneath the image of Teulanic, whimpering in their guttural tongue, asking the Great Mystery to bless Hankasi's warring in the coming season. Not to bless the nets, Senecwo had noted with dismay, or the harvest, or the mothers. Theirs were gods who seemed to want nothing but sorrow. To feed on it as men feed on the fruit of the vine.

The godwood was a grassy clearing named for the ring of white birches that encircled it. It was oriented around a central mound, the top of which stood more than twice the height of a man. At its summit the mound collapsed into a concave hollow wherein the magi had installed an ominous wooden pole that seemed to erupt from the grass like the groping ambition of some giant seed.

Three captives waited at the foot of the hill, their hands tied, their necks bound with iron collars. Recently brought up from the king's pits, they were covered in scabs and leech-wounds and barely able to stand. One of the captives was an emaciated young boy whose ribs stood out individually against the taut, yellowed skin of his abdomen. He shivered despite the warm breeze. His nose ran like a spring stream and his feet were black with dungeon rot. The other two prisoners were hardly less pitiful: a hunched, balding wretch with a potbelly wearing nothing but a dirty loincloth, and a bow-legged fellow with wiry coils of gray hair. The old man wept openly, tears running crazily across his cheek where the flesh was branded like a cow's.

Senecwo stood to one side, arrayed in her finery. She was present only as a figurehead. Hankasi had demanded she come and then ignored her all morning. Seeing the prisoners, the young queen felt an aquifer of shame welling within her. In another life she might easily have stood where they did.

After the muttering prayers had gone on for some time, the High

Mage's acolyte came forward and took up the rope attached to the boy's neck to lead him to the post atop the mound. The acolyte was but a boy himself with not a hair to be seen on his cheeks. He moved deliberately, seeming neither reticent nor eager to perform his bit part in the day's events. Perhaps if he had moved faster everything would have been different. As it was Senecwo had just enough time.

She stepped forward and took hold of the rope. The acolyte bowed low and let the lead fall from his hands. As he backed away, Senecwo stared at the grimy urchin standing before her. The child was no less terrified now than he had been a moment earlier. His eyes were wide as a deer that has heard the hunter. Senecwo had no plan, having acted on pure compulsion. Uncertain and almost dazed, she turned to find Hankasi looking at her in astonishment. His surprise at her audacity was so great that for a moment he simply stood and watched along with the High Mage. It seemed she should say something, at least to the boy if not the crowd. But her tongue stuck to the roof of her mouth and her heart fluttered wildly, a hummingbird trapped in a basket. A pane of throbbing silence slid across the grove.

Hankasi had arrived at the ceremony in a new robe of midnight blue adorned with many moons, and it billowed behind him now as he covered the distance to the mound in a few long strides. He looked like a bull preparing to charge.

Throughout the morning the shaman had been crouched on his haunches at the edge of the circle, watching the proceedings in silence. He looked like some kind of bird, squatting in the dirt with his charcoal-banded eyes, beak-like nose, and cloak of feathers. His own acolyte, the girl named Canowic, was sitting just behind him along with the pack of wolves that accompanied him everywhere he went. Canowic wore her deerskin cape, the pelt's head pulled up over her own. Finely wrought tattoos traced her hairline and jaw, stylized vines illuminating the sharp angles of her cheekbones.

Senecwo was so focused on Hankasi's approach she did not notice the shaman rising quickly, his cloak whispering like rain in tall grass. He arrived at her side a moment before the king, interposing himself between them. The king was livid, but the shaman held his gaze without flinching. In fact his hooded eyes seemed to convey that he was not overly concerned by the young king's anger.

"Am I not Lord of Lords," Hankasi said, his voice low and salted with danger, "and speaker for the gods?"

"Lord you may be," the shaman replied. "Though of certain things only, and those for whom you presume to speak are not what you imagine."

Having drawn close enough to hear this, Ixiltical spat in the sand. Hankasi looked over his shoulder at the High Mage, who now threw back his cowl, revealing his skull-like head, and let out a shriek of rage. Senecwo's skin crawled. The shaman turned to face his true enemy, ignoring the king. Ixiltical raised his ceremonial knife and drew it across his own arm, bringing forth a bright ribbon of blood.

"You have dwelt in your hole by the sea too long, dog," the High Mage shouted, pointing his bleeding arm at the shaman. "You have forgotten yourself. Teulanic will requite you with doom for your heresy!"

"By whose authority do you rebuke me?" the shaman asked, his voice as powerful as the mage's though he had not seemed to raise it.

"The Mystery of the Desert," Ixiltical snarled. "He will not be mocked."

"Yet he makes a mockery of justice and of life itself," the shaman said, reaching out to touch the shoulder of the young slave boy, who immediately stopped trembling. Ixiltical's face was becoming disfigured with rage. He began to walk toward the shaman, brandishing his long white wand. Senecwo drew back and ducked, raising her hands to cover her face.

The blood on the mage's arm was turning black and steaming, but the shaman only raised his chin, like a man in a street fight daring a drunk to punch him. The feathers of his cloak fluttered in an unfelt breeze and the light in the grove dimmed, as if someone had thrown sackcloth across the sun. A white light seemed to emanate from the shaman's scalp. Senecwo felt an intense heat radiating outward from the holy man. When he spoke, his eyes blazed with terrible fire.

"I defy your curse, black one. You hold no power over me."

Ixiltical only laughed.

"The judge of the worlds will run you through his jaws," he said, his voice distorted now, sounding as though it came from underwater.

"Speak not to me of judgment," said the shaman, "for you yourself will one day stand upon the trial stone."

Just as it seemed to Senecwo that sparks must soon ignite both men and trigger a terrible conflagration that would consume them all, Hankasi raised his hands with the bravery of a fool.

"Enough!" he shouted, looking at the shaman. "All men know that to strike a holy fool is to throw a bad number upon one's own head. You are unworthy of my time, old one."

With that he turned to lead the young slave boy the rest of the way up to the whipping post atop the mound. But before the king had gone three steps the shaman raised a hand towards his back. Hankasi slowed, then stopped altogether. His head drooped down, chin touching his chest. When he raised it back up a moment later there was a different lambence in his eyes. The anger was still there, but dulled, as if the burning iron of rage had been plunged into a barrel of cool water. He held the halter to the boy's neck loosely in his hand. He was clearly confused, trying to understand why he had stopped walking. His brow furrowed, then smoothed as he held the rope up for the shaman to see.

"Do you not understand that I can be merciful too, old man?"

The shaman said nothing, merely bowing his head. Hankasi dropped the lead and stalked back down the mound. Ixiltical stared at the shaman with knowing fury, but he was clearly exhausted. Sweat stood out on the shaman's forehead too, though he was not as spent, or at least hid it more artfully. Taking the boy's hand, he escorted him down the mound and outside the circle of trees. The people murmured as he went, but Hankasi seemed not to notice. Gathering the other magi, Ixiltical sliced his hand and dripped his own blood onto the pillar stone beneath Teulanic's totem. Two slaves came forward bearing armfuls of wood, and soon the smoke of their infamies was rising toward heaven.

. . .

Senecwo still remembered the slave boy's terrified expression, and the way his trembling had stopped when the shaman touched him. Now in the hour of her need, she longed to feel comforted like that. She reached out and took Wiwoka's hands in her own.

"Let us see what the morning brings."

The light was fully gone now. Senecwo carried a lit taper with her as she padded quietly into her daughters' bedchamber. The girls were sprawled together in Leokita's bed, limbs tangled together. The queen knelt beside them. How beautiful they were in repose, she thought. How perfect. She brushed the hair from their foreheads and kissed them both before moving to the crib where Kisoko lay swaddled. Senecwo envied her babe's ignorance. She wished she could unlearn all of life's brutal lessons. She wished there had been no need to be taught them.

After her handmaidens helped her undress, the queen dismissed them to go their own chambers, but they begged her to let them stay for the night. If anything were to happen to her they feared they would be divided like meat amongst dogs. She let them, of course. They curled on the furs at the foot of her bed while she lay down and descended into a dark and troubled dream.

Chapter Ten

YENGWA

. . .

Yengwa lifted the grimacing boar's iron tongue and let it fall with a resounding boom against the door at the base of the tower. The stones of the Meatsellers Quarter had been warm beneath his feet on his way over, the cobbles retaining the heat of day long after sunset. In contrast, the door radiated cold. Yengwa stepped back and craned his neck up toward the shard's dizzying tip. When Hankasi had first given the magi the run of the tower it had extended perhaps fifty feet above the highest pinnacle of the castle's main building. It seemed to have doubled since then, groping like a dark thistle toward the sky.

Half a mile back in the direction he had just come, the Council was sequestered in their lodge. Yengwa pictured them tumbling over one another like bees in a hive. As much as he disdained their endless talking, he knew they were not weak men. Many had been warriors in their day. They must have hated who Hankasi had become as much as Yengwa himself. He also knew many of them shared his low opinion of the magi, and given the chance would do what was necessary. No, the problem was not the Council, nor even the magi. At least, not the first problem. The first problem was the queen.

That foreign bitch. It made Yengwa seethe even now to think of such a royal bloodline as Teshuwa's being watered down and mixed with the worthless seed of the mountain peoples. Had the Ancagua kept their blood pure for centuries for nothing?

Kulkas had manipulated Hankasi into having his own physician treat the sickest of the sick in the very courtyard of his own castle, beneath his own balcony. The custom of the people, at least in Yengwa's lifetime, had been to take those who were beyond help or too old to fend for themselves and leave them far out on the barren coast south of the city. In this way they would no longer be a burden to their families. The queen actually wanted to treat these hopeless cases. That Hankasi had let her was a powerful reminder of how even the most potent of men might be warped under the yoke of a woman.

Despite all this, both custom and law called for Kulkas to now take the throne. But the Council would not give him any trouble there. They did not want a foreigner on the throne any more than he did. Any of them that did could be dealt with. Perhaps they already had been. Yengwa had revealed his suspicions regarding Iyaye during an earlier meeting and the sorcerer had promised to handle the problem. His lack of hesitation also told Yengwa the High Mage would have no qualms about trying to eliminate him at some point too. Unlike Iyaye, he would be ready.

He had just grasped the boar's tongue and raised it to knock again when the door swung silently inward. Yengwa crossed the shadowy threshold. A cool breeze blew down the tightly spiraling stairs, carrying hints of old stone, cobwebs and something he could not place. Bitter and sweet at once, it made the hairs inside his nose prick up. He lifted a hand and gingerly examined the deep wounds marring half his face. Several of the deepest cuts were starting to close, but many of the craters where huge bubbles had risen and burst were still weeping. The breeze irritated the raw skin beneath the eye he had been lucky not to lose. He blinked, shifting the weight of his war hammer where it was slung across his back, and began to climb.

The stairway was dim, the only light coming from an occasional guttering torch in a wall bracket. A rough orange glow would sputter and bleed down on him from above as he climbed, eventually appearing around the endless curve only to fade away behind him as he rose further into the darkness. The brush of his boots against the stone echoed down the shaft. Hemmed in by the tight angle of the stairs, he wouldn't have been able to use his weapons if he'd wanted to. This was the mage's way. He made you feel uneasy before you even reached him.

As he climbed the tower's throat, Yengwa's mind wandered back across the years that had led to this day. He still found it hard to believe how weak Hankasi had become. It had been painful enough to see his old friend, a man of such great potential and lineage, deluded by the magi. Anyone with two eyes could see the red-robed witches had no love for Aghuax or its inhabitants. They sought only to control and enslave. But Yengwa would be no man's slave. He had waited on that first day in the throne room for Hankasi to give the signal. Or better yet, to skewer the High Mage himself when he transformed his staff into a host of vipers. Yet he had stood by, both then and ever after, allowing the magi to run riot over their people's most sacred traditions.

No one would mistake Yengwa for a holy man, but he kept the rites and observed the festival days. He was Ancagua. He did not fear the gods of his fathers, but he knew they were there, in the seas, the earth, and the heavens, and that they favored men of action. The rhythms of the ancient faith had kept the city stable for aeons. This alone was a mark in its favor. Hankasi had given the godwood over to a band of outsiders and their blood cult for no reason.

Yengwa finally reached a second, smaller door at the top of the endless stair. It was time to put certain thoughts aside. He rearranged his face into a mask and raised a hand to knock, but again the door swung open before he could.

The High Mage's chamber held neither chair nor bed, the only piece of furniture being a large table covered in star charts. Bundles of dried herbs hung from the rafters, and the circular walls were covered from floor to ceiling with shelves crammed with ominous tomes, strange instruments, and jars containing things unborn or long dead. Ixiltical stood with his back to the door, looking out at the moon-white sea through a window that was scarcely more than an arrow slit.

"You are wounded," said the High Mage.

The two men had not spoken at the funeral despite their proximity. Yengwa touched his face again, involuntarily, his fingers grazing the melted flesh.

"She is only a child," Ixiltical went on, still looking out the window. His voice held a rattle that was not quite a laugh.

Yengwa was stunned, though some part of him knew he ought not be. He had not spoken with the High Mage since the day he had received his scars a fortnight earlier, just before leaving for raiding. There was no way he could have known how he had come by them.

"And no," Ixiltical continued, "the shaman does not know, for she has not told him and he will not read her mind against her will."

Yengwa understood what the mage was trying to do by throwing him off guard, but all he needed was to keep the pretense of their cooperation up for a few hours longer. Rather than playing into the mage's hands, he ignored the provocation and spoke plainly about the task at hand.

"It is time."

For a moment his words seemed to hang in the air, thick and substantial. He imagined he could almost see them turning in the gloom. Ixiltical finally swiveled to face him, the hem of his crimson robe whispering against the stones. Dozens of candles ignited themselves all around the room, untouched by human hands. Staring into the mage's face, Yengwa found himself wondering whether the creature before him was a man at all. Perhaps a demon or some avatar of the other world. He could feel the mage's heavy eyes crawling through his brain.

"So tonight is the night," Ixiltical said, with a hint of condescension. "You have come to let me know."

Yengwa kept his face impassive.

"Even now I am on my way," he confirmed.

In the moonlight the sorcerer's gray eyes were like dull pearls.

"I am with you," Ixiltical said. "I would only remind you of our earlier conversation."

Yengwa raised his eyebrows slightly, asking for clarification.

"I seek only one thing," Ixiltical said, his tone inviting Yengwa to recite that one thing.

"Your gods can slake their thirst," Yengwa said. "I will not stop you."

"It is a particular thirst they have," the High Mage said. "Wherever you reach the queen and her brood, you will find the shaman waiting with them."

"That goat," Yengwa sneered. "How does he know?"

"He is a magician," Ixiltical said, his voice dripping with contempt and perhaps a hint of resignation. "He knows many things. He will try to interfere, but my servant will deal with him. Afterwards, you will bring the shaman's acolyte to me."

"No." Yengwa shook his head firmly. "The girl is mine."

Ixiltical cocked his head. He was not used to being denied, but he could go to the abyss as far as Yengwa was concerned. The girl was his by all rights of vengeance. He had claimed her. Now he noticed a feeling in his forehead, a prickle growing quickly to a persistent itch. The air was oppressive, cold yet fetid at the same time, like the too-close staleness of a fishing skiff's hold.

The mage was boring into him, trying to enter his mind and violate his will. Yengwa funneled all his energies into a bulwark. He was conscious of the hammer and spear slung across his back, yet knew neither would reach the mage, even if he were to hurl them with all his strength and accuracy. Before things escalated any further Yengwa felt himself released. The relief he felt was as real as if the mage's hands had been clenched around his throat.

"As you wish," Ixiltical said, his voice threaded with soft menace. "Bring me one of the other girls."

Yengwa simply stared at him, refusing to give the sorcerer any satisfaction. Having said what he came to, he turned to leave. Ixiltical's voice stopped him at the door.

"You will take Glimmer with you."

Yengwa bridled. The last thing he needed was another mage keeping track of him. At the same time, loathe though he was to admit it, extra help might be useful where the shaman was involved.

"He can join us when the time is right."

Ixiltical smiled mirthlessly and turned toward a small set of stairs near the window. Yengwa looked at them in confusion. Had they been there all along? The High Mage had already begun climbing, not bothering to see whether Yengwa would follow. Ixiltical's hands were filled with the hem of his robe as he lifted it to avoid tripping, and his back was wide open to attack. But again Yengwa was stayed by a doubt that any mortal weapon could kill the mage. He waited a moment longer, meaning to leave. Then curiosity bested him and he followed Ixiltical up the stairs and through a trapdoor onto the roof.

The wind tugged gently at Yengwa's cloak as he emerged. The stars were spread out above them like a great host of ships floating in a black sea. From this height the entire beach was reduced to one long smudge of blackness at the edge of the sea. He drew a deep breath of salty air, hoping to clear his head.

"You once had a great love for Hankasi, I think," Ixiltical said. The mage was facing him, arms hidden in the voluminous sleeves of his robe. "Like that of a man for his brother. But it has faded."

It was true that he had loved the king. Contrary to the mage's assertion, that love had never faded. The magi had corrupted Hankasi, and none more so than Ixiltical himself.

"You overstep yourself," Yengwa said.

The mage dipped his head.

"Forgive me."

Yengwa offered no forgiveness, and the mage went on, untroubled by having given offense.

"If you rule the people, how will you know what is best for them?"

"When I rule the people," Yengwa said, "they will know what is best by virtue of what I decree."

"The king's word is law," Ixiltical said, nodding gravely, but Yengwa could sense the mockery in his reedy voice.

"The king's word is law," Yengwa echoed.

"And yet, perhaps you think Hankasi's words, his decrees as you call them, were less than perfect."

Yengwa shrugged, again refusing to step into one of the mage's traps. "Hankasi has gone to the hall of his fathers. I will not sit in judgment on him." He looked back toward the trapdoor where they had emerged. "Time is of the essence."

"Time," Ixiltical sighed. There was a hint of fatigue in his voice. Yengwa was not at all certain that time meant for the mage what it meant for him, but it did not matter. All men could be defeated, even the immortal. Strength was all that mattered. Strength and will.

"You will hear from me," Yengwa said, taking a step toward the stairs.

"May you find success," the mage said. As he spoke these parting words the heft dropped out of his voice. Yengwa turned back and saw Ixiltical staring slack-jawed at the stars, transfixed. The High Mage let out a gasp and pointed a bony talon at the sky.

"Ah!"

Before their eyes a star fell as if struck with an arrow, its red tail cutting the glassy dark.

Chapter Eleven

CANOWIC

. . .

Six months earlier the shaman had brought Canowic along with him to an audience at the castle. This was when Hankasi was still allowing the shaman into his councils and before he stopped coming at all. Master and acolyte had waited at the end of the throne room, patient as beggars seeking alms, while the king's ministers discussed plans for the coming year. By late morning Canowic was indignant on her master's behalf. The old men had been talking for hours, yet no one had asked the shaman's opinion on a single issue. All this talk of money and war and a possible treaty with the eastern tribes, and they did not deign to ask the oldest and wisest among them for his views. It was a disgrace. It was an insult.

Canowic searched the faces of the advisers and warriors gathered about the throne. Proud visages with hawkish brows and flinty, smoking eyes. The elders were all puckered old men, the light of their strength and glory veiled by age. Several of the warriors in the king's inner circle were long-lived for men of action. One of the youngest of these was Hankasi's captain, Yengwa. There was no denying he was handsome, even beautiful. The proportions of his face were perfect. The thick waves of hair, the high cheekbones, the vivid eyes shot through with dusky light.

While Canowic was watching him he happened to turn in her direction. His gaze snagged on her like a floating cottonwood seed caught by thorns. She tried to tear her eyes away, but for a long moment found she could not. When she finally succeeded she tried to pretend nothing had happened. The shaman had not seemed to notice. Perhaps Yengwa would let it go. The audacity of an acolyte making eye contact with the First Spear was grave. But her master hadn't seen. Everything would be fine. Then she heard footsteps.

Hankasi had been droning on about something. Now his voice died off. Canowic could feel the entire room turning to follow Yengwa's progress down off the dais and across the long floor. She heard the shaman stand beside her, but still could not bring herself to look up.

When she finally did, Yengwa's war hammer was in his hand and he was only a few strides away. His face had gone two shades darker. The knot of advisers had fallen silent. They did not understand what was going on. Canowic knew if it had been just the two of them he would have killed her without a second thought and left the mess for the stewards to clean up. She tensed to run, but then Yengwa hit an invisible wall. His face contorted, as if a wave of nausea was rolling over him.

"Let me pass, old man," he rasped, his eyes focused on Canowic. He sounded as if he was struggling to catch his breath. If he had been able he could have reached out and touched her with the head of his war hammer, he was that close.

The shaman had taken up a protective stance in front of her, hands hanging loosely at his side. He said nothing in response to Yengwa's demand.

"How dare you meet my eyes!" Yengwa barked at Canowic.

"Is it really the place of a warrior to quarrel with a child?" the king asked from his throne.

If Canowic was surprised by Hankasi's words, it was nothing compared to the look of astonishment that appeared on Yengwa's face.

"She has disrespected me," he said. "I will not brook arrogance from a whelp."

The shaman spoke at last. "Only the insecure see those weaker than themselves as a threat."

These words had an immediate effect on Canowic. Something began happening in her gut, a softening as the heat of indignity warmed tense muscles. The idea that she would be harmed, even killed, for merely looking at a man... it was too much. She felt her head lifting, her eyes rising to meet Yengwa's. The First Spear's nostrils flared as she stared at him. For a moment everything was still. Then he drew a sharp breath and let out a bellow that seemed to shake the roof beams, the tendons in his neck standing out like cords. He was straining with all his might, but he could not get past the invisible barrier holding him back. Hankasi rose and slowly walked down off the dais.

"You dare to taunt my warrior?" he asked the shaman. "You, who have given so little to the people in this season of great and joyous change?"

"I feel no joy at the changes the king has wrought," the shaman said bluntly. "Though I remain his true servant."

Hankasi snorted.

"This," the shaman continued, lifting a hand toward Yengwa, "was not your father's way."

"Do not invoke my father in the midst of defying me," Hankasi said, "lest I have your head on a pike."

"Do not threaten my daughter," the shaman said, his voice rising a notch.

Hankasi laughed and said something about orphans and whores, but the king might have been a mile away for all the attention Canowic was paying him. She couldn't believe her ears. *My daughter.* She blinked and realized there were tears on her cheeks. Yengwa was saying something else, joining the king in deriding her, but the shaman's words had taken the sting out of their slurs. He had called her daughter in front of all of these men.

The shaman was turning to go, his face hard and troubled as he showed his back to the king. All Canowic could do was follow. It had always been her master's way to avoid conflict whenever possible, and yet she marveled anew at his self-control. If given his powers she would have blasted Yengwa into the other world.

She looked back as they walked away and saw Yengwa struggling to come after her. He would have slain her if he could, but the magical shield held him back. At the last instant, before the guards' pikes closed behind them and the door to the throne room slammed shut, she permitted herself a mocking smile. Yengwa's scream of rage came through the closed doors. She thought the shaman might smile at this, but his face was like the sky before a storm.

"Now it begins," he said. She could not tell if he was speaking to her or to himself.

· · ·

Canowic expected Yengwa at the cave for the better part of a month. Her feeling of triumph had quickly worn off and was replaced by a sense of constant trepidation. Anytime the shaman left her alone, even for a moment, she went into a state of hyper-vigilance. She kept the cave wall at her back and a heavy branch on hand, and she never let the wolves out of her sight. As weeks turned to months she gradually dared to believe she might be safe. A feeling of vindication tempted her to let her guard down. Why should she bow down before a man like Yengwa, or accept the unspoken laws of his people, which said women could not look where they pleased? She grew careless. This was a mistake, for men like Yengwa have long memories.

A day came when the shaman left on an errand, taking the wolves with him. Canowic might have thought the danger had passed, but the shaman knew it never would. He instructed her to remain at the cave, and left his seeing stone with her.

"If anyone comes, or any danger arises, speak my name while holding the stone, and I will hear you."

She knew the master's name, his true name, but she would never have thought to profane it by speaking it aloud.

"Call and I will answer," he said, seeing the hesitation in her eyes. "Otherwise, wait for my return."

She reminded him it was a market day. She could go into the city while he was busy and purchase what they needed. He told her not to worry, he would bring back everything they required. She bridled at the restriction. He would bring back something the wolves had hunted, he meant. She was tired of venison. Why didn't he trust her to go collect the herbs they needed or buy a piece of mutton and a skein of cord for the mending? He thought she was too young. Well, she would prove him wrong. Once the master and the pack were out of sight she slipped off.

The market was full of wild color and incredible smells and a thousand people to watch. The citizens of Aghuax could seem standoffish, even cruel, but most of the time she slipped through them unmolested. This was never more true than at the market, where everyone was preoccupied with the wares and entertainments on display. She watched a man juggle a set of steel daggers, and thrilled to run her hands through a basket of dried long beans.

At the eastern edge of the market she came upon a stall manned by an old woman with a necklace of fuzzy antler tips. A block of pure diamond sat on a piece of ragged velvet in front of her. Canowic watched as a fisherman reached out to touch the block, which glowed from within as if with the light of a star. He recoiled in shock as soon as his fingers touched the surface.

"How is the fire held in such quiet?" he exhaled.

The old woman shook her head and claimed that what had burned his finger was not fire, but water cut from the edges of a mountain river. This was ridiculous of course, but Canowic was fascinated by the spectacle.

The shopping was no trouble. In addition to the cord, she picked up some star fruit and a new flint, and talked a rank-smelling farmer down to an acceptable price on a leg of mutton. She had just left the sheep pens and was turning into a narrow alley to take a shortcut back to Diamond Gate when a shadow fell across her from behind. She turned and saw Yengwa standing a few feet away.

He smiled, revealing a mouth full of white teeth that shone like alabaster. Something was seeping into Canowic's stomach, a sour dread that penetrated to her core. Yengwa took a step forward and she turned to run, tripped over a rock and sprawled face-first in the dust, sending the mutton flying. She rolled over in desperation to find him already standing over her. Yengwa glanced quickly over his shoulder, scanning the mouth of the alley. Canowic was riveted by his face. The pores of his nose were tight and clean, the skin smooth.

There was something in his eyes she had not expected. Something that frightened her more than pure rage would have. Yengwa leaned in close and she could smell the sweetness of his breath. He was panting lightly and she caught the aroma of ripe figs. He reached for the edge of her dress. For a moment all she could think about was the fact that she had left the shaman's stone at the cave.

Then Yengwa's fingers touched the cloth and Canowic felt something begin to well up from deep within her. It felt blue. This was the strangest sensation, but the color was there. At first it was a prickling sense of indigo beneath the skin of her abdomen. Then the energy began to push outwards, building to a coursing flow that turned first violet, then peach, orange, and finally red. She felt her eyes widening. Yengwa's hand was on her thigh now. He had not sensed what was happening within her until now, and something shifted in his eyes, registering alarm, and now the redness was blossoming, uncurling, bursting forth in an eruption of all-consuming, white-hot energy that slammed outwards from her eyes and her ears and her fingertips. Her head was flung back, her limbs went rigid, and for a moment she was utterly changed into fire. Then she knew nothing.

. . .

When she came back into herself Yengwa lay on the ground in front her. His face was charred. The skin looked like the side of a mountain torn loose in a mudslide and come to rest again all tumbled and ruined, mashed wetly together. It could not have been long, for the sun had barely moved overhead and no one seemed to have come across them. She gathered the things she had dropped and stumbled away.

When the shaman returned at dusk he immediately sensed something was wrong. But ask and cajole and demand though he might, Canowic would not tell him what had happened. She went to bed without eating and kept to herself for days afterwards. Her earlier fear had been nothing compared to this. Now she *knew* Yengwa would be coming for her. She knew just as clearly that she must tell the shaman, for anyone who came for her would come for him too, but she was ashamed, and afraid of whatever had poured itself out through her. Whenever she tried to work up the courage to tell the shaman she was overwhelmed and could not bring herself to do it.

She prayed the darkest prayers. That Yengwa would die. That he had been rendered a simpleton or lost the ability to speak. Rumors filled the city, but no one seemed to know the true story of where or how the First Spear had been so horribly disfigured. Some said he claimed to have fallen into a fire. Others speculated the magi had cast a spell on him. Canowic wondered why he did not come for her. Less than a fortnight after the encounter in the alley the war band thundered out through Char Gate to open the spring raiding. Canowic hid herself in the crowd and watched as Yengwa rode by at Hankasi's side, his once-perfect face now a mask of death. She was certain that when they returned everything would be different. She could not have known how right she was.

Chapter Twelve

CANOWIC

. . .

C anowic turned in time to see the shaman free himself from the cords of whale gut. She raised a hand in greeting as he stood, but he ignored her completely. He was still in thrall to his trance. As he passed by on his way out of the cave, magic curled in his wake, its potency making Canowic tear up as if she were smelling a freshly cut pepper. He waded into the water and the wolves followed. Sea and sky mirrored one another, both the bright scarlet of seal's blood.

Canowic knew her master had induced this trance himself. She also knew that, having given himself over to it, he now had no choice but to follow the spirit journey to its conclusion. Like a stick borne along a torrent, he could not turn back. A spark of uneasiness leapt in her heart. The city was in unrest. What would happen if he tarried too long before returning? What if someone came to the cave that night while he was away? She took a deep breath. *The wolves will still be here.*

The shaman was up to his knees in the water. He had been wearing only his loincloth and now he removed that too, dropping it into the waves. He stood with his hands open, divested of all raiment, long hair hanging down across his back. He would take nothing on his journey. Neither food nor any stone for seeing. While Canowic watched, he raised his arms to the just-appearing stars and made a whimpering sound. Then he hunched forward like a man whose heart is seizing and lurched sideways out of her field of vision. She heard a rustling sound, like rain rising quickly on the surface of a lake.

As Canowic scrambled out of the cave, trying to see what had happened, she was buffeted by an invisible pulse of energy that swept past her, popping her ears. He was gone. The wolves were skipping through the waves splashing one another, yipping like pups at the magic in the water, which was suffused with a strange golden light.

Canowic shuffled slowly back to the entrance of the cave and looked down at her unfinished meal. Her appetite was gone, replaced by a twinge of dread. She stared out at the bay, which had already returned to a rhythmic calm. There was no way of knowing how long the shaman would be away. As this truth sunk in, Canowic turned slowly toward the back of the cave, where the shaman's seeing stone lay unattended in its velvet shroud. She had used it numerous times in his presence, but never alone. The master had not expressly forbidden her to do so, so why did the mere thought leave her feeling furtive? After a few long moments of standing there, illicit feelings seeping into her spine, she made her decision.

Part of her protested, but she pushed her misgivings aside and looked back to see where the wolves were. She found them tracking her with their keen eyes. A few of them had their heads cocked sideways in a uniquely lupine display of curiosity. Surely they would have bared their teeth if she was in danger, or if the shaman would not have wanted her to look. That is what she told herself. But their tacit approval did nothing to stop the pounding of her heart as she pulled aside the shroud and looked down at the stone.

The crystal orb lay dull in its bed of cloth. Canowic dared to reach out and brush a finger across its surface. The stone's interior rippled and undulated at her touch, as if filled with water. She hesitated, then reached out and picked it up in both hands and quickly carried it to the front of the cave, out of the heavy shadows. Darkness had fallen.

Soon she was heading up the beach with the stone and an armful of sweetwood. The wolves did not accompany her. Nothing could make them leave the cave before the shaman returned from his long journey. Canowic was not too worried to be leaving their protection. The stone had pushed her fear of Yengwa aside. Besides, he would not think to look for her where she was going.

The sand held a memory of the vanished sun, and the warm breeze carried notes of kelp and gull dung. Had she looked behind her she would have seen the lights of the city glowing red in the darkness. She followed the curve of the beach, trudging along through the sand. By the time she finally reached the path that zigzagged up the chalky cliffs toward the bluff where the magi's totems held court above the sea, the sweetwood was growing heavy in her arms. The pomegranate seed stars bathed the path in even, silver light. She quickly reached the arch of willow switches marking the edge of the godwood, and paused at the threshold.

The day's events had stirred a layer of sediment from the bottom of her soul. She could feel the longing that had been growing in her for months unlimbering itself. Perhaps this would be the night when she would finally get some answers to the questions she wasn't sure she even knew the depths of. Where did she come from? Did her family still live? Who *was* she? The blood thrummed in her ears and she shivered despite the warm breeze.

She could feel something reaching out to her from across the threshold. Reaching out to whatever was inside her. The power that had scalded Yengwa wanted to spread its wings. She could feel it in her ribs and her legs and her heart. What if she was being inhabited by some demon or minor god? Part of her wanted to turn and run, but she desired answers even more. She would not be content with just another set of random symbols to interpret. No, tonight she wanted something clear and unmistakable. A whirlwind or a bolt of fire. A thunderclap and a clarion voice telling her what she longed to know. She gripped the shewstone tighter and felt power streaming through the willow arch, tugging at her cloak, beckoning her to come in, come in.

The shaman had warned her of the corruption the magi had brought to the holy place. Their wickedness and cruelty were on display for all who had eyes to see, and Canowic had learned to fear them. But could they truly have corrupted a place as sacred as this, one that had been hallowed since long before their arrival? If the elder gods still held sway over the treadings of the universe, then surely the Ancient One—if he was the true Lord of the World—would not allow such a wellspring to be defiled. Perhaps he would even reveal himself here at this ancient seat. For though his signs and wonders were all about her, she had yet to see him with her own eyes. Perhaps here, where the pathways of the immortal and the dead touched the world of men, she could find news of her family and hear from the Torchbearer all at once. The wind was pushing at the trees, causing them to bend like penitents toward the shadow-soaked totems. Canowic took a deep breath. If death found her now she would meet her family on the other side of the great waters.

All it took was a small step. The air shifted subtly as she stepped under the willows and crossed the threshold into the godwood. She began walking slowly around the clearing's edge. The grass was soft beneath her boots, the air humid. Everything was quiet, as if she had stepped beneath an upturned bowl. As she walked she looked up at the giant carvings arrayed along the cliff's edge. Teulanic's idol gleamed in the starlight. His bulbous eye seemed as if it might blink at any moment. Canowic was staring in dread fascination at the rippling lizard's endless rows of teeth when she sensed movement to her right. She spun wildly and nearly dropped the shewstone, the muscles in her back tensing as she prepared to run. She peered into the darkness, trying to see who was there.

Down at the far end of the row, Remerac grinned impishly, looking for all the world as though he had just climbed, laughing, back into the wood of his idol. He stood with one hand outstretched as if beckoning for something. His cape and tousled hair seemed to blow in the stiff winds of the crag where he had met his doom. Remerac had climbed to the upper slopes of Kulia, disregarding the wisemen who had warned him against the mountaintops. Dancing there along the crater's hem he fell into darkness. Yet the gods had pity on him and made him as one of their children, and he is reborn anew in each generation.

Satisfied that she had seen nothing, Canowic turned from the idols and climbed to the top of the mound at the center of the clearing. Sitting down on the close-cropped grass, she laid out the sweetwood and struck a flame. She settled in with her back against the whipping post, holding the shewstone in both hands, and inhaled deeply as the fire came to life. The smoke smelled of incense and fresh seaflowers, crushed pepper and trailing vines. Her head felt light.

The sweetwood burned quickly. Already the flames were dying down, the wood collapsing into a bed of glowing coals. Canowic had sat down with her back to the idols, and now, watching the firelight play across the crystal in her lap, she felt their eyes searching her. She inhaled again and looked up at the vault. The stars hung low and fat like fruit waiting to be picked. It was time. Gathering her courage, she slowed her breathing and leaned forward to look into the stone. The world fell away.

· · ·

She awoke disoriented, legs scissoring in the sand. Her head felt as though it had been stuffed with a hundredweight of cotton. The wind gabbled in the birches. It was fully dark now and for a moment she wasn't sure where she was. As she looked around, trying to reorient herself, she saw the shewstone lying at the edge of the coals that now throbbed dimly, red eyes glowering from hummocks of ash.

She lurched forward to bat at the stone, heedless of the flames, and was surprised to find it cool to the touch. It must have rolled from her hands at some point during her vision. She shuddered to think what the master would have done had he returned to find she had harmed it.

The shewstone's previously translucent surface had turned a solid black. This did not mean it was damaged, as it often changed colors and appearance. When at rest it was usually opalescent, shot through with veins of pink and red quartz, but Canowic had seen it mist over into a dark blue, as if overtaken by heavy clouds, or flash pure white. When the master gazed into the ball he could turn it to the purest, transparent glass. Nonetheless, the stone's newly blackened exterior seemed ominous.

Hugging the stone to her stomach, Canowic bit her lip and tried to focus. She was covered in a deep sweat and started shivering as the wind picked up. The chimes of bone in which the magi claimed to hear the voices of their gods were rattling and moaning in the breeze. Shaking uncontrollably, she rolled over on her side and vomited. The wind was kicking up to a roar, flattening the grass and blowing her hair around, but she paid it no heed. She was lying on her back, transfixed by the sight of stars falling by the dozen. Their long tails blazed as they rocketed toward the sea, all heaven catching fire.

BOOK II

...

Chapter Thirteen

SENECWO

. . .

Senecwo was a girl of fifteen winters when the Ancagua came creeping up from the gorge below her village with knives between their teeth. It had been late summer, when the harts leap from rock to rock in the still mountain air. She remembered her last moment of peace perfectly. She was sitting in the dirt floor of her family's hut plaiting husks with her mother and sisters while they waited for the men to come home from the terraces. Unbeknownst to her family, she had also been waiting for something else.

In the quiet hour after eating and before sleeping she would volunteer to take the scraps to the goats. It was a chore none of the girls liked, ensuring no one would deny her. Eyan would be waiting for her at the edge of the pen.

"What are you smiling about?" Her mother asked.

"Nothing," Senecwo said, grateful for the half-light. She could feel the color rising to her cheeks. When her mother deemed the men sufficiently late she sent Irin, the youngest girl, to fetch them. It was not uncommon for the men to stay in the fields after dark, working by the light of a bonfire to mend a wall or repair the sluices. Normally they would send someone to tell the women to eat without them. When they failed to do so Senecwo's mother became annoyed.

Irin had barely left the hut when the evening stillness was cut by a scream so torn and primal at first Senecwo thought it was an animal. She was the first to run outside, ducking through the goatskin flap and nearly stumbling over her little sister in the process. Irin was lying on the ground, her tiny legs kicking feebly, blood seeping from her mouth. An arrow protruded from her back, its black feathers scratching erratically across the ground as she struggled to breathe. The image of her writhing in helpless agony seared itself into Senecwo's mind.

Then Irin tried to speak. Senecwo leaned in close, putting her ear next to her sister's mouth. Irin drew a rattling breath and tried to push the words out, but the only thing that rose to her lips was a froth of pink foam. Her eyes were wild as bees, darting back and forth across Senecwo's face. Behind them something whispered in the grass. Senecwo whirled, squinting fearfully into the gloom.

She was just about to turn back to Irin when a wraith-like form rushed past, barely discernible against the outer darkness and visible only as a void against the navy soup of star and sky. Senecwo felt Irin squeezing her hand and looked down in a panic. Her sister was fading. She laid a hand on Irin's forehead and bent down to kiss her, whispering in her ear as she did.

"Sleep now, my heart. Be still and sleep."

Then the night cracked open. A multitude was suddenly upon them. Tall warriors with painted faces rose like spirits from the darkness, crowing in an unintelligible tongue. Senecwo threw herself across Irin but was immediately dragged off. She clawed at the earth, trying to stay with her sister. Irin's legs were sawing feebly, as if she were attempting to run while lying down. Tears ran down her face, mingling with her blood in the half-light.

Then Senecwo was jerked to her feet and shoved down the path into the village. She tried to hit the warrior behind her but he cuffed her sharply on the head and simply shoved her again. Disoriented, her senses muddied by rage, Senecwo darted off the path toward the trees, getting no more than a few paces before she was tackled. As she lay breathless on the ground she dimly registered the sound of anguished shouting. Then she was being pulled to her feet again. She tried to look back at Irin, but the warrior who had tackled her screamed in her face and bumped her with his chest, nearly knocking her down again. Again, he pointed toward the village.

Senecwo stumbled forward, trying to think. She was being swept along amidst a stream of villagers. Burly figures were firing the huts and the smell of burning grass was pungent on the wind. Weird shadows clawed across the villagers like swarming bats. Women and children sobbed hysterically.

The village was perched atop a cliff, and at its edge some of the men were trying to make a stand. A few of them had formed a line of defense in front of their wives and children. Hopelessly outnumbered, they called to one another in strained voices, searching for bravery and finding it. Tayuna, one of her father's oldest friends, brandished a hand scythe as the raiders circled, waiting for their opening. Torchlight slid across the greasy black paint on their faces. It was hard to tell in the shadows, but the skin of their bare chests and arms seemed impossibly dark. Senecwo watched helplessly as a raider feinted in from the left, drawing Tayuna's attention, while another came in hard from the right wielding and felled the old man with a savage blow to the head.

Senecwo searched the chaos in vain for her family, or for Eyan. He would know what to do. But she didn't see him anywhere.

Mothers were casting their children into the abyss to keep them from being enslaved and used wickedly. There at the edge of the cliff with her heart darting about madly like a thrush seeking to escape from a cage, she realized she was going to jump. She whispered a final prayer, steeled herself, and sprang forward. Just before she could jump, iron arms encircled her and held her close. She bit deep, puncturing flesh and finding bone. Then she was struck on the ear and knew no more.

Senecwo woke with the blood throbbing in her head and gasping with a terrible thirst. Her hands and feet were bound with hemp. Suffering and only half aware, she opened her mouth and croaked in a lizard's voice. Then the memory of what had happened landed on her like a boulder. She clenched her eyes instinctively, afraid of what she might see. A smell hit her as she lay there, a sweet reek tinged with something sharp like rotting venison.

When she finally opened her eyes and rolled over, she saw the bodies of half the people she had ever known tangled in a heap a few yards away. There were children in the pile, their little faces bloated, limbs hanging askew like demons in a dream world. Tiny Hona. Fat, cheerful Intis. Senecwo whimpered and longed for death. The sky was just beginning to lighten in the east.

Time passed. The sun rose, casting the same light on the carnage of the morning as it had on the peace of the day before. A shadow fell across Senecwo's face and she looked up to see a tall warrior with a sharp, arrowhead nose and a bandaged hand looking down at her where she lay in the dirt. His skin was the color of an earthen jar, and his throat and the lower part of his face were covered with thick black war paint. She tried to stand, but before she could get her feet under her the man knelt beside her and said something soft in a barbed language. She spat full in his face. The warrior froze for a second. Then he wiped the spittle from his face and pulled a bladder of water off his shoulder. He hefted it in one hand, as if weighing whether to let her have a drink. It took all her pride not to beg him for a sip. Finally the bandaged warrior held the bladder to her lips.

She was ashamed at how thirstily she sucked on the opening. When the warrior put a hand behind her neck to help her she wrenched her head away. This caused some of the water to spill on the ground, and the warrior pulled the bladder away. He said something else, tracing the outline of her cheek with his finger. Again Senecwo jerked her head away. The man laughed as he stood and walked off toward a knot of warriors.

Before she could formulate a plan the warrior returned with a knife. For a terror-filled moment Senecwo thought he meant to scar or even kill her. Then he was bending and there was a quick tension on her legs followed by a snicking sound as the ropes binding her feet fell away. The warrior gave her a pointed look that could not have been clearer—*don't run.*

All around them the other raiders were striking camp. The tall warrior bound her at the neck with a length of rope and started walking, forcing her to fall in behind him. The rest of the war band took up positions in their wake. Buzzards floated effortlessly in the perfect blue morning. As they passed the still-smoking ruins of the village longhouse, Senecwo saw the charred remains of villagers who had run inside for shelter, only to be trapped and burned alive.

There was a noise from the edge of the forest, and a moment later a warrior emerged dragging another girl. Senecwo recognized Kikoya, Tayuna's youngest daughter. She was weeping and a trickle of blood ran down her leg. There were others. Selpowac. Tantawelae and her twin sister Hochelaese. Up ahead at the edge of the village Senecwo saw Wiwoka. The girl's long black hair was blowing in her face. Senecwo wanted to call out to them, to offer some word of encouragement, but she was overcome. Wincing, she looked down to see blood dripping from her balled fists.

She unclenched her hands and found moon-shaped wounds where her nails had cut her palms.

Most of the village's men were missing. Aside from those Senecwo had seen die at the cliff there were hardly any men among the corpses. She felt a tiny flicker of hope at this realization. Perhaps her father and brothers had escaped. Perhaps they were watching even now from the forest, planning a rescue. She stole a glance at the tree line. Nothing but emptiness. An ominous quiet blanketed the hills and pooled in her heart.

The train of captives was led from the village. Senecwo's senses had largely returned and she kept her head up, alert, trying to fix everything in her mind no matter how terrible. She knew she would never see this place again. Even when they passed by her family hut she did not turn away. The structure had been burned to the ground. Her mother's feet were sticking out from what had been the doorway, and her skirts had been pulled up around her hips. Irin lay wide-eyed in the grass where Senecwo had left her. There were birds perched on her shoulders. As the warriors approached they flapped away, soon to return.

From the edge of the village it was just a short walk to the standing stone. There at the far edge of the field Senecwo saw where the men of the village had gone. They were hanging from the limbs of half a dozen trees, strung up in a neat line like washing left to dry. Her father and Eyan were next to each other, swaying limply in the breeze. Their arms were tied behind their backs and their tongues hung out, swollen and distended. A sob tore loose from somewhere deep in her chest. It was the sound of something breaking off and dying. She took off running toward her father. His face was purple, his eyes half-open. He was in agony. He needed relief.

When the rope snapped tight it nearly broke her neck. Gasping in the dirt, Senecwo did not hear the warriors laughing or calling impatiently, just as she did not hear the other girls crying at the sight of their own dead fathers and brothers. She drew down into herself like an animal curling into its shell. When the tall warrior came to check on her she did not respond to his touch. He let her stay on the ground for a moment before trying to help her to her feet, but she was limp. With a sudden lurch gravity gave way as she felt herself picked up and thrown over the tall warrior's shoulder like a sack of yams.

Chapter Fourteen

SENECWO

. . .

For a while Senecwo floated along, half-aware, jouncing dumbly on the warrior's broad shoulder. At some point he put her down and she started stumbling along behind him. They walked all day. Each step she took was like a tiny dagger in her heart, each plodding footfall increasing the distance between her and the only home she had ever known. For a long time her mind remained back at the stone, tarrying behind her body like a calf on a tether. She pictured its glassy surface, carved with runes already ancient before her grandmothers' grandmothers were children.

She had been taught all her life that it was a thing of power, a magic wayplace. There must be some key in the stone, some power to unlock the riddle of the day and put everything back to where it had been. She agonized and prayed and tried to focus all of her energies on the stone. But the warriors just kept walking and the women around her kept weeping until she finally realized it was all over. Her father and her brothers had died in sight of the stone and it had been powerless to save them. No fire or avenging spirit had issued from it. The thing was useless, and it would not save her either.

Her neck was one raw wound where the rope had seared it dry, and the itching of the rough fibers on her wrists was starting to drive her mad. She tried to distract herself by counting the warriors. They numbered somewhere around two score. In the light of day she could see them clearly. They had long, tawny legs and black hair braided up with feathers or painted twigs. Their faces were painted with black handprints or stripes. Upon their persons they carried all manner of weapons and ornaments, long knives stuffed into their belts and short lances and war hammers trimmed with horse mane and bows and quivers armored in the scales of fish that jangled softly as they walked.

By mid-morning they reached a boulder-choked river in high flood that cut through the valley floor. Senecwo was surprised to hear the knickering of horses above the roaring water. They rounded a final bend in the trail and she was greeted by a sight that broke her heart all over again. A clearing by the riverbank filled with more than a hundred other captives seated in rows. Most were women but there were a few children, all of them light-skinned like Senecwo. They had mud in their hair and their faces were stricken with looks of impotent rage or despair. The captives were attended by an additional host of warriors.

Everywhere there were horses. Senecwo had seen wild stallions a handful of times in her life, but these animals were larger and better fed. Lightning bolts and other designs decorated their flanks. As her group stumbled into the clearing Senecwo understood with jarring clarity that the raiders who had stormed her village were only a small group split off from this larger host. What kind of people sent out war bands of this size?

Within minutes of their arrival the camp had been struck. Before Senecwo realized what was happening she had been separated from the other girls and shoved into the larger train of captives behind a short, trail-weary woman with dead eyes and filthy feet. Any chance she'd had to communicate with her friends was gone.

The tall raider who had given her water and carried her on his shoulder had disappeared when they joined the larger group. Now, as another warrior worked his way down the line, using a long chain to connect each prisoner at the neck, she heard the drumbeat of hooves. The tall warrior reappeared atop a brilliant white pony, the pelt of some exotic cat fluttering around his neck. The other raiders raised their voices in a cheer as he thundered past toward the rear of the column. Then the rope around her neck went tight, forcing Senecwo into a slow run.

She wasn't sure she could keep up, but it turned out not to matter. The white pony was already pounding back up the trail. The tall warrior pulled up next to her and held out a beckoning hand. Senecwo looked away, fixing her gaze on the head of the woman in front of her. The warrior, who she now realized must be the leader of the entire war band, called out in a harsh voice and slapped his thigh. Still she ignored him, even when he dismounted. He pulled her roughly out of line, cut the hemp from her wrists and neck, and threw her up onto the back of his horse. Senecwo was already more than tired of being treated like a basket of vegetables. She heard Hochelaese scream something, but her cries were drowned out by the white pony's hooves.

She rode all day behind the tall warrior who she was beginning to think of as a king. Having secured her presence on his pony, he proceeded to ignore her completely. He spent much of the morning talking intermittently with another warrior with a strikingly beautiful face who rode beside him. This second warrior wore upon his belt a collection of human ears. Some were fresh.

In the afternoon they reached a break in the tree line. The trail turned sharply along a sheer cliff, affording a long view down to the waters of a narrow lake. Senecwo had seen it from this vantage before.

Her brothers would sometimes hunt the shore in autumn when the harvest was over. From the path she could see the lake's wind-driven surface peeling like the skin of an onion.

Her captor dropped from his horse and lifted his hands to help her down. Senecwo's hips were sore and her inner thighs chafed, but she refused his help, dismounting awkwardly on her own. The king appraised her with unmistakable hunger. His handsome second said something in their thick tongue and the king laughed and said something in return without ever taking his eyes from her.

The other captives had been allowed to sit and rest for a few moments. Senecwo scanned for her friends, finally spying them huddled together near the cliff's edge. The girls were all sitting except for Hochelaese, who stood off to one side, looking across the valley at the place where the sun struck the pines on the opposite slope. She had been wearing only a thin shift when driven from her home the night before. Even at a distance Senecwo could see the fullness of her friend's curves beneath the soot-streaked cloth, and recalled the king's ravenous gaze.

As Senecwo watched, Hochelaese started walking away from the other girls. The closest warrior was busy fishing a handful of leaves from a pouch on his belt and wadding them carefully into his cheek. Hochelaese did not seem to be paying any attention to whether she was being watched or followed. She left the trail and wandered dangerously close to the cliff's edge. Senecwo opened her mouth to call out a warning to her careless friend only to be shocked into silence when Hochelaese took two final, decisive strides and plunged over the cliff.

For a second there was total silence. Senecwo imagined Hochelaese falling in a long arc towards the boulders at the bottom of the cliff. Then Tantawelae let out an otherworldly scream. Startled, the warriors turned to see what had happened. Two of them had to restrain Tantawelae from running after her sister. The king stared impassively and motioned to the rest of his men to get the captives up. They were on the trail again within minutes.

. . .

At dawn the light came sideways through the trees, glistening in discrete bars of gold. Senecwo woke curled in on herself. She could feel the cold ground through her dress but she did not move or stretch. She just lay there listening to the cries of strange birds pierce the canopy.

After the evening meal the king had carried her off into the darkness beyond the fire. She had screamed and resisted, knowing what was coming, but he had held her down and had his way. When he was finished he had hobbled her legs like a horse and covered her with his cloak before rolling over and falling asleep. Senecwo sobbed quietly, silent tears cutting channels through the dirt on her cheeks.

Now the warriors began to stir. A bright yellow songbird tumbled from a branch above her and soared into the blue. Senecwo sat up in time to see the king approaching with a haunch of deer. He was looking at her with curiosity. She couldn't interpret his look, but assumed he was wondering how easy it would be to take his satisfaction the next time. He set the meat down on a leaf and walked away without a word. Once she was confident he wasn't watching she tore the venison apart, and was overcome with self-loathing.

She only saw the other girls once that day, when the king rode back along the entire column, inspecting the line. They had descended to the lake and begun picking their way along its rocky shore, finally turning south as the sun began to die. The column was spaced out, with Senecwo's friends towards the back. When they finally came in sight the king did not slow down, leaving Senecwo just enough time for a quick appraisal of the girls' condition as the white pony swept past.

What she saw frightened her.

Selpowac had the high cheekbones and blue irises of their people, and always looked noble. But her normally effusive eyebrows, which could arch like lightning strikes at the faintest hint of joy or displeasure, were knitted in pain above eyes that had lost their glitter. Wiwoka's braids were dirty and matted, striking her back woodenly as she limped along. A fly crawled on Tantawelae's forehead yet she made no move to brush it away.

Upon reaching the end of the column the king had a brief word with the rear guards before turning the pony back toward the front. This time Senecwo was ready. When she was within earshot of the girls she cried out.

"Strength!" she yelled. Her friends' heads whipped up. "Be strong! In time we will find a way home!"

That was all she got out before the king elbowed her in the face. She could feel the welt rising instantly. Tears swarmed to her eyes. Perhaps Hochelaese had been the wisest among them. Maybe all they could do to fight back was die.

Chapter Fifteen

SENECWO

. . .

She woke to panicked shouts. Cringing, she looked through her fingers at the ashes of the previous night's fire. Overnight the small hollow they had camped in had filled with tendrils of mist that snaked around sleeping bodies and settled in the low places. The cries that had woken Senecwo were quickly devolving into screams of rage. A powerfully built warrior with half his head shaved in an intricate design was pointing emphatically at the man still sleeping next to him. Senecwo wondered what the warrior on the ground had done to so enrage his companion, and how he could be sleeping through the uproar. And then she realized he was not asleep. He was staring up at the trees as flies swarmed around a sagging gash that had been his throat. An apron of blood spread out across his chest.

The king took charge, quickly dispatching a ring of sentries into the surrounding underbrush. He had the captives gathered together in a knot and stationed the remaining half of his warriors around them in an outward facing circle. Finally, he walked over and examined the dead

man himself. After only a moment assessing the body he stood and began walking straight toward Senecwo. She was afraid, yet even in her fear
and disgust she could not deny the king's beauty. His dark chestnut skin
glowed despite the cloudy morning and his powerful strides tore through
the mist.

"Someone is following us," he said, pointing back at the dead
warrior. Senecwo registered the anger in his voice, but she was too
shocked at hearing him speak flawless Odmarsim to pay attention to what
he was saying. "They seem to want you."

His words sunk in a moment later. *Someone follows.* Senecwo felt
an uneasiness come over her. Was someone watching from the trees even
now? If so, who was it? A survivor? If someone was out there, why had
they not cut the girls loose and helped them escape? The king raised
his eyebrows expectantly. He seemed to want some kind of answer. When
none was forthcoming he pursed his lips, causing the skin beneath that
strong arrowhead of a nose to turn white.

"They will all die," he said, pointing at Wiwoka and the other
girls. Senecwo turned to look, but the king grabbed her chin and forced
her eyes back to his. Any trace of patience was gone, wiped away in an instant as he stared into her, searching for any sign she'd been complicit in
the killing. Finding nothing, he stalked away.

Scouts trickled in one by one all morning, catching up with the
main party as they beat a forced march south. Each time the king received a report his face turned a shade darker. The landscape was changing, and as they began to leave the mountains Senecwo was assailed by a
feeling of inevitability. In other circumstances the wilderness might have
filled her with wonder. But with no control over where she was led, each
new vista was an offense. She was now farther than she had ever been
from home.

They passed along the edge of a foggy marsh containing

multitudes of fluorescent birds swooping low over the reeds. She caught glimpses of leaping dog-like creatures with luxurious tails and white circles around their eyes that lent them a look of constant surprise. Mist rose from the dark water in ominous wreaths.

That night the forest came alive with the creaking and chirping of unseen beasts. The raiders tripled their guard and stoked the fires high, keeping their prisoners at the center of a protective ring. The horses sensed something was wrong and whinnied uneasily. Senecwo picked her way among the frightened women looking for her friends. When she found them, Tantawelae's face made her realize the march had to end soon, or they wouldn't make it.

Tantawelae's eyes were bloodshot and half-closed. She was doing nothing to keep herself clean. Bits of food had gathered in the corners of her mouth, and if they weren't being given starvation rations the stains on her gown would have been worse. Senecwo had them all lie down next to each other. She put her arm over Tantawelae and felt her friend's heart beating in her chest. She was still alive in there.

When Senecwo finally drifted off to sleep her father came to her. He was carrying her mother in his arms. His face was blue from hanging and when he opened his mouth to speak he could only spit out blood. After a time he left and Eyan appeared in his place. Her parents had not known about Eyan. She had done everything she could to conceal her feelings for him, knowing they would have said she was too young to marry. The women of the Odmarsim were given in marriage once they had passed into womanhood. Senecwo had been bleeding for two years already, but her father doted on her and had been reluctant to agree to a match. Not yet, he had said. One more year at home, then we will find you a man.

It was fine with Senecwo; she knew who she loved. Eyan may have been young like her, but he was more capable than most men in the village. He could do anything he set his mind to. Someday he would inherit his father's terraces and herd. He stood before her now, darkness above and below him. She could see stars reflecting in his eyes but no matter what she said, no matter how she pleaded with him, he would not open his mouth. Finally she reached out to push him away, but her hands passed through his ghostly body.

She woke sometime in the night. The fires were burning brightly, the guards talking in soft voices. Horses pulled up tufts of grass with gentle ripping sounds. She listened to the sounds of the night and wondered if the phantom was still out there. That slashed throat had clearly not been the work of an animal. Perhaps whoever was following them had been injured, or simply given up, leaving the girls to their fate.

. . .

Prior to her capture, Senecwo had seen the same view every day—the steep green slopes and snowcapped peaks that ringed the village. She'd seen many new things during the previous days' walking, but none of them had engendered in her a feeling quite like the one she was having now. The woods had begun to thin in earnest as the column wound its way across a long spur curving down out of the foothills like a talon. A remarkable smell had been wafting in on an easterly breeze all morning. Something about the scent taken with the change in foliage gave Senecwo the impression they would soon be leaving the mountains behind altogether.

She took a deep breath, relishing the strange new aroma. Tangy and fresh, yet faintly sour at the same time, something in its bouquet promised invigoration and renewal. She was lost in her reverie, staring at the puffs of dirt kicking up from the hooves of the king's horse, when the air was pierced by a whistling sound followed by a crack like ice snapping in a freeze.

Just up ahead, the path they had been following dropped in a gentle switchback toward a wider chalk road. The mountains were giving way to rolling hills. The final tip of the spine they had been following petered out a mile to the west against a farther, gentler ridge. The view was impressive, but Senecwo's attention was arrested by the sight of a giant cedar log coming up the road below them.

Dust billowed in the tree's wake as it trundled slowly across a bed of smaller logs laid out perpendicular to its length. A team of slaves three score strong powered the huge log's forward movement, straining at long ropes wound about its bole. In addition to these tow-men a separate group was busy making a perpetual circuit from the rear of the trunk to its head. They picked up the rollers as they were spat out behind the log and ferried them back up front, creating a fresh bed in an endless loop. Each roller took the full strength of two men to lift. It looked so exhausting, Senecwo assumed the men must all be on the verge of collapse.

The slaves were overseen by a crew of lash-wielding guards, and as Senecwo watched, one of the slaves on roller duty stumbled and dropped his end of a log. Harsh shouts rang in the cool air and a guard cracked his whip, eliciting a cry that could be heard half a mile away. Unlike Senecwo and her friends, the men pulling the log were even darker than the warriors guarding them. Their skin was almost black, and their fuzzy hair stuck out from their heads in soft, misshapen orbs. Despite their intense efforts the log was moving slowly and the war band soon overtook them. The slaves dared not pause or even look up from their labor. The king guided his horse out of the road and around the spectacle. The white pony nearly trampled two old men lying in the dirt who looked to have collapsed from exhaustion. Flies worried their eyes.

A nearby guard leaned on his spear and bowed to the king, ignoring the fallen elders. As they passed, he removed a gourd from his waist and took a long drink of water. Senecwo called to the old men in her own tongue, not knowing whether they would understand her. They lifted up their faces, confused, trying to pinpoint her voice. She told them to take hope and was soon rewarded in the same way she had been the first time. The king turned and cuffed her upside the head, this time hitting her so hard she tumbled backwards off the horse, landing on the ground with a whuff as the breath was knocked from her lungs.

The king dismounted and strode over to where she lay gasping in the dirt. Standing over her, reins held loosely in one hand, he struck his chest and shouted a single word in his own tongue. Then he pulled her roughly to her feet and put her back on the horse. This time he jumped up behind her. Despite riding behind him the entire journey, she had never once put her arms around him. Now his burly forearms encircled her waist and his chest grazed her back.

Before long the cries of the guards and the creaking of the log faded. Senecwo clenched her teeth and rode quietly, struggling to contain her feelings of rage and helplessness. Her skin crawled at the king's touch but she would not let him see her cry. Lost in her private misery her eyes fell back to the road. It was not until one of the warriors called out in excitement that she jerked her head up to discover the hills had parted and a floodplain been opened to view. Shining in the center of the plain like an inexplicable pearl lay a great city the size of which she could never have imagined had she not seen it with her own eyes. Wilder still, the city's mighty towers and sprawling buildings were hemmed in and dwarfed by that which lay beyond them; a glittering plate of endless blue so vast and beautiful it made her heart catch in her throat. Try as she might, Senecwo could not keep the tears from rolling down her cheeks.

Chapter Sixteen

SENECWO

. . .

A t dawn on the day of her wedding, Senecwo was sick in her spacious marble washroom. A month had passed since she had first seen the city, a month during which she had been nauseous every morning without fail. She wiped her mouth with an exquisite linen cloth and looked out the window at the city spread below.

The first time she had seen Aghuax and the great waters it sat beside she hadn't been able to decide where to look. Buildings rose from the floor of the gently sloping tidal flat in a spiraling helix of multi-colored stone. At its center, like the hub of a giant wheel, a sweeping collection of parapets and slender castellations towered above the rest of the city. To the east, a curved dome that looked to be woven of sticks rose hump-like above a network of lower buildings. The smoke of cookfires drifted on the wind along with the lowing of unseen animals. Senecwo had never seen so many structures in one place, let alone as many people as their presence implied. Miles below, tiny figures could be seen approaching a huge gate set in the city wall. The proportions seemed impossible. The people were like grasshoppers.

For all the city's majesty, Senecwo's eyes had soon passed beyond it to the blue plain commanding the horizon. Her people were a people of mountains. She had never seen a body of water larger than the long lake, and now her powers of perception nearly failed her. That the blue plain was comprised of water was something that, at first, she hardly dared guess. The lines of white chaff pulsing around its golden-white rim suggested movement or fluidity, but away from the edge there seemed to be nothing but still emptiness. Looking out across the surface was like falling into the unblinking eye of a god. It frightened her.

She was jolted from her contemplation by the warriors' ululating cries, which soon came reverberating back to them from the guards atop the gate's twin towers. The entire caravan stopped inside one of the last folds of land before the final approach to the gate. The warriors took their time reapplying war paint and tightening the braids in their ponies' manes. While the king was having his face paint redone, Senecwo took the opportunity to look behind her at the long train of slaves.

The other girls from her village had been moved closer to the front. Kikoya motioned to her, trying to indicate something. For a terrified moment Senecwo thought Kikoya was about to run, which would have led to death or worse. Senecwo shook her head as discreetly as possible, trying to discourage her. Their only hope was to survive and wait for an opportunity. Perhaps the king could be manipulated and the favor he was showing Senecwo used to their advantage. Kikoya kept motioning, and Senecwo kept not understanding.

When they finally passed through the city gate Senecwo was pierced by a chill that came from more than just the shadow of the huge stones. Crippled beggars lined the portal, their blighted eyes weeping as they stared sightlessly up at the passing retinue. The streets were lined with people. Women and girls with skin the same bloody red as the raiders threw flowers in their path, while the men of the city lifted their hands in greeting. Everyone was shouting and calling out to the warriors, who answered with blood-curdling victory whoops. For their entrance the king had resumed his place in front of Senecwo, the better to display himself to the people. The crowds kept shouting something, the same words over and over, but she did not understand.

Little boys, their hair worn long like the warriors they hoped to one day become, darted amongst the horses, striking the captives on the legs. Senecwo looked out into the sea of people and saw a man pulling a rotten yam from a basket on his arm. She watched as he hurled it at a young captive's face. Something tightened in her chest at the sight of the filth dripping from the girl's cheeks. A wrenched cry cut the air, full of fear and pain. It took Senecwo a moment to realize it was not the girl who had been hit with the yam. It was Wiwoka.

A group of warriors were hustling her friends down a side street. Senecwo could just see the top of Wiwoka's head between two ponies. Selpowac and Kikoya were vanishing around the corner of a squat building. Tantawelae was close behind, being dragged by her hair. Just before they all disappeared, Wiwoka's face bobbed into view a final time.

"Stay alive!" came Wiwoka's voice. "Stay alive!"

Senecwo raised a hand in acknowledgment, but Wiwoka's guard had already muscled her out of sight. Senecwo couldn't hold the tears back any longer. The crowd lining the streets roared, taking in the drama. By now the king had drawn his mount up and turned to see what the noise was. Senecwo cringed, but he neither struck nor admonished her. He simply watched, impassive, as her last shreds of hope detached and drifted into the air like a dandelion being scattered before a hurricane.

· · ·

The castle had awed her. It was elegant and mountainous at once, with beautiful towers and foundation stones the size of her family's hut. Senecwo had a difficult time envisioning how men might have constructed such a thing. As they passed into the courtyard she looked up at the row of decomposing heads atop the wall. A row of slaves in dark green robes greeted them inside. One of these stepped forward and bowed low as the king's pony clopped to a halt.

"Nantawi het Hankasi," he said, spreading his arms wide.

Most of the war band had dispersed by now, and the people of the city had been kept outside the castle gate. The king dismounted and began walking into the castle while the slaves remained behind with the horses or returned to their tasks. Senecwo found herself following the king into a cool stone hallway draped with rich fabrics. The slow and steady beat of drums thudded in the distance, celebrating the war band's return.

They walked for what seemed to Senecwo like an impossible amount of time, ascending wide staircases and crossing in front of endless doorways, each leading onto magnificent halls of dark wood. At one point they passed large kitchens and the aroma of cooking meat filled the air, awakening Senecwo's hunger.

The king walked in silence, and Senecwo did not know what to do other than follow along. She could have run off at an intersection and tried to hide, but she would have been instantly lost. She walked with the resignation of someone headed to the executioner's stone. Finally they turned yet another corner and the pavement beneath her feet was replaced by a ribbon of soft red fabric. Soon the king stopped in front of a set of heavy mahogany doors and threw them wide.

Senecwo found herself staring at the most beautiful room she had ever seen. The floor was a river of creamy marble and the walls were constructed of exquisitely set stone. Tapestries depicting giant fish were lit by the sunlight flooding in through windows twice her height. Elaborately carved chairs gathered around a beautiful wooden table that could seat twelve. Other doors led off this first chamber into other rooms. Through one of these Senecwo could see a huge bed canopied in silks and covered in furs.

The king touched the fingers of his right hand to his breast.

"I am Hankasi," he said, once again speaking in Odmarsim.

He waited for Senecwo to respond but she had nothing to say. He had slain her family and raped her repeatedly. What did he want? To somehow win her? All this luxury was nothing but trash and rags as far as she was concerned. Hankasi was visibly annoyed, but Senecwo would have had to work hard to care any less whether he was pleased with her. She turned away and looked out one of the open windows.

"You would do well not to ignore me," he said. When she continued to do so he reached out and turned her face toward him with a firm grip that seemed to promise he would not hesitate to snap her neck if that was what it took to make his point. She stared at him, pouring all her hate out through her eyes. He could make her look him in the eye, but he could not change her. He finally let his hand drop and left without another word, leaving the door open behind him. Senecwo knew there was nowhere for her to escape.

She made her way slowly through the rooms. One of the smaller suites had a table in the corner with a large object attached to the back. Senecwo walked in front of this on her way to the window and caught a glimpse of someone staring back. She let out a stifled whimper of terror and stumbled backwards. Only after several long minutes and an excruciatingly slow crawl back in front of the thing did she realize she was merely seeing herself, as in the surface of still waters.

That same room had an antechamber the size of her childhood home containing dozens of dresses. Senecwo's first thought upon seeing them was to wonder if she could use them to set the room on fire.

She was starting to feel crazed, like a wild animal penned in a cage. Wandering to the windows, she looked down into an inner courtyard filled with lush fruit trees and a small pond. If she jumped she could end it all. There was no one to stop her. But she knew that if she did things would go badly for her friends.

Later that night a servant delivered a meal of hot bread and soup brimming with flavors she had never encountered. She devoured the food, trying not to think of the other girls. What if they were in a pit somewhere? When it became apparent she was going to be left alone all night, she lay down at the foot of the opulent bed and quickly fell asleep on the warm marble.

She was woken in the morning by Hankasi's disbelieving laughter.

"What is this?" he said from the doorway. "I have given you everything. You are surrounded by the wealth of a nation. Why have you slept on the stones?"

"Where are they?" Senecwo said, her face flushed with anger. "I want to see them. I want to see my friends."

Hankasi looked out the window, ignoring her demand. The mountains of Senecwo's youth gleamed white in the unreachable distance. When Hankasi spoke again it was as if he was talking to himself as much as to her.

"You will be the queen of all that can be seen from this window."

Senecwo had been trying to push away the very suspicion the king was now confirming. There was clearly some reason why she was being given preferential treatment. But... a *queen*? How could you make a slave your queen? To make someone whose family you had killed your wife was a perversion Senecwo could not comprehend.

"One month," Hankasi said. She wondered where he had come by his Odmarsim. "In one month, we will be wed."

The next words out of her mouth were careless.

"If you do not bring the other girls here tonight," she said, "you will find me dead in the morning."

"If I find you dead," Hankasi replied evenly, "I will spit your friends on the wall." He shrugged. "Alive."

She had played right into his hands.

That night she caved and crawled between the silk sheets, pulling them up around her neck, hating herself for how good it felt. She wondered how far she would get if she climbed out the window and ran, but before she could finish the thought she was asleep. The ensuing days brought little relief. Senecwo could not take any pleasure in the water that flowed, like magic, through special sluices into the stone pool in her bathing chamber. Nor could she enjoy the rich foods she was served, knowing her friends were being held somewhere else.

For that first month she had been left alone. Servants delivered her meals, but she was otherwise left to dress and occupy herself. The first time she tried to leave her room she discovered guards posted outside her door. They permitted her to leave but followed at a close distance. She began exploring the castle, knowing the king would no doubt be informed of her reconnoitering but resolving not to let it stop her.

On one of her forays she came upon a rooftop garden dominated by a large palm. From its shady vantage she could look out west over Aghuax toward the water. She spent many evenings there, watching the waves roll toward the shore and wondering where her friends were. She whispered prayers on their behalf and listened to the breakers hiss with a rhythm that never quite calmed her.

· · ·

Senecwo had just finished washing out her mouth on the morning of her wedding when there came a knock at the door. She opened it to find a slope-shouldered eunuch waiting in the hall along with another man sporting the shaved head of a slave. The eunuch helped Senecwo into a dress embroidered with green arrows. The other man went to work on her hair, gathering the thick waves up into an elegant arrangement on top of her head. They washed her feet and anointed her arms with perfume. When they were done they stood her in front of the mirror to admire herself. Senecwo could not deny she looked beautiful and it nearly made her sick again. She loathed the thought of being presented to Hankasi like this.

The attendants led her out the door of her chamber, and their trio was quickly enfolded in a rectangle of guards. The warriors steered them down a staircase, into a tunnel, and back up another set of stairs. At the top of this second flight there hung a curtain through which Senecwo could hear the gabbling of a great multitude. The warriors stopped and she stepped through the curtain alone. She was standing on a wide dais, a sea of faces spread out below her. The crowd grew silent at her appearance.

Hankasi waited in the center of the platform, his long hair blowing free in the wind. He wore white boots and a white robe that hung open, revealing his powerful chest. A single piece of jade hung from his neck on a thong. He held out a hand toward her. With nowhere to run, Senecwo walked forward to meet her fate.

The ceremony did not last long. Hankasi took her hand and turned to the people, raising her arm as if proclaiming a champion. The crowd roared in response. The marriage was presided over by a holy man of some kind, a skeletal figure in a crimson cloak. The man's face was completely devoid of hair. He had sunken, mesmeric eyes that pulled Senecwo in, and when he drew close his breath smelled like fetid roses.

The priest reached out to bind her hand to Hankasi's with a ritual cloth, and as the old man's skin touched hers she felt a numbing surge of energy shoot up her arm. The holy man produced a shard of bone with which he transcribed a strange symbol in the air in front of Senecwo's face. A foreboding sense of warmth began spreading from the crown of her head down towards her heart. Before she had time to react, the priest reached forward, gripped her jaw with one hand, and pierced the soft skin at the bottom of her nose. He was finished before the pain hit with a lancing shock that brought tears to Senecwo's eyes. She was close to panicking as the priest began shouting in a shrill voice,

Kulkas! Kulkas! Kulkas tixecana ha owino e!

Hankasi shook his head as if starting from a dream. Senecwo wondered if he was under some kind of spell. She looked out at the sea of people, their faces animated with a strange combination of hatred and excitement. She felt exposed and robbed of her agency. Like a marker in a game being pushed around a board. Then she saw Wiwoka and everything else stopped mattering.

Senecwo had been so focused on the crowd and the priest that she had not noticed Hankasi gesture towards someone behind a curtain on the other side of the dais, identical to the one she had stepped through moments earlier. Now another pair of slaves with the same shaved heads and feminine body language as the two men who had dressed her were leading a line of women out onto the dais. The women were wearing dresses that matched Senecwo's. She blinked twice, unsure if what she was seeing was real.

Wiwoka's face was haggard, but her skin was clean and her hair gleamed in the sun as if freshly washed and oiled. The other girls from the village stood next to her, their hands clutched knuckle-white in front of them. The king's voice was buzzing in her ear, saying something. After a moment Senecwo realized he was looking at her expectantly.

"They are for you," he said, raising his chin toward her friends.

So they were a gift. The king was presenting her friends to her as a set of matching handmaidens, as if he had not enslaved them and killed everyone precious to them. Senecwo felt a great well of rage breaking open inside of her, surging fire rising from the floor of the canyon of grief that had been steadily dredged out of her chest over the last few days. She nearly lunged forward to scratch out Hankasi's eyes. Instead, she bit her lip and attempted a broken smile for her friends. They were alive. That was enough for now.

A moment later she was being ushered off the dais to the delirious screams of the crowd, who were busy showering the king—not her, she knew from day one that she was a figurehead at best—with rose petals. The other girls were waiting in the side tunnel. Selpowac's eyes brimmed with tears of relief. Senecwo gathered them close, wrapping her arms around them. A tiny flicker of something other than utter doom kindled in her heart. Perhaps there was hope.

They held each other tight, crushed together in a knot of solidarity, their noses running, their heads bowed. When they finally let go and prepared to leave, Senecwo took one last backward glance at the crowd. That was when she saw him for the first time; an ancient father, older than old, with sagging earlobes and a chest full of wiry gray hair. He was standing off to one side against the castle wall at the edge of the crowd.

The people were giving him a wide berth, which probably had something to do with the pack of wolves fanned out at his feet. His face was like weathered stone, with a craggy nose and great jutting chin dominating the cliff of his face. Bright onyx eyes glinted in the shadows beneath his hatched and wrinkled brow. Despite the appearance of age the man seemed vital and strong, invested with an indomitable energy. A clasp fashioned from an eagle's talon held a cloak of black feathers about his neck. He touched his forehead and nodded at her. Senecwo turned for the tunnel without acknowledging him, unsettled but somehow unafraid.

144 · Ben Bishop

Chapter Seventeen

SENECWO

. . .

When they were finally left alone for a few moments, the newly crowned queen insisted that her friends disrobe in front of her. Although the girls had been cleaned up and presented in immaculate dresses for the wedding ceremony, Senecwo quickly discerned that they had been mistreated. A dark bruise the size and color of a pomegranate marred the small of Selpowac's back. There were welts on Wiwoka's inner thighs. Senecwo wept at the sight of these cruelties. She fell upon them, hugging their necks, and they wept together for the dead and for the disintegration of their world.

"I'm sorry," Senecwo finally managed to say between heaving breaths. "I'm so sorry."

The other girls had been given quarters just down the hall, but they would not leave Senecwo and she would not have let them go. She insisted they take turns sleeping in her giant bed, three at a turn, while the others took the exquisite bed coverings and spread them out on the floor. They all slept like the dead those first few nights, except for Senecwo, who turned restlessly in the darkness, her world drawing down into a small seed of hatred.

She filled the hours between dusk and dawn with fantasies about how she might snare Hankasi and his warriors on merciless hooks of vengeance. The scenarios were endless. She stabbed, burned, and drowned her tormentors a thousand times. She impaled, beheaded and burned them. She threw them to ravening serpents. She cut off their manhoods as they gasped in breathless horror. It brought her no relief. She woke each morning covered in sweat and ran to void her stomach, her frayed nerves betraying her.

Six days after the wedding she made up her mind. She had overheard the guards joking about the ceremonial period of purity. On the seventh day Hankasi would come to consecrate the marriage. There was a sickening irony in this, given what she had already suffered on the journey back to the city. She felt like an animal with a burning taper bound to her tail. Not knowing where else to turn, she took Wiwoka into her confidence, though she was loathe to expose her to danger. She had a plan.

On the afternoon of the sixth day the two of them climbed down from the window of Senecwo's apartments, disguised in robes Wiwoka had stolen from the head cook's closet. With the hoods up over their heads they looked like kitchen assistants and passed out of the courtyard without incident. They headed towards Char Gate as the sun began to disappear into the sea.

. . .

It had not proved difficult for Senecwo to ascertain the identity of the weathered old man who had sent a lightning bolt down her spine on her wedding day. A host of attendants had cycled through the royal apartments that first week, teaching the handmaidens how to do for the queen what she must never again have to do for herself. A heavy woman with arthritic hands and burst veins in her nose showed them how to fold Senecwo into the white hide dresses and fitted silks in the closet, while a young boy demonstrated how to work the levers and pumps that brought water to the marble bath. But it was an even lowlier page, a fair-skinned little slave boy tasked with removing the queen's chamber pots, who ultimately sated Senecwo's curiosity about the old man in the raven feather cloak. The boy had been on his way out of the bath chamber one morning when Selpowac came around the door unexpectedly and startled him.

"Forgive me," the boy murmured, scurrying around Selpowac quickly, clearly eager to complete his task and leave. Senecwo was sitting at the table talking with Wiwoka when it happened.

"What did you say?" Senecwo called.

None of the servants spoke the language of her people and they relied on gestures to communicate, yet she had understood this boy. As far as she knew Senecwo had never heard him utter a single syllable before. He stood frozen in the doorway, clutching the two long feathers he used for dusting in nervous hands. His eyes were locked on his scabby feet.

"It's alright, child," Senecwo said gently. "Do not be afraid."

The boy couldn't have been more than six winters old. He looked so frightened she felt sorry for stopping him. She got up from the table and walked over to him. When she touched his shoulder he began trembling visibly, having been instilled with the threat of a beating or even death should he ever fail to discharge his duties in silent perfection.

"It's alright," she said again. The boy's chest heaved and he nearly burst into tears. He was light skinned like Senecwo, yet had a completely different facial structure than the Odmarsim, with a broad nose, full lips, and tight, curly hair that was soft as lambswool under her fingers. Senecwo wondered if he had been born in captivity. Tears rose unexpectedly to her eyes along with a strange sense of gratitude at this tangible reminder that she and her friends were not the only people suffering in this kingdom.

The boy struggled to catch his breath. Senecwo waited patiently, rubbing his back. When he was finally able to speak he told her, in a dialect similar enough to her own that she could understand him, that he was sorry for speaking out of turn. She reassured him again that everything was fine and he would not be punished, for he had done nothing wrong. And then Senecwo realized the boy could help her. She asked him if he knew of the old man with the wolves. The boy's face lit up like a lantern, and he proceeded to tell her about the shaman who lived in a cave by the sea.

· · ·

With the light fading in earnest, Senecwo and Wiwoka had skulked through rubbish-strewn side alleys and slipped out of Char Gate just before it closed for the night. The guards had jeered at them as they went, shouting lewd taunts about what would happen to two women out alone on the road at night. Senecwo almost uncowled herself and demanded to be taken to the king, who would either have beaten her or castrated the guards or both. She constrained herself with the knowledge that the other three handmaidens would likely be tortured if she was discovered missing. Time was of the essence.

Once out of sight of the gate they gathered their robes about their knees and ran until they came to a lonely bend in the road. Checking to see no one was watching, they turned off into the sand and began weaving through rolling dunes toward the water. Coming within sight of the black boulder the slave boy had described, they saw a tendril of smoke rising through the clear night air. Senecwo felt a tremor of doubt, but she was determined to make contact with the shaman. If she did not remedy her situation quickly she would die. With Wiwoka close by her side she stepped around the side of the boulder and into the light of the fire.

The shaman sat with his back to the stone, whittling. He had taken off his cloak of feathers and his shoulders were the sloped, sun-spotted shoulders of a very old man. He was surrounded by a loose arrangement of wolves. Wiwoka let out a little gasp at the sight of the animals.

"Your majesty," the shaman said, his hands going still as he looked up. He had not startled when they appeared. It was almost as if he had been expecting them. "You honor me."

Senecwo realized she wanted him to say something else. To tell her what to do, where to go, how to carry on, and all of this before they had even been introduced. She wanted him to admit that he too had felt something pass between them on the day of the wedding. But he just sat there, appraising her with his lightning-tinged eyes, saying nothing about the fact that she was out on the beach at dusk without a guard, wearing a cook's robe.

"I have come seeking your name," she said at last. To her surprise, she found it was the truth.

The shaman nodded, the hint of a smile appearing at the corners of his mouth.

"There is great power in a name, and you are shrewd to seek mine. But how shall I know my name is being given to one I can trust?"

"I am Kulkas," the queen replied, drawing herself up with what she hoped seemed like self-possession. The name slid across her teeth like oil and she recoiled at the sound of it, as well as at her sudden impulse to brandish a status she detested. Perhaps something in the name the magi had given her was clouding her judgment. Perhaps it was simple fear. If the shaman noted her internal struggle he gave no indication. He had already resumed whittling.

"The wolves wonder if you are staying," he said.

Senecwo blinked. The wolf nearest the shaman's feet, a beautifully dappled animal with wet black lips, yawned powerfully, revealing a mountain range of gleaming white teeth. The schick of the shaman's knife across the wood was soft and rhythmic.

"I wonder too," he said.

The stars were bright overhead and the moon was rising above the water. There was little time. Senecwo was seized by the temptation to tell the old man everything in her heart. She clenched her fists and tried to remember why she had come.

"Who are you?" she asked.

The smile was gone from the shaman's lips, but somewhere in the depth of his eyes a flicker of merriment danced.

"I am a keeper of ancient ways," he said, reaching over to toss a new log onto the smoldering fire. "And a very old man."

"What ways?"

"The ways of my people, though many have strayed from them."

One of the wolves lifted its head without warning and gave a soft howl. It only lasted a second, but Senecwo nearly fell down so great was her fright. Wiwoka clutched her arm.

"They howl for the coming of the stars," the shaman said, craning his head up toward the sky. The Swan loomed on the horizon, her wings still half underwater.

"Miraba," Senecwo said, following his gaze.

"I have not heard her called that in many years," the shaman said, leaning back against the wall of the cave. "If I am not mistaken, it was high on Merwa, in the glades of the Odmarsim."

So he had heard of her people. It shouldn't have surprised her, but it did.

"The Ancagua," he continued, "among whom you have fallen, no longer revere her as they should. They used to appreciate the virtues of her tale, but now they seem to have no need for stories about salvation coming to little girls."

Senecwo knew the story. Her mother had told it to her many nights as a girl. Miraba, a young princess, is saved from certain death and defilement at the hands of her father's enemies when the gods transfigure her into a swan, enabling her to fly away.

"You speak as if you are not one of them," she said.

"And yet I am."

"My name is Senecwo," she said, her voice coming out in a whisper.

She had spoken without thinking. Vouchsafed her name to a foreigner, a man who for all she knew may have been more powerful than any of her captors.

"The Helper," the shaman said, finding her eyes with his.

Senecwo felt a wave of nausea rise out of nowhere and overwhelm her. She fell to her knees in the sand. Wiwoka tried to catch her and they both went stumbling down together. The shaman was already reaching for a skin of water as she felt the sickness rising in her gorge. The last thing she remembered before blacking out was the feeling of his gnarled hand cradling her head.

Chapter Eighteen

SENECWO

. . .

S enecwo had known from the beginning that her sickness was a
manifestation of the child she carried. She and Eyan had conse-
crated their relationship in a spray of straw behind his father's
goat pen one night not long before the raid, when all things were still
possible. She had been waiting in the woods near the pen, afraid to be
seen by Eyan's father and so intent on staying hidden she hadn't heard
him sneak up behind her. Eyan had grabbed her and she'd screamed with
fright before he covered her mouth, dying with laughter.

Then they were tumbling in the straw. Eyan's hands were calloused and his legs were spattered with mud, but he was so gentle. Gentle
when he touched her face, gentle when he caressed her back, and gentle when he finally pushed her dress aside. In the moment he entered
it had hurt. There was ecstasy in the pain, but there was also the pain
itself. Then she could feel his essence surging into her. Lying in the straw
afterwards with Eyan holding her tightly, Senecwo's heart nearly broke
with joy.

She knew she was carrying new life when she stopped bleeding. The moon had waxed and waned three times since then. The nausea had started in the second month and been accompanied by a growing sense of dread and a powerful nesting instinct she had no way to indulge. Then Hankasi's raiders had swept across her life like a fire, burning down everything she had ever loved. Everything except for the child growing within her.

. . .

When Senecwo opened her eyes on the morning after her clandestine visit to the beach she found herself lying in bed. Wiwoka knelt next to her, applying a cool cloth to her forehead. Senecwo asked how she had come to be back in her own chambers. Wiwoka told her that after she fainted the shaman had picked her up and carried her in his arms along the beach until they reached a clutch of vines at the base of the city wall.

"He stepped through and disappeared," she said. "I was scared but I couldn't leave you, so I followed him in. There was a tunnel behind the vines. It was cold and dark and there was water running along the floor. There was some kind of light coming from his hand. I couldn't see what was casting it, and it only shed enough glow for us to see a step or two in front. We walked and walked, through dripping passages that twisted and turned until I was completely lost. Finally I felt fresh air on my face.

"We were in some kind of chamber. I could see out through a grate into the inner courtyard and hear the guards talking around their fire. The old man waited until they left to make their rounds, then pushed the grate up and climbed out. He carried you all the way up here."

"What of the guards?" Senecwo asked. There was always a pair of guards stationed outside her chambers, day and night.

"They were asleep," Wiwoka whispered, though there was no one around to hear. "Or not *asleep*. Passed out. The old man muttered some words before we came around the last corner. I heard metal hitting stones and then we rounded the bend and the guards were sprawled out like they were drunk."

Senecwo felt a chill run through her body despite the thick furs on her bed.

"Then what?"

"Then he left."

. . .

That evening Hankasi came to Senecwo's chambers. He arrived soon after sunset, entering unannounced. Selpowac and Kikoya looked up as the door swung open. When they saw who it was, their eyes darted back and forth from Senecwo to the king. The queen dismissed them to their own chambers with a firmness bordering on harshness. They looked heartbroken, but she had to get them safely out of the way before they did something foolish trying to protect her. She was grateful Wiwoka and Tantawelae were out on an errand. They would have put up a fight.

Hankasi smiled at the handmaidens as they passed him. Senecwo was still seated at the table where she had been mending one of her slippers.

"There are servants to do that," Hankasi said, moving across the marble floor. As he walked the silver ornaments on his wrists chimed softly. Before he could reach her, Senecwo stood and moved to the bed, letting her robe fall. She would not allow him the pleasure of unclothing her or prolonging what was to come.

Hankasi had scented himself with myrrh and cloves. When he reached her she was trembling with fear and the coolness of the breeze coming in through the open window. He guided her onto the bed and sought to pleasure her. His touch was gentle and she hated him for it. Though her heart was a rampart of flame, her body betrayed her by responding to his ministrations. She turned her face aside and made no sound. Soon the king moved on to taking his own satisfaction. He moaned with increasing urgency until his face went slack and he was finished. Though her head was turned away from him, Senecwo could feel Hankasi's eyes burning into her. His lust satisfied, there was nothing but contempt in his gaze.

She thought he might say something, but in the end he just stood and drew his robe around himself, strolling slowly from her chambers without another word. When he was gone she rolled over to the edge of the bed. This time the foulness that spilled from her mouth had nothing to do with the baby in her womb.

· · ·

It was not long before Hankasi realized she was with child, and not by his seed. Her stomach began to swell in earnest, and while she could conceal it a while longer in the folds of her dresses, she could not hide it in the king's bed. After that first night in her chambers he began summoning her to his own. At first he had her stay the night, though she never engaged him, never did anything other than roll over onto her side when he was finished. Eventually, realizing his attempts to win her heart were only hardening her all the more, he turned caustic. He still had her brought to his chamber where he forced her to perform all manner of acts that disgusted her. When he was finished he would send her back across the castle, escorted by a pair of guards whose mocking stares seared the back of her neck.

She feared Hankasi would kill her child as soon as it was born.

It did not occur to her that his forbearance might be part of an even darker plan. One day when she was just two moons from giving birth, there came a knock at her door. When Wiwoka opened it two magi swept past her, ignoring her protestations. The sickly sweet odor of incense that clung to their vermilion robes made Senecwo light-headed. The magi were accompanied by a short woman with a huge mole on one cheek. The woman wore a cape of faded purple velvet and walked with a pronounced limp. The trio floated toward the seated queen, who reflexively lowered her hands to cover her belly.

"You have no business with me," Senecwo said.

The first mage, a gaunt man with gray lips and a lazy eye, smiled faintly.

"Your majesty is with child."

"The child is healthy," Senecwo said.

"As you say," the mage said, spreading his hands in deference. "We are here at the king's request. He wishes only that we monitor your health and the child's."

"Make no mistake," Senecwo said. "If you try to put your bloodstained hands on me, I will kill you."

Behind the magi she saw Wiwoka's eyes widen, but she didn't care. There were certain things she would not abide. A cool grin crawled across the mage's face. His loose eye wandered toward the ceiling.

"Your majesty enjoys the company of her handmaidens," he said quietly. "Companionship is important in this vulnerable time. It would be a shame if anything were to befall one of them."

The second mage stared queerly at Wiwoka. The witch began limping towards Senecwo.

"It will only take a moment your majesty," said the first mage. "Just a check of your skin."

Senecwo raised a hand as the witch drew near, causing the

woman to stop.

"I swear by the gods of my people, should any of you touch me or my attendants, your hand will adorn my mantle."

For a moment Senecwo thought the witch would proceed despite her threats. Instead, the mage inclined his head in mock deference.

"As you wish," he said, a thread of barely restrained laughter in his voice. The magi retreated slowly from the chamber and the witch limped after them. As Wiwoka slammed the door behind them Senecwo was murmuring to her child that it was safe. As if it could hear her. As if she could truly protect it. Nothing had happened, and yet a seed of fear had been planted in her heart. In that moment, she was struck by a bolt of total clarity.

She knew what she had to do.

. . .

When the time for the birth drew nigh Selpowac prepared a mixture of hyssop and oil, which she gave to Senecwo to drink at sundown. The apartment door had been barred for the night and the washroom prepared in secret. Kikoya doused the lights in the outer chamber and they all huddled together, the expectant mother lying in the makeshift bed her friends had prepared for her in the marble tub. Selpowac crouched at Senecwo's feet with a stack of clean cloths. Wiwoka held her hands as the contractions began to come. Senecwo bore down and they slipped a piece of leather into her mouth for her to bite.

She felt as though the child would never come, that she was ripping open and dying and the world was only a place to be escaped. She passed out of her body and back into it, the pain overwhelming her senses but never shutting them down. Eventually she heard the child screaming. She was delirious and did not notice the looks her handmaidens were giving one another, the fear in their eyes as they looked at the blood filling the bottom of the tub.

"A name, a name," Senecwo cried. "She needs a name."

Selpowac was trying to soothe the babe. Tantawelae had stuffed towels under the washroom door to keep the child's cries from reaching the guards, but she was loud. *She*. Senecwo had given birth to a girl. Selpowac held her close and Wiwoka draped a heavy cloak over them. They waited in tense silence. Tantawelae's face was white as birch bark. The guards never came. Senecwo passed into delirium.

· · ·

Wiwoka crept through the black tunnels, holding the newborn in one arm and a torch in the other. Drops of flaming pitch fell noisily into the trickling stream at her feet. It was the darkest hour of night and it was black as a tomb beneath the city. Wiwoka stumbled through the junctions where tunnels crossed, praying she was headed in the right direction. When she finally saw a lighter square cut out of the blackness ahead, she dropped the torch into the water with a hiss and emerged onto the beach. The stars seemed blinding overhead and she worried the guards would see her. She crept along the base of the wall until the distance between her and the surrounding woods was shortest, and then ran.

She breathed heavily as she picked her way through the scrub brush toward the beach. She could scarcely believe what she was about to do, but Senecwo had been adamant. An owl hooted somewhere nearby and she paused, holding the nameless baby close. The child was warm against her breast. Wiwoka looked down at her. Even in the darkness she could make out Senecwo's features. She doubted herself. How could she go through with this? Somewhere in the darkness a branch creaked. Wiwoka leaned down to kiss the child and then forced herself to keep moving.

She left the cover of the forest and crept into the outer dunes. When she came within sight of the cave she stopped to observe. She knew she did not have long until sunrise. The shaman's wolves were nowhere in sight. When she finally dared to set out she stayed low to the sand, every muscle and shred of intention focused on silence. She drew closer, then closer still, until she was hard against the boulder's side. She laid the baby on the ground and kissed her forehead one last time. The child began to awaken.

Wiwoka had only just escaped back to the dunes when a wolf emerged from the cave. It trotted curiously over to the bundle of cloth and peered down inside. Wiwoka watched in horror, unsure what to do. The shaman appeared a moment later, sweeping the beach with his gaze. Wiwoka sucked back against the shoulder of the dune she was hiding behind, not breathing, not even daring to blink. She heard shushing and then the baby's cries were dampened as if she had been taken inside the cave. Wiwoka scrambled back into the woods, collapsed against a fallen tree, and shook soundlessly.

BOOK III

...

Chapter Nineteen

THE SHAMAN

. . .

Long streaks of fire arced across the glass of the ocean's surface as the shaman swam back toward the air on the last of his energy. He watched the blurry cinders burn through their parabolas without understanding what they were until something about the curving trajectories finally made him realize what he was seeing. The stars were falling.

When he had disappeared beneath the surface of the bay he had been warm and rested. He had started strong, churning powerfully through schools of iridescent fish as he moved away from shore. He swam deeper and deeper, the light fading and the cold intensifying as he traveled away from the sunlight. Icy currents buffeted his frame and probed his thick fur and still he continued to swim. Eventually the water grew so dim he could barely see his huge white paws in front of his face. He was allowing himself to sink as much as swim by now, guiding himself in a controlled descent. At some point total darkness fell and the shaman stopped swimming altogether. He dropped through the freezing pitch blackness. Time vanished. He seemed to fall forever. Fathoms piled up like weights above him, pressing down on his lungs and the very blood in his veins. At last he collided with the seabed. He could feel his paws sinking into muck. He began plodding forward, guided by instinct.

The silt was thick and exhausting to walk through. It sucked at his paws as he trudged through the darkness. Several times he felt the brush of unseen scales against his flank and wondered if he would have the strength to fight off a monster of the deep if he were attacked. The frigid waters had long since pierced his fur, penetrating to his muscles and bones.

When he first saw a flicker of light up ahead he thought the darkness was deceiving him; that it was a memory of the sun or a sign of blindness setting in after staring through utter blackness for too long. But then the flicker appeared again and held steady, a glimmer on the underwater horizon. The light grew brighter as he walked and gradually a form took shape in the distance. He was approaching a pile of rocks, an underwater citadel of boulders and steaming vents lit from within by soft pink light. As he reached the rocks a voice called out from somewhere within the formation.

"Hail, Henyawé."

The bear-shaman bowed his shaggy head. When he lifted it he saw Kulan hopping up onto the rocks, his condor wings folded about him like a huge tent waiting to be spread. Sheleth the Terror was there as well, the stripes on his body rippling in the water as he stretched luxuriantly. The shaman marveled to see his predecessors, whom he knew only through Anharay's stories. His own master was there as well. Unlike the others Anharay appeared in his human form, his missing hand restored, the gray hair the shaman had braided on feast days now black as ebony. He was vital and renewed and when he saw his former acolyte he laughed, lifting his arms from atop the rocks.

"Hail, Walks the Stars," Anharay called again, an otherworldly light in his eyes. "We have come at your call from the mountain of the other world. Speak to us of your need and we will counsel you."

The shaman wanted to soak in the moment. Just the sight of his master filled his heart to the brim. There were many questions he might have asked, but there was little time to spare.

"The people are suffering," the shaman said. He felt his strength returning, the presence of his ancestors refreshing him. He could feel their magic reverberating steadily from the castellations of stone. "Though they scarcely know it, having allowed themselves to be blinded and bound. Now I fear Aghuax and all who dwell within her hang in the balance."

In all his years the shaman had never called on his predecessors. Not during the great plague a century before, nor when the magi corrupted the godwood. He did not know what they saw of his world, or whether they were concerned with it any longer, having passed from its shore of sufferings. The elder shamans listened as he spoke to them of his own acolyte, the wickedness of Hankasi, and the foreign queen whose life now seemed as though it would surely be forfeit. He concluded by telling them of his own dreams and what he had lately read in the stars. When he finished they remained silent a time. The shaman found himself wondering if they were pondering his words or simply deciding what to reveal to him. He felt certain they must know at least something of what the future held.

Kulan turned his crow head sideways to appraise the shaman and Sheleth's tail swished rhythmically in the pink waters as though he was deep in thought, but it was Anharay who finally broke the silence.

"It is not for you to know all the dooms of men," he said. "Yet there are things we may speak of. Take care not to forget that what seems imminent may yet be undone, and the impossible may soon be accomplished, for good or ill."

Then Anharay revealed to his former acolyte some part of the fate that awaited him. When he concluded, there was a shifting in the light and the shaman sensed his audience was drawing to a close. As the elders turned to go, he felt a great sorrow and lifted a hand toward his old master.

"Bless me, master," he said. Anharay's eyes lit up with compassion. His robes fell straight around him, as if the water had no power to move them. He raised both hands, including the one the shaman had seen cut off with his own eyes.

"Rise now to meet your fate. Whether in suffering or in joy, hold fast to the light, for it is not death that threatens the pure of heart, but corruption. Soon you will stand among us. Prepare yourself and be filled with hope, though the moon falls and the sun is hidden in obscene darkness. You are worthy to have inherited my mantle. Now go forth, knowing you are strong enough to die with honor."

· · ·

When his snout finally broke the surface the white bear let out an explosive breath, sending a cloud of vapor into the air. The wolves rushed into the water, baying wildly. Sensing the shaman's weakness they helped guide his huge frame toward the beach. Stepping back onto dry sand he shook himself out, sending great sheets of water flying. The wolves licked his face and barked with joy.

The shaman looked up at the sky. Stars rained westward, their tails sparkling ominously as they plunged toward the sea. He took this great portent in for a moment. Then his eyes rolled up into his head and with a violent shudder he transformed back into a man. When he returned to himself he noticed a change in the wolves' barking. He turned to see a young woman in a traveling cloak standing by the cave, shaking visibly at

eir eyes had widened as she named the various oracles they were to
ng back with them, but they had not protested. She expected their
atest obstacle would be getting out of the castle. If her suspicions were
rect the guards had been instructed to keep them locked in, prisoners
the pretext of safety. Instead, when Senecwo opened the door, steely-
d and ready to talk her way past anyone, she found the hall empty.
e guards had vanished, leaving nothing but the torrid light of the falling
s pouring over the flagstones. It was worse than she had thought.

She sent her handmaidens off with a kiss on the cheek and
red the doors tight behind them before returning to the balcony. A
ved screen shielded the balcony from the street below. Great beasts
ulated on its wide panels, rolling heavily amidst the wooden waves.
kasi had commanded the panels be set up soon after their wedding
and ordered his young wife to remain hidden behind them, citing the
gers of the street and the prying eyes of his enemies. She would be
lded from the arrows of assassins and her honor protected at the same
. Senecwo wondered why he bothered pretending to consider her to
anything more than a piece of property, a fetish to be fondled in pri-
and kept hidden from other men.

The screen made her feel even more like a prisoner, its violently
ing beasts serving as a constant reminder of the demands her captor
e of her. But he was gone now, and for one night at least she would
ree. The screen was lighter than she had expected. She slid it aside
ease and stood at the railing, exposed at last to the street and a royal
. The city spread out below her, but she ignored its dark grandeur.
eyes were fixed on the dragon tails shearing the sky.

The stars were falling in even greater numbers now, burning
ugh the atmosphere in eerie silence. There was nothing to do but
and so she stood at the railing for the next several hours, watching
brilliant wakes phosphoresce in the black kettle above her. At last

the sight of the wolves' bared teeth. Her wide face was illuminated by the crimson glow of the phoenix stars. The shaman raised a hand to silence the wolves and began walking towards her, retying his breechcloth around his waist as he went. The stranger bowed low at his approach.

"Her majesty Kulkas requests your presence and that of your acolyte in her chamber. She asks that you would come with great speed, returning with me even now."

So soon, the shaman thought. *Scarcely have I returned and already the wheels of fate begin moving.*

"What does the queen require?" he asked in his deep drum voice.

"Alas, my lord," the handmaiden said, sounding genuinely forlorn, "she has given me no further instruction." She looked at the sky as she spoke. The reason for the queen's request was evident enough. And yet if that was the case, why did he feel the prick of a familiar doubt?

. . .

There had been a handful of times over the years, almost always near dusk, when the shaman had sensed a watching presence near the cave. It was always when Canowic was nearby, plaiting rope beside the fire or playing in the surf with the wolves. It had not been difficult for him to determine where the watcher sat, though she thought herself well hidden. It was always the queen.

She had summoned the shaman and his acolyte to the castle on several occasions, ostensibly to get the shaman's opinion on the princesses' health. She seemed to value his opinion above the king's physicians. Yet no matter what she asked him about, or how clearly he discerned her true concern for her daughters, the shaman sometimes had the sense during these visits that the queen was not fully listening to him. It was not the feeling of being mocked or merely humored. He would not have continued to answer her summons if that had been the case. No, it was something else entirely. She seemed distracted. There was no one else in the room during their meetings besides the princesses, the handmaidens, and Canowic.

For years he had entertained various theories about what was going on, but he had always refused to sate his curiosity through the use of his stone. Then one day in the autumn of Canowic's thirteenth year something had happened. Master and acolyte had been standing in the king's throne room listening to the elders discuss the harvest, when the shaman happened to look over at the queen. A loose piece of hair had fallen across her face and she tucked it behind her ear using only one finger. Though the shaman had never seen her do this, the motion was instantly familiar. He had seen it a thousand times somewhere else. In that moment, understanding had bloomed in him like a rose.

· · ·

"As you see, my acolyte is not here," the shaman said, gesturing to the empty cave. "I await her return."

He looked toward the cliff at the end of the beach where a small figure could be seen picking a path down its flank. He left the queen's messenger staring at the sky and stepped into his cave. When he re-emerged his cloak of black feathers was gathered about him like night itself. He looked at the wolves and uttered a phrase in a tongue the hand-maiden did not know. The wolves became agitated and started barking. The shaman shook his head and repeated the phrase, but it did not seem to help. The pack began to howl.

Chapter Twenty

SENECWO

· · ·

Senecwo was disoriented, falling down into her body clouds of a dream so real the world had seemed into flame. She sat up too abruptly, her forehead sli limbs tangled in the silken sheets. *The palace was catching were next door!*

But... wait. She felt her heart thudding as she str her breath. There was nothing but silence coming from room next door.

Only shadows.

Pieces of light danced around the room, mottle sliding across the floor and walls. As Senecwo looked arou woka awake and standing by the door to the balcony. Fea eyes like ashes from a funeral pyre. The queen stood and her friend, pulling on her robe as she went. The two of th to the balcony together, and discovered the source of the st

Within minutes Senecwo dispatched three of he

she heard the sound of the door being unlocked, followed by a restless shifting of feet and the low murmur of voices. Wiwoka slipped onto the balcony.

"They have arrived, my lady. All who are coming."

"The shaman and his acolyte?" Senecwo asked.

"She is here my lady," Wiwoka said. "They are both here."

Senecwo nodded and looked back out over the sleeping city. From her vantage she could see other rooftops with other stargazers, all of them riveted by the same sight she was. The clammy smell of day old fish and offal drifted up from the Meatsellers quarter like the scent of fear itself.

"Wiwoka," she said, eyeing the roof of the royal stables across the street where a clutch of magi huddled over their tubular looking glasses. Her voice was quiet and almost wistful. "If we had not come to this place we might have lived out our lives in the peace of the mountain kingdom."

Wiwoka bit her lip. "I dare not entertain the thought, lest it slay me."

"You would not have called me queen," Senecwo went on, turning from the railing with a sigh. "Nor would I have had to wear the rough name these buzzards have chained me to. I would have been only Senecwo, and you Wiwoka. Our daughters would have been free before the wind."

Wiwoka's head bowed in sorrow and it was all Senecwo could do to maintain her composure. To see her friend so distraught was almost enough to undo her. Her heart surged painfully against its seams, but then she composed herself. She could not fall apart now. There was the girl in the other chamber to think of. All of them, really, just girls.

She put a hand on Wiwoka's shoulder and spoke softly, pouring her voice out carefully, like milk into a dish, lest she lose herself in her own sorrow and fail them all.

"We were brought to this place, against our will. And you, beloved sister, have acquitted yourself well."

Wiwoka's head shook silently as Senecwo bestowed her blessing. Then Senecwo drew her friend into an embrace in which they were perfect equals again, two frightened girls holding onto one another through the darkness of a long night. When Wiwoka had dried her eyes, Senecwo sent her back into the audience chamber ahead of her. She needed a moment alone.

She wedged the stones back into the dam of her soul, tightening them, sealing her heart as best she could against weakness. She had not asked to be a queen, but now she must rise to the moment. She went to her dressing room and chose a blue gown shot through with luminous silver threads and a shimmering grey cloak. She put up her hair in two tortoise shell combs and painted her face lightly, but took no ring upon her finger, disdaining the diadem of six stars and leaving the other jewels of the throne heaped together in their box. When she was ready she looked into the mirror above her dressing table.

"My god," she whispered. Then she took up her scepter and swept through the door into the audience chamber in the final hour before dawn.

Chapter Twenty-One

THE COMPANY

. . .

The roof of the world was tearing loose in fiery chunks. Canowic raced back to the cave, terrified, hoping against hope the shaman would be there when she returned. When she caught sight of him standing at the water's edge she was flooded with a sense of relief. So much so that it wasn't until the very end of her sprint up the beach that she remembered to hide the seeing stone beneath her cloak. She was so focused on her master she didn't register the ominous black-robed figure behind him until the last minute. Her eyes widened and she shouted a warning but the shaman remained calm.

He explained that the queen had summoned them, and Canowic realized the cowled stranger must be one of Kulkas' handmaidens. She didn't want to go to the castle. She wanted to sit with the shaman and tell him everything she had seen in her vision. Only he would be able to help her. She opened her mouth to explain, but the master stopped her with a raised hand. His face was clouded with concern.

"What is this?" He was looking at the place where she had

clumsily hidden the stone inside her cloak. "You have sought a vision in the godwood?"

Canowic nodded miserably and pulled the stone out. There was no use hiding it anymore. She set the crystal in her master's outstretched hand. There was something grave in his countenance, but it was not anger. He looked down at the stone and then back at her. His eyes were impenetrable.

"Come, we must not keep the queen waiting."

Without another word he turned and set out toward the city wall at a pace that had Canowic and the handmaiden running to keep up.

. . .

The shaman was not the only interpreter of dreams amongst the Ancagua. There were others who sought to commune with spirits or walk the planes of the other world; the oracle of the forest, living in her woven basket amongst the cedars; the rivermen, who gave themselves over to the ecstasies of possession by the river wights, their hair turning green and mossy, eyes heavy-lidded as stones from a stream; the cartomancers who read the Deck of Dreams on street corners, shuffling their bright cards and explaining the fates implied by the Lady of Arrows, The Doe, or The Runner. In the dark corners of the forest there were all manner of magicians who would read the lines in a person's face, or spin basilisk eggs over the abdomens of pregnant women. Rather than deterring these holy ones from their labors, the magi's persecutions had merely driven them deeper underground.

Standing on the flagstones of her private audience chamber, Senecwo surveyed the array of seers she had summoned. Here was the dwarf who lived beneath the royal forge and read the embers of fires and the leavings of tea. She had first seen him at one of Hankasi's wild parties. He had been waddling bowlegged among the guests on the portico, clothed in the skin of a lion he claimed to have killed himself. Hankasi had called him over to where he was reclining with his concubines and made him read the stories in their palms. The dwarf's fingers were small and fat like a babe's, yet he had the fine, oiled beard of a full-grown man. His head was so overlarge Senecwo was surprised it did not pull him over like a gourd atop a twig.

She had shaken her head in disgust at the dwarf's ludicrous play-acting. Later, though, she learned his knowledge had proven uncanny. He had predicted the pregnancy of one of the king's concubines three months in advance as well as the death of a chambermaid. He was rumored to be a great interpreter of dreams.

Two anchorites from the hold of Atelan had come. Raiders had long since overrun most of the old holdings, but Atelan had survived, in large part because of its location. The cluster of ancient fastnesses was situated on a rocky headland a two-hour ride south of the city. Hemmed on three sides by crashing surf, Atelan was sealed off from the mainland by a huge wall. Senecwo was surprised the message she'd sent with Kikoya had convinced the famously reclusive anchorites to come.

Despite having spoken openly with the shaman on more than one occasion about his gods, and born witness over a period of years to the eccentric rituals and powerful rites performed by the various sorcerers, wizards, holy men and hermits who dwelt among the Ancagua and on their fringes, Senecwo had never quite fully grasped the demarcation that existed between the deities the shaman sought to honor and those to which some of the others owed fealty.

This included the anchorites of Atelan. She knew they had little contact with the outside world, and that some amongst the Ancagua believed them to have become lost in their studies, fallen prey to an esoteric theology that had led them astray. The first of the two men, a towering eunuch with thin arms, stood blinking slowly in the weird light rippling through the room. His companion was an old, shriveled man twisted by a wrecked hip. His face was dominated by a lumpy forehead and a pair of cobra-slit eyes.

A young man huddled in the corner beneath a trio of potted palms, apart from the other seers. The youngest of the region's oracles, he lived alone in a tree some distance outside the city. Senecwo only knew the general area where he might be found and was impressed Tantawelae had located him. The oracle was bent over, slumped against the wall in obvious pain. Veins meandered across his pale skin like small rivers across a map. His beard was patchy and his long hair clotted and clumped. Senecwo could smell him from where she stood.

The young man seemed to be in the grip of some kind of fit. He was muttering to himself, oblivious to the scene around him. The muscles on his neck stood out taut as cords and spittle ran down his chin onto the armless burlap sack he wore as a shirt. The dwarf stared at him with open disdain. As Senecwo watched he raised a claw-like hand and rammed his calloused knuckles into the side of his head. She winced, but he seemed not to have felt the blow.

Lastly, there were the shaman and his acolyte. The old man's face was just as she remembered it; channeled and pocked, dominated by eyes as placid and deep as a river pool at first light. A face to exhort kings and defy gods. Canowic wore a linen dress under her deerskin cape. The animal's glassy eyes stared at Senecwo with life-like intensity.

The girl's features marked her as an alien. Like Senecwo, she had the eyes of the mountain people, and the same light skin and elegant neck. The women of Aghuax wore their hair up, braided and pinned atop their heads in intricate assemblages of cord and feather, but the shaman's acolyte let her long black hair fall down her back, cascading beneath the deerskin nearly to her waist.

It was not until Canowic looked up at her that Senecwo realized she had been staring. As their eyes met a spark leapt across the gap, connecting the two of them amidst the dread light of the dying stars. Senecwo thought her heart might burst if she did not say something to the girl. It was not time though.

Her survey of the room had only taken a few moments. When Senecwo spoke her voice was hard and bright. The voice of a queen.

"The king is dead and the stars fall from heaven like chaff. This very night I have dreamed a dream of surpassing clarity. Honor and riches await the one who can interpret its true meaning."

She gauged the assembled seers for their reactions. The dwarf's eyes shone with a furious light and she could see the crumpled old anchorite's mind whirring through its gears, no doubt trying to ascertain what kind of riches she might be referring to, but it was the eunuch who spoke first. His birdlike voice seemed out of place in one so tall.

"Tell us what you have dreamed, o queen, and we will interpret its meaning."

"I have dreamed four dreams in one," Senecwo began. "Oxen drawing a plow that turns a city street rather than a field; a blind ragman beset by thieves; a broken glass for the keeping of time; lastly, a banner flying in a strong wind."

As she spoke Senecwo noted a change in Canowic. The girl had shifted her weight in one sudden motion, rocking back on her heels as if hit by an invisible wave. The eunuch tilted his head sideways as he considered the queen's words, concentration shadowing his face like a cloud above water. The dwarf's brows knit themselves into a furious thatch, his lips moving soundlessly as he formulated and discarded ideas. Meanwhile off in the corner, the young oracle gave no sign of having heard anything.

The shriveled old anchorite clasped his mottled hands together and made an unpleasant attempt at a smile.

"Allow me one moment of reflection, your majesty, and I shall tell you the meaning of your dream."

The dwarf snorted.

"I do not need a moment," he said, sneering at the anchorite. "I will prophesy now."

When the queen had begun explaining her dream, Canowic's heart had leapt within her. A great thing had befallen her, was befalling her even now. Dizzy with anticipation and dread, she felt a strange warmth spreading down her arm, like sunlight pouring onto her skin. Turning her head, she saw the shaman had laid his hand on her shoulder. He only left it there for a moment, so briefly that the others did not see, but a fortifying calm continued to flow through Canowic afterwards.

Now the dwarf stepped forward and cleared his throat, holding up both hands like an orator and scanning his audience dramatically before beginning. When he spoke his voice was harsh, like shears cutting tin. The dwarf held that the plow was a symbol of the city's coming prosperity, the earth of commerce being tilled and made fresh anew. The ragman symbolized the weakness of the surrounding nations upon whom the Ancagua would soon fall, just as brigands had fallen upon the beggar. The hourglass, he ensured the queen, was a symbol of the timelessness of Hankasi's throne, which, though the king had died—thus the fracture in the glass—would continue without end. The banner? It was the flag of victory, of course. He added in closing that the falling stars visible through the open window were a guarantor of the dream's import. Finished, he dropped his hands and bowed at the waist. Canowic could not tell from the queen's face whether she gave any credence to this last claim, although it struck her as aggrandizing and unnecessary and therefore dangerous.

The elder anchorite had listened indignantly, angry at having been cut off. But as the dwarf rolled out his interpretation the corners of the old man's lips had slowly lifted in a mocking smile. No sooner had the dwarf finished speaking than the anchorite extended an arm magnanimously.

"Esteemed Kulkas," he began, "the dwarf's interpretation is a true interpretation. I would correct him in but one thing."

The dwarf rolled his eyes at this bit of gamesmanship and crossed his stubby arms.

"The hourglass is a symbol not of the endlessness of the king's throne, but of your own. Soon you will ascend to the royal dais and take your place over the city."

The dwarf actually laughed out loud. If the queen found it unlikely that a broken hourglass implied something fortuitous for her or her heirs she did not show it. Instead she turned to the eunuch.

"What say you?"

Beads of sweat were clearly visible on the slender giant's lip. He wiped his mouth with the back of his hand and blinked heavily, looking as though he deeply regretted his decision to come.

"The plow d-does represent newness, your m-m-majesty," he stammered, trying to gather momentum. "Though whether newness of commerce or of something else I cannot say. The ragman is indeed a traditional symbol of poverty, so it may be the dwarf is correct and poverty will be beset by wealth." The eunuch looked to the dwarf for approval, but the dwarf simply stared back, hunkering down behind the barricade of his prodigious brow. "Or it may not."

The dwarf shook his head slowly in disgust and the eunuch's shoulders sagged.

"As for the hourglass," he went on miserably, "it is a symbol to counteract the idea of prosperity. It is the tool of the scribes, and its fracturing may indicate difficult foaling and hard trading ahead."

The eunuch winced as he spoke this last pronouncement,

the first openly negative interpretation anyone had offered. He squirmed under the queen's gaze, which had neither softened nor hardened since he began speaking.

"The fourth image, that of the banner," he continued, in apparent torment, "portends that whether in times of abundance or difficulty the kingdom shall endure."

"The kingdom shall endure," the queen repeated. The eunuch hung his head, a wrung-out cloth. The oracle in the corner moaned. The entire company turned to look at him, but he only struck his head against the wall and convulsed.

Everyone had spoken but Canowic and the shaman. Canowic turned to her master to see what his interpretation would be, but he only gave her a reassuring nod. She realized what she had to do. There was no time to waste. She stepped forward. As she did, words came to her, spilling from her lips like a spell that demands to be cast.

"O queen," she began, "your dream is a fell dream of doom for you and your kingdom."

A chorus of protest from the other seers. The dwarf threw up his hands.

"Will we be mocked by a child?"

"She speaks a lie, your majesty!" cried the ancient anchorite.

"This cannot be," the eunuch moaned. "The stars have said nothing."

"Cut her tongue out!" The elder anchorite shrieked. "And that of her soothsaying lord. He has never been held in esteem by the seers of Atelan. He speaks poison in her ear!"

The shaman's presence suddenly filled the room, huge and searingly radiant. His eyes flared like liquid silver in a crucible and the anchorite staggered backwards. The queen held up a hand.

"Peace," she said firmly, her eyes fixed on Canowic. "I would hear what she has to say."

In an instant the shaman's aura vanished, leaving nothing to indicate it had been real save the volcanic glint in his eyes. Canowic gathered herself again.

"I come this very hour from a vision of my own," she began,
her voice clear in the freshly sown silence. "I went to the godwood alone.
There I made a fire of sweetwood and fell into a seeing trance. I was
vouchsafed a series of images. These images mirror your own dream, your
majesty."

· · ·

As the flames died down, Canowic had gazed into the shewstone and descended to that place where the passage of time slows to a crawl, like
heavy sludge inching toward bedrock. She had stilled her breath as the
shaman had taught her, focusing on the place at the edge of her nostrils
where it came in and went out, putting aside all other thoughts as she
opened herself to the other world.

Sometimes when an image first came to her it was as if disparate
veins within the stone were slowly being stitched into something clearer,
the scratches of a child's rude drawing gradually cohering until something
clear could be discerned. This time was different. This time the images
had come fully formed. And they had moved.

First she had seen the blade of a plow churning through broken
ground. Then her field of vision widened and she saw the full plow and
the team of oxen that pulled it. Instead of passing through a field, the
blade was breaking up the middle of a city street. A dark figure walked
behind the yoked oxen, cracking his whip as the hard earth of the road
turned over in dark furrows.

Next came the image of a hunched wanderer, cloaked and

hooded with a long cane in hand. The wanderer was tap, tap, tapping his way down a dark and desolate road. Again her vision expanded. Now the road the figure walked was revealed to be a lonely path passing between high banks in a desolate place. Canowic watched as the groping wanderer was beset by thieves. They stole his purse and beat him with his own cane until he lay unmoving in the ditch.

The third image was an hourglass like those used by sailors to mark the watches of the night. The instrument lay on its side, its glass bell broken and sand pouring from its side like blood from a wound. The entire scene was spotlighted inside a narrow beam of light around which thick blackness swirled like storm clouds.

After the hourglass receded she saw a banner snapping in a stiff breeze against a bright blue sky. The flag was emblazoned with a wreath of lilies and flew from the battlement of a great castle.

The final image in Canowic's vision had been a stone door of the type the ancients fashioned for portals. Two standing stones with a lintel stone placed across their top. This mighty gate stood on a hill of green grass shot through with small white flowers waving in a gentle breeze. The stones were carved all over with runes written in an alien tongue Canowic could not read. From her vantage point she could see through the door. Although the grass and the delicate flowers looked the same on the other side, she knew that to pass beneath the lintel would transform her forever.

"The plowed street represents the destruction of the kingdom," Canowic said. She could feel the eyes of everyone in the room upon her, but she kept her gaze locked on the queen. "The city will be razed to its foundations and the fields sown with salt. This will come about through a great treachery. The ragman is you yourself, my queen. You will be beset by wicked men and put to death. The broken hourglass signals that the time for your death draws nigh. Even now doom stands at the gate, beckoning to be let in by the night watchman.

"Lastly you saw a flag. You did not say, but the flag was flying from a great rampart and emblazoned with a wreath of lilies. I do not know what the lilies represent. Only you know this."

Canowic saw a spark of recognition illuminate the queen's eyes. She pressed on, allowing the words to flow out of her like water from a spring.

"The battlements and the fact that the banner was flying on a clear morning foretell that when you die you will climb to the ramparts of heaven and be seated with your father and mother at the feast of the dead. This is my interpretation."

As she spoke Canowic was filled with a strong intuitive sense that the final image she had seen, the door of stones, was not a part of the queen's dream, but was instead a sign to her alone and one she must hold close for the present.

Now she waited silently. The room had gone so utterly still that palm fronds could be heard whispering outside the open window. The queen looked at Canowic for an endless moment that seemed encased in amber, suspended beyond time. Before she could respond the stillness was broken by the oracle in the corner. His face jerked towards the ceiling and his eyes rolled back in his head. When he spoke it was with the deep, wrenched voice of a demon.

"They are coming."

From the courtyard below there arose a sudden shouting and the crooked bray of horns.

Chapter Twenty-Two

SENECWO

• • •

The brazen ring of the war horn hung in the air like a spell, transfixing them all. The shaman alone seemed unaffected. He moved quickly, placing his hands on the door's heavy crossbar and muttering an incantation before the horn's echoes had even faded. Not a moment too soon. The wicked horn blast was now followed by rattling spears and the tramp of running feet.

"Your words ring with the clarity of fate's bell," Senecwo said softly, looking at Canowic. "Where others have sought to flatter me or conceal their lack of knowledge, you alone have spoken the truth."

The other seers stared at the queen. The dwarf grimaced in indignation, and the eunuch's legs trembled violently as a newborn foal's. The elder anchorite was just opening his lips, one finger raised in his defense, when the queen silenced him.

"Hold your tongue, worm. The sacred laws of your own people state that he who presumes to speak assurances or divinations which come to light as false shall meet with swift punishment." Senecwo felt the fury of a stolen lifetime kindling within her. Her daughters, woken by the tumult, were crying in the next room. She stared at the anchorite pitilessly. "And there shall be none to bury him or assign him a place with his fathers at the gate of Usthil."

In the end it was the dwarf who ran first, bolting straight into the shaman's arms like a skittish animal running toward the butcher. The rest of the smaller man's misshapen frame seemed to disappear behind the cloak of raven feathers, leaving his face disembodied, eyes rolling and lips sputtering as he fumed like a tin of coals. Without looking to the queen for approval the shaman took the dwarf's oversized temples in his hands and wrenched a quarter turn to the side. The sound was like the splintering of a dry tree limb.

As the shaman dropped the dwarf's lifeless body to the floor, the elder anchorite was already flinging his hand forward and screaming a word of power. The shaman's arm began to bubble like a shred of dough in an oven, but he quickly loosed a counter-spell and the anchorite's robes burst into flame. Lapping currents of fire quickly spread to his beard, transforming him into a grotesque, living torch.

The anchorite spun in a circle, screaming like a stuck sow and beating the air with his fists. He stumbled to the ground and continued to thrash in agony, calling upon his gods to save him. But they must have been busy on other errands for he continued burning. In his last moments the anchorite begged Canowic to slay him, but she only stared at him, her dark eyes wide with horror as the skin melted off his face and arms onto the floor. When he finally stopped kicking, a miasma of burning flesh filled the room. Without a word the eunuch jogged lightly to one of the tall windows and jumped out. He hit the cobbles of the courtyard with a sound like splattering melon.

This was followed immediately by the sound of heavily armed men running in the hallway, as if they were all but actors in a farce and the eunuch's suicide had been the cue for their entrance. There came a terrific pounding on the chamber door. A man was screaming, demanding the bar be lifted. Somewhere in the back of her mind Senecwo wondered why Iyaye had not sent word of the Council's decision. Surely he would have warned her if he could. The rest of the elders had been so open in their hatred of her—a hatred that seemed entirely predicated on her being a foreigner—that it was almost hard for her to think of their failure to oppose Yengwa's coup as treachery. It occurred to her that Iyaye must be dead. Then the thought was driven from her mind by the wail of axes striking the heavy oak door.

"Behold," she said. "Even now my enemies stand at the threshold."

It dawned on her that this might be The Moment She Had Been Waiting For, but before she could act a sudden wave of nausea overtook her. Canowic was grimacing too and even the shaman looked gray. They felt it too; evil had entered the hall. Some slinking wickedness emanating noxious power. The heavy iron bands of the door vibrated at a new frequency but held fast thanks to the shaman's fortifying magic.

"Wiwoka," Senecwo called. "Prepare the girls for traveling, quickly."

Always faithful, Wiwoka vanished into the princesses' chambers without questioning where they could possibly be going. Senecwo knew it was time. Her moment had come. Without further delay she ran to her dressing room.

At the back of the closet where all her robes and finery were stored, hidden beneath a particularly heavy chair, there was a small trap door she had discovered soon after her capture. She had always assumed it was a vestige of some past queen's need for secrecy. She reached down into the darkness of the secret compartment and withdrew an ornate wooden box. Though battered and soiled it was still beautiful, its intricate lid tooled with a delicate circle of lilies.

She returned to find Wiwoka ushering the princesses into the main room. The handmaidens busied themselves with pulling on the girls' boots and folding them into thick cloaks, as if they were not completely surrounded with nowhere to go. Upon seeing their mother, Leokita and Mictanta broke away and ran to her, throwing their arms around her legs in terror. Senecwo set the box on the table and bent down to hold her daughters close, whispering words only they could hear. Then, with the girls still huddled close to her flank like chicks against the wing of a beautiful swan, she stood and lifted the box's lid.

Time had affixed it to the rest of the box and now it separated with a crack. Bits of dust and excelsior flaked away onto the tabletop. Setting the lid aside Senecwo looked down and exhaled with wonder. For though she knew what the box contained she had never opened it. She reached down and gently removed a crown of pure white ivory that no one save its maker had ever seen.

· · ·

From time immemorial it had been the custom of the women of the Odmarsim to have *weyawen*, helms of immortality, prepared for them by the crown-maker of their village. The crown-maker was an elder, always a woman, who had been taught the art by another before her. Packed in its ritual box and stored against the last days of a woman's life, the weyawen was to be unsealed and put on only when death was imminent. The crowns were said to be worked with great enchantments for the stirring of courage and hope, for the Odmarsim were not concerned with the inescapable fact of death, as much as with the way in which one died.

The crown-makers of the Odmarsim were renowned for their craftsmanship and the fineness of their tools, though few had ever seen their handiwork. Many women never unsealed their crowns, their deaths coming unexpectedly or with little warning. When this was the case, a woman was buried with her box undisturbed. No two crowns were alike, though they were all variants on the same image, rendering in great detail the parapets, streets, banners and gates of the holy city to which Senecwo's people yearned to fly upon death.

Three months before the raid that changed her life forever, the crown-maker of Senecwo's village came to her hut. Emtahet was older than the hills and nearly blind. Her eyes were cloudy white and her chin was covered in a rubble of moles and stray hairs, but her voice was warm and melodious; a comforting voice. She appeared in the doorway one afternoon while the men were in the fields, holding a circular box in her arms.

"I am here for Senecwo," was all she said.

Senecwo's mother looked at the old woman in surprise, and then quickly gestured for her daughter to rise. Senecwo stood from the mat where she had been weaving and reached out to take the box from Emtahet. For a moment both their hands were touching the enameled surface.

"May the day for this crown's unsealing be far away," Emtahet said, still holding the box. "May it be held at bay until all the days numbered for you have come and gone in peace."

Senecwo felt a weightiness settle on her shoulders like a cloak. There were tears in her mother's eyes, but she did not seem afraid.

"I made your mother's crown," Emtahet went on. "And I bestowed the same blessing on her that I now bestow on you. One day your time of dying shall arise. It may come slowly, through illness or old age, or arrive suddenly like a beast lunging from tall grass. Whenever that day comes, unseal this box and set the crown upon your head. Then you will be filled with courage, and know it is a good day to die."

After Emtahet left, Senecwo's mother had helped her wrap the box in cloth and bury it next to her own in a shallow hole beneath their hut. When she was marched out of the village in chains Senecwo had written the crown off as lost forever.

Then one day several years into her reign, she had received a gift. A basket of fruit had been left on the ground near the courtyard guardhouse with a note indicating it was intended for Queen Kulkas. The fruit would have been consumed by the guards and never mentioned to either king or queen had Wiwoka not happened to pass by in the early morning just as the basket was discovered. She immediately recognized the fruit, and brought the basket with her back to the queen's chambers. When Senecwo saw what the basket contained she stopped braiding Mictanta's hair and locked eyes with Wiwoka.

Having caught wind of this strange gift, Hankasi insisted his cupbearer, a sallow-faced young fellow with drooping earlobes, sample each piece of fruit to make sure none were poisoned. The king himself never laid eyes on the fruit. If he had, he might have recognized it as Fire Lace, a delicacy of the mountain valleys from which he had plucked his bride.

Once the cupbearer left Senecwo parceled out the slender fruit so each of her friends and daughters had a piece. Biting into her own segment brought a shock of tangy juice and an aroma that instantly evoked a memory of her grandmother's knobby hands folding pieces of the bittersweet fruit into the small cakes she baked at harvest. Where had it come from? Had someone survived the razing of their village? Even if they had, how could they have known where she had been taken? Two luxurious bites later Senecwo's teeth caught on something pulpy. She spit out a small piece of gossamer-fine hide.

Once unraveled, the hide was found to contain a message with an invitation to meet on a lonely stretch of beach north of the city. There was a promise of information. Senecwo sent Wiwoka to the rendezvous. She returned bearing the box and a story. Wiwoka had arrived at the location and camped there for three nights. During that time no one came to explain the note or anything else. On the third day she woke to find the white box sitting next to her on the ground. She shouted at the trees and the waters of the bay, begging whoever was there to reveal himself, but all she received in response was a flurry of wings as frightened birds rose into the sky.

During Wiwoka's absence Senecwo and the other handmaidens had entertained numerous theories about the writer of the note. They recalled the morning when they had woken to find that one of their captors' throats had been cut, but it was impossible to know whether this had anything to do with the basket of Fire Lace. When Wiwoka returned with the box, Senecwo had taken it from her with trembling hands. She remembered the day when Emtahet had given it to her, and the look that had passed across her mother's face at the thought that one day her own daughter would die. Senecwo cleaned the box as best she could and then hid it carefully in the secret place within her closet, and no one had spoken of it since.

. . .

The crown was carved from a single piece of ivory. As Senecwo lifted it out of the box and plunged it into the undulating red light of the falling stars, she felt a surging connection to something that had existed long before her and would continue long after. Emtahet had used the finest tools, rendering in incredible detail her own vision of the heavenly city's cobbled streets, its spiraling turrets and domes, the windows all thrown open to allow in the eternal light. At the front of the crown stood the city's storied gate, beyond which no evil was suffered. Upon this gate was carved a lily. Likewise, a tiny pendant emblazoned with a wreath of lilies flew from the rampart of the city wall, snapping in an invisible breeze. Upon seeing the twinned lilies Senecwo remembered Canowic's prophecy.

While the queen had been busy retrieving the crown, the hammering on the door had continued unabated. One of the metal bands now groaned, finally giving way. A corner of the door began to cave in and the princesses shrieked in terror. The shaman shuddered as his protective ward was fractured. The voices in the hallway were suddenly clearer, carrying graphic threats of violence.

The shaman raised his hand toward the door and let out a guttural howl. An answering bellow sounded from the hallway. Senecwo saw the shaman wince, his face drawn with pain, and knew the end was drawing near. She set the crown upon her head and stretched out her arms.

"Canowic." Her voice was husky, choked with a bramble of emotion. The shaman's acolyte was staring at her in confusion, not understanding why the queen would use her name. The girl looked to her master for help but he was staring at Senecwo.

"Canowic," Senecwo repeated, barely able to get the words out. "Forgive me."

Canowic's eyes searched her face, unsure what she was being asked to forgive.

"I have kept from you and your master these many years a secret so great I have not known how to tell it. Now I fear a final hour is upon us, and I cannot hold my tongue any longer."

The shaman's eyes were like paper lanterns blossoming with light from within. Canowic reached out for him and he took her hand in his. Then she turned her bottomless, heartbreaking eyes back to the queen.

"You are my daughter," Senecwo said. She had meant to declare it boldly but the words came out in a torn sob.

"Yes," she gasped, unable to stop, hoping to somehow use her words to bind up the wound she was in the very act of creating. "You are my daughter and the child of my womb. I bore your father's seed within me when I was captured and brought here to be an unwilling bride.

When the time came to give birth I feared Hankasi would slay you, so I left you on the strand before the shaman's cave."

Canowic began to sag toward the ground. The shaman moved quickly to support her, putting an arm about her waist. The thing in the hallway bellowed again, sending a shudder through the chamber's torches.

"I never told your master," Senecwo went on, willing Canowic to raise her eyes again and look at her though she knew that gaze would slash her heart. "I never admitted it was I who had set him the task of raising you. I only hoped he would accept."

Her words were like sawdust in her mouth. Could there be any justification for what she had done? She wondered now if she had really protected her daughter at all, or if she had merely acted out of fear for herself. It was the most fraught moment of Senecwo's life, filled with a white-hot mixture of love and shame. The girl before her was so beautiful and so afraid. It was too much to bear. Senecwo's heart roared as it caught flame. But there was one more thing. One more truth that, even if she died a moment hence, her daughter must know.

"You have heard me called Kulkas," the queen said, "but that is a name the men of this kingdom gave me. My true name is Senecwo."

The door began to give way completely. Unable to hold the enemy off alone, the shaman ran to the far wall of the chamber and lifted the rich tapestry that hung there. He pressed his hands against the granite and the mortar began to crumble, the stones slotting in upon themselves. The wall parted to reveal a secret passageway even Senecwo had not known of. Beyond the opening there was nothing but darkness and a rumor of cold wind. The head of an axe burst through the door with a sound like snapping tinder. In the corner slumped the breathless oracle, his fit having run its course.

"It is time," the shaman said. "We must fly."

Chapter Twenty-Three

CANOWIC

. . .

The tapestry fell back into place, plunging the tunnel into pitch darkness. Canowic thought she might retch. It was all too much; the revelation that the queen was her mother, the deaths of half the people in the room, the evil flooding the hallway, all of it running together and threatening to drag her under. She had ended up directly behind her master as they piled into the tunnel. As she struggled not to panic she heard him rustling in his cloak. A moment later a white light appeared, emanating from the shaman's cupped fist. He began moving swiftly down the tunnel and Canowic hurried to keep up.

The passageway was narrow and smelled of cold earth. Roots stabbed downwards, grabbing at her hood as she ran. Whoever was behind her kept clipping her heels and nearly sending her sprawling. At one point Canowic thought she felt a breeze against her cheek. How deep were they and where did this tunnel lead? The princesses whimpered in the dark, their echoing sobs seeming to come from everywhere at once.

Soon the path began slanting steeply downwards. Canowic was

about to ask the shaman where they were going when a hellish boom sounded from back up the tunnel, its reverberations overtaking them like a shockwave. The handmaidens moaned in fear. Whoever pursued them had surely gained entrance to the queen's chambers now. How long before they found the entrance to the passage? Behind her one of the handmaidens gave breathless voice to her own question.

"Who pursues us?"

Before anyone could respond Canowic ran into the shaman's back, and the rest of the group quickly piled up behind them. While they untangled themselves Canowic peered around the shaman to see what had stopped him. The light from the master's fist illuminated a heavy iron door. Its surface was inscribed with a circle made of two serpents, each devouring the other's tail. The shaman placed his hand in the middle of the serpents and exhaled a long sigh. Having expelled all the air from his lungs, he croaked a word of power. The door groaned open and Canowic was blinded.

The darkness of the tunnel had dulled her vision such that even the dim light now flooding her eyes was overwhelming. She found herself squinting into a spacious underground grotto. Dawn had arrived somewhere above them, sending shafts of red sunlight streaming down through openings in the rock to refract off the surface of an underground river running through the chamber. Fog played across the surface of the water like steam rising from a witch's bath. Canowic and the others followed the shaman through the door and out onto a stone dock that descended in five broad stairs to the water's edge. The lower portion of the dock ran out some thirty yards before ending against the wall of the cave where two small boats were tied to an iron ring.

"What is this place?"

Canowic looked up to see the queen standing beside her. But no, not the queen... her *mother*.

"An ancient refuge," the shaman replied, already climbing down the stairs. "Its stones have seen many things. Not even all the kings of Aghuax have known of its existence."

Senecwo looked down at Canowic and gave her a reassuring smile. That alone would have buoyed her heart, but then her mother put an arm around her shoulder and guided her down the stairs. Canowic thrilled at the touch of her hand. Down on the dock the queen headed for the boats. Canowic started to follow but then felt a tug on her arm. The shaman pulled her aside. His face was shadowed with concern or sorrow.

"My child," he began, speaking clearly but quietly so only she could hear him. "I have loved you like my own life."

His voice was strained in a way Canowic had never heard. Raw fear erupted in her heart like a weed punching through soft soil.

"Time is of the essence," he went on. "You are about to set forth on a great journey." He reached down and took her hand in his own. She felt something smooth, and looked down to find a small crystal ball in her palm, like the shaman's shewstone in miniature. It weighed hardly anything at all. "A traveler's stone. Light enough to carry on the way."

She flicked her eyes from the stone's veined surface back to her master's face.

"I do not understand," she frowned, her vision blurring with tears. "Where am I going that you do not lead the way?"

"You must see the princesses to safety," he said. "If it is allowed me, I will come behind you."

Canowic shook her head violently, trying to forestall the implication in his words. "What do you mean if it—"

She was cut off by a massive clang from the other side of the serpent-charmed door. At the end of the dock the princesses were being passed into the boats from one handmaiden to another. Now the queen raised her voice.

"Sisters, the time has come for us to cast off the chains of this kingdom. Hurry. Our freedom draws near!"

At that moment the bronze door was battered again and crumpled in on one side. An arrow flew in through the opening and struck Wiwoka in the throat. She fell into Senecwo, pulling them both to the ground. Kikoya leapt back out of her boat onto the dock with Selpowac close behind.

The shaman threw his hand toward the door as if hurling a stone. A bolt of shimmering air slammed into the newly opened hole, followed by the sound of screams from the tunnel. Canowic could feel the thick, suffocating presence that had harrowed them from beyond the door of the queen's chamber. She turned and ran toward her mother.

The shaman had only bought them a moment—already more arrows were whistling through the hole in the door. Senecwo held Wiwoka's head in her lap, helpless to do anything as her friend's blood poured out onto the stones. The shaman retreated to where they lay. He knelt and put his hand on the place where the arrow protruded from Wiwoka's throat. The flow of blood seemed to slow. A moment later she sighed and grew still. Senecwo reached out to close her friend's eyes but the shaman was already pulling her to her feet.

"Quickly," he rasped. "To the boats."

Too late. As Senecwo stood, another black-fletched arrow whistled through the echoing grotto and buried itself in her side. She dropped to her knees with a gasp. Canowic froze. Senecwo looked up at her, a smile twisting her mouth even as she grimaced in pain.

"Your prophecy is proved right. Today is my day of dying."

Her crown caught the diamonds of light being tossed from the surface of the rippling water and was transformed into a thing of white flame. So it was that Senecwo, the Helper, Daughter of the Odmarsim, lately crowned Kulkas, Empress of the Broken Moon, was mortally wounded by the warriors who had once carried the footstool for her feet.

"Beloved!" she cried, blood running from between her fingers. The princesses had climbed back out of the boat and were running to their mother. Senecwo drew them close, even as she slipped back onto the stones.

"I must leave you now," she said, "and make my journey to the land beyond the darkness. How I wish I could stay and see you grow!"

She looked up past the princesses to fix Canowic with a look of longing that was a blessing in itself. "Now I fly to the city of the lilies, dwelling place of our ancestors. I will wait for you there beyond the far waters, in the land where all tears are dried. Be courageous, fawns of my heart. May the sons of your virginity possess the towers of all who hate them."

With that her head fell back and she went down to the gate of eternity singing her deathsong, her voice echoing eerily about the chamber. Her remaining handmaidens ran to her side, released from the spell of horrified stupefaction in which they had been suspended. Even as they did, the door to the grotto broke open and a host of warriors swarmed in led by Yengwa, Hankasi's captain and First Spear of the Ancagua. Something trailed behind them reeking of evil.

Canowic felt her lungs constricting, the panic and grief of the moment threatening her ability to breathe. She registered the warriors flooding the cave, but it wasn't until she made eye contact with Yengwa that she snapped out of her own stupor. His face was painted in the half-black motif of battle, the scars and blisters on the ruined side of his head still oozing. Some of them gaped as if they would never heal. When he saw Canowic he let out a howl of rage. In response, the shaman stepped in front of her and roared with the strength of a full-grown bear.

Nothing about his transformation was hidden this time. Canowic witnessed her beloved master's metamorphosis with terror. His arms dislocated grotesquely as they enlarged, the skin breaking out in sheaves of white hair. The nails of his feet grew into great claws. All of his raiment, including his loincloth, his cloak, and the amulet around his neck, burst off and fell to the ground as he swelled in the space of a few heartbeats. His face was turned away, but Canowic could still see the side of his jaw unhinging and distorting into a muzzle.

The bear rooted himself directly in front of where Canowic and the handmaidens were gathered about the queen. Just before the warriors reached them, he turned to look at Canowic with the same bottomless black eyes she had gazed into every night of her childhood. It was *him* beneath all that muscle and claw. Then he roared again, and in that roar Canowic heard his voice telling her to fly. Acting on instinct, she reached out to take the infant from Tantawelae's paralyzed arms and leapt into the boat, pushing the princesses ahead of her. She unlooped the cord from the iron ring and cast off into the stream.

Back on the dock the bear reared onto his hind legs as a warrior hurled himself forward. He swiveled to one side at the last moment, his massive paw crushing the man's head like a rotten lime. Canowic cried out for the handmaidens to get into the other boat but they seemed not to hear her. Passing the infant off to the eldest princess, Canowic grabbed a paddle from the bottom of the boat and dug into the water, trying to add to the current's speed. There was a shout from the dock and moments later a swarm of arrows hissed into the water all around them. Several hit the boat, including one that lodged in the seat next to her. The tunnel bent around a corner just up ahead. Canowic dug hard twice more before risking another look back. The bear was still standing his ground above the queen's body, throwing men into the water as if they were dolls. Several arrows now protruded from his arms and chest, and the handmaidens lay slain around him.

Yengwa had hung back at the bottom of the stairs like a coward while the first warriors attacked. As he strode forward and prepared to close with her master, Canowic felt a visceral rage come over her, breaking through the panic buzzing in her ears. She wanted nothing so much as to see Yengwa disemboweled on that dock. So much so that she now took the paddle and tried to slow the boat. The bear slammed his chest with his paws and bellowed, inviting his enemy in. Just before they clinched, the powerful current carried the little boat around the bend.

The screams of men and animals rolled around them. The princesses clapped their hands over their ears and put their heads between their knees but Canowic kneeled upright, staring back at the rock wall. She was shaking uncontrollably and the paddle fell from her hands. The noise of battle continued for some time until finally a long howl sounded, like the cry of a dying animal.

BOOK IV

...

Chapter Twenty-Four

CANOWIC

. . .

Rain pelted down out of the blackness, hammering the broad-leaf ferns the girls had crawled beneath. While water assaulted them from above, an arresting cold seeped up through the frozen ground, driving them together into a knot of arms and legs as they sought to stay warm. The ferns, like the girls themselves, were huddled at the foot of a huge ash tree, deep inside the primeval wood that swept down the spurs of Merwa and carpeted the winding vale at the mouth of which Aghuax lay like a dim jewel.

After sunset the forest had fallen swiftly into a blackness so complete the girls could not see their hands in front of their faces. Before the light died Canowic had tried to think of what the shaman would do. She had assessed the princesses, taking stock of their condition, and remembered the day she had seen them for the very first time in the king's court. Gikzil, the eldest, had projected an air of self-possession.

Today's events had cracked that poised exterior. Gikzil had cried quietly as they set out on the trail. Canowic would not have blamed her if she had wept for days after all they had seen, but soon her tears had stopped. She and Canowic had traded off carrying the baby, and Gikzil had also comforted her younger sister. Ontec had trudged in silence behind them all day, her thick black hair closing off her face like a sheaf of vines.

Now in the darkness the princesses huddled together with Canowic for warmth. Canowic could feel Gikzil drawing her cloak around her sister, trying to cinch it against the cold. She followed suit, attempting to wrap the girls tighter, grateful for the warmth of the infant against her chest. All four of them were already shivering. Canowic feared for the baby most of all. What were they to do with her? They had no milk, nor any way to get some. It was a problem for the morning, along with anything else that required sight. They had made no fire for fear their pursuers might see them. With nothing to distract her from the freezing wetness, the rocky ground, and the memories of the day, Canowic closed her eyes and tried to sleep. But sleep eluded her, and all she was able to think about was whether death could be worse than what she felt.

. . .

The underground river had carried them down the tunnel. The ceiling was so low that if they had tried to stand in the little bark boat they would have struck their heads on the rock. After the final soul-wrenching scream the grotto had fallen silent behind them. Before long they rounded another bend and the glittering dimness of the tunnel was informed by a promise of daylight. Shadows danced along the walls in unpredictable patterns. Gikzil was sobbing uncontrollably, clutching the baby to her chest. Fearing she would suffocate the child, Canowic reached out and gently peeled her arms away. Ontec was gripping the side of the boat with rigid fingers and staring blankly ahead as if in a fit.

Eventually they came to the mouth of the tunnel and drifted through the overhanging vines, as if passing through a ceremonial barrier demarcating the life they had known from an uncertain future. The vines trailed across them like slippery arms, and then they were being greeted by a newly risen sun casting the world in pink and white and blue.

They had been spit out into the bay. As she looked out across the water Canowic smelled smoke on the breeze. She swiveled north toward the city and saw black clouds rising above the castle. Ontec let out a fragile, cracking sound. Turning to comfort her, Canowic found herself staring at the shaman's wolves, who were arrayed amongst a stand of pampas grass above the entrance to the tunnel. They gazed silently down at the bobbing girls with an unmistakable air of sorrow.

For a moment Canowic just stared at them. Then Gila, the snowy wolf-chieftain, barked. Canowic blinked. They were in mortal danger. She snatched the paddle from the floor of the boat and struck out hard for the beach. After helping the princesses onto the sand and instructing them to wait with the wolves, she threw off her garments and paddled back out into deeper water. The rising sun was warm against her nakedness. When she thought she was far enough from shore she broke the paddle over her knee and jammed it down through the tender bark. Water welled up around the gash. She repeated the action, making another set of holes, before wedging the paddle halves into the first set so they would sink along with the boat. She wanted to leave no trace for anyone following them. Finished, she slipped over the side as the papery craft disappeared silently behind her.

Back at the beach, wet hair steaming in the cool morning air, she took stock of the situation. They needed to get off the beach quickly, but where could they go? Her head felt full of lead. Before she could decide anything the wolves began loping up the beach, looking back over their shoulders expectantly as if wanting the girls to follow. Canowic was more than happy to let them lead.

The pack soon turned into a gap in the tall grass at the edge of the beach. Just before they plunged into the grass Canowic looked back a final time, scanning the jagged outline of the city. The shaman's cave lay hidden from view on the other side of a headland, but the castle was in plain view. Greasy smoke gathered in crowns above its parapets. Canowic wondered what was happening in Aghuax, and with whom the balance of power lay. She noticed the Dark Star still hanging heavy above the bay, its orange nimbus visible through the smoke.

The wolves led them into the forest all afternoon. They were decisive navigators, and Canowic trusted they had some destination in mind. Having known and loved the animals all her life, it was still remarkable how different she felt in their presence without the shaman around. She could see the grief in their eyes. Here were Little Buli and Serouac, who had stayed behind on the beach to erase their tracks, Red Wing and his mother Gila, and a host of other familiar faces. Canowic had never felt more grateful for their presence than she did now.

The exertion of a long, hurried walk over broken ground soon banished the chill of morning. Within a few hours Canowic's feet ached. She could only imagine how much the princesses must be hurting. At least she was accustomed to running on the beach and swimming. They had only known a life of confinement in the castle. To her surprise, they said little all day. Finally in the afternoon Canowic heard a soft yelp behind her and looked back to see Ontec had fallen behind.

"Come," Canowic said, stopping in the middle of the path. "Let us rest a moment."

They left the path carefully, crossing a cascading slide of gray shale that would leave no tracks, and hid behind a huge fallen tree. The fresh smell of the earth still clutched in its root ball suggested it had not been down long. The wolves arranged themselves around the girls in a circle, some hiding in the foliage while a few remained close at hand.

Canowic felt the first stabs of hunger in her gut, but they had no food and there was no water about. Still, sitting felt good. The girls slumped against the trunk's scaly bark, Ontec's head hanging down against her chest like a broken doll. Gikzil unslung the infant from her back and wiped her face with the hem of her dress. Canowic reached out and put a hand on Ontec's arm, but the girl didn't acknowledge her. Gikzil then handed the baby off to Canowic and drew Ontec in, stroking her hair and murmuring in her ear. Canowic leaned back with the infant and looked up at the sky. She was surprised to see how far gone the sun already was. The light was starting to thicken and grow buttery. They couldn't wait long—this was not a place to spend the night. Soon she got them moving again.

Kirin, youngest of the wolves and swiftest by far, had vanished a while back. Half a mile up the trail she reappeared, her black head popping out silently from between two ferns. She mewled once before disappearing again. Canowic pushed in behind her, following her lustrous black tail through the thick undergrowth until they reached a depression at the base of a hoary ash tree bearded with skeins of moss. It would be a good place to spend the night.

When she returned with the girls, Canowic exhorted them to move slowly, taking care not to break a single branch or step on moist ground, lest they leave a footprint. Kirin's fern-cave was additionally hidden from sight by the trunk of a massive fallen cedar. Unlike the other log they had rested against, this sentinel had fallen years earlier, as evidenced by the row of feathery saplings sprouting from its side.

After installing the girls in their temporary shelter, Canowic left them with the wolves and went scavenging. Scanning the ground for mirror wort or edible roots provided a distraction, but thoughts and images from the day kept creeping up on her. Had it really been just that morning that everything had happened? It didn't seem possible. If ever there was a time to practice staying in the moment—just as the shaman had taught her, focusing on her breath until fear fled from her mind like rain clouds before the wind—it was now. But she found she couldn't.

Questions came at her like a knife-fighter, slashing, feinting, then stabbing from another angle. Had she really just met her mother? Her *true mother*? Surely the shaman had not known. He would not have kept that knowledge from her. She'd never know, for now he too was gone. Not just gone but... *slain.* She shuddered stiffly and looked up toward the tops of the trees, where the uppermost branches were still bathed in light. She breathed deeply. The scent of rain was heavy on the wind.

When she looked back down at the darkening undergrowth her eyes snagged on a burst of color; sprigs of mentati jutting from between the roots of a host tree. She plucked several of the berry-laden twigs and then slipped back to their makeshift camp. On the return journey she found a bit of canthis root sticking out from under an embankment. The canthis could not be eaten, but sucking on it would dull their hunger.

Back under the ferns she found the girls bedded down amongst the wolves. Ontec was already asleep with her face nestled into Red Wing's auburn fur. Gikzil was cradling the baby in her arms and leaning back against Serouac. Canowic tried to give Kisoko some of the berries but she spit them out. Next she tried holding a piece of the canthis root in her mouth and letting her suck. Soon the child's breathing slowed and she grew still. Canowic ate a few of the berries and passed the rest to Gikzil.

The forest went dark with shocking speed. Canowic could feel the day's heat evaporating, but feared building a fire lest the light of a flame betray their position. So they all piled together as night fell, wolves and girls overlapping like bear cubs in a winter den. Canowic had just closed her eyes when she felt a warm blast of air on her cheek. Haifax, the oldest of the wolves, was pressing his gray head up under her chin. She could feel his ancient wolfheart beating through his tatty coat, which was still soft despite the years.

"Hello old friend," she whispered. Haifax blinked slowly, his lone good eye a comforting flash in the darkness.

"Do they have names?" Gikzil said softly.

Canowic smiled to herself in the darkness.

"Yes. This old fellow is named Haifax. You're leaning against Serouac."

"Mother was right," Gikzil said. "She said there is power in a name. They seem too magical not to have names."

Canowic was grateful for the darkness now, for she could no longer hold back the tears coursing down her cheeks.

"She told you her name," Gikzil observed. Canowic ran it over her tongue again. *Senecwo.* Such a beautiful name. She wondered what it meant.

"We have names too."

Canowic released a slow breath and tried to compose herself.

"What are those?"

"Mother gave us secret names, different from those the magi gave us. Mine is Leokita. Ontec's is Mictanta. They called our baby sister Kulza, but her real name is Kisoko."

Canowic wished she could see her sister's face. Maybe it was just the lack of food and her fatigue setting in, but she thought she could feel something swirling around them.

"What wonderful names," she said. "I will call you by them with your leave."

"I'll never answer to that other name again," Leokita said.

This was the end of their conversation. Soon Canowic sensed all three girls were asleep. Slipping her hands into the pockets of her cloak, she felt for the stone the shaman had given her. It weighed less than she would have expected for a stone of its size, for it was enchanted and shift-ed subtly in shape and weight to fit the needs of its owner. It had seemed light as a feather in her pocket as they traveled. Now, with her fingers closed around it, the stone seemed to gain density and weight. She felt a strong desire to look into it, but the darkness beneath the ferns was com-plete. Without light to refract she knew the stone would remain dark and inert. Still, it felt warm to the touch and she kept her hand closed about it.

She had pulled her deerskin hood up for warmth, and now she fancied she could feel the animal's eyes peering out from atop her head. Tilting her face upward she discovered a small gap in the ferns through which a tiny sliver of sky was visible. She could just make out a pair of constellations. There was the three-pointed stem of the Rose, and directly above her, the twisting leaves of the Vines.

The Vines of Life, those enchanted tendrils that twined across the lintel of the door she had seen in her vision at the godwood. The shaman had told her the story of the Vines many times. It was said they had sprung from the earth at the feet of Asmat when the Torchbearer named her as his wife, and had been growing ever since, constantly seek-ing a new way forward, straining toward the light. Anyone who could cut a piece of their stalk for himself and eat it would be healed of any wound, no matter how grievous. They were a symbol of the power of the seers. It was these same vines that had been inscribed on Canowic's face when she was a young girl.

The shaman had tapped out the pattern meticulously over the course of a long afternoon using bundled needles dipped in squid ink. The searing pain had seemed to last forever, the master endlessly tap-tap-tapping a precise pattern into her skin with his small wooden hammer. He paused every so often to reload the needles with ink or wipe away the blood beading on her scalp and later her jaw. When the ceremony was finally over he had presented her with the deerskin hood. In her youthful ignorance she asked if she could have a staff. She winced now to think how impudent she had been.

"The magi have them," she had said.

"You do not need tools like the magi," the shaman had replied calmly, holding out a bundle for her to take.

"But the stones are tools."

The shaman had nodded. "They are, and the magi do not use them. Our tools are different from theirs, as are our ways different from their ways."

Canowic had taken the bundle and shaken it out, revealing a cloak made from the hide of a young deer. The animal's head had been lined and fashioned into a hood. She pulled the cloak on, marveling at its softness.

"The hood of an acolyte," the shaman said. "So no one will mistake you for anything else."

In the darkness of the forest, frightened and uncertain and feeling so far away from that warm day on the beach, Canowic pulled the cloak tighter around her and clutched the stone in her hand. As she did so, she felt an unmistakable warmth begin to emanate from its surface. A murmur rose in her ears like the congress of innumerable bees. Pulling the stone from her pocket, she saw it was lit from within by a faint rosy glow. She stared at it, captivated.

She felt herself being pulled down, drawn irresistibly toward the orb's shimmering surface. Then she was passing through, descending through the dark stuff of the stone itself toward an approaching hill of grass. She was moving at great speed yet she felt calm and alert. The pink light leavened the darkness extending into infinity around her. Soon she was alighting on a lawn sprinkled with white flowers. There, dominating the hilltop before her, stood the twinned stones of her earlier vision.

The runes in the door's side were clearer now. She could almost understand them. In fact she felt she knew this place. This hill was familiar to her. Looking through the door she could see the rosy sky beyond, and understood that she was inside the stone. She started walking forward, wanting to get a better glimpse of the carvings and whatever message they held, but before she'd gone two steps she felt a pulsing within her chest, a liquid presence trying escape. Suddenly her hands were tingling, then burning, and then shimmering tongues of lightning burst from her fingertips.

For an instant the ferns were illuminated as if at noon. The wolves snapped awake, startling out of the seashell shapes they had curled into. Mictanta's eyes flew open and then the tableau fell back into darkness, an image of the princess's terrified face frozen in Canowic's mind. The baby began to cry.

Canowic struggled to breathe. The door was gone and she was no longer inside the stone. Never had a vision ended with such violence. She felt disoriented and hollowed.

"What happened?" Leokita asked, trying to calm the baby.

"I... I do not know," Canowic said.

"I'm frightened," Mictanta said plaintively.

"I am frightened too," Canowic managed to say. "Here. Lie back." She passed Mictanta a piece of canthis root. "Suck on this. It will ease your heart."

Canowic felt a memory rising within her, a memory of a tale she had been told long before.

"Listen," she whispered, as the wolves licked their chops and hunkered back down around the girls. "Listen, and I will tell you a story. High in the highest mountains, in a shifting place, there stands a door that leads to the other world."

Chapter Twenty-Five

A TALE OF THE
MOUNTAIN PEOPLES

. . .

L ong ago, when the tribes of the Highest Mountains had not yet been scattered and still dwelt together in the lofty vales, a young shepherd decamped to the moors with his flock for the summer grazing. He wandered through the highlands for several days until coming upon a mere beside which he made camp, for the grass was plentiful and the waters of the mere sweet. Days turned to weeks and the animals grew fat on the green grass. At length, seeing his herd was well bulked against the coming of winter, the boy roused them and turned for home.

On the last night of their return journey, the clouds to the south glowed orange like a heated kettle. The next morning the boy rose early and drove his herd onto the trail. He kept them moving quickly all day, eager to come again to his father's hearth. As he jogged behind the sheep he smelled something strange on the breeze.

Upon rounding the last bend in the path the boy's heart seized in his chest. His village burned before him, garlands of harsh smoke rolling up from the ruined huts. Bodies littered the ground. The boy saw riders retreating down the valley, miles away. He could make out captives being driven before them on foot. Turning away with the fear of a young child, he retreated all the way to the mere, bringing his sheep with him.

There by the water's edge he cried to the gods of his people and to his ancestors in the voice of a child, bewildered and pitiable. Wandering in grief along the far shore of the mere the boy came upon a rough shelter with a crude pen attached for stock. He installed his flock in the pen and waited, not knowing what else to do. Soon autumn passed and heavy snows began to assail the mere, burying the pen and causing the boy to bring the sheep into the shelter with him. Despite his best efforts many of them died. Finally, snowed in and subsisting on roots, having killed and roasted the last of his flock, the boy despaired of life and lay down to die. The wind howled outside his shelter, seeming to mock him. His last thought was of his parents and sisters.

The boy awoke to see dawn light streaming across a field of spotless snow. The wind was gone and the storm had abated. Rising from his blanket the boy set out, weak with hunger but driven by a compulsion the origin of which he did not understand. He headed toward the rim of the depression in which the mere was situated, forcing his way through the drifts. He thought to look upon the world from a high vantage and perhaps see a new thing before he died and flew to the banquet table of his elders.

At dawn everything had been calm, but by mid-morning the wind picked back up and a new storm descended. Snow and ice assailed the boy. He stumbled on until his strength gave out and he fell into a snowdrift just feet shy of the rim of the depression. He could feel his body's warmth dissipating. He knew he was about to die and was afraid, but part of him was too tired to care. Soon he would see his family again and the burning cold would be gone.

Just as he was about to shut his eyes for the last time, the boy found himself warming, his limbs pulsing with radiant heat. Looking up, he saw a figure standing at the top of the ridge, holding a torch that cut through the storm's boiling darkness.

Filled with a new and mysterious energy that decanted itself into him like wine into a vessel, the boy arose from where he lay and followed after the torchbearer who had just crested the ridge. As he crossed over himself, the boy was confronted by a mighty doorway. Its massive stone posts were carved with runes of life and fire. Rather than question the appearance of the huge door, which stood alone amidst the virgin snow, the boy began walking toward it. The torchbearer had disappeared. The boy did not know whether he had vanished through the door or been but a figment of his imagination. As he passed beneath the lintel stone the snowscape of the mountains vanished and he felt bright sunshine on his face. He emerged from the door's shadow into the light of a cloudless day, and found himself surrounded by his family at the table of a great feast in the land of the morning stars.

His father ran to embrace him and his mother and sisters covered him with kisses. The boy refreshed himself with food and drink, and listened as his father sang the song of thanksgiving. For three days and three nights he remained in the bosom of his family. On the third day he was ushered into the halls of the elders where he saw his grandsires. As they were greeting him, the hall was filled with the presence of the Ruler of all Mountains, and the boy fell down to the ground as one who is dead. Yet his head was lifted up, and he was told of a mighty quest for which he had been chosen. For the young shepherd was destined to become Wahathanash, *He Who Comes From Beyond The World*.

He became the first of the children of men to return from the other world, gathering the remnants of his people who had been scattered by their enemies. He ruled justly for many years, and took Qulina the Red as his wife. But the memory of the land of the morning stars never left him, and as the years went by his desire to return there only grew.

Finally one day when he was yet hale and the vigor of his limbs remained unchallenged, the king set the circlet of his royalty upon the ground. Taking his wife with him, he journeyed high into the mountains where he found once again the ever-shifting doorway and passed out of the world of men a second time. To this day the magic doorway of the Highest Ones is open to those who have need of it, and it is ever-moving, and cannot be found by searching, but rather only by those whom are led to it by One who is higher than they.

Chapter Twenty-Six

CANOWIC

. . .

T he boy went to the city in the sky," Mictanta said, her voice tenuous in the darkness. She had spent the day in desolate silence and now Canowic waited for her to say more. Instead, it was Leokita who spoke next.

"Mother told us about the city in the sky. The place beyond the door of life where the dead go. That where she is now."

Canowic had heard the story of the boy and the doorway from the shaman. It was one of numerous tales he had told her involving holy thresholds and magic doors and dividing lines from beyond which men could not return. Some came from the lore of the Ancagua. The shaman had explained how the arch of sacred willow switches leading into the godwood served dual purposes, hallowing the circle of ground within while also reminding all who passed beneath it of the door that leads out of the world of men. When Hankasi's warriors had lifted his concubine upon his shield, it was in the hope that she might look over the flames of his pyre and receive a vision of this ultimate door for which the arch of willows was but a pale reminder.

In Canowic's moment of need the story about the young shepherd had come to her, and it had been a comfort to tell it. But now Leokita's words brought back thoughts of their mother's final moments and Canowic felt the comfort bleeding away.

"The magi spoke of the rivers of fire," Leokita continued, as a steady wind made the branches sigh eerily above them. "Our father said that is where my mother's people go when they die. He says everyone who does not honor the lords of the magi with blood is made to swim the rivers of fire."

Canowic had heard the magi speak like this as well. They portrayed the other world as a place of grinding teeth and endless torment for their enemies. All who failed to appease Teulanic in the first world would reap a doom of anguish and tortured isolation in the second. They spoke of their own Door of Life through which fallen warriors passed on their way to everlasting rewards.

Canowic had once asked the shaman about how the Ancagua and the mountain peoples and the magi all told stories of enchanted doors. He had turned the question back on her.

"What do you say?"

She had shrugged. "Perhaps such a confluence means some part of the story is so deeply true it is evident in some form to all peoples."

He had smiled one of his old crow smiles and tilted his head in acknowledgement without explaining exactly what he thought. Now, with the blackness of the forest and the tendrils of despair both encroaching on her, Canowic revised her view. She wondered if perhaps all men were deceived by the same perverted hope, borrowing from one another without understanding what they were doing as they fashioned their towers of delusion. But then what to make of her own visions?

"I do not know where your mother has gone," Canowic said

quietly. "I know only that she was brave, and loved you more than anything in the world of men. Surely the one who guards the door to the city she hopes to enter will know this."

As she finished speaking there was a rustling in the brush nearby. Forgoing caution, Canowic spoke a word of light. Her fingertips glimmered in the blackness, revealing Elil emerging from the shadows with a dead rabbit clenched in her jaws. Canowic's legs had been trembling with fear, but now she was filled with gratitude. Elil laid the hare silently before her, and Canowic touched her forehead to the wolf's in thanks. She thought of building a fire despite the risk, but then she heard the sound of heavy breathing and realized the girls had already fallen back asleep.

It was getting on towards dawn now. Canowic looked up at her narrow patch of sky and saw the Ship sailing across the vault, her mind connecting the relevant stars with a web of invisible lines. The constellation was associated with journeys and quests, though an interpretation of its nightly angles would require a wider field of vision than she had. She watched the blackness begin to soften in the east, as the world's edges were hammered and heated in the forge of the sun. Soon saffron light heralded the approach of day.

Chapter Twenty-Seven

YENGWA

. . .

T he bear's body was studded with arrows, the feathered shafts protruding from his chest, his neck, and his limbs in a dozen places, yet he would not fall. Yengwa marveled at the animal's strength and the will of the one whose spirit animated it. Yes, he knew who this was. As he leapt through the breached door into the riverside cavern, he had seen the shaman transform before his eyes into a white bear of impossible size.

Seeing the old man change shape so violently had been a shock. His leathery, mottled skin had exploded into hair while his jaw distended with a snapping sound like dry branches cracking underfoot. But Yengwa's battle-tempered instincts had kicked in quickly, suppressing the upwelling of primal fear all men experience in the presence of profound magic. He allowed his momentum to carry him through the shattered bronze door and down the steps of the waterside quay. He paused at the foot of the stairs, allowing several of his warriors to streak past and probe the bear's defenses. When they were dispatched with sobering efficiency

Yengwa gripped his war hammer and stepped forward, glad to meet a worthy enemy. The bear pounded his chest and roared, his voice shaking the grotto as Yengwa broke into a run.

As he drew near he lifted the head of his war hammer, a mass of star-iron forged in the shape of a snarling boar, and brought it down with all his strength. The bear threw up a forearm at the last moment, deflecting the blow and causing the shaft of the hammer to vibrate as if Yengwa had struck a rock. The impact sent him stumbling backward, but he pirouetted artfully, regaining his balance. Two more arrows struck the bear's leg in the interval. By now he was bleeding from so many places he seemed to be turning red. Yengwa gritted his teeth and decided to end things.

It only took a moment of renewed combat, though, to realize the bear's wounds had stoked his rage as much as weakened him. They circled one another, probing and testing, each seeking the opening that would allow for a deathblow. Yengwa feinted toward the water but the bear was not fooled. Next he whirled the head of his hammer up from below in an attempted surprise, but again the bear sidestepped easily before counterattacking with a swipe of his paw that ripped the battle amulet from about Yengwa's neck. The razor claws had missed his face by a hairsbreadth.

Yengwa pivoted and swung again. This time the bear ducked and lashed out with a leg, catching Yengwa's knee. He stumbled backwards and the bear instantly pressed in with a blow that would have relieved him of his nose had he not tripped and fallen out of reach just as the paw whipped through the space where his head had been. As he went down onto his side, Yengwa felt death nearby. He was preparing to go out with a final swing when he saw movement in his peripheral vision. It was a pair of his strongest warriors, Mekoche and Irirat, whirling in to defend him with battle-axes.

Perhaps the shaman sensed his work was finished. The foreign bitches all lay dead and the girls had escaped for the moment. Or perhaps his god-like strength was finally waning. Whatever the reason, he had not pounced on Yengwa to finish him off. Instead he weaved where he stood, sides heaving as the warriors sprinted toward him. He let out one last deafening roar as his attackers launched simultaneous converging blows. He somehow swung wide of one blade, only to have his side sliced cleanly by the other, triggering a great geyser of blood. The blow would have instantly killed even the strongest of men, but the bear somehow stayed upright, staggering toward the pair of burly warriors momentarily caught off balance. He collided with them, wrapping his arms around them in a crushing embrace.

These were huge men—Yengwa had seen Mekoche throw a twelve-weight stone the length of Hankasi's horse enclosure—yet the bear lifted them like they were little boys. Their toes searched desperately for the ground as the bear forced the air from their lungs. He roared again, flecks of red foam spraying the men's faces, and then began stumbling towards the river with his human cargo, one shaky, agonized step at a time. The archers looked on, helpless to do anything lest they strike their brothers. When the bear reached the edge of the dock he collapsed backwards into the rippling waters without ceremony, still clutching his enemies to his chest. Yengwa ran to the edge of the dock and looked down, but all he saw was his own reflection in the mirror of the surface. As he stood there peering into the depths he felt something invisible tugging at him from behind, and turned to look back.

. . .

Assembling his men in the courtyard the night before in preparation for what he had hoped would be a simple storming of the queen's chambers, Yengwa had been on the lookout for a mage in a red cloak. He had agreed to allow Ixiltical's emissary to join his war band, not because he anticipated needing any help in subduing his prey, but as a way to keep the peace. When the time was right he would deal with the High Mage, but for now it would be easier to countenance one of his lick-heels. Let this "Glimmer" tag along if he could keep up. Perhaps he would even catch an arrow in the confusion.

Yengwa had been standing on the cobblestones while his men quietly checked their weapons, and was utterly unprepared for the sight of the pale beast that came striding through the arch of the king's colonnade. He immediately knew this was Glimmer. The men he had hand-picked to join him in the grim task at hand—hardened warriors up to the task of butchering infants—drew back as the beast entered the courtyard. Clad in nothing, the creature's shoulders stood half a head taller than the crown of even the stoutest warrior's head. It stood on powerful legs thick as young cedars. Its hands and feet were nearly identical, something like the hand of a man bred with the claw of an eagle, with long talon-like nails. Short spikes of horn or bone traced its spine.

Yengwa's revulsion at the beast's appearance was matched only by his disgust at having allowed himself to be played by the High Mage. Glimmer's skin shone with a light that did not come from the moon alone. An infernal luminescence like that of the fish said to inhabit the deepest parts of the sea shone from within the creature's very body, except for its eyes, which were the utter black of wet coal. Mekoche had looked at Yengwa with a warning, but he had turned away without answering and signaled for the man with the war horn to sound his blast. There would be no leaving Glimmer behind. The only thing to do was get on with it.

From the beginning things had been more difficult than they should have been. Ixiltical had told him to expect the shaman, but Yengwa had assumed the old man wouldn't give them much trouble. After forcing the door, he and his men would kill everyone inside except for the acolyte and one of the princesses, who would be the High Mage's to do with as he pleased. But when they reached the door they found an invisible barrier blocking their way. The magic sickened the men as they lay into the door with their axes.

When they couldn't penetrate the timbers after a few swings, Glimmer stepped forward and held up a claw-like hand inches from the door. Something fearsome began to emanate from the beast, an invisible, eye-watering essence more noxious than whatever spell the shaman had cast. Yengwa controlled himself, but the man beside him retched. Yengwa watched, mesmerized, as the door's lacquered surface began to bubble and smoke. Moments later the axes started to gain purchase and soon they were through.

The warriors had been shouting in excitement, making it impossible to hear what was going on inside the chamber. When Yengwa first rushed in, leaping nimbly through the splintered remnants of the door, he half expected to see no one at all. The women would be hiding in one of the smaller rooms. Instead, he nearly tripped over a small body. Yengwa looked at it in confusion. It was the dwarf who sometimes attended Hankasi's parties. He was dead, his neck twisted at a grotesque angle.

While Yengwa tried to get his mind around who might have killed the dwarf, and what he had been doing in the queen's chambers in the first place, he took stock of another body lying nearby. It was an old man. He had been charred beyond recognition. Confoundingly, though the man's robes still smoked, nothing else in the room seemed to have been so much as singed.

A quick sprint through the various rooms revealed the women were gone. Yengwa returned to the main room in time to see Glimmer vanishing behind a tapestry. Yengwa dove in behind, whistling for his men to follow. At the bottom of the tunnel it was again Glimmer who pushed them through, blasting the iron door with a spell that overcame whatever enchantment the shaman had lain upon it. Yengwa charged ahead and become engrossed in combat, not realizing Glimmer had held back.

Now the monster walked over to where Yengwa stood at the edge of the dock and joined him in looking down at the place where the white bear had disappeared. Up close, Yengwa could smell something deeply wrong wafting from Glimmer. The creature's raw, unmolded lips might have been grimacing, but its face was otherwise a blank, unreadable tablet. It was the eyes that frightened Yengwa most. As he watched, the two black stones hatched like chrysali with an ember of consciousness, as if something, or someone, was stirring inside the giant. Yengwa wondered if the creature was but an avatar of the High Mage, and whether Ixiltical was seeing what those black eyes saw.

What they saw, unless they could penetrate the water in a way Yengwa's eyes could not, was nothing. Meanwhile, the remaining warriors milled behind them. Several of the men had made their way over toward the corpses of the women and were leering down at them. Yengwa waved them off. The corpses could not be desecrated, at least not yet. He would display them publicly in order to demonstrate his seriousness to anyone who might contemplate opposing his accession to the throne. There was also Hankasi to consider. Were the dead king to retain an interest in the affairs of his kingdom from the other world he might understand the pragmatism of Yengwa's exterminatory campaign, but nothing good could come of disfiguring his woman's corpse. Before he could ruminate any further on the threat of revenge from beyond the grave, Yengwa's mind was blown blank by a geyser of white water.

The bear landed on the stones of the dock with an incendiary howl that left Yengwa's ears ringing as if he had been crushed between a hammer and anvil. The bear was still filled with arrows and the gash in his leg had rendered the limb almost useless. He'd nearly landed on top of Glimmer and immediately fell forward toward the monster, both claws windmilling. The element of surprise, his incredible mass, and the ferocity of his attack almost carried the day.

Glimmer retreated before the onslaught, sliding backwards as the bear came on. The creature was driven all the way back to the steps, ducking away from the snapping jaws and absorbing several blows with its own huge forearms, until running out of room. Stepping back one last time, Glimmer's foot slipped on the bottom step of the staircase and the creature stumbled sideways. The bear dove in, burying both claws in Glimmer's flank and raking downwards, scoring the thigh to the bone.

The bestial scream of pain and rage that tore from Glimmer's throat was harrowing not only for its primal qualities but because it indicated vulnerability in something that had seemed invincible. It was almost too much for Yengwa to take in. The shaman had risen from the dead and the High Mage's champion been proven imperfect in the space of a single breath. But he was a man of action, and he managed to keep his wits about him. Standing with his hammer at the ready, he waited for his chance.

He moved sideways, trying to put himself in a better position as the bear dislodged his claws and reared back for another strike. Before he could land it Glimmer lashed out with the speed and accuracy of a viper, and delivered a crushing blow to the side of his head. The bear crashed to the ground, blood pouring from a caved-in temple. Glimmer staggered upright with a hot sound of pain and limped over to the bear. Then the creature stooped, levering its arms to get purchase beneath the bear's body, and straightened its back. Huge muscles went taut as anchor cables. At first the bear did not budge. The monster kept on straining, veins bulging, until it succeeded in slowly winching the bear's huge body from the blood-soaked stones. Staggering under the outrageous weight, the creature walked to the edge of the river and hurled the bear in with a final scream.

As the bear's body sank into the cold waters for a second time Yengwa sprang into action. Dropping his hammer and drawing the knife from his belt, he dove into the river. If he swam quickly he could still catch the girls and finish this. The tunnel echoed around him as he swam. When he turned the corner that had carried the girls' boat out of sight he was greeted by a scattering of coins as the tips of wavelets stirred by his passage caught the diffuse glow of the newly risen sun. Reaching the tunnel's mouth, he braced himself against the wall and peered out through a thick row of vines hanging down across the water at the beach beyond. He cursed quietly. The sand was empty.

He waited until he was satisfied the girls were indeed gone and not just hiding before he swam to the beach. He saw no footprints, but he could tell the sand had been disturbed. His warriors began arriving. They emerged dripping from the water with their knives at the ready, looking around in expectation. Glimmer was not with them.

"Where is it?" Yengwa asked.

One of the men shrugged, knowing who he meant. "It went back up into the tunnel."

"What of the bear?"

"He stayed down."

Yengwa wondered if he ought to go back and dredge the body up, just to be certain. Dismember it and scatter it across the beach where the gulls could have their fill. While he contemplated this he stared at the beach's high water mark, beyond which thick grass rose in waist-high swells. The shushing of the waves upon the sand and the wind in the grass were the only sounds. Where had the girls gone?

"Alon," he called out. A slender warrior with a knifeblade nose and charms in his ears walked over in response, his gait a rolling fisherman's stroll. Yengwa pointed at a narrow opening where a game trail cut away from the beach towards the green darkness of the wood. He assumed this was where the girls had left the sand, but his master tracker might be able to glean something more from the scene. As Alon knelt and stared at the ground Yengwa looked up to see the High Mage sweeping across the beach, his fiery robes motionless despite his movement. Glimmer limped in his wake.

"Strange," Ixiltical said as he floated to a stop. He was looking off toward the trees, brow furrowed as if in confusion. "I had thought they were but small children."

Yengwa's face betrayed nothing, but he knew his men had heard the taunt.

"Hold your tongue, mage," he said. "I will not be mocked."

Ixiltical's eyelids flared. It was only a moment, just enough to reveal how rarely he encountered a demand for respect.

"You have already been mocked," the mage said, his voice plummeting dangerously. "I merely note the fact. A trio of little girls has eluded you."

At this juncture Alon said something quietly to Yengwa, and pointed to a faint shape in the dirt at the head of the narrow deer track leading off the beach. It was a fragment of a paw print.

"It seems they are with the shaman's wolves," Yengwa said, meeting the mage's eyes. "The old man is dead."

Ixiltical smiled thinly. Yengwa wondered what he knew about what had transpired in the grotto. He had correctly predicted the shaman would be waiting with the queen and her daughters. Yengwa hated to admit it, but he had also been right about Glimmer being the one to finally deal with the bear. What had he said? *He will try to interfere, but my servant will deal with him.*

Yengwa looked at Glimmer. The beast stood behind the mage, as impassive now as it had been filled with bloodlust moments earlier. Nothing had that level of self-control. Those eyes, solid black with no pupils, made it impossible to know where it was looking. Yengwa wondered if it could even speak.

Ixiltical did not reveal what he knew of the shaman's end. He raised his right hand and the sunrise was snared in the violet stone of a ring upon his forefinger. At this signal Glimmer set off into the grass, returning moments later with a squealing cock. The mage slit the bird's throat. Then with the blood running down his arms he opened his mouth and began to speak in a strange, womanly voice. The High Mage made invocation to Remerac. Though wily and seldom concerned with the things of men, the god of turning coins and shifting twixtplaces sometimes deigned to give the gift of farsight, and it was this grace for which Ixiltical now begged.

At the end of his incantation, Ixiltical gripped the bird's legs like the handle of a whip and began sawing it up and down towards Glimmer, spraying the beast with hot blood while choking out something guttural. Glimmer roared in what seemed to be agony, straining against invisible chains. Yengwa wondered at how potent a spell Ixiltical must have had laid on Glimmer in order to constrain so fell a beast. Some of the warriors were visibly disturbed by this exposure to raw sorcery, but Yengwa stood his ground, if for no other reason than to spite the mage.

"They journey toward the heart of the wood," Ixiltical crooned, his voice once again his own. "You will find them again in the company of one you are not expecting."

The claw marks on Glimmer's hip were still bleeding at a rate that would have killed an ox, but the creature stood calmly by, awaiting further instruction. It was as if it had merely been bitten by an insect. Now the mage held a hand out toward the wounds and Yengwa saw them healed at a distance, the flesh closing in over itself, leaving horrible scars. Glimmer winced but remained quiet. This, more than any of the gore or witchery that had preceded it, was the sign that caused Yengwa to question who he had aligned himself with.

"When you do," Ixiltical said, "you will remember our agreement.

The princesses are mine."

Yengwa stared at him for a long moment, neither affirming what he had said nor denying it. Then he turned his back on the mage and spoke to his men.

"We will overtake the pups by night. He who brings me the shaman's acolyte may enjoy whichever of the girls he desires before we slay them."

The warriors crowed in anticipation and Yengwa took off at a brisk run without so much as a backward glance. His men fell in after him as they entered the forest. He did not have to look back to know Glimmer followed close behind.

Chapter Twenty-Eight

CANOWIC

· · ·

In the gory twistings of the hare's entrails Canowic found the Skull, a symbol of death. Given her present circumstances this was unsurprising. The person she loved most in the world had died while standing over the body of the one person she had most longed to know. Twice in rapid succession she had fled from chambers filled with corpses. Now death almost seemed preferable to whatever the warriors might have in store, should they find them.

The velvet fur of the hare's belly had been soft in her hands as she slit it open, spilling the guts on the ground for reading. The stomach was perforated where Elil's fangs had punctured it, but an undamaged portion of the grayish surface held a clearly visible circle. Canowic interpreted this as the Well. Often a symbol of hope and perpetual life, it could alternately be a forewarning of entrapment. Taken together the two signs were ambiguous at best, grimly inauspicious at worst.

The hare's lifeless eye stared up at her plaintively. She took the stick she'd been using to prod the guts and set about fashioning a spit.

Her hips and knees burned in protest as she shifted her crouch. She had lain awake through the early morning as thick fog rolled in, smoking in the branches of the trees and creeping along the ground.

Somewhere above the fog line the sun was burning, but down on the forest floor it was cold. Canowic held her stick, now heavy with the rabbit's thighs, above the tiny fire she'd risked and peered out through the ferns. Somewhere out there Yengwa and his men were puzzling over a lost trail, trying to discover the thread that would lead them to the girls. She cupped the back of her neck with a hand and kneaded the muscles. The master would know what to do.

But he wasn't here and he never would be again. He had fallen into darkness, leaving her to forge ahead alone. Double hammers of grief and loneliness pounded her soul. Then there was the convoluted mixture of affection, responsibility, and even resentment she felt toward the girls sleeping a few feet away. Canowic sighed with exhaustion and thought of the door from her vision. Its vibrancy and power had moved her. If only it hadn't been merely a vision.

She forced her mind back to the present. Where were they going? Perhaps the wolves could help them gain a pass somewhere on the flanks of Merwa through which they could escape into the land beyond, where striped horses were said to roam the steppes in herds that stretched as far as the eye could see. Perhaps they would all be dead by the time the sun reached its zenith in a few hours. It was no good. She shoveled the jumbled mass of thoughts to the back of her mind and roused the princesses, taking the baby from Leokita and passing her the meat.

The baby felt cold to the touch. Canowic felt a dagger of fear in her heart but dared not show it. Instead, she wrapped Kisoko in her cloak and encouraged the other two girls to eat as much as possible. She scarcely had anything herself, knowing she could forage along the trail and that she was stronger than they were. When they had finished Canowic prepared to leave the cover of the ferns, only to find her way barred by Red Wing. When she tried to sidestep the auburn wolf he moved with her, blocking her in. Canowic raised her arm in frustration, but Red Wing only bared his teeth.

"What!" Canowic hissed quietly. "What do you want?"

In response Gila trotted to a spot further around the edge of the hollow, looking over at Canowic to make sure she was watching before taking a few steps into the undergrowth. She reappeared a moment later, the same look in her eyes. The effect was unmistakable.

Follow me.

The wolves were trying to keep them from going back to the path. Canowic realized they must know of another, safer way, or even sense the war band nearby. She had long ago learned to trust their uncanny woodcraft and unerring intuition. They were right, of course. It would be madness to follow the path in broad daylight, not knowing whether their enemies were ahead or behind. She bowed to Red Wing.

"Brother, forgive me. You were only trying to keep me from my own folly. Lead on."

· · ·

They spent the morning traversing a long, steep slope carpeted with thorny underbrush. Vines stretched taut as wires between the trunks of trees. It took hours to reach the top, at which point the girls were exhausted from constantly stooping under snagging limbs and clambering over fallen logs. After cresting the ridge they found themselves descending gently to the shore of a clear lake. Towering cliffs rose straight out of the water on the opposite side, their faces bare as a castle wall. The lake was long and knifelike, stretching out of sight ahead of them.

The girls fell to their knees at the water's edge and slaked their thirst. When they had finished they began walking up the pebbled shoulder of the lake. The sun ticked overhead, pushing toward midday. They scavenged berries from bushes and sucked the last of the hunger-killing canthis root from Canowic's pocket. The princesses walked without complaint, although their lack of protest was starting to frighten Canowic more than encourage her. She assumed the older girls' silence must be evidence of bone-deep exhaustion as much as determination. The baby had fallen asleep again on her breast.

After they had been walking a while, Canowic realized a strange silence had fallen. Thrushes had filled the air with their courtship all morning, chirping as they looped through intermittent beams of light, but now the only sound was the soft murmur of the wind across the lake and the gentle cracking of stones underfoot. She looked at the wolves and her heart dropped to see them standing stock still, ears keyed toward the woods. Then she heard it too.

Instantly she dropped to all fours, cradling the baby in one arm and praying she would not wake. She motioned for the other girls to get down. They were horribly exposed out on the rocks, but she forced herself to remain motionless as she strained to listen. The scrap of sound that had sent her diving to the stones had held a man's voice. Her shins burned where they pressed against the stones at strange angles. Gila crouched beside her, eyes riveted on the tree line. A moment later the wolf shot off like a bolt, heading straight for a patch of blackberry bramble to their right.

There was no time to think. Canowic took off behind her at a sprint. When she reached the bush she turned to see Leokita helping Mictanta across the broken ground. The younger girl was struggling. A few of the wolves had stayed back to protect them while the others had vanished into the woods.

Canowic heard the voice again, closer now. Then the crunch of a snapping twig. The girls weren't going to make it. With a supreme effort of will she set the baby down inside the bush and ran back to the princesses. She picked Mictanta up and carried her back to the thicket, her heart nearly bursting with fear and exertion. They all tumbled inside, shaking the dry thorns with a noise that sounded like a hailstorm to Canowic's frightened ears. There was no way their pursuers hadn't heard them.

The interior of the thorn bush held a small hollow just large enough for them all to cram into. It seemed like a miracle to Canowic, who did not know that many brambles have just such an opening at their heart. Her lungs ached, but she fought to take her breath in short sips. None of the wolves had come into the bush with them and Canowic felt blind. There was nothing to do but hold perfectly still and listen. More sounds trickled in now. Pine needles being ground into the dirt. Whoever was out there was mere steps from the bramble. Then they heard a man's voice and Canowic ceased breathing altogether.

Yengwa was asking someone else whether the girls might have hidden themselves in the bramble. The shore was a bed of stones from the water's edge all the way to the bush, so they had not made any footprints, but it was entirely possible they had left a trail of splashed water or some other unmistakable sign of their passing. The place where they'd entered the bush must be clear as a painted sign. The seconds slunk by. At any moment Canowic expected a flaming torch to drop onto the bush.

Then Yengwa's companion expressed doubts. Canowic was shocked. Could the wolves have woven some enchantment about the place? In any event, no enchantment had been laid upon the baby. She squirmed and began to awaken. Canowic clamped a hand over her mouth as a rustling sound came from outside. The warriors were testing the bramble's density.

Canowic watched, helpless, as the baby's face turned the color

234 · Ben Bishop

of a dry beet under her hand. She could feel Kisoko sucking at her palm, desperate to breathe, but she couldn't let her. It would mean death for all of them. Finally, after what seemed an eternity, Yengwa left. No explanation had passed between them. Perhaps there had been none. Perhaps the finger of a god had flicked dust in their eyes. The unseen warriors passed around the bramble, joking, unaware the girls could have reached out and touched their legs.

At length everything went quiet again and still Canowic kept her hand firmly over the baby's mouth. When she finally lifted her hand away Kisoko did not cry or gasp or move at all. Canowic sensed the tears running down her cheeks, but she felt nothing at all, save a strange lightness as the blood drained from her limbs. She seemed to be hovering above herself, looking down on her own crumpled form as she started to shake silently.

"What is wrong?" Leokita asked, pulling her around to check on the baby.

Canowic held out the dead girl, shaking like a palsied beggar.

"Have mercy on me. Have mercy. I have slain your sister to save our lives."

Leokita let out a snapping moan and pulled Kisoko's loose form to her breast. She began to weep and Canowic thought the warriors, not far gone, would surely hear them, and she did not care.

Chapter Twenty-Nine

CANOWIC

. . .

L eokita would not let her touch the body, so Canowic could only watch in despair as her sister strapped the tiny corpse to her back with two strips of fabric, knotting them across her chest like a woman headed to the fields. The baby's head lolled to the side, pulled down by its own weight at an unnatural angle. Thick clouds that had boiled in soon after the warriors' departure now broke open, drenching the shore with freezing rain.

The warriors had continued up the shore of the lake, so the wolves led the girls back into the woods, where they were soon hacking through thick foliage again as they climbed the steep slope of the valley. The wolves were subdued, sober in the way of animals. They communicated their grief through their huge, liquid eyes.

Mictanta shut down completely. She had seemed like a joyful child the few times Canowic had seen her before Hankasi's funeral. Jumping up and down in her mother's shadow at the annual harvest festival when the entire city performed their maize dances, her dark hair jouncing around as she watched the huge bonfires roaring on the beach. The memory of her joyfulness made it that much more excruciating to see the evisceration in her eyes. She followed Leokita with her head down, feet shuffling absently through the dirt. Several times she walked into fallen trees or rocks she might have avoided if only she had looked up. Her face was tracked with tears and pieces of moss were caught in her hair. She was a husk that might blow away at any moment.

They labored uphill all afternoon, sweating in silence, scratched and torn by thorns and branches. Just as Canowic began wondering whether they would have to sleep beneath some random tree, they pushed through a particularly thick stand of scrub and broke into a long, open field flooding with cherry dusk. The red light drenched the grass, and slathered itself across the surface of a tall stone standing at the center of the field. Smooth and black, it felt like something fallen from the stars or spit from the throat of the past. It was larger at its top than where it sank into the ground—a fang fallen from the mouth of a giant and stuck in the earth.

Before they left the cover of the trees they scanned the field. It would be madness to walk out there without knowing whether they were being watched. They never could know, of course, and it would never be safe given the circumstances. But they were children, and the stone held an attraction they could neither name nor deny. As the red light began darkening toward a vinous purple they stepped out of the woods.

The stone seemed to sing in the gloaming. A soft, high-pitched energy hummed from its bulk like the call of an insect. When they drew close, Canowic saw the surface of the stone was covered all over with strange runes and figures that may have been animals. She was studying the figures so intently that at first she did not notice Leokita turning and walking away, Mictanta trailing obediently behind. By the time she did the princesses were halfway back to the tree line. For a moment Canowic simply watched them go. She felt numb and so, so tired. But the stone had pricked at her, and the sight of Leokita loosening the makeshift sling and pulling the baby into her arms woke her up even more. It didn't take her long to catch up.

"Leokita."

Her sister ignored her. Canowic looked ahead, trying to guess where she was headed. At the edge of the field near where they had emerged, the silvery branches of a giant celicia tree spread in terraces toward the sky. Soft gray bark peeled in great strips from the trunk.

Leokita stopped at the foot of the celicia. Through some miracle of altitude, temperature, or pure grace, Kisoko's body was still intact and had not yet begun to smell of death too strongly, though the odor was there. Now Leokita bent forward and kissed the little corpse on the forehead. There was an opening at the base of the tree, a tiny cave where a diversion in the roots created a recess safe from wind and rain. Leokita gently committed Kisoko's body into this hollow. After laying her to rest, she straightened and spoke a simple word of blessing over the grave, with one arm outstretched and the other drawing Mictanta in close.

Canowic stood silently by, feeling more alone than she ever had in her life. The princesses eventually scavenged rocks to raise a cairn that would protect their sister from beasts and spirits. They finished as full dark set in. After a final moment of silence Leokita moved toward the woods. Canowic let them go, but took note of where they lay and made sure several of the wolves bedded down with them. She nestled down a few paces away, pulling dry leaves over herself to ward off the chill. She closed her eyes, but sleep took its time in finding her.

Chapter Thirty

YENGWA

. . .

He was sure they would catch the girls within minutes of leaving the beach. They wouldn't need whatever magic Ixiltical's bloody rite had bestowed. These were children alone in a wood. But then the minutes stretched to the better part of an hour. Then two. At first his blood had surged with the thrill of the hunt, any frustration only stoking his pace. He had pounded along the path winding into the dark wood, marking the subtle signs that betrayed the girls' passing. A broken stick here, a bent leaf there. Then the signs had ceased. After a while he reluctantly ground to a halt beside a gnarled root-ball straddling a rise in the trail.

He called for Alon and the slender man appeared at his side a moment later. Yengwa spoke quietly so only his tracker could hear.

"I have seen nothing for the last quarter mile."

Alon dropped to his knees and sniffed the dirt. He dragged a finger across the ground and tasted the tip.

"They have turned aside," he observed dryly.

"We would have heard them crashing about," Yengwa said, shaking his head. "These are not wood sprites. They have never left the castle."

Alon nodded without agreeing, his face a cipher. "The shaman's acolyte. Perhaps she possesses some woodcraft."

Yengwa thought again of the partial wolf-print they had seen at the beach. The animals had always pricked at him. They followed the shaman wherever he went, slinking around the old man's feet like greasy water. If it had been up to him he would have poisoned them long ago. He knew the wolves possessed some magic. Perhaps they had laid an enchantment on the girls' trail. He looked off into the dimming foliage. The sun was setting. They would be obliged to spend a night out in the open.

Damn you into the fire, Hankasi, he thought. *Even in death your rats vex me.*

· · ·

In the morning Yengwa split his men into two groups. They would slow down, spread out, and flush their prey like hunters stalking game. While giving a few curt instructions, he glanced over at Glimmer. The giant had taken up a position at the back of the group upon leaving the beach, seemingly content to slip along in their wake with a silence that impressed Yengwa. When they stopped to make camp, Glimmer went off toward a low granite outcropping some distance from the rest of the war band. The creature dug a small hole in the ground, and proceeded to rub wet mud onto its legs, arms and back, as if packing itself for the evening. Some of the men were visibly unsettled by this bizarre ritual. The fishwives would have them believe that being out on Merwa's flanks at the end of summer, when spirits were loosening from their summer lairs to roam free before being gathered at harvest, was an invitation to mishap. Yengwa did not put stock in fishwives' tales, though. He rolled himself in his cloak and fell into a dreamless sleep.

He broke his fast with a cold meal at dawn, chewing dried venison while explaining his plan to Shanset, the warrior he had tapped to lead the other half of the party. They would slip over the ridge and into the valley beyond. Shanset's group would follow the line of the ridge north to see if they could discover where the girls had crossed, while Yengwa and the others forged straight across the valley. They would meet on the far slope before sunset. Yengwa was crouched on his haunches, drawing a map for Shanset in the dirt, when a flash of purple light erupted behind them and a low cracking sound pierced the morning.

Yengwa whirled to see black fog swirling around the granite where Glimmer had spent the night. Two shining crystals appeared amidst the dissipating shreds, and moments later a long, powerful body materialized. The lizard surged across the rocks like a serpent on four legs. Its head was shaped like a diamond and its tail was as long as a man. Moments later a twin appeared, jet black and slithering in Glimmer's shadow as the giant strode out from around the rocks. It was whispered that the magi and their servants could make use of invisible pathways, but Yengwa had never believed it until now.

The lizards' heads rolled sinuously as they crawled, their forked tongues flickering in and out. Their lantern eyes roved to and fro across the ground, moist black nostrils probing the air. Suddenly one of them snapped to attention, head high. A moment later they both took off at a run. Glimmer followed without even looking in Yengwa's direction. Yengwa sensed his men were as confused as he was, but there was no time to waste. He seized his hammer and set out after the strange trio.

They ran all day, occasionally passing through gaps in the canopy that let them feel the thin warmth of the mountain sun. Squirrels rustled in the underbrush and leaves whispered overhead, but strain though he might Yengwa never heard the cry of a child. By noon they had covered so much ground he began to seriously doubt whether the girls could have even come this far. It didn't matter. They were moving too fast for Alon to properly cut for sign, putting themselves completely in Glimmer's hands. If they missed something or lost the trail they could travel miles in the wrong direction. Yengwa somehow doubted they would.

Rather than being reassured, he felt hot anger welling in his chest. He could not believe the princesses had dragged him this far. When he caught them he was going to make the little rats regret having ever slipped from between their mother's legs. Then there was the mage. Ixiltical was playing him for the fool, sending him far afield while he remained free to capitalize on the chaos in the city. Glimmer, while undeniably potent, was undermining his authority. Yengwa wondered which would be more difficult; killing the monster or leaving it behind.

All morning his rage sustained him, keeping him fresh despite the hard night's sleep. Soon after the sun clipped its apex they came to the edge of the Great Knife Lake. A few hundred yards up the shore Glimmer pulled up. The lizards were poised on the loose stones of the shore, testing the air with quick sips. Yengwa's sides were heaving, but Glimmer and the lizards seemed fresh as if they'd only just started out. Looking at them now, Yengwa realized they were like wingless versions of the great beasts populating the stories his grandfather had told him as a boy, tales of Xigura and Tectalon the Destroyer.

Yengwa looked around. After the closeness of the forest the open air was refreshing. Blue wavelets lapped gently at the rocky shore. Up ahead a large section of blackberry bramble spilled out from the edge of the forest. In the same moment he noticed the thicket, Yengwa felt his head begin to throb dully. The lizards felt something too. They shook their heads as if they smelled something foul.

"Those things don't know where they are any more than we do," Alon murmured.

Yengwa turned to the tracker. "Where would you have gone?"

Alon looked up at the broken cliffs across the lake.

"They won't be up there," Yengwa said, following his gaze. "The little rats can't swim." He looked around, turning his attention back to the blackberry bush. "No, they're close."

From where he stood the bramble seemed to be an impenetrable tangle of thorns. He walked over and began a circuit of the perimeter, searching for an entrance point.

"If it were me I'd hide in here," Yengwa said quietly. He was just considering lighting the bush on fire when he was struck by an overwhelming sense of being watched. His head jerked up toward the trees. He could feel an intelligence being trained upon him as clearly as if the watcher were standing right in front of him, yet all he saw were a million gently waving leaves. Glimmer had also stiffened and turned to look at the same patch of forest. For a moment all was tense and silent. Then the demon shook its head as if being released from a spell, and stalked into the woods. Yengwa looked back down at the blackberry thicket and tried to remember what about it had so captivated him. Soon he and Alon were following Glimmer into the trees.

They kept running all afternoon, climbing steadily upward out of the lake's valley on a narrow ladder of switchbacks that eventually spilled into a field dominated by a great black stone. Yengwa felt a rush of familiarity. He had not seen the monolith in years. The last time he had been here he had approached from a different direction. Now, standing in front of its rune-filled sides, memories flooded back; the night they had captured Kulkas; women tossing their children off the cliffs into the gorge below; the sound of the infants' cries receding as they dropped away into the blackness. He looked off into the trees at the far edge of the field where he had hung the queen's kinsmen all those years ago.

Lost in his thoughts, he did not immediately notice Glimmer and the lizards had stopped. Either the stone had impressed them too, or they had come to the end of the trail. The lizards sat side by side, staring at Yengwa with languid menace. He ignored them.

"What?" he said, addressing Glimmer. "The trail has ended?"

But Glimmer was already moving again. When they had almost reached the trees on the opposite side of the field Yengwa turned and saw the setting sun igniting the leaves of the forest into a thousand shining spearheads. A moment later his eyes widened and he motioned violently for his men to flatten themselves. They melted into the high grass just as the girls emerged into the field.

There was nothing to keep them from taking the girls now, yet something held him back. Caution is like a spear in the hand, as the proverb said, and while Yengwa had had never been one for proverbs this was no ordinary situation. The idea that he had somehow passed by the girls seemed incomprehensible, yet here they were. He remembered something about a headache at the lake, but the memory was strangely vague. He motioned his men back toward the trees.

The shadow of the forest was a great slab being shunted across the field by the setting sun, making it difficult to see what the girls were doing. They had come out to the stone before turning back unexpectedly and then stopping under a celicia at the tree line. The elder princess had deposited something under the tree, and they had then raised a mound of rocks over it. At length they finished and melted into the darkness pooling beneath the trees.

"Shall I mark them?" Alon asked.

Yengwa shook his head, eyes fixed on the place where they had vanished.

"No. Better to face the wolves in the daylight."

He was not afraid of losing them again. The stone would call them back in the morning.

. . .

He rose before dawn and sat motionless as the sun revived the field. An hour passed, then two, and still he did not doubt his plan. If it had only been a matter of tracking the girls, he and Alon would have found them days earlier. There were clearly greater forces at work. He must use them to his advantage as he would the lay of the land. As the day wore on he knew his men must be growing restless, but they said nothing.

The girls finally appeared as the sun was beginning to set. They stepped out into the field with the wolves spread around them. One of the dogs was letting the younger girl ride it like a horse. Yengwa could not see the infant and wondered about the burial under the tree the night before. As he watched the girls cross the field, he was drawn to the shaman's acolyte. The girl seemed to have aged a year in the last day. She shuffled along a few steps behind the princesses, her face as drawn as a pallbearer's. The sideways light made the vines on her jaw and forehead stand out like black letters. In stark contrast to her apathy, the white wolf seemed intensely alert. Yengwa was surprised she had not smelled him and sounded an alarm. Then he remembered the lizards and another proverb; *water flows two ways*. Perhaps the demons' magic was countering that of the wolves.

Behind him a small river burbled merrily. The girls and wolves had passed the stone and were now halfway to the trees. As they drew near Yengwa slipped off to the hiding place he had prepared. When the unsuspecting refugees finally pushed through the last of the reeds at the river's edge he sprung his trap. He had spread his warriors all around, in the tall grasses, the surrounding trees, even the river itself, where he and several others were pressed up under a ledge, chest-deep in the freezing water.

The younger princess slipped off the wolf she'd been riding and knelt at the water's edge, her hands cupped for a drink. The image of her face appeared on the surface directly in front of Yengwa. There was a moment as she gazed down into river, before her hands disturbed its surface, when she saw him and was transfixed with a look of horror. Then Yengwa exploded upward, grabbing her wrists and pulling her into the water.

The rest of the war band launched themselves from low hanging branches, or surged dripping from the reeds. Yengwa tucked the shocked princess under one arm and shoved off. Reaching the other side of the pool quickly, he hurled the girl ahead of him onto the bank. There was a splash behind him and he turned just in time to see the wolf she had been riding about to close its jaws on his leg. He spun artfully, bringing his hammer down in the same motion and crushing the animal's skull. The princess was screaming in abject terror by now, but Yengwa ignored her cries and quickly surveyed field of battle. The trap had not fully closed.

When he had pulled the princess into the water the other two girls had not yet been close enough to the warriors in the reeds. The wolves had instantly launched a counterattack. A huge black wolf already had one of his men, Akwesu, pinned to the ground. Beyond Akwesu's kicking feet, Nasha was busy grabbing the remaining princess. The acolyte clawed viciously at him from behind, but then Ipenat was there to help, freeing Nasha to hustle the princess away. Ipenat swatted the acolyte's head before kicking her feet out from under her with a powerful leg sweep. She went down in a heap.

Ipenat was pulling his loincloth up and reaching for the acolyte's dress when a flash of blue-white light went off. Yengwa instinctively touched his face and flinched at a memory of searing pain. When he opened his eyes Ipenat was rolling in the dirt, his head encased in flame. The acolyte was staring at him, struck dumb by whatever had erupted from her. Her stupor didn't last long. She soon scrambled to her feet and picked up Ipenat's war hammer. Yengwa watched, incredulous, as she struggled to raise it over her head. When she dropped the hammer Ipenat's flaming head exploded like a rotten cabbage. Yengwa leapt back into the river. He should have finished this long before.

The acolyte looked up at him in a daze as he sprinted towards her. There hadn't been much distance between them to begin with, and he had already cut it in half when an arrow struck the girl in her chest. She tripped and crashed to the earth, hitting her head against an exposed root as she fell.

Yengwa felt everything slowing. It was a common feeling in battle. Sometimes things felt unnaturally clear, as though he had all the time in the world to avoid a coming blow. At other times it felt as though he was trapped in a river of sap, unable to get to where he needed to be. Today he burned, as if it was his head and not Ipenat's that had been set aflame. He was still barreling toward the acolyte, focused only on finishing her off, and the rest of the world had momentarily disappeared. So he was completely blindsided when the white wolf hit him.

She blasted him backwards into the water where he landed face first. He scrambled desperately to his feet, whipping the hair from his eyes, ready for combat. But the wolf had trampled straight over him on her way toward the archer who had shot the acolyte. The warrior had just knocked a fresh arrow and was beginning to pull the string taut when the wolf tore into him at full speed.

Yengwa looked back at the acolyte to find three wolves circling her. One licked her face while the other two barked viciously at him. He howled with frustration but knew it was time to retreat. He ran back to where he had left the princess on the riverbank. She had tried to crawl away but he picked her up easily and threw her over his shoulder. At that point Glimmer loosed the dragons.

Something streaked across Yengwa's vision, crossing the river in a single bound and ripping into a mottled gray wolf in the act of separating a warrior from his axe. The lizard eviscerated the gray in seconds, but a second wolf quickly came to its rescue, followed by a third. Then the other lizard arrived like a lightning bolt striking the earth and the entire fray careened into the reeds where the animals were hidden from sight behind a wall of shaking cattails. Vicious snarls and barks commingled with something like the keen of a diving hawk. After a period of escalating clamor the reeds shook violently one final time and everything went still. The lizards emerged. One of them had the dripping head of a wolf in its jaws.

Yengwa dimly noticed the princess beating against his ribs. He hit her hard, once, to shut her up. Some of the wolves had run off, but he wasn't about to chase them. He whistled for the surviving warriors to circle up, motioning to Nasha to bring the other princess. He cast one final backwards glance at the acolyte's motionless body, spitting towards her and her guardian wolves before heading off into the darkening woods.

Chapter Thirty-One

CANOWIC

. . .

The first thing Canowic saw upon regaining consciousness was Kirin's body. The light was almost gone, but she could see well enough to make out the halo of blood spreading out from the wolf's crushed skull. Canowic gasped and went to move, but as she did she felt a sharp pain in her breast. She pulled aside her cloak, fearing the worst, but the arrow had struck the shaman's stone in her pocket. The pain she felt, and the vicious purple bruise on her chest, were the result of landing on the stone as she fell. Her head throbbed. She reached up to investigate and found blood in her hair, then saw a matching smear on a nearby root. A warrior lay beside her, his skull badly fractured and his own war hammer lying beside him. She tried to remember what had happened.

The grass all around her had been flattened in whorls. Broken reeds fell at crazed angles across two dead warriors. Their eyes were the eyes of fish, bright in death, the blush of vigor still fresh on their cheeks. Serouac lay between them, his stiff flank feathered with arrows. A few feet away Haifax was sprawled out beneath the shimmering arms of a willow tree. A thick trail of blood indicated where he had crawled from the river. In a perverse trick, sunlight was slipping through the canopy and burnishing the dead wolves' coats to a lustrous shine, transfiguring them into wolves of gold and steel. Their black lips curled back from their teeth in final snarls. Canowic looked at them and wept.

Time inched along. Her mind felt like a draughty, forgotten hall, haunted by cold winds and half-filled with sand. The earth was cold against her cheek. Finally, with a gargantuan effort, she rose. The princesses were gone. It did not make sense to her why she had been spared. Perhaps the warriors had thought she was already dead. Surely they would have checked. She wondered where the other wolves were.

She could not have lain unconscious all that long. The sun, which had been going down as they left their hiding place, was only just now fully setting. She started to stumble away from the river back towards the field, then quickly thought better of exposing herself and instead wandered off the path into the underbrush. She had to find somewhere safe to rest. There—a fallen log hidden behind the bole of a great white oak. It was half rotten with damp, and saplings and redcap mushrooms sprouted from its mossy surface. Canowic crawled inside and was asleep before her eyes were closed.

When she woke a tiny shaft of moonlight had threaded itself through a knothole. The beam crept across her cheek and up the opposite side of the log. Chains of thunder began snapping in the distance. Grubs crawled over her. She fell asleep again, murmuring feverishly for the Torchbearer to either save or take her.

The cold woke her a second time. It had seeped up through her thin clothes, trying to lay hold of her. She had to move if she wanted to live. If she fell asleep again she wouldn't be waking up. She emerged from the log into a thin rain. The trees waved their hoary arms above her with a sound like spirits talking. The log's surface had acquired a fine patina of white frost in the night. A snuffling sound caused her to turn around.

The remaining wolves surrounded her. Canowic knelt and took Red Wing in her arms, burying her face in his bright fur. He shuddered and she saw he was favoring a foot. Several of the others were wounded too, their flanks scored, their bodies pierced by spears. She snapped an arrow in half and withdrew it as gently as possible from Asha's hind leg as his brother Syrxes looked on.

She had never been so exhausted. She remembered the outpouring of magic that had set the warrior's head ablaze, but didn't know what to make of the fact that power had come out of her again, and with such astonishing violence. Or maybe she did and was just frightened. There was something inside of her. Even if she was just a conduit—a vessel, the shaman would have said—the thought that something or someone was sending its might sluicing through her was terrifying. Her heart spun wildly, like a water wheel overwhelmed by a river in flood. If this was what it meant to be like the shaman, to be a true prophet, she was not sure she wanted it.

"It is too much," she whispered to Gila. "Too much."

At length Canowic stood again and began weaving unsteadily toward the field, leaving the wolves behind. The stone was a dense slab of black cut out of the dark clouds behind it. Drawing near, she felt the monolith's nighttime shadow envelop her. The rain was falling in gently billowing sheets. She raised a dripping hand and placed it on the stone's wet surface. Something within the fabric of the rock throbbed, tightening the skin on her palm.

As she stood there tethered to the stone, recrimination piled up in her heart. Doubt reached out its skeletal hand, telling her it would have been better if she had joined her mother in death. She turned her face up to the rain and closed her eyes.

"Master."

The word was bitter on her tongue, like a shock of onion.

"If only you had been here, we would not have fallen into darkness."

She waited, not so much out of hope for an answer but because there was nothing else to say and nowhere else to go. Thunder cascaded from the weightless mountains hanging above her. She stood there for a long time.

The wolves had let her have a moment in the field alone. Now they watched with curiosity as she returned and began hunting in the underbrush until she found a short, thick branch. The rain was growing heavier by the moment, the drizzle giving way to annihilating sheets as Canowic took her branch and began to dig.

To sleep within the bosom of the earth, where the worm travels and the chill of death draws near, was a path of last resort. The shaman had made this clear to Canowic on the one occasion he had spoken of it. The ritual was a powerful means by which to loose the bonds between this world and the other, though the loosening came at great cost. Some souls could not take the strain and never woke.

Using the branch like a trowel, she began to clear a trough out of the matted leaves and soggy twigs. The mud was somehow stiff and wet at the same time. It quickly soaked her robe and overwhelmed her boots. She had to pause frequently to remove frozen stones with her hands, a chore that quickly sucked the blood from her fingers and left her barely able to maintain her grip on the branch.

When she had scraped out a rough hole large enough to lie in she cast the branch aside. The wolves had watched her without intruding, the wounded and the unscathed all huddled together for warmth, their eyes following her every movement. Now Canowic turned away from them, as if turning away from the hope of comfort, and looked up through the trees toward the witness of the night. In a clear voice she spoke the invocation that would bring on a sleep like that of mortality. Then she wrapped her cloak about her legs and lowered herself into the shallow grave, scooping and dragging the mud back in on top of herself until she was almost completely buried. Rain struck the mound above her body, carving tiny valleys in the mud.

In the last seconds before she lost consciousness the cold seemed to seize her heart. She felt her breath slowing. She closed her eyes and something swarmed in her mind. Then she slept, and in sleeping she dreamed a dream of wonder.

Chapter Thirty-Two

CANOWIC

. . .

A rrows of sunlight pierced the canopy overhead. The sudden warmth felt so good on Canowic's skin that it took her several moments to register she was no longer buried in the ground, but standing next to the log in which she had recently lain hidden. With her hand resting on the rough bark she bent over and looked inside, where a bed of bright green moss hosted a trio of brilliant butterflies.

She had closed her eyes at night and opened them—in what seemed like the next instant—at mid-morning. The rain was gone and the wood awash in thrumming birdsong. The colors around her seemed more vivid than those of the waking world. Perhaps her vision was just sharper. The hundred different greens of the forest, the exquisite relief into which the shade-soaked ranks of trees receded, the sweet smell of fallen wood, the flicker and buzz of winged insects darting through a lattice of ferns: in contrast to the swirling gauze that sometimes obscured her visions in the seeing stones the world here seemed ready to burst into fire.

Despite the beauty of her surroundings, Canowic's heart was taut as a bowstring. She left the clearing and began walking back toward the bend in the river where she and the princesses had been waylaid. Even though a part of her knew she did not need to fear being seen or heard, her stomach still filled with a coil of dread as she came to the final elbow in the trail. Before she could round the bend shouts rang out followed by the sound of wolves crying.

She ran past the last few bushes just in time to see herself fall to the ground with an arrow stuck in her cloak, cracking her head against a root as she landed. The sight of her own shade, a perfect replica down to the same dirty robe, the same felt boots, the same deerskin cloak, was the most disjointed moment of her life. She recognized her face, having seen her tattooed reflection in pools of water and the black circle of the seeing stone. But this was like looking at someone else, and her appearance was not what she had imagined. Canowic wondered uneasily if perhaps it was *she* who was the shade; a spectator permitted to watch the dumbshow of her own life being replayed.

She was perfectly positioned to see the battle unfolding before her. The meaty thwacking of hand-to-hand combat echoed through the perfect morning. Wolves snarled and slavered. Leokita screamed in fear as she was grabbed and hustled roughly across the river. Canowic felt a powerful urge to run over and tackle the warrior who held her, but she knew it would do no good.

She understood she was in the midst of a living vision—she could feel the corners of her mind glimmer and warp—but she also felt acutely awake, more vividly grounded, more present to each and every moment than she ever had been. Everything she was watching unfold had been lost to her after she passed out. She saw the wolves tear into the war band with a frenzied counterattack. Just when they seemed to be prevailing, an intense feeling of sickness cascaded over her like a deluge of rotten water. The wolves seemed to feel it too. They turned as one and looked up at the low rise above the opposite bank.

Canowic had never laid eyes on whatever it was that had cast the pall of evil in the castle, but she knew the signature of its presence. The massive creature stepping into view was clearly its source. Its face was a death mask with eyes like deep black wells, a chest like a cooper's barrel, tree-trunk limbs, and yellowed tusks. Its pale flesh glowed pearlescent in the half-light and its hands were enveloped in tongues of blue fire that neither consumed nor harmed the skin beneath. Taller than any mortal man, it went naked and seemed to have no sex between its legs. Invisible sorcery roiled from it, causing Canowic to gag. At its feet a pair of black hell-dragons slithered powerfully.

Canowic crouched instinctively though she knew she was invisible. While she cowered, one of the lizards flashed down the bank and leaped over the river. Serouac rose up to meet it but the lizard disemboweled him with one thrust of its razor claw. As he lay dying several other wolves ran to defend him. Then the other lizard screamed in, and the force of the ensuing collision carried both lizards and wolves into a stand of reeds. These shook as if blasted with a storm wind and desperate sounds spun outward while the hidden combat churned the water into waves.

The reeds ceased to shake and Canowic tensed. The stalks parted with a rustle and one of the lizards emerged into the sun, water dripping from its jet scales. Lowering its rhomboid head, shaped like a child's coffin, it sniffed the wet earth for news. When it proceeded to Canowic's helpless body and began probing her hair she nearly retched. The air was rent with a bird-like scream as the other lizard emerged. Now Canowic could not help but cry out, for this second lizard held Buli's decapitated head in its jaws. The little wolf's eyes were vacant. Blood dripped from the bottom of her disembodied head, soaking the ground ochre red.

At the sound of her exclamation Canowic covered her mouth in horror. Both lizards whipped their heads around and stared straight at her where she crouched in the middle of the path. She stared back, unable to look away as their red eyes drilled into her, clawing at her, trying to reach her in her cocoon. Though not present with them in the flesh, she feared they could somehow discern her presence. Interminable moments passed. Finally she managed to rip her eyes away and looked across the river at their pale master.

He too had fixed her with an unblinking stare. Canowic felt her head start to split at the side. Horrified, she reached up to her ear to feel the broken skin and was disoriented to find everything intact. The iron flavor of dark magic was thick in her mouth. She doubled over in pain and heard a splash. The lizardmaster was crossing the river. So this was how things would end; strangely, in a dream from which she would never awaken. She was defenseless, with neither a weapon nor strength to wield it. Her body would rot where it lay buried while her spirit flew to the other world.

But the giant stopped at the water's edge. It scooped up a handful of mud and slapped it on the first lizard's side, causing it to writhe in pain and snap its jaws angrily. The giant snapped back, revealing fangs like those of a wolf to match its tusks. Canowic saw now that the lizard's flank was scored with claw marks. It had not escaped its battle with the wolves untouched. The pale monster stood, but instead of continuing on toward Canowic he turned and crossed back over the river with the lizards in its wake.

As she watched them disappear into the forest Canowic heard a sound in the reeds and turned to find Red Wing nipping playfully at Buli's tail. She was stunned. The dead wolves all stood before her at the water's edge. Haifax took a long drink from the river while Serouac sniffed the air as if waking from a nap. Their coats gleamed as if lit from within. Canowic looked behind them at the corpses strewn about. The living wolves before her were the identical twins of those lying dead in the water and reeds. Buli's head had rolled into the grass beneath the willow, yet here she stood, leaping playfully at her companions, dancing sideways through the grass as if she was aware of the wondrous grace by which she had been reanimated.

Canowic knew she was beholding the deepest kind of magic. She might be a temporary projection in her present form, but the wolves were something else—the spirits of those that had passed through the gate of death. She felt the edges of the world smear and a shiver passed through her, reminding her of the frozen earth that held her body. Then the wolves dove into the river without warning, shocking her out of her contemplation. They burst out on the far bank and sprinted off down the path in the direction the war band would have gone. Canowic stumbled into the river behind them, hurrying to catch up.

They coursed along the pathway, the wolves running swift and silent and always a few steps ahead until Canowic rounded a particularly sharp corner and found them crouched low to the ground, looking off toward a stand of pine trees. Though the interwoven branches moved gently as anemones in a tide pool, betraying nothing, she knew what she would find inside.

This section of the path was bordered by an embankment, with the copse laying downhill of its foot. Canowic paused to scan for sentries. Seeing nothing, she slipped down the embankment and began stalking through the undergrowth, flitting from cover to cover. Golden white sunlight streamed down through the canopy, trapping dust motes in the fragile glass of its slender columns. With the preternatural calm of a dream Canowic noted the wolves had stayed behind. Apparently this task was hers alone.

The final approach to the copse was a stretch of open ground. She was steeling herself for the run when she saw Mictanta walk slowly from the trees. Although Canowic was watching her from behind, she somehow sensed the princess's face was composed. Mictanta never looked over her shoulder as she walked steadily toward a further curtain of trees, and no one pursued her.

Canowic hesitated, paralyzed by a sense of dread that swept over her like a summer squall overtaking the bay. Mictanta disappeared into the far trees, though whether it was a shade or the princess herself Canowic did not know. There had still been no sound from within the copse. Canowic turned back to look at the wolves in the half-hearted hope they would have some guidance for her, and that was when she saw him. There, arms folded beneath his cloak of feathers, stood the shaman.

His face was creased with the same hatchmarks and crows feet it had always borne. It was difficult to tell at a distance, but his eyes seemed to shine with a new light. There was no wound or mark visible upon his body, though Canowic had seen the white bear pierced with many arrows and bleeding from his snout at the end. How could he be here now, looking so unscathed? His cloak of black raven feathers was now trimmed with a border of crimson plumes, and he wore a wreath of reeds upon his brow. The crown glistened in the sun as if wet with oil or water.

Canowic threw caution to the wind and broke into a headlong sprint back towards the trail. She tripped in her haste, falling, rising again, heedless of the noise of her crashing, heedless too that no one could hear her. Her self-awareness had fled along with any sense of being in a dream, her vision narrowing into a tunnel focused on her master's face.

The shaman watched her run, his features set in the stoic look she remembered so well. She called out to him with a breathless shout, but he only watched and waited. Then, when she had scrambled most of the way up the embankment and could almost have reached out and touched his feet, he turned away. Canowic cried out in confusion, losing her footing in the process and sliding backwards down the muddy slope, tearing out weeds as she went.

"No!" She cried. "No! Master, wait!"

But he was moving steadily away down the path, pulling the wolves in his wake. Canowic dug her hands into the mud to stop her descent and began clawing her way back up the embankment in a frenzy, churning on all fours like a beast. As she reached the path again the shaman was just disappearing. She set off after him at a dead run.

When she rounded the bend he was already vanishing again around the next corner. A fist of despair began to close around her heart, squeezing tight. Why would he appear only to leave her? Why did he not wait? Something in this line of thinking jogged her memory and she registered again, as if for the first time, that this was all a dream. Her body was buried in the cold wet earth. The shaman was dead. Yet he was here in some form. That was all she cared about. Only he could explain himself. Only he could explain all of this. He would know how to proceed, and without him she was lost.

Canowic redoubled her efforts, sprinting up the path and shouting herself hoarse, but the shaman did not stop. He seemed to float ahead of her on wings. Just when it seemed she had fallen hopelessly behind she came around the root ball of a fallen oak and there he was, standing in front of an opening in a dirt bank bordering the path. The door-sized opening was overhung with ferns. Canowic rushed forward with her arms outstretched. But just before she reached him the shaman stepped into the opening, the wolves slipping in around his feet.

Canowic paused at the threshold, confused.

"Master!" she cried, her voice breaking with frustration and a deadening sense of rejection. "Why do you flee me?"

Cold, dry air whispered from the opening. She felt afraid, but she had come too far. Pushing aside the trailing ferns she stepped across the threshold and plunged into darkness.

. . .

She fell through a field of stars. The hardpack of the trail was gone from beneath her feet, as were the sounds of the forest, the warmth of the sun, even the hunched darkness of the tunnel itself, which had instantly been replaced by an expansive, bottomless black, at once thicker and less claustrophobic. A sharp wind streamed through her cloak and hair and drew tears from her eyes. Distant pinpricks of light illuminated the nothingness extending around her in every direction, both formless and impinging.

She had no idea how far she might already have fallen. Perhaps she was plummeting toward broken rocks in the throat of the canyon that separates the other world from ours. Perhaps she was not falling at all. Before she had a chance to worry, one of the pinpricks began to grow larger. It swelled, flaring at its edge like burning parchment, until a circle of light hurtled past Canowic like the lip of a basket and she was screaming through a dizzying vortex of fountaining light and liquid dark that thrashed and tossed and spun her like a rag doll while a hurricane roar filled the air.

Suddenly everything was gone. The stars, the leaves, the cataclysm. She had alighted upon a cliff at the mouth of a cave, a bright shield of blue sky brilliant above. The shaman stood before her and this time he made no move to leave. The wolves milled silently at his feet, while far off in the distance the peaks of the mountains whose foothills she recognized as those in which she had left her mortal body shone white with snow. The master raised a hand to touch her face.

"My child," he said. His voice was gentle.

She leapt at him then, throwing her arms about his neck. Dream or not, he felt substantial. The coarse hair on his chest was rough against her cheek. He returned her embrace, his arms providing a greater reassurance than any words could have. Canowic began to sob. She wept for her mother whom she had not known, and her sisters whom she had failed. She wept for the wolves who had given themselves for her. She wept for the shaman. And she wept for herself.

"Where have you been?" she demanded, her voice jagged with sorrow and anger, her body still shuddering. The shaman moved his hands from her back to her shoulders and held her at arm's length.

"I have been on a journey," he said, "to a place I have longed to see."

The familiar rasp in his voice had never been so reassuring.

"You dream, young one. And in dreaming you are blessed to see both things that are and things that may yet be."

"Please speak to me plainly," she begged. "I do not have the strength for mysteries."

"I have gone ahead of you across the dark waters," the shaman said. "I have seen many things. Some of these are not for me to reveal, but some pertain to what awaits you."

A cloud seemed to pass across the liquid of his eyes.

"You will wake to great sorrow, my daughter. But take heart. There is a hope set before you that is greater still. Soon you will meet a helper, one who will set your feet upon a new path."

Dread curled in her heart like a worm.

"What sorrow? What do you mean?"

"It has not been given to me to tell you," the shaman said, shaking his head.

"Then why have you told me anything at all?" Canowic asked. She started crying again. "Why have you come to me, if only to put fear in my heart and confuse me?"

"On the night of my death," he replied, "I journeyed far beneath the sea to the Rock of the Ancestors. There I met and spoke with my own master, Anharay. There were many things I desired for him to say, yet he could only give me that which was allowed."

It was not what Canowic wanted to hear, but she could see by the look in the shaman's eyes that he ached for her. She remembered that look. It was the same one he had had on the night he told her the story of finding her abandoned on the beach.

"I have not come to frighten or confuse you," he said, his steady voice calming her again. "I have come to you in your hour of need to give you that which will sustain you."

He reached out and took Canowic's sweaty hands in his own.

"Soon you will wake," he said. "Not long after you will encounter a helper who will aid you on your way."

"I have asked you to speak plainly," Canowic pleaded. "Who will this helper be?"

"My daughter, I speak in mysteries for they are the words that have been given to me, and because I cannot see all that will happen."

"Do I speak with a shade?" Canowic asked. "Are you my master or an impostor?"

"I am Henyawé," the shaman said, pulling aside his robe to reveal deep wounds on his ribs and thighs. Canowic remembered her last glimpse of the white bear, arrows protruding from his bloody fur. "Though I have tasted death, I live."

"How will I proceed," Canowic asked, "when I do not know the way?"

"The way will be made known to you."

"The way to where?"

The shaman lifted his arm toward the sky. "Look for the Swan. When your hour has come it will guide you onward, and lead you to the place you must go."

"I am tired of riddles," Canowic said. She was still holding the shaman's other hand. She never wanted to let go. "I am tired of running. Where am I going? What do I seek?"

"I know you are tired," her master said. "But let your heart be encouraged. You seek the door of our people. The door that leads to the other world. I do not know when or where it will appear, but you will find it. You will find it, my daughter, this great thing I myself have longed to see."

She smiled sadly.

"Will I find you on the other side of this door?

The shaman took her other hand again and renewed his grip on both.

"You have found me now, and you will find me again, though there are miles to tread between now and then."

"And what if I fail?" she said, her voice breaking as she thought of all the dead.

The shaman again lifted a hand to her cheek.

"You may suffer, sorrow, even die. But you will not fail. Your heart is too full of love."

His grip on her shoulder was growing strangely light and insubstantial. Canowic cried out in a sudden panic, sensing he was about to leave and begging him to stay, but he was already vanishing along with everything else, cave, cliff and sky all dissipating into grey wisps as she felt herself sucked up, up, up, with a sound like a body sliding off silk sheets, back through a tunnel of gentle white snow which faded into a field of blackness as unknowing settled upon her in great waves.

· · ·

She woke up choking. During her gravesleep the wet sludge of the earth had settled in around her, drawing out her warmth. Freezing mud had paved over her pursed lips and nearly clogged her nose. She clawed her way out of the grave with great effort, rocking her body back and forth pitifully as she gasped for air. When she finally popped loose with a great sucking sound she had no strength left at all. She rolled over on her side in the cold rain and curled into a ball.

The branches above her rattled like wet bones in an offering tree, slung back and forth by a piercing wind. She had woken several of the wolves. They loped over to where she lay and began licking her muddy face with warm tongues. They nudged her with their snouts until finally, with great effort, she stumbled to her feet and began to weave unsteadily toward the path back to the river.

Chapter Thirty-Three

CANOWIC

. . .

The rain had started too late to capture the warriors' footprints. It didn't matter. They would have followed the path, unafraid of pursuit. The act of running was itself a kind of battle for Canowic at this point. More than once she stumbled, but each time Gila was there, a strong presence at her side. As she reached the river the sky was rent by a jagged sword of incandescent light. The grass on the near bank was flattened just as it had been in her dream. Thunder stampeded down through the trees as Canowic gazed upon the disfigured corpses of warriors and wolves. Lightning lit up the forest again, searing the image into her memory. Gila barked and bounded further down the trail. There was no time to spare.

The woods crowded in closer around the path now, shielding some of the rain. Intermittent flashes of lightning revealed the wolves frozen in mid-stride, their bodies stretched out or coiled tightly, ready to explode forward. They were hunting, given over to that urge and dream for which they had been fated since the dawn of the stars.

As they sprinted through the dark, Canowic had to use all her powers of perception to keep from tripping and sprawling headlong. She came close several times, grazing her shins against a hurdled log or nearly snagging a root. The wolves bounded easily through the inky blackness, surefooted as goats on a crag.

At length Gila slowed, trotting along a section of the path bordered on one side by a sloping embankment. Canowic recognized the place immediately. Hidden in the darkness beyond the foot of the bank was the copse of trees from which Mictanta had emerged in her vision. Canowic peered into the starless black beneath the trees. It was *so cold*, and the path beneath her feet was hard as stone. A familiar fear took hold of her bowels as she considered what she might find in the trees. But the shaman's words were now working on her like a warming draught of liquor. Pulling the soaked hood up from her back and nestling it onto her head, she stepped off the path and ran down the embankment.

The final approach to the copse was unprotected, just as it had been in her dream. Despite the cover of darkness she was wary of the crossing. It was impossible to know whether Yengwa had set a lookout. Finally, hearing nothing and knowing time was of the essence, she pushed off and sailed out onto open ground. After a few breathless moments she raised her hand and reached out to grasp a branch. She'd made it to the edge of the copse. The feel of the sharp pine needles anchored her, drawing her focus to a razor point. The strong scent of the trees brought to mind the festal days when every door in Aghuax was hung with fresh cut boughs.

That she had made it this far undetected meant she was either entering a trap, or the men she stalked were preoccupied with pursuits that had temporarily blinded them to the threat of ambush. No sooner had this thought entered her mind than she heard the sound of a man's voice. He was asking for a number. She began to creep closer, straining to listen while taking extra care in the relative dryness beneath the trees not to make any noise. A second voice replied to the first, and Canowic began to piece together what was going on. The men were casting lots.

Having insinuated herself halfway into the copse, Canowic saw firelight. Shadows crouched around a pit, settled on their haunches or standing under branches out of the rain. Dull red tongues flickered up from hissing logs. She could see the faces of the men on the opposite side of the circle. They were mostly obscured by darkness and war paint, but the occasional flare from a pine knot illuminated their features.

As the warriors waited on the outcome of their lot-casting, Canowic scanned the darkness at the edges of the firelight, trying to find the princesses. She had not heard their voices, but they must be close by. She tried not to think about what it would mean if they were not here in the copse. She was straining to see between the gloomy boughs when the second warrior spoke again.

"Twelve. I choose twelve."

The first warrior, the one who had asked for a number, nodded slowly. He was seated cross-legged in front of the weakly spitting flames with his back to Canowic, but now she recognized his voice.

"Taking the girl's age as your number," Yengwa said, glancing at the darkness off to his right as he began shaking a set of bones in his hand.

"I shouldn't be letting any of you have a taste. None of you brought me the shaman's little pup."

Canowic began moving toward the spot Yengwa had marked with his gaze. Within a few steps Leokita came into focus. She was lying on the ground with her arms tied behind her. She was staring at the fire without blinking. For a moment Canowic's heart stopped. Then she saw the tracks on her sister's cheeks reflecting the bloody light of the flames. She blessed the tears as proof Leokita was still alive.

The men leaned in as Yengwa tossed the goat knuckles. Time was running out. Canowic desperately canvassed the shadows as she continued moving toward Leokita. She would have to act soon, but she still hadn't located Mictanta. She could make a sound in an effort to draw the warriors off, or lead them away from the fire where the wolves could get at them. But what if they did not all follow? What would they do to the girls? Her brain was trying to handle too many things at once, such that she had not realized Leokita was staring intently at a fixed point. Following her line of sight across the fire Canowic saw what she had previously missed. A bundled shape she had mistaken for a log, buried in shadow. Two small feet, stripped of their felt boots, stuck out from a roll of cloth.

She opened her mouth to scream, then clapped it shut again, biting her tongue and tasting blood. Her head felt suddenly light and she stumbled, grabbing for a tree branch. She was sure the warriors would hear, but they were preoccupied. The bones clutched in the mud and a collective groan went up.

"Twelve," Yengwa rasped. "The gods favor you, Shanset, even if no one else does."

A warrior missing half an ear unwound himself from his crouch and started toward where Leokita lay. Canowic was stepping forward to block him when a howl went up from outside the copse. The sound came from everywhere and nowhere at once. The cry of the single wolf was soon joined by another, and then another, until it sounded as though the entire pack were lifting their challenge to the stars. The warriors cursed and reached for their weapons.

Leokita was temporarily forgotten as the war band circled up with their backs to the fire. The warrior named Shanset was positioned directly in front of Canowic's hiding place. She had moved out of the darkest shadows, and now her only hope was to remain still as a boulder.

But she blinked, and a look of concentration tightened on Shanset's face. He squinted and opened his mouth to call out, but then a new sound cut the darkness—a whimpering snuffle followed by a piteous growl. The sound of an injured wolf.

"It's wounded," a warrior muttered while pulling a burning brand from the fire. "They're crying over one of them that's wounded."

Another gurgling howl slipped through the trees. Spurred by the first warrior's confidence, several others pulled torches from the fire. They looked to Yengwa and he nodded, giving permission. Armed with light and heat and dreaming of wolfskin cloaks they trotted out of the glade, passing within feet of where Canowic stood.

Yengwa remained behind. Canowic wondered if he sensed something. Unlike the others his eyes were trained upward, as though he expected to be fallen upon by hawks or spirits of the air. The angle added thick creases of shadow to the black paint already covering his throat. While he was studied the treetops and Canowic wondered how she might use the wolves' disruption to her advantage, an explosion sounded from the outer darkness. The screams of men commingled with the snarling of wolves.

"No!" Yengwa shouted when some of the remaining warriors started to run after the others. "It is a trap! The shaman's dogs have come for the girl. Stay by the fire!"

He reached down and threw several branches on the dwindling fire, which burst into renewed brightness. Then he began moving towards Leokita. Canowic no longer had the luxury of waiting. She reached out her hand toward the freshly stoked fire and shouted a word of power no acolyte should have used. The wetly hissing branches erupted in a roaring cone of white flame that rushed upwards to touch the tops of the trees. Canowic staggered backwards as a great dome of smoke and cinders unfurled above the copse in the shape of a phoenix.

The warriors who had stayed behind were blown about like chaff. Shanset alone was somehow still standing, gripping his spear and turning in a circle as he tried to locate their attackers. Canowic burst into the fire-light, sacrificing her cover in favor of the shortest direct line to Leokita. Shanset's eyes widened in fear and Canowic wondered what she must look like to him, covered in mud with her hair full of twigs. He drew back his spear as she dove forward in a desperate roll. Every muscle in her body clenched in anticipation of the spear's impact. When she wasn't skewered she looked back just in time to see a shadow dragging Shanset into the darkness beyond the fire. A black figure pulled him from behind, one arm around his neck and the other hand clamped over his mouth.

Canowic pulled Leokita up and shoved her into the ring of trees before sprinting over to Mictanta. She tore back the blanket to find her sister staring up at her with lifeless eyes. She wanted to somehow take the body, but then she saw another of the surviving warriors drawing his bow. His first shot whistled past her cheek and vanished into the trees. Before he could draw a second sparks began raining down from the phoenix. Its wings were flapping while its flaming tail swished side to side, propelling it slowly upward. Several of the molten sparks landed on the archer, igniting him like a torch. His screams pursued Canowic as she barged into the trees.

Branches tore at her. She ran into a tree and was knocked down, but got up and kept running. A few seconds later she broke free of the copse and passed Asha, the ever-youthful twin of Syrxes, heading the other way. He was impaled with a spear and blood was streaming from his lips as he ran back into the copse. Canowic watched dumbfounded as he vanished into the trees, dragging the spear behind him.

Leokita was calling out from somewhere up ahead. Her voice was tight with pain, and when Canowic caught up with her she saw the princess was hobbling. There was no time to ask why, or to saw off the ropes still binding Leokita's hands behind her back. There was no time to do anything but run.

In addition to the glowing phoenix behind them, strange twin lights were now bobbing swiftly through the darkness off to their left. Obscured by tree and bush, the lights danced like carried torches, yet had none of the angry darkness of burning pitch. Theirs was a blue-white glow, like starlight trapped in ice. They were still some distance off but closing quickly.

Canowic was spent. Great power had gone out from her and she was not sure how she could go on. But she knew she would, if for no other reason than she could not fail a third sister. She squeezed Leokita's arm.

"Hurry!"

A swarm of wolves materialized out of the darkness, flowing around the girls in a protective arrowhead. Canowic was grateful for their presence, but realized it meant they had broken off their diversionary skirmish. The rain had slackened a bit and the darkness was just lightening with a hint of dawn. Gila's coat blazed in the dying shadows. Canowic took one last look over her shoulder and in so doing saw the source of the blue light.

A massive figure swept around the edge of the copse, a shadow against the shadows. She caught a glimpse of skin cratered like wet sand, and protean, burning eyes. It was the monster from the river, flanked by the two arrow-headed lizards. The creature's hands glowed gelid blue in the darkness. It raised one of them as if to strike her down from a distance.

Something shot past close over their heads, close enough for Canowic to feel the withering heat of black magic. Ahead of them a tree exploded in cold flame, but they swerved around it. They reached the path again and started sprinting, but Leokita struggled to match Canowic's pace. She sensed the wolves urging them on, holding back from the speeds at which they could have run. Around the next bend a small stream crossed the path. The water was falling off into a pool, and for a moment Canowic thought of jumping, but they were running headlong and it was too dark to see how deep the water was. The moment passed.

Canowic felt the vines on her face aching. It seemed the shaman had been wrong. This was the hour of her doom. If so, it would be better to stand and face death rather than be cut down from behind. She would fall back slowly so Leokita and the wolves would not notice. They could run on ahead while she delayed the monster chasing them. She would find a rock by the side of the path, speak a final spell, and then fly to join her master in the other world. It would all be over quickly.

She was about to slow down when a ghost dropped onto the path in front of them. It was too late to do anything, including move out of the way. The figure was not a shadow so much as a pure sable void that devoured all light. Leokita was about to run straight into it. But the figure somehow turned sideways in the eyelash of an instant before impact, thrusting out a knife as it did. Canowic screamed as the blade came up.

There was a snicking sound and the bonds on Leokita's wrists flew off with an audible pop. Canowic had already launched a blow at the shadowy figure's head, but it dodged easily, grabbing her wrist in the process and jerking her forward as it started to run. Pulled forward, Canowic stumbled into a renewed sprint. The entire episode had taken a few seconds.

The stranger was dressed head to foot in black, including an assassin's headwrap that left only a slit for the eyes. After a few yards the path turned again and they found themselves staring straight into the red eye of a god. It was the worst of luck; backlit by the rising sun and blinded at the same time. Without hesitating, the black-clad stranger veered off the path and into the underbrush. Canowic followed, trying not to break branches but mostly just running for her life. The wolves floated around them effortlessly. Canowic was surprised they hadn't pulled the stranger down.

She'd lost track of how close their pursuers were. Surely they had almost closed the gap. Up ahead the stranger headed straight into a dense thicket of scrub. Canowic pounded in close behind, bursting through a wall of foliage and skidding to a stop as the stranger lifted a fallen birch branch that turned out to be the handle of a trapdoor. Somewhere close an inhuman voice screamed. The stranger was beckoning her forward. There was no time to think. Canowic pitched forward, trusting she would not end up in a pit of vipers or impaled on a stake.

She landed on soft sand and heard Leokita tumbling in behind her, followed by the stranger. The trapdoor fell shut, plunging them into darkness. Canowic's heart was pounding like Merwa on an eruption day. A scraping sound, then light. They were in a low underground warren. A badger's den fit to human size. The stranger set the freshly lit candle down and began to unwind the headwrap. Canowic and Leokita gasped.

Chapter Thirty-Four

YENGWA

. . .

The child hung limp at Yengwa's side, jouncing against his hip as he ran. Less than a quarter league up the trail he spotted a circular stand of blue pine separated from the surrounding forest by a clearing. Just what he'd been looking for. Not that he was worried about being found. The few remaining wolves couldn't have much fight left in them. He signaled with his free arm, stepped off the path, and a few seconds later was standing in the center of the copse. The thick grass bore no evidence of previous fires.

When he dropped the girl to the ground she did not cry out. He looked down with curiosity, wondering if she was still alive. He knelt and pulled back the hair hanging in a filthy curtain across her face.

"Touch her and I'll have your fingers for a necklace, you pig!"

He looked over at the other girl, the one Nasha had been hauling. Her face was a mask of rage. Nasha had wisely tied her hands behind her. As a result, she had no way to break her fall when it was her turn to be dropped. The look of contempt on her face as she lay gasping for air reminded Yengwa of a look the queen had given him on many occasions.

"You have your mother's eyes," he said, before returning to an examination of the younger princess. She was dead. He must have killed her with the second blow. He rolled her in her own cloak and carried her to the edge of the clearing.

"What have you done to her!"

The other girl was screaming, her voice so hoarse she could barely get the words out. Yengwa ignored her question and posed his own.

"Where is your other sister? Where is the baby?"

He walked over and squatted down next to her. "Where is the shaman's brat?"

The girl spit in his face. He had planned on killing her quickly, but now, wiping the spit from his cheeks, he decided she deserved something else. He stood and began loosening his belt. The sun had run off between the trees and darkness was spreading through the grove like cobwebs. He had just pulled out his manhood when he was interrupted by a flickering blue light that cut through the gloom. Yengwa re-cinched his breeches and reached for his war hammer, motioning for his men to spread out. A pair of twin flames danced through the shadows beyond the trees. They disappeared for a moment and then the wingless dragons emerged into the firelight, followed closely by Glimmer.

It had started raining lightly and moisture glistened on the giant's pale skin. Ignoring the other warriors, Glimmer leveled an accusing finger at Yengwa. The beast's jaw opened wide, far wider than seemed possible, the bones unhinging with a snap until the entire lower half hung strangely loose. Then words came forth from the creature's throat, though its lips never moved. The source of the witchery was soon obvious.

"You have failed more completely than I would have expected."

The voice belonged to the High Mage.

"On the contrary," Yengwa said. "My work is nearly done. Two of the princesses are dead and the third is bound beside me even now. The shaman's bitch is hiding in the dark somewhere."

"My servants have done what you and your men have failed to," Ixiltical boomed, the words reverberating bizarrely from Glimmer's chest. "Now time runs short."

"Then it is good things are drawing to a close."

"Aghuax is in flames," the mage said. Yengwa's mind kindled at the thought of what Ixiltical might have done in his absence to desecrate the city of his youth.

"If you still desire the place in the new kingdom we have agreed upon, finish what you have as yet been unable to," Ixiltical said.

"The speed at which I return will not affect my place on the throne," Yengwa said. "Do your seeing pools tell you that? Or have you forgotten I am a warrior?"

It took a moment for Yengwa to realize the sound coming from Glimmer's dislocated jaw was the High Mage's laughter. It was a dry crackle, the sound of leaves catching fire. The mage thought all things had fallen under his hand. But his power was undermined by an arrogance that had nearly overwhelmed Yengwa since the day he had placed Hankasi under his spell. The exigencies of the moment were all that had bound them together. Yengwa had stood by while Ixiltical bewitched his best friend and ensnared the elders, but now he felt the fibers of that bond tearing. He pointed at Glimmer, assuming the mage could see him through the beast's unblinking eyes.

"If you are so eager for me to finish the task at hand, then answer me. What do the night skies have to say about where the shaman's acolyte hides?"

"The night skies have nothing to say." The mage's tone was scornful. "My servant was turned back by the dogs' magic. It will break with time, but for now she is hidden. She is of no consequence. Forget her. Kill the other rat and be done with it."

Yengwa laughed. "Even in death the shaman bests you with his magic. You are useless to me. Leave a man alone and he will do a man's work."

The other warriors around the circle nodded at this. The mage may have sown doubt in their minds, but they were loyal. Glimmer's face shifted, the huge jaw snapping back into place with a sickening crack. Yengwa tensed, ready for an attack, but Glimmer only turned and melted into the trees, the lizards trailing soundlessly behind. Yengwa looked up at the night sky. For a moment he could see the stars the Odmarsim called the Swan hanging directly above the grove. Then the clouds closed again and the rain began to pick up.

Nasha had started to make a fire and Yengwa sat down beside it. He needed to return to the city quickly, but he could not seem overly concerned with the mage. His confidence might be all that was holding the war band together at this point. He would make time for a bit of sport. Perhaps the acolyte would trickle in and join them at some point. As Shanset threw sticks on the fire, Yengwa pulled a pair of goat knuckles from a pouch on his belt.

When everyone who wanted a chance at the young doe had taken a number he rolled. He looked over at the girl to see if she understood what was about to happen, but she was staring at her sister's body. Shanset let out a grunt of satisfaction. He'd won. The lucky bastard was just standing up, a look of smoldering lust in his eyes, when a howl went up from outside the grove. This was not the far off sound of a hunting pack carried on a scrap of wind. The wolves were just outside the trees. Yengwa's hand flew to the haft of his hammer, his mind racing. There'd been something about that howl. Something *off*.

"It's wounded," one of the men called out, grabbing a brand from the fire. Several others were keen to join him, and Yengwa nodded his approval. Killing off the remaining wolves would mean one less thing to worry about on the journey home. There were more howls, and they did sound pained. Half his men ran out of the trees, eager for a kill. They hadn't been gone five breaths when a sound like a snare exploding from its trip-thong sawed through the air of the grove, followed immediately by cries of pain.

Yengwa called out to prevent anyone else from following, and hurried to throw more wood on the fire. He noticed the princess coming out of her stupor. It was time to end this foolishness before anything else happened. He drew his longknife, and began walking towards the girl. As he did he noticed a flash of movement in his peripheral vision. He had just registered the flutter of the acolyte's cloak when she made a tossing motion and everything went white as dawn.

He woke facedown in the mud, yards from where he had been. His warriors were scattered around the clearing like cordwood. A weird light was in the air. He rolled over and tried to sit up, only to feel a scalding sensation on his left thigh, like a hot pan being pressed against his flesh. Looking up, he saw the source of the strange light. A giant bird hung above the clearing. Molten rain fell from its outspread wings. It was a drop of this rain that had burned him. He scrambled toward the tree line for cover, digging a handful of mud from the ground as he went and slathering it on his leg to cool the pain.

The girls couldn't have gone far. He was about to run out of the copse after them when he saw a pair of pale blue lights moving quickly through the trees.

Chapter Thirty-Five

CANOWIC

. . .

They had been saved by a woman. Canowic sat perfectly still as their rescuer finished unwinding the strips of cloth from about her head. She fully expected the roof to cave in at any moment and extinguish all three of them in suffocation and darkness. Finished, the stranger ran a hand through her short hair, leaving it standing on end like wheat stubble.

"What is that thing?"

Canowic said nothing, willing the crazed woman to be quiet with her eyes.

"Whatever it is," the stranger said, tossing the cloth aside, "it won't bother us down here."

Canowic did not believe her. It was difficult to judge the woman's age. A thick scar ran from the corner of her left eye to the middle of her cheek, where her nose started to rise towards its elegant bridge. She had thin lips and luxuriant, steeply peaked eyebrows. Even in the guttering light of the candle stub it was clear she was deeply tanned.

The stranger reached behind her and slipped a square of hide from a fold in her shirt. She passed it silently to Canowic who caught a whiff of something tender. She held it to her nose. Jerked venison. Canowic tore off a hunk and passed the rest to Leokita, content to wait for answers. If they were about to die they might as well do it on a full stomach. When Leokita didn't take the meat Canowic looked over and found her staring bitterly at the stranger.

"Who are you?" Leokita asked, not bothering to lower her voice.

"The one who saved your life," the woman replied.

"What are you called?" It was an insolent phrase, although Canowic was not sure the stranger would understand that. Then again she apparently spoke Caguazi, so she might.

"You speak to me like you would speak to a dog," the stranger noted, returning Leokita's stare.

"I speak to you like one I do not know."

The stranger kept staring, until the tension grew so taut Canowic felt compelled to puncture it. Before she could, the woman spoke again.

"Cuscanta."

"What kind of name is that?" Leokita asked.

"An old woman's name," Cuscanta said.

"An old woman," Leokita repeated, sarcasm soaking her voice. Canowic wondered why her half-sister was so angry with this woman who had just saved them. Before she could steer things back to calmer waters Cuscanta reached out and slapped Leokita full across the face. The princess's hand flew to her cheek.

"Among my people, a child respects her elders," Cuscanta said evenly. "More so when her life has been saved."

Leokita's jaw clenched and her nostrils flared but she said nothing. Canowic saw her hands ball into fists and reached out to stop her from doing something that would get her killed.

"Peace," Canowic said, taking her wrist. Leokita wrenched her hand free. She was quivering, tremors shaking her lips. Canowic sank backwards, at a loss. A long minute slipped by. The cramped confines of the warren left Canowic feeling short of breath.

"Now, who are you?" Cuscanta asked. "What are you doing out here alone?"

For a moment Canowic was not certain how to answer. She was not certain she *had* an answer to that question.

"The men you rescued us from want to kill us."

"And why is that?"

"They have already killed our mother." Canowic left out any mention of their sisters, the shaman, or the handmaidens. Naming one death was enough for now. "She was a great queen. They seek her throne."

"May she sleep in peace," Cuscanta murmured. Her brow furrowed and she cocked her head, her eyes moving between the girls. She pursed her lips as if weighing something. The candle guttered and bent, carving her face with shadows. Then something kindled in Cuscanta's eyes and the corners of her eyes softened.

"I have been waiting for you," she said at last.

"You have not been waiting for us," Leokita whispered, shaking her head. Canowic heard something in the rejection and began to understand. The broken, jagged thing that smoldered agonizingly in Leokita's heart was being turned against this woman, the very person who had cut her loose from her bonds and hidden her safely away. Perhaps Cuscanta knew this, for she did not rise to the bait. She simply restated herself.

"I have been waiting a long time," she nodded. "Ever since I watched a girl who would become a queen being marched from her home in chains."

Cuscanta drew one leg beneath her and cocked her other knee beside her face, encircling it with both arms. She looked the part of an assassin in her skin-tight black wrappings and leggings tucked into sable felt boots. Even covered from neck to foot it was obvious she was flexible as a sapling and toned as a leopard.

"I am Cuscanta, daughter of Telbaha and Omant. I have lived my entire life in the glades of the Odmarsim." She lifted an arm as if to imply these self-same glades were all around them. "Thirteen summers ago our people were beset by Ancagua raiders. When they launched their attack I was coming home from checking my brother's snares. He had been over-taxed since our father's death and working the fields left him with little time to see to his traps. The sun was setting as I came over the last rise in the trail with a pair of hares slung over my shoulder. I remember see-ing the whole village bathed in orange shadow.

"I was only a stone's throw from old Izil the widower's hut when I saw men with long knives and hammers coming down out of the trees on the far side of the village. They were slinking through the grass, not wanting to be seen. If I had cried out I could have warned everyone else. I might even have survived, for they would have fallen on the village be-fore getting to me. But I was a coward. I ducked down and crawled back into the woods, leaving the hares in the dirt.

"The screaming started soon after. I turned and saw the door to Izil's hut bang open. He ran out with a hoe in his hand, wearing nothing but a breechcloth. He had over fifty summers to his name but he ran out into the unknown with the courage of a man half his age."

Cuscanta hesitated for the first time in her telling.

"When the fires started I forced myself to leave the woods and get down around the back of the village. I stayed out of the light, running from shadow to shadow. I thought maybe I could find a way to get to my family's hut, to find my brother and mother. Then I saw the women mill-ing like frightened sheep at the edge of the cliff. The men were trying to form a wall around them."

Cuscanta was speaking calmly, but her eyes were eclipsed by a vision Canowic and Leokita could only imagine.

"Mothers started throwing their children from the cliff to save them from slavery. I bit my arm to keep from crying out. Then I saw Senecwo, and I wondered where my brother was. While I was watching she tried to jump, but a warrior caught her and knocked her unconscious."

Leokita covered her mouth at this revelation and made a gagging sound.

"I don't understand," Canowic said, scanning from Leokita to Cuscanta and back again, though a realization was already starting up somewhere deep inside her. Senecwo. How did this woman know their mother's name? Her skin felt like it might burst into flame. The dark warren made her want to scream. She closed her eyes and sought her breath. A hand closed on her wrist. She opened her eyes to find Leokita gripping her arm tightly. Cuscanta was staring at the candle flame.

"After that I ran back to the forest and hid beneath a stump. In the morning they hung my brother and the rest of the men of the village in sight of the waystone. The dogs laughed while they strung them up. They urinated on the waystone, but they could never harm its magic. It was a good place to die.

"The warriors slaughtered almost everyone, but they took a few slaves, including Senecwo and some of her closest friends. Girls I had known my whole life. I followed them for three days. They were not trying to hide their tracks, nor were they moving quickly. I would sleep for a few hours during the day, then run to catch up. At night I crept in and watched how they guarded themselves.

"On the third night, I slipped down from my tree in the hour before dawn and crept into the middle of the camp. I did not care if I died, but I knew the girls might be killed if I was discovered. They were sleeping together, all huddled in a ball like pups. For a moment I thought

284 · Ben Bishop

about waking them but the urge to kill was too strong in me. I clamped a hand over a warrior's mouth and opened up his neck with my blade. The blood sprang up like water from a well and his eyes shot open as he was born anew in the other world. I was certain the others would wake up, but he did not make a sound. Afterwards I fled.

"After that they moved faster and guarded the girls too closely for me to try a second time. I cursed myself for not taking the chance to free them when I'd had it. I followed them all the way down the shoulders of Merwa until I saw the walls of a great city. The forest thinned, making it harder to follow in secrecy. Finally I turned back, hopeful that I knew where the girls had been taken.

"Senecwo was sick several times on the journey to the city. I had seen her and my brother one evening, laughing behind our family's goat pen. It was a chance thing and I did not linger or spy on them, but I knew what they were about. Watching her on the march to the black city, I wondered if her sickness meant she was with child. Now I know she was."

Canowic waited for her to explain, but no more words were forthcoming. Cuscanta had fixed her with a penetrating gaze. Finally, she asked the obvious question.

"How did you know?"

Cuscanta's mouth curved in a faint smile. "Because you look exactly like your father."

Chapter Thirty-Six

CANOWIC

. . .

Cuscanta smiled sadly in the flickering light and adjusted her position against the opposite wall of the warren.

"Your mother was a calm girl, sure of herself in such a way that she rarely felt the need to speak. When she did, others always listened. She was beautiful. It seemed as though every boy wanted her. There was a rumor that men from all the surrounding valleys had asked for her hand, even a chieftain from a raven clan. Her father had supposedly turned them down, claiming she was too young. Girls far younger than her were married all the time, of course. I was jealous of her, but she was difficult to hold a grudge against.

"Some of the boys called me the fish," Cuscanta said, touching her scar. "They said I looked like I had been hooked. I would be lucky if an old fisherman would have me, they said. Senecwo never joined them. She never pitied me either, which I would have hated even more than being mocked. In the fall we would help drive our families' sheep over the ridge to the gathering of the tribes. The last time we went she shared her sweet corn with me and we made fun of my brother."

Canowic listened in breathless silence. Here were stories more precious than anything she could hope to possess. She was afraid to say anything, lest Cuscanta stop talking. She wanted her to go on forever.

"I didn't know Eyan fancied Senecwo until a few weeks before the raid. Each spring after the gathering, when all the sheep had been sold and bought and all the corn and honey traded, the men would set up a course in the bowl of the valley and there would be footraces. Boys from all the surrounding villages would test themselves. Eyan was not the swiftest boy or the strongest, but he was close."

Canowic recognized the turn of phrase. She had heard Senecwo use it to praise one of her handmaidens. To name the strongest or the purest of heart as such was to invite the evil eye.

"That year he elected to run with the men," Cuscanta went on, "though there were some boys older than him still running in the lower race to improve their chances. In the weeks leading up to the gathering Eyan had come home later than usual several nights. He would not tell me where he had been, and I had no idea until I saw him lining up for that race. The other men were stretching and jumping and slapping their legs to warm themselves. Not Eyan. He just stood there, looking down at the ground, arms loose at his sides. When the starter called for the runners to toe the line I saw my brother look straight at Senecwo, as if he'd known exactly where she was standing. I saw her meet his eyes and I knew then where my brother had been those evenings he had been late coming home."

Cuscanta's eyes took on a faraway look, as if she were back on that field. She spread her hands wide, conjuring the starting line.

"There were a full score of men in the field that year, most of them a head taller than Eyan. The race was set at three times around the circle. When the flag dropped and the runners sprang forward Eyan was jostled and fell to the ground. Some men would have given up right then. There was no chance he could catch the others, but he rolled to his feet and started running anyway. The whole first lap he trailed the field by a full twenty paces. My stomach nearly turned itself inside out, I was so worried about the shame he would feel at losing that badly. He wouldn't live it down all year.

"I was still afraid watching them come back through the first turn, but then something happened. Eyan actually started to gain on the man ahead of him. He caught him on the second turn. As they passed the line again and started the final lap people began screaming his name in disbelief. The rest of the field was flagging now, looking over their shoulders to see what the noise was about. Eyan kept gaining speed, picking up momentum as if he was being carried along in the talons of an eagle. His feet barely touched the ground. When he crossed the finish line I was screaming like a stuck sow. He collapsed into our father's arms and I worried his heart would stop right there.

"When they gave him the victor's crown he acknowledged the cheers for a few moments. Then he slipped the leaves from his brow and started walking down the edge of the crowd. I've never heard a gathering go quiet so suddenly. When he set the crown on your mother's head they murmured like brush fire, whispering and laughing at his audacity. It was the first time I had ever seen Senecwo lower her eyes. She turned red, but she was smiling. I wondered if her father would be angry. He came and stood beside her. His face was stern, but there was a light in the old man's eyes."

Cuscanta looked at Canowic. "Your mother was not much older than you are now."

Canowic waited for her to finish, but there was nothing else.

"You returned here after the raid," Leokita said. There was accusation in her voice. "Just made a new life and left your friends in chains."

Canowic knew where the rage came from, but she was appalled at her sister's timing. She was going to break the fragile spell that had fallen over them. In that moment, Canowic did not care what Cuscanta had done with herself in the intervening years. She just wanted to hear more about her parents.

"I returned home," Cuscanta said, acknowledging Leokita without taking up her challenge. "The ravens and foxes had set upon the dead. I cut the men down from the trees and buried everyone. My brother. My parents. Every member of my village. It took me the best part of a week to send them all to their rest."

"It seems you were more concerned with the dead than the living," Leokita said.

"I couldn't stay in the village afterwards," Cuscanta continued, letting another accusation go uncontested. "It had been razed to the ground. Not a hut was left standing. I dragged a half-burned piece of roof thatch into the woods and built a lean-to. A few weeks after finishing the burials I went back to the village to strip it of any supplies I could. Emtahet was the oldest woman in the village and our crown-maker. At the back of her hut, hidden in a hollowed space, I found the boxes of a dozen death crowns, all unopened, with names carved on the outside. They were all for women who had been killed in the raid. Crowns she had not yet finished or had a chance to give to their intended owners."

Canowic thought of the moment in the queen's chamber when she had opened the box and pulled out her beautiful crown, the heavenly city in radiant miniature.

"I knew what I must do. I journeyed to the city and slipped inside with the crowds entering on a market day, disguised as a beggar. The people buzzed with rumors of their new queen. I found a few slaves who spoke Odmarsim. They told me this new queen was a war prize, captured just weeks earlier, and that the people could not comprehend why the king had taken her as his wife. Then I understood what had happened.

"It was not difficult to spy on them. Senecwo had been put in an apartment with the other girls. I tried to look in from a building across the way, but a screen hid their balcony from view. I stayed several days, sleeping in alleys and remaining near the gate of the castle courtyard. I kept the hood of my robe up and the people seemed to pay me no mind.

"Senecwo never left the castle, but one day Tantawelae emerged from the gate with a basket on her arm. I followed her towards the market, planning to pull her aside as soon as she was alone. But then I realized how well fed she looked. Her dress and hair were clean, and she had new sandals on her feet. I thought of myself, living in the woods outside the ruins of our village, tempted to eat grass. I thought of burying her parents. Would I really have been rescuing them if I had found a way to get them out of the city? It may sound strange to you, but in that moment I thought perhaps they did not need rescuing."

"You could have asked her," Leokita said, her voice trembling. "You could have at least told her you were there. She deserved to know. They all deserved to know."

"You are right," Cuscanta said, her jaw clenched. "But I did not. I was troubled in spirit. I returned home to the forest and lived alone for many years. Your mother and her friends sometimes came to me at night, asking why I had left them to rot. There were many springs when I considered journeying to the walled city again, slipping inside the castle, and murdering the king in his bed. The fear in his eyes as I kicked him awake would have been sweet. He would have died slowly, alone and in agony."

Cuscanta sucked in one cheek as she contemplated this scene.

"But in the end I held to my original decision. I can tell you it was not out of cowardice. The life I have lived alone has been worse than any death at the hands of my enemies would have been. But now, looking at you, I wonder if the gods of my fathers have not held me back for such a time as this."

Leokita gave no indication of whether she found this explanation satisfactory.

"The seasons came and went. I abandoned the village to the animals and the forest. Weeds sprung up along the path. I could neither fully leave nor bear going there. Then one day I arose and it was if my feet carried me back of their own accord. I had not set foot in the village in many, many seasons. Something led me to the end of the path where it turns and empties into the waystone's field. I stepped into the wreckage of the last hut. Your mother's hut. Sticking up from the mud underneath was something white. I dug out another of Emtahet's boxes.

"I returned to the city a final time, and paid a boy to leave a basket of Fire Lace in the castle courtyard. I had pinned a note to it saying it was for the queen, and hidden another message inside the fruit inviting someone to meet me outside the city. When Wiwoka actually arrived at the place I had named I found I could not face her. I was ashamed I had done nothing to save her. To save any of them."

"They would have forgiven you," Leokita said.

Cuscanta looked up at the dirt roof above them and blew out a long breath.

"Perhaps. I know it must have eaten at them to know I was out there but to never see me. In the end I left your mother's box next to Wiwoka while she lay sleeping."

"I know," Canowic said.

Cuscanta tilted her head. "You know?"

"I know the queen received her crown."

"How could you know this? None save Senecwo will ever see that box or the crown within."

"As I have told you, our mother is dead," Canowic said. "We saw her slain with our own eyes. Before she was killed she opened the white box and found the crown it contained. A crown in the shape of a city."

For a long interval Cuscanta remained motionless, saying nothing. Then she closed her eyes and her head collapsed to her chest. Canowic imagined visions of childhood dancing through her mind. When Cuscanta opened her eyes again she leaned back against the wall and reached down to untie a ribbon cinched around one of her legs, releasing a black bag. From within this bag she produced a long-stemmed pipe with a bowl of horn. After filling the bowl with tobacco she lit a splinter in the candle flame and brought the leaf to a yellow glow with steady puffs. Thick smoke plumed upward from her mouth to crawl along the ceiling and a sweet, piney smell filled the chamber.

Canowic felt herself growing drowsy. She punched her cloak into a pillow and stretched out. Cuscanta did the same while Leokita curled up in the corner. Canowic felt lightheaded, drunk on all the new stories she had heard.

"Were you not afraid of the spirits?" Leokita murmured.

"Afraid of the spirits of my ancestors?" Cuscanta replied.

Leokita nodded. "Were you not afraid they would hound you?"

"That is an idea of the people who enslaved your mother and are themselves enslaved by lies. The dead do not hound the righteous."

Leokita's voice was strained, but no longer with rage.

"The magi say the dead are forever lingering. That they suffer and need help in easing their pain."

Cuscanta shook her head softly as she looked at the ceiling.

"No, sweetness. The dead do not linger. The dead are safe."

Chapter Thirty-Seven

CANOWIC

. . .

W hen Canowic woke she felt Cuscanta examining her with a penetrating look that suited her falcon face. The woman's keen eyes knifed through her, probing, searching for something. Leokita slept in the corner, her features troubled.

"Who pursues you?" Cuscanta said, her voice quiet but firm.

Canowic rubbed the sleep from her eyes. She wasn't sure where to begin.

"I know they're from the city," Cuscanta went on, "but beyond that I am lost. I would know who, or what, I am dealing with."

Canowic's mouth felt dry as a grain sack, and when Cuscanta handed her a skin of water she drank gratefully. Afterwards she wiped her mouth on the back of her hand and cleared her throat.

"The king who captured my mother and her friends was named Hankasi," she began. "Less than a fortnight ago he was wounded in battle and succumbed to the injury soon after. Upon his death his chief captain, Yengwa, sought to kill us all."

"Even you?"

"I was with the queen when she died," Canowic said. "I was there with my master, a great shaman, to help interpret one of the queen's dreams. I only learned in that final hour that she was my mother. My master died trying to protect us all. He too was killed by Yengwa's warriors with the help of a fell beast."

"The nightmare that chased us through the wood last night."

"The same." Canowic recalled the sight of the beast and his attending lizards from her vision. "I do not know what he is, nor what name he goes by."

"Clearly he, or it, is possessed of great magic," Cuscanta said.

Canowic thought of the otherworldly blue glow coming through the trees and the pine tree shattered by ball lightning. "I fear it is a servant of the magi."

"The magi?"

"Deceivers. Grim lords who usurped much of the king's power in his last days. I know the aroma of their presence, and they are a part of this, most likely through the beast."

"So they have another name," Cuscanta said.

Canowic was confused.

"Rumors of these magi have penetrated even here. They left a trail of evil behind them when they crossed the mountains. Even the animals carried word of them."

"There are some who thought they came down from the stars," Canowic said.

Cuscanta snorted. "Some stars are evil, but those bastards come from a real place. Some hellmouth coughed them out in a land beyond Merwa." She spit on the ground, indicating her feelings about the magi's homeland. Its location on the map of Canowic's mind was as hidden as the dark corners of the underground warren, which, had it not been for

Cuscanta's candle stub, would have been as dark now in the morning as it had been in the dead of night. At least Canowic assumed it was morning. She felt a rumbling in her stomach, but all thoughts of food were driven away by Cuscanta's next words.

"This Yengwa, the leader of your pursuers. I will never forget him. I can picture him shining in the light of a burning hut all those years ago. Back then half his face was not peeled away."

Canowic said nothing. If Cuscanta noticed her discomfort she didn't let on.

"What is your plan from here?"

"We have no plan," Canowic said. She thought of the door from her vision. It had never left her mind, even before the shaman had reaffirmed its importance. She knew it was vital to her journey, she just wasn't sure how. She did not reveal any of this to Cuscanta, for reasons having to do with the delicate balance of dreams and visions, as well as her own lived experience which told her that the heart's hope, once spoken, begins to wither like a flower freshly cut.

Besides, she spoke the truth. She had no plan other than flight. Cuscanta was reading her face, weighing what she said, sifting it like wheat. Leokita breathed steadily in the corner, her slow breaths forming the heartbeat of their little womb.

"I will lead them away," Cuscanta said at last.

Canowic stared at her, hearing but not understanding. Leaving the hole to lure the war band away would be almost certain death. She started to shake her head but Cuscanta was already shaking hers. Canowic was surprised to see anger in her face. Or perhaps it was deep sorrow.

"Wait a full day. When you leave, head east over the mountains. In the valley beyond you will find another city where you will be safe."

"You can come with us," Canowic said. "There is no need for you to die."

Cuscanta nodded, as if not denying this. "But my home is here and I cannot leave after all this time. You are young, with your life ahead of you. You will find the way on your own."

"This is not your fight," Canowic said, her voice starting to rise. "They will kill you and it will not end quickly."

Cuscanta smiled grimly. "It has been my fight since before you existed. No one takes my life from me. I offer it up willingly."

wrapped in a black sheath. She gripped the pommel in one hand and flexed her other, unlimbering the tendons.

"Hide yourself, and do not emerge no matter what you hear."

"What if I will not?" Canowic replied.

"You will have your time to fight," Cuscanta said. "Perhaps even to die. That time is not now."

Canowic shook her head again, and was surprised to hear Cuscanta laughing with genuine joy.

"Your father's fire burns strongly in you." There was something like pride in her face. "To bring vengeance on your enemies is a worthy desire. But the pleasure it brings is fleeting. Whatever may come, you will have a chance for glory. Do not throw away your life. If your gods can make a stone sing," and here she pointed cryptically at the place where Canowic had kept the shaman's traveling stone hidden in her cloak, though she had never shown it to Cuscanta, "then they can show you something new in these old hills."

Before Canowic could protest, Cuscanta lifted the warren's trapdoor a crack, then tossed it aside and boosted herself out. After a few long moments the sound of shouting came through the door, as if from far away. Canowic could not make out the words. Not long after she heard wild screams followed by a sound like rolling thunder.

Chapter Thirty-Eight

CUSCANTA

. . .

C uscanta flew through the pines silent as a doe. The only sound accompanying her passage was the nearly inaudible hum of air shearing along the naked blade in her right hand. In her left she carried a heart-sized stone she had picked up from beside the trail. To her surprise, several of the wolves had followed her. They streamed behind her like a tailing banner, fluid and sure-footed. The thin air burned her lungs, but the sun was warm on her face. Leaping over a fallen log she ground to a halt, the blood pounding in her ears. Someone was nearby.

"Hail, warriors of the Ancagua!" she shouted. "I am Cuscanta, daughter of the Odmarsim!"

Her voice echoed from the hillsides, reverberating in the stillness.

"You and your kind raped my mother and slew my family! I am ready for redress! Come at me like men!"

With that she lit out again, cutting upslope. She was running at full speed when the first warrior stepped out from behind a moss-covered boulder. His black-banded eyes widened as he swung his war hammer.

Cuscanta sidestepped easily, letting her momentum carry her knife cleanly through the man's stomach. He fell to the ground with a breathless gasp.

She heard the twang of a bowstring and flung herself to the ground just before an arrow ripped through the space where her head had been. Rolling to her knees, she hurled her rock up into the branches of a nearby pine. Guided by skill or luck, the stone struck her second attacker square in the mouth, knocking him out of the tree. The wolves were on him before he could cry out.

By now the trunks were thinning and Cuscanta could tell the tree line was just up ahead. She decided to turn west instead of coming out into the open, but as she was about to change her trajectory she burst between two cedars and found herself plunging over the lip of a steep embankment. She skidded nimbly down the loose dirt toward a dry creek-bed, the wolves piling in after her. Her first thought was that she might continue up the gully, using it as cover. This plan dissolved when warriors appeared on both sides of the channel.

The warrior with the ruined countenance stood directly above her at the lip of the gully. The bottom half of his face was covered in war paint but she could still see the scars warping his skin underneath. One eye looked like it was ready to fall out of his head. The man stared at her and Cuscanta felt cold waters wash over her heart as he raised his arm. He dropped it, and the thrum of bowstrings filled the air. Cries of pain rang out all around her.

Cuscanta turned to see a huge black wolf pinned to the ground with an arrow through his paw. He snapped the arrow in half with a snarl as a second volley hissed into the sand around him. They were trapped like fish behind a dam. Cuscanta was gathering herself for a charge up the embankment, gripping the pommel of her knife with both hands like a sword when the wolves began rising through the air.

They were not merely leaping with great dexterity, nor were her eyes betraying her. The wolves were flying; soaring through the air as on wings, shooting out of the defile, up, up above the warriors before falling like striking hawks cutting into a flock of pigeons. Their fur rippled in the wind and their eyes sparked with wild fire. Cuscanta realized she had been running with enchanted beings. The raw fear of battle was matched by a sense of awe as she watched a speckled gray wolf hurtle towards a warrior, easily dodging the panicked release of his bow and fastening her jaws around his leg while another wolf plowed into his chest.

The massive black wolf landed beside a warrior who had abandoned his bow in favor of a war hammer. Half an arrow shaft dangled from his forepaw. The warrior waited until the wolf lunged and then swung with all his might. But the black somehow changed course mid-strike in a way that should have been impossible, dodging the club and knocking the man backwards over the lip of the embankment. He tumbled down, crown over sole, and landed at Cuscanta's feet. Blood ran from his nose and his eyes were wide open, staring up at her. He tried to roll to his feet, but before he could find his balance Cuscanta kicked his legs out from under him and sank her knife into his chest. Froth bubbled up from his mouth as he tried to say something. Cuscanta reached down and pulled the knife from his chest, releasing an upwelling of blood. A moment later something crashed into her and she was tossed aside like straw in a gale.

Spinning out of control, she skittered down the soft sand of the streambed and finally came to rest in a tuft of high grass. She'd somehow held onto her knife. She gripped a hunk of grass with her other hand, the feel of softly ripping roots bringing her back into the moment. Her entire right side ached. She shook her head, willing the world to come back into focus.

When it did she found herself staring into a nightmare. A black dragon was hissing at her from less than an arm's length away. She tried to bring the knife up but it was too late. The demon flashed forward and sank its teeth into her knee. There was an eruption of excruciating pain followed by the snap of tendons and breaking bones. The creature was a hot weight on top of her. Something was happening behind her eyes, a terrible pressure building and building until her mouth shot wide open and she screamed.

Suddenly she was weightless. Rolling over in agony, she dimly noted a pair of wolves locked in battle with the dragon. It was as if she was gazing at them through a thick piece of amber glass. They scored the ground with the fury of their combat while she lay on her side, trying to catch her breath. The pain in her leg was so great it had gone numb, as if to spare her.

Cuscanta watched as the sleeker of the two wolves darted in and worried the dragon's flank. The dragon spun and lashed out with its thick tail, sending the attacker spinning but temporarily losing its focus on the other wolf, which now crashed into it from behind. So it went, feint, attack and counterattack, until the sandy streambed was thoroughly raked and all three animals were covered in wounds. Cuscanta was not sure who would carry the day until the very end when the larger, auburn wolf opened its mouth and a great tongue of flame gushed forth, enveloping the dragon's head. Even at this the creature did not die. It stood up on its hind legs and screamed, swatting the air as if begging for battle rather than relief. Finally it collapsed in the dust with a boneless flop.

By now Cuscanta had managed to get an elbow under herself. She looked groggily up at the lip of the streambed, which was smoking like the rim of a crater. All of the warriors she could see were dead. She scanned the corpses for the captain as the huge black wolf picked its way back down to the bottom of the streambed. The wolves' presence comforted Cuscanta, though she knew deep within her that the time of her death was drawing near.

As if confirming her intimation, a pale monstrosity appeared at the lip of the streambed and looked down on the carnage. Here was the thing she had saved the girls from in the grove. Amazingly, the creature seemed as massive in the light of day as it had at night. A hulking god glistening with the wetness of one used to hidden places. It flexed its huge hands, each surrounded by the coruscating blue flames that had glowed so eerily in the darkness the night before. The creature fixed its eyes on Cuscanta and she felt she was being opened up with a saw. Any moment now she expected the beast to launch forward and savage her. Instead, as the wolves watched in wary anticipation, the giant raised one of its glowing blue hands, palm up.

The sky cracked with thunder and the world went red. Great forks of lightning hit the ground, sending molten earth fountaining into the air. The devouring fire slammed into the wolves and lit them like torches, enveloping their bodies in flames. They writhed in agony as Cuscanta watched. Her face was scorched and she threw up her hands to defend herself, feeling as though she were in the midst of a potter's kiln. After an eternity the shattering noise subsided along with the sheets of flame. She looked up to see the monster descending in silence through the air toward the streambed, as if riding an invisible wire. When it touched down it began moving among the inert wolves, slaying as it went.

A second dragon slithered ahead of the giant, powerful hips swaying hypnotically from side to side, searching for survivors. While the dragon and its master were focused on their grisly work, Cuscanta noticed movement in the foreground. Somehow the giant black wolf was still alive. Blood ran from his mouth and eyes as he staggered, trying to rise. Now the remaining dragon saw him too, and it did not wait or give any quarter. The dragon sprang forward, scoring the wolf's flank with its claws as it passed. The black wolf mewled pitifully as he fell. Meanwhile, the dragon's momentum carried it straight on towards Cuscanta. Acting on pure instinct she flung her knife, sending it tumbling end over end like a swordsman executing a trick throw. It struck the dragon full in one eye, killing it instantly.

The pale monster was momentarily rooted by surprise, and in that moment the black wolf leapt up and bit one of its glowing hands clean off. As the wolf fell, crying in pain, the pale creature loosed a scream that sent an avalanche of sand and gravel cascading down the side of the gully. With blood pouring from the stump of its arm, the beast turned and strode over to Cuscanta. In her last moments she looked around, trying to locate the scar-faced captain's corpse so she might spit in his direction one final time. But she did not see him anywhere. Then the monster's shadow fell across her and she looked up to face death with her eyes wide open.

Chapter Thirty-Nine

YENGWA

. . .

Yengwa crawled to the edge of the gully in time to see the end of the battle. He was stunned. As Glimmer stood over the Odmarsim woman, blood streaming from the stump of its arm, Yengwa scanned the battlefield. Men and animals lay tangled together, limbs askew, variously rent by fearsome teeth or filled with arrows or scorched by the incendiary stuff that had spewed from the throats of the wolves. Smoke rose from blackened fissures in the ground. He refocused at the sound of Glimmer's voice.

It was not a voice so much as a noise, a violent hiss underlain by thick bubbling, like red-hot rocks being dropped into a cauldron of boiling water. Bleak syllables fell from the creature's lips. Yengwa recognized the cadence of the black tongue the magi used in their divinations. He felt a crawling sensation on the back of his arms and looked over his shoulder, but there was nothing but dirt and scrawny pines and a dead wolf.

. . .

After the debacle by the fire he had followed Glimmer into the forest. He had been a fool not to check the acolyte's corpse, and doubly a fool not to kill the eldest princess when he'd had the chance. This time there would be no hesitating. Both girls were exhausted and the acolyte had a head wound. They couldn't have gone far, even with the few remaining wolves.

Sunrise broke cold and crimson through the trees. It was clear where the girls had left the path, but then they had vanished. An arcade of thin pines spread out in every direction. There was no scent on the wind, no bent branch or crushed pinecone to serve as a clue. Yengwa looked up into the trees. Maybe they had climbed away from him. Maybe he would have to burn this whole forest down.

Glimmer stood perfectly still a few yards off, waiting for something. The creature seemed to be staring straight at the sun. Yengwa imagined the High Mage whispering to it through some inner witchery, feeding it instructions from his high tower. They returned to the grove and Yengwa gathered the remnants of his war band. He sensed doubt in them, even dissension. He could not spare anyone, but he would have to make a brutal example of the first man to question him.

They combed the woods for a mile in every direction from the point where the trail had gone cold but found nothing. At midday Yengwa abandoned the search and turned the party uphill in the direction he thought the girls had most likely gone. Glimmer and the lizards followed along all morning, the latter sniffing and pawing and cocking their heads as if searching the ground for clues, though Yengwa could not shake the suspicion that Glimmer had already given up, and was merely bearing witness to the war band's failure. By mid-afternoon they'd left the tree line far behind and were approaching the first in a series of ridges that would eventually lead up to Merwa's peak. Yengwa crested the ridge and immediately realized his folly.

A further series of ridges stood ranked before him, marching off toward the east. The eastern plains were rumored to be fertile and wild, and he had thought the girls might be trying to make their way toward this abundance. But they would never live to see the plains. The ridges before him were tall and flecked with snow. Long scars where rockslides had torn away the trees were the only lines of any kind on their slopes. There were no trails, no clear path to the top. The girls were wounded and without food. The wolves could only do so much for them. They would die out here.

And what if they did make it? It would matter nothing if they escaped. Did he really fear the princess returning at the head of some foreign army? Ridiculous. How had he let things go this far? Why had he left the mage such an obvious opening to consolidate his power? Though he would never admit it, he realized pride had blinded him.

They made it back to the tree line again by dusk. They had been up the entire night before and the men were exhausted. Yengwa gave the order to camp on the edge of a small streambed. The following day they would begin a forced march back to Aghuax where the High Mage would face a reckoning.

In the morning they woke to stillness and ate quickly. Yengwa felt well rested. He had just knelt beside Alon for a brief consultation on the quickest path back to the city when a woman's voice called out, strong and clear, from somewhere downslope.

"Hail, warriors of the Ancagua! I am Cuscanta, daughter of the Odmarsim!"

Something sparked in Yengwa's mind. A distant memory. He quickly pointed at two of his best remaining men and gestured towards the trees. As they disappeared into the wood he retreated to the far lip of the streambed, leaving half the war band hidden across from him on the other side. They'd only just assumed their places when a figure clad neck to toe in black like an assassin from the ancient stories shot from the trees and skipped over the lip of the embankment along with several of the wolves.

Yengwa was surprised at how quickly the woman had arrived, indeed that she had gotten past the ambushers at all. He stood up and raised a hand. As he did, the woman continued to stare at him defiantly. She knew she was trapped, but the look on her face was not one of fear or even anonymous hate, but of a loathing that spoke of recognition. Yengwa had the strange sensation he was on the receiving end of a memory. Despite her distinctive features and the pair of ugly scars adorning her cheek, he could not place her. He would have time to examine her more closely in a moment.

Yengwa let his hand drop and the warriors unleashed a rain of arrows. His eyes remained fixed on the woman, who looked like she was getting ready to make a final forlorn charge up the embankment. He beckoned to her with his free hand, holding up his war hammer in the other. But then the wolves began rising into the air, and moments later he was bowled over by a ten-stone weight of pure muscle.

The wolf's momentum carried them end over end into a thorn bush growing beside a stunted pine. Yengwa only just managed to get his hands up in time, gripping the snout in one hand and the lower jaw in the other. Fangs punctured his palm. He grunted with exertion and the wolf slavered at him, drooling and rolling its yellow eyes.

Pine needles rained down on them as the wolf scrabbled viciously at his stomach with its hind legs. Finally Yengwa rammed a desperate knee up and there was a whumph of air as the wolf lost its breath. For a moment the tension went out of its jaws. This was all Yengwa needed. He pulled the wolf closer, slipping one hand under its jaw and grabbing the fur at the nape of its neck, and wrenched sideways.

Yengwa flopped back, panting heavily, the dead wolf lying on top of him. He examined his hands and found the gashes were not as bad as he had feared. After a few more deep breaths he pushed the animal's corpse off and rolled to his knees. Down in the streambed he could still hear the sounds of fighting. Where was his war hammer? He spotted it under a nearby tree and stood to retrieve it. As he did, the world was riven in two.

His head snapped back and his spine arched like a man in a fit. The sky went blood red and something burned his nostrils as he was flensed by pure white fire. Then the lightning cleaved away all awareness. The searing, skull-shattering agony winked out and he was floating in a sea of blackness.

When he woke the world had been put together again. His body felt strange and mismatched. He wondered how long he had lain beneath the pines, staring up at the robin's egg sky with his legs twisted beneath him. He sat up slowly and squinted, trying to focus his eyes. A shadow passed across his face and he flinched involuntarily. Glimmer was floating through the air, shimmering like a god. The beast was angling down into the streambed and soon passed out of sight. Another man might have run, but Yengwa had never been one to shrink from fate. He crawled to the edge of the gully and peered in.

One of the lizards was dead. It lay between two wolves, a lump of slag where its head should have been. The remaining lizard had slithered down the embankment and was now stalking slowly ahead of Glimmer, who was striding amongst the wreckage, finishing off survivors. To Yengwa's surprise, an enormous black wolf was trying valiantly to get to its feet. Blood streamed from multiple wounds where its fur had been stripped by teeth or flame. The wolf was trying to maneuver into a position where it could shield the Odmarsim woman, who was lying wounded a few yards farther down the streambed.

The lizard wasn't interested in waiting. It struck with sudden ferocity, stabbing and slashing in a quick pass that left the wolf sinking back toward the ground with fresh wounds. The lizard's charge sent it sailing past the wolf and towards the woman in black. She reacted so quickly Yengwa didn't fully register what had happened until the lizard was lying dead with her blade buried to the hilt in its eye.

A weightless moment followed in which the black wolf jumped up with the last of its strength and bit one of Glimmer's hands off above the wrist, then fell to the ground, howling in pain as its stomach distended and began to glow with a sickening light. Blood poured from its nose and anus. Glimmer loosed an otherworldly scream. Ignoring the dying wolf, the High Mage's avatar stalked over to the Odmarsim woman and crushed her throat without ceremony. Yengwa approved of the way she died, looking up in defiance.

When Glimmer began rumbling in the magi's choked language, Yengwa saw the chance that lay before him. Shanset lay slain nearby. Yengwa quickly crawled to his side and retrieved the dead man's bow and quiver. Notching an arrow to the string, he peered back over the lip of the gully and saw Glimmer still lost in communion with the High Mage. Rising to a crouch, Yengwa anchored the bow against the outside of his thigh. He would live or die by a single shot. He had just brought the bowstring fully taut, the arrow quivering at the corner of his eye, when Glimmer spoke three words in a loud voice.

As Yengwa loosed his arrow, a point of light appeared in the air above the pale behemoth's head. The shaft struck Glimmer in the back of the neck, directly at the base of the skull. The giant head slumped forward as if a cord had been snipped. A moment later the beast pitched forward onto the sand, shaking the ground as it landed.

Yengwa held his breath, not daring to hope. Meanwhile the point of light was growing into a line, a seam falling open in the air. Light poured from inside and he felt a sudden blast of heat, as if someone had opened the door to a furnace. After all he had seen Glimmer endure, Yengwa found it difficult to believe the creature could have been killed with a single arrow. He picked his way cautiously down the embankment, another arrow notched and ready.

He approached the huge body slowly, circling it once before drawing close. Glimmer's mouth hung slightly open. One of the yellowed tusks was stuck in the sand. The black eyes stared into the dirt, chilling as ever. Yengwa looked up at the seam of light. The initial heat had dissipated but a powerful glow still throbbed from within. He finally let the tension out of his bow and hurried to retrieve his war hammer. Appropriately armed, he returned to Glimmer's body and leapt up into the seam.

He landed on solid ground and scanned quickly in every direction, war hammer at the ready. Nothing but gray mist spreading away on all sides; neither sun nor moon above nor grass on the ground, which was covered with the same fog that obscured his vision. The air was utterly still. The seam had vanished along with its light, and for a heart-stopping moment he wondered if he had fallen into a trap. Then he spied a mark on the ground, a slash of black attended by a faint light that bobbed above it like a torch with no torchbearer. He walked over to investigate. Standing beside the mark he saw another some twenty strides away. The light began to move toward the next slash of black, as if inviting him to follow. It seemed he had little choice.

He passed dozens of the black marks before the light stopped above an iron ring sunk in the ground. Yengwa looked around. The same blank grayness hung like a curtain all about him. There was nothing for it. With his war hammer in one hand he reached down and pulled on the ring. It gave way like the plug of a drain. A hole began to open beneath him. Yengwa stepped back warily, peering down into the darkness, but there was nothing to see. No fetid air gusted out, no screams, no flashing eyes of demons. For a moment he hesitated, fingering his hammer. Then he jumped.

Chapter Forty

CANOWIC

. . .

After Cuscanta's departure and the dim concussions that followed there had been nothing for the better part of an hour. Canowic waited in the darkness, letting Leokita sleep on while straining to hear anything through the dirt overhead. When she couldn't stand sitting still any longer she pulled the seeing stone from her pocket and breathed a gentle word of power over it.

The crystal came to life in her hand, pulsing with a soft mineral glow. She set it at her feet and tried to clear her mind, but faces kept flashing at her; the shaman, her mother, little Kisoko. She was glad when Leokita stirred. The princess rubbed her eyes and looked at the glowing stone.

"Where did she go?" she asked.

"To lead the warriors away," Canowic said.

"When will she return?"

Canowic looked up at the dirt above them, something hot tickling the back of her throat. She could feel Leokita staring at her as the truth sank in.

"So," the princess finally said, "it is down to you and me."

. . .

When they finally lifted the sod hatch and crawled out of the hole it was past midday. Gila sat next to the opening, quietly conning the depths of the surrounding forest while she waited for them. The white wolf bared her teeth in what seemed like a grimace, and for a moment the reassurance Canowic had felt at seeing her was shaken. But then she looked into those green eyes and felt sympathy as she realized even a creature as indomitable and regal as the one sitting before her could feel sorrow. Gila had known the shaman even longer than Canowic. Now she alone was left out of her pack.

The sun was bright where it pierced the canopy, but its rays were quickly being swallowed by a vortex of clouds churning in from the north and east. Thunder rumbled from within the murk, and Canowic wondered if they might be better off waiting out the storm in the hole. But Gila was already moving. Perhaps there was some other danger nearby, something they needed to escape more than snow or rain. Leokita set off in the wolf's wake and Canowic followed.

They slipped through the woods, returning to the grove where Canowic had unleashed her fiery phoenix. The trees breathed peacefully in the wind but the place was tainted and they did not tarry. Gila loped ahead of them, silent as a ghost. Despite having slept all night, Canowic was exhausted. Cuscanta's jerky had been the only thing she'd eaten in two days.

Gila stopped a few feet short of a sudden break in the forest. They had been traversing a rise and the trees had been thickening, their overlapping branches crowding out the light. Now they gave way

altogether like a curtain quickly hoisted. There was nothing obviously strange about the gently sloping field before them, yet Canowic felt a
sense of foreboding.

The wreathed crown of Merwa was clearly visible, a cape of trees
pinned to its neck by a brooch of snow. While Gila tested the air Canowic
scanned the field. To the west a black shape peeked up over a hump of
ground. She recognized it immediately as the tip of the standing stone.
Just beyond was the celicia under which Kisoko was buried. They were at
the extreme end of the field. Canowic checked with Leokita to see if she
had realized, only to see her already following Gila out into the field at a
run.

The wolf led them way from the stone, up the rising slope. Canowic felt horribly exposed as she charged after Leokita, but they were committed now and all they could do was cover the distance as quickly as
possible. Gila turned north, swerving between two gentle hummocks, and
soon they were in the midst of a scattering of ruined huts. Canowic found
herself running down a path through the heart of an abandoned village.

Despite her anxiety she felt her footsteps slowing, until she came
to a stop altogether and stepped off the path into the grass. She did not
call out to the others to stop or worry about whether a pursuing warrior might be closing from behind. The world had receded. She knew this
place despite having never seen it.

The hut she had stopped in front of was almost entirely gone,
its footprint implied by what little remained of the wattle walls. They had
burned to the ground except on one side, where a charred portion still
reached to Canowic's waist. A shrub grew hard against this remnant, shel-
tered from the mountain wind.

Canowic walked out into the ambit of packed earth that had been
some family's living space. The dirt was still tamped enough from years of
use to have resisted the encroaching grass. A blackened ring of stones sat

on the ground. Canowic crouched down and reached out to touch one of the rocks. She closed her eyes and took in the moment. When she opened them again, her eyes caught a gleam of white from underneath the shrub in the lee of the ruined wall. Frowning, she scooted over on her knees and pushed aside the shrub to reveal a brilliant white plant, its snowy leaves punctuated with sprays of bright red berries. Hartstongue. For a long breath Canowic just stared at the cold leaves shimmering in the dull, stormy light.

She knew what the plant could afford her. She reached out and fingered a cluster of the white leaves, letting their razor edges tickle her fingers. Just one of them would send her to the other world in less time than it took for a candle to blow out in the wind. The pain would be terrible, yet last only an instant. Then everything would be over. She could sleep forever.

She felt a tugging in her mind, and thought of Remerac. He Who Tempts Towards Doubt. She shook her head and looked up, blinking in the wind. Leokita was waiting for her at the far end of the village by the husk of another hut. Canowic wondered which of the ruined dwellings had been their mother's. The one she knelt in now? The one her sister stood beside? She drew a deep breath and stood, leaving the hartstongue behind. The smell of rain was heavy on the wind and the sun was preparing to set.

· · ·

The raft of stormheads had dropped in, obscuring Merwa's jagged saw. Gila led them back to the forest where they made camp moments before a thick wall of cloud rolled into the forest and passed over them like surf. The little trio was engulfed in a bath of whiteness that blotted out the world and covered everything in a cloak of silence.

They made no fire, and did not speak as they shared a meager handful of mushrooms Canowic had foraged. Afterwards the girls rolled themselves in their cloaks while Gila sat up to keep watch. Canowic was beyond tired, but rocks dug into her side and her legs ached after crouching in the warren for so long. Her stomach protested its hunger.

"Are you asleep?" Leokita whispered.

Canowic grunted in response.

"Do you believe what that woman said about the dead?"

Canowic tried to remember what she was referencing.

"About the dead not hounding the living?"

"Yes," Leokita said, her disembodied voice earnest in the dark. "Do you think it's true?"

The air was cold as the flat of a sword. Canowic drew her cloak tighter around her and exhaled a steamy breath.

"I believe it must depend on your soul. The righteous may be ready to fly to the other world. Perhaps the unrighteous have a reason for tarrying."

"So you think we have a say in it."

An image came to Canowic's mind of Leokita's sisters—her sisters—standing together with their mother on the other side of a shadowy arch. She wanted to believe they had been ushered immediately through the gates of the city depicted in the queen's beautiful crown. She hoped they had not hung back, even to comfort her or Leokita. Surely they had fled the threshing floor of this world as soon as they were free. Or were they already free in death, such that no amount of tarrying could dampen their joy?

"I don't know."

An owl queried the darkness.

"What do you think?" Canowic asked after a long silence. But Leokita was already breathing heavily.

When she finally fell asleep Canowic dreamt she was flying silently amongst the stars. She woke in darkness to find a strong wind had blown the fog and clouds away. Gila was staring off into the woods. Canowic stood and walked slowly back out to the edge of the field, still wrapped in her cloak. The stars were a river of white flame above her. Low in the west, where the land fell away toward the sea, a host of constellations splayed across the dome. Her eyes were drawn to a form low along the horizon. She remembered her master's words as she followed the elegant line of the Swan's neck. She knew where it was pointing. She knew where she had to go.

Chapter Forty-One

IXILTICAL

. . .

T he waters of the seeing basin rippled as Ixiltical stretched out his hands and uttered the incantation to open the passage. Small wavelets began lapping against the edge of the stone bowl, and then Glimmer's portion of the spell dropped around him with a sound like hot brands being plunged into cold water. Ixiltical felt the thrum of summoned energies course through his body, vibrating in the stones beneath his feet.

The queen's vermin had been eliminated. More importantly, Glimmer was about to dispatch that fool Yengwa and his remaining warriors. A grim smile settled across the High Mage's features without touching his eyes. His fingers danced like a man playing the lyre and he began to chant.

> *O Teulanic*
> *Open the dying way*
> *That men might stride forth*

Just as he completed the spell something went off with an explosion in his face, snapping his head back. It felt as if he had been struck in the temple with a hammer. Then the pain shifted colors and his head slammed forward, crushed against his chest. A moment later everything released and he crumpled to the floor.

The spell connecting him to Glimmer had been viciously severed, but the passage they had created remained open. Ixiltical could feel it humming as he lay helpless on the stones. Gradually the pain subsided. With great effort he pulled himself upright using the basin's pillar. He leaned over the water, breathing heavily, while drawing on the vast energies available to him. Soon he was strong enough to walk over to the shelf of earthen jars he kept ready for such an emergency. He reached inside one of these and pulled out a hard black object with a teardrop shape. A lizard scale.

Holding the scale in one hand, the High Mage closed his eyes and plunged his other fist into the waters of the basin, which instantly began to boil with a dim red light. He felt himself pulled, his very being contorted, crushed, squeezed through an impossible opening.

. . .

When he opened his eyes the world was dim. He could only just move his head. It felt impossibly heavy, like a ten-stone weight. With a tremendous effort he managed to drag his eyes downward and was rewarded with the sight of his stubby black legs and armored underside. He could feel the dying lizard's body growing cold. It was only alive by the slimmest of margins, and the animating spirit was about to flee.

A few yards away he saw the explanation for his pain. Glimmer lay facedown in the sand, a black-fletched arrow standing straight up from the base of the creature's skull. The shaman's wolves were scattered around him along with several of Yengwa's warriors. Directly next to Glimmer lay a human corpse, clad all in black.

Above the carnage a bright sky was giving way to the forerunning arms of a storm. Ixiltical turned the lizard's head and saw the tops of blue pines rising above a sandy embankment. He was in a streambed. Now the point of light that marked the opening of the passage he and Glimmer had created was widening in the air. The mage heard footsteps in the sand behind him. The lizard's vision grew dimmer and Ixiltical fought against the darkness, struggling to hold on a few moments longer so he could see the mysterious assassin who had blindsided Glimmer. He could not stay in the lizard's body once its spirit flew.

Too late.

The light winked out and he was being crushed again, pressed against the ocean floor of his soul. He opened his eyes to find himself back in the dark tower's pinnacle. His gaze flashed to the ceiling. Someone was coming through. Retrieving his wand he hurried to the staircase and up onto the roof where a hard wind whipped his blood red robes about his legs. He hastily scanned the stars. Had he been so busy preparing for the following day's ceremonies he'd missed an obvious sign? He looked again. No. There was nothing. All the stars were aligned, and not one was out of order. It was a test then. Teulanic allowing him to prove his worth again on the eve of victory and consummation.

A set of stones had appeared three days earlier down on the bluff where this weak people had once worshipped their weak gods. It was a strange portent, but no cause for despair. He would destroy the stones tomorrow while ushering in a new era for the Ancagua, bringing them under the full dominion of the Desert Mysteries.

His attention was brought back to the present as a patch of air before him began to shimmer. A point of light appeared a few feet above the stones of the roof, falling downward like a woman opening for birth.

Heat and light spilled forth and then a figure tumbled out. Yengwa landed on his feet like a cat and deftly rolled to one side. It must have been a shock to step out of the gray monotony and find himself in his enemy's lair, but he had kept his wits about him. He gripped his hammer warily while Ixiltical leaned on his wand like an old man. The two men locked eyes. For a moment there was silence as they took one another's measure, the disfigured captain and the pale sorcerer, each clutching the implement of his power.

"So," Ixiltical said at last, concealing his surprise with disdain. "The lone survivor."

Yengwa was already sliding sideways across the flagstones, as if he believed he could outflank the mage.

"I will admit," Ixiltical continued, "I did not think you capable of what you seem to have accomplished."

His words were complimentary though he felt nothing but contempt. Glimmer had been his greatest creation, an incarnate testament to his power.

"You have enslaved my people," Yengwa said, continuing to crabwalk sideways.

Ixiltical laughed in disbelief.

"Who? The people you left to my devices while you were off hunting mice? The people I have held dominion over since long before Hankasi's fall? You have nothing to say about my influence over *your people*. You do not care for them. You care only for yourself. You were waiting for your lord to die. Now it is time to find out if you are stronger than he was."

Yengwa pointed with his hammer, baring his teeth.

"Foreign dog! Your words hold no power over me. You do not know the Ancagua. You do not own us."

Ixiltical smiled mockingly as Yengwa crept closer.

"Perhaps the question is not who owns your people, but whether they still own themselves." He stretched an arm out towards the city below and Yengwa chanced a glance over the tower's edge. Ixiltical saw him registering the flames smoldering below.

"What is this witchery?" Yengwa muttered.

Ixiltical was still leaning on his wand. "Truly, you and your people are the fools I took you for. You believed you could defy my gods while ignoring your own."

"Your gods are not gods," Yengwa said. "I have killed one of them just now."

"Glimmer was no god," Ixiltical replied. "In Glimmer you were simply brushing against the shadow of Teulanic."

"Then why is there fear in your eyes?" Yengwa asked, inching forward. The head of his hammer was quivering back and forth in anticipation of a strike. Ixiltical let him come closer.

"You cannot hope to contain the immortal," the High Mage said. "Only to serve it. No man has ever wrangled a god to his own will."

"Open your eyes, fool!" Yengwa snarled. "The gods honor those who take the snake by the tail. Man may have the breath of the gods in him, but they never hewed him a path."

"Quite the path you have hewn for yourself," Ixiltical observed. "Treachery and murder."

"I have set my hand against the wheel of fate and bent it," Yengwa said. "Soon the fires you have set will be extinguished, and you along with them."

"On the contrary," Ixiltical said, sliding subtly backward, "like all men, it is your fate to choose in life whom you will serve in death. And you have."

Now Yengwa was within arm's reach. His eyes were bloodshot and he stank of unwashed travel and the terror of battle. The scarred side

320 • Ben Bishop

of his face drooped down hideously, giving him a flat, discarded aspect.

"You speak as though you were not a man," the warrior said.

Ixiltical smiled. "Now you begin to see clearly."

"Enough talk, traitor," Yengwa hissed, lunging forward.

Ixiltical made no attempt to fend off the attack, and the head of Yengwa's hammer slammed into his ribs with killing force. But at the moment of impact its fearsome weight shattered, spraying starstone across the roof. Ixiltical barely felt the blow. It was as if a child had tossed a pinecone against his robe. As Yengwa stared at the decapitated shaft of his hammer, his brows twisted in a look of bewilderment and fear, Ixiltical raised his wand.

In this last moment, as the mage flicked his willow switch forward, just before the hideous strength of his spell picked Yengwa up and cast him over the edge of the tower to hurtle to the stones below, a look of resignation came over the warrior's face. His disfigured features slackened for an instant and a black light dawned in his eyes as he realized how impotent he was. Then he was gone and the High Mage was alone upon the tower, listening to the laughter of the wind.

Chapter Forty-Two

CANOWIC

. . .

C anowic caught a rumor of the sea while they were still some distance off. The faint stench of seaweed followed by a brisk note of salt. The smell lifted her spirits, evoking memories of all the nights she had fallen asleep in the sand listening to the sighing of the bay. When they finally came within sight of the city she gasped.

They had avoided the lake on their return, tracing a new route back to Aghuax. Canowic found herself looking over her shoulder less frequently as they went. She was beginning to worry more about what lay ahead than who might be pursuing them from behind. While she walked her thoughts returned again and again to the shaman. She knew he was not a god, that he did not control events or fate. But another part of her, a vocal minority in the council of her mind, believed he could save them even now if he wanted to. That he could descend on wings like an eagle and carry them to safety. She could hear his voice with perfect clarity, explaining the principles of divination as they sat together by the evening fire. She longed to feel his hand on her shoulder one more time.

They snuck down through a final stretch of forested slope and stopped where the woods plunged over a sheer drop. Far below the waters of the bay broiled against the base of the limestone cliffs. They were just north of Aghuax. From here they could see the entire crescent of the beach.

Fully a third of the city had burned. Blackened timbers poked up like ribs from the carcasses of buildings. The entire Meatsellers Quarter had been incinerated. It looked as if fire had passed through a field of wheat. The Lodge of the Elders was cracked open to the sky. Meanwhile the castle stood untouched, vaulting amongst the wreckage. Canowic's brow furrowed as she eyed the tallest of its towers. Surely it had not reached that high before. The slender talon shot skyward, a malignant finger accusing the heavens. Its stones seemed darker than when she had left.

The Swan had burned through the previous day, its eerily visible stars hanging above the city like a cluster of lanterns. Equally portentous was the disappearance of the Dark Star. It had been the last thing Canowic saw before vanishing into the woods on the day they had fled the city. Now Axal was gone from the sky.

"I do not know what I hoped to find," Canowic said. "But half the city burned..."

"Have they been invaded?" Leokita wondered.

It was a reasonable question, but Canowic shook her head.

"This is the work of the magi."

Two tiny figures were visible atop Cripples Gate. It was impossible to discern their dress or appearance. Were they Ancagua? If so, who were they faithful to? Had the remnants of the city's war band driven the magi out in the aftermath of Yengwa's attempted coup, or were the men guarding the gate in the thrall of the red-robed seers?

Leokita was thinking similar thoughts.

"Whoever is in power, they will not be pleased to see us."

"We should not risk both our lives," Canowic said. "I will go down to the city and gather what news I may. When I return we will make our plans.

Leokita's brow tightened. "Why should I leave you to take all the risks?"

"I am swifter and more skilled at woodcraft—"

"No," Leokita cut her off. "No. The choice is not yours to begin with. I am coming with you."

Canowic thought about contesting this point, but found she didn't want to.

"I am glad," she said. "I have no one else."

Leokita looked at her curiously, her frown softening. Just after sunset they scurried out from the tangle of trees at the north end of the beach and sprinted to the shaman's cave. Rounding the front, they were confronted with a clutch of burnt debris. Someone had filled the cave with trash and built a bonfire in the entrance. A slur had been carved into the soft stone of the interior wall. Without thinking, Canowic picked up one of the charred sticks and hurled it into the water with a scream.

The waves were silent in response. Canowic's shoulders heaved as she struggled to contain her rage and sorrow. She looked out over the surface of the bay where the moon was rising in tandem with itself, twin orbs of gold shining like eyes. While turning back to the cave she chanced to look down the beach towards the godwood. That was when she saw it. There, half hidden by the crown of trees, stood two huge stones crossed by a third.

Chapter Forty-Three

GILA

. . .

The first light of dawn was paving the streets with gold as the magi filed from the base of the black tower. The High Mage brought up the rear, just as he had on the day of Hankasi's funeral. At the head of the column walked Bal, a mountain of a man who had been Hankasi's executioner and keeper of the dungeons. His back was laced with thick white scars and his long hair was shaved on one side. He had a sword strapped to his back and in his hand he held the reins to a train of prisoners.

Gila watched the procession from the shadows of a nearby alley. She scanned the captives with a knowing eye. Most were foreigners captured in raids, or slaves who for one reason or another had been imprisoned instead of killed outright. Of the dozen trudging captives, most had the sores and vacant stares of those who had languished in the pits beneath the castle for months or years, but there were a few Ancagua among their number who seemed relatively fit. Recent additions.

There was much Gila did not know about what had transpired

while she was away. It was clear Ixiltical had taken control of the city, but how this had come about she could not be sure. One thing was clear. He had not granted the general amnesty some conquerors might have. Indeed, the High Mage seemed only to have added to the number of prisoners in Hankasi's dungeon.

As Ixiltical stepped from the tower the heavy iron door clanged shut behind him. The High Mage swiveled his head, casting around with his furnace eyes as he descended the steps to the street. The mage could sense Gila's watching presence, and it pained him visibly not to be able to locate her. She felt his spirit probing, chafing under the thorn of her gaze, but she had cloaked herself with her own great powers of obfuscation.

The procession wound its way through the city via a circuitous route. Gila projected the column would eventually head toward Arrow Gate, but they were taking their time getting there. They turned unnecessarily into various side streets, threading their way through narrow lanes where drying sheets hung like flags and old crones looked down from their windows in scorn. It was as if the magi wanted to be seen by as many eyes as possible.

While she shadowed the procession, Gila eyed the people lining the streets. They were mostly women and children, the mothers' faces clouded with anger and resignation. As a rule, the occupier ignores the rage of the occupied at his own peril. But Gila knew these Tomic sorcerers—she had contended with them before and would contend with them again before the age was done—and they were not concerned with the perils of men, nor with their hatred. For them the fate of the Ancagua was a foregone conclusion.

Crouching in the broken shadow of what remained of the Lodge of the Elders, the white wolf watched the procession roll by and wondered again about what had happened in her absence. She imagined Ixiltical presenting himself at the entrance to the lodge on the day after Yengwa's departure, informing the elders that he would now be guiding the people. Perhaps he had attempted to awe them with signs and wonders. Perhaps he pretended his rule would only be for an interim period. Either way, the elders would have balked. The Ancagua were crafty and wise, ever trying to outwit their opponents, ever wary of being tricked themselves. When they prickled at his outrageous declaration he would have slain them without pity or hesitation. Gila envisioned a spray of green fire from the High Mage's wand igniting the timbers, sending all of the old men to the other world together. Their families would have picked through the wreckage later, hoping to retrieve the bodies so they might bury them with their ancestors, but finding nothing save cinders and ash.

With the elders gone, would others have tried to stop the magi? Gila noted how the tight cluster of streets known as the Sword Quarter, where most of the king's household guard and their families had lived, had been completely slagged, the very stones in the street melted as with brimstone. The white shields of the household guard were conspicuously absent from the array of warriors posted along the processional route.

Whatever form the quelling had taken, Gila tried to imagine what Ixiltical had said to the people after it was all over. Perhaps he had stood on the pinnacle of his tower and spoken in a voice that echoed supernaturally throughout the city, amplified by dark arts so as to reach even the ships in the bay.

Your leaders have betrayed you. They have failed to honor Teulanic, but he is longsuffering and will be pleased to purify you.

Gila studied the eyes of the warriors guarding the route, seeking a clue as to their loyalty. The warriors of the Ancagua often looked grim, but now even the rumor of laughter was gone from around their mouths. Even if there was some threat of rebellion from within the war band, Gila doubted Ixiltical was concerned. The people's acquiescence or resistance was not important to him. They were already consigned to his ravenous god as living sacrifices. All who hindered him would die and in death be set free from their reticence.

There were several hundred people waiting when the procession reached Arrow Gate and prepared to head out of the city. The breeze ruffled Gila's fur. It occurred to her that perhaps she should take the mage now, sprint out from her hiding place and sink her teeth into his neck. For now her own magic kept his perception at bay, though if she charged he would quickly detect her and she would die with him. But she was not concerned with death. Death was not extinction.

The crowd on the beach parted before the procession, opening to allow them to pass and then falling in behind. Gila thought better of attacking. Instead she took off in the opposite direction, running back into the city. She made her way by alleys and warrens to a forgotten place between the back of a tannery outhouse and the stones of the southern wall where a rough-hewn hole was almost entirely concealed by trash. Soon she was running through the brush above the beach, headed for the godwood.

. . .

Gila arrived at the grove well ahead of the procession, in plenty of time to join Leokita and Canowic where they had hidden behind a rock at the cliff's edge in the shadow of the totems. Leokita was tense, her eyes flickering everywhere. Canowic seemed placid by contrast. Her eyes were fixed on the approaching parade. Gila wondered what would happen to this girl who had grown up before her eyes.

From their hiding place they had a perfect view of the doorway. Gila had been amazed when she first saw it. Even she, who had wheeled with the stars and journeyed the face of the earth for countless lives of men, was filled with wonder at the sight of the door of the Nameless One standing here, in a once holy place now desecrated by perverse violence and the blackest of magic. Unable to be ignored. Impossible to deny.

As the line of hooded figures passed through the arch of willows with their captives and entered the godwood, the king's herald blew a mournful note on his horn. The people of the city remained outside, spreading out around the perimeter of the sacred grove. Gila was not worried about being discovered. The people feared the totems. No one would come this far.

The magi bowed to the idols upon entering. One of them started removing the chains from the necks of several captives. A second mage produced a whetstone from within his robes and held it up to Ixiltical, who began stropping the blade of his ritual knife across its face. One of the unchained prisoners, a light-skinned man with stars tattooed on his feet and the mark of a thief branded on his hand, cried out and turned to run. Bal knocked him down easily. Ixiltical looked at the executioner and jerked his head toward the mound at the center of the grove. The doorway had appeared atop the mound, one of its two standing stones obliterating the sacrificial pole the magi had installed.

The prisoner struggled miserably as Bal dragged him up the grassy slope, while at the base of the mound the magi formed a half moon and started a low chant. Once Ixiltical finished sharpening his knife he started towards the mound himself and Gila's hackles began to rise. A murmur started up in the crowd. Perhaps they realized what they were about to see. Perhaps they were finally awakening, questioning whether they wanted to be party to this sickness. Yet no one stepped forward. Gila was disgusted. The shaman had always had a higher estimation of this people than she had. They were fickle, vicious, and in the end, cowards.

Ixiltical climbed all the way to the top of the mound, stopping before the threshold of the stone door. For a moment Gila wondered if he would walk through, and what would happen if he did. Now he raised both hands and the other magi fell silent.

"People of Dust," he called out, "animate for a brief time and only with the leave of the gods, you are greatly blessed. Today you will witness a wondrous thing. The final victory of Teulanic over the gods to whom your fathers gave worship and thereby condemned themselves in this life and the next."

The people watched in silence as Ixiltical pointed his knife toward the totems.

"The Lord of the Sands is not one to share the spoils of war. The usurping queen is dead along with her whelps. Today, from out of your midst, the Lords of the Desert will ordain a new king over the Ancagua."

At this mention of her mother Leokita sucked in her breath and Gila turned to look at her. There were tears in the corners of the girl's eyes, but her mouth was turned down, her teeth nearly chattering with rage. The High Mage was speaking again.

"Soon one of you, yes, even you who are gathered here today, will be called forth for anointing."

He turned to address the door.

"But first this abomination must be felled."

Ixiltical gestured to Bal, who forced the prisoner down onto his knees. The High Mage looked up into the sky above the door and raised his ritual knife.

"Come, Teulanic!" he cried. "Free your people!"

The sun caught the knife's blade and set it shining like a bar of flame. For a moment everything was perfectly balanced—past, present and future all burning on the tip of a needle. The High Mage opened his mouth to utter the words of an immense and ancient spell. But he was cut off by a voice from the shadow of the totems.

The voice of a girl.

Chapter Forty-Four

CANOWIC

. . .

Stop."

Canowic's command rang in the air as she stepped from behind the rock. Ixiltical stared down at her from the top of the mound with a look of incredulity on his face. His features quickly contorted with hate, but Canowic had seen through him. He did not know all things or foresee every eventuality. He had not anticipated her return.

Within moments a group of warriors surrounded them. The men were wary of Gila, who bared her teeth and snarled ominously. They leveled their spears, keeping a healthy distance between themselves and the wolf. There was nowhere to run.

"You are just in time," Ixiltical called out. "In a moment this pitiful shrine will be shattered, and everything your master gave his life for will be proven a lie."

Canowic did not respond. She was looking at the crowd ringing the grove. Ixiltical followed her gaze.

"Your people!" he crowed.

Canowic wondered at how he seemed to understand the ambivalence she felt in that moment. In the faces of the throng she saw raw fear and apathy, dread of the imminent crowding out all else. Maybe there was more in their hearts, but she did not have time to find out. All she knew in the moment was that no one in that crowd loved her.

"Your master thought he could save them," the mage shouted. "But they have made their choice. Now Teulanic has claimed them as his own."

The man about to be sacrificed was weeping. Canowic took a step toward the mound, still having said nothing more. The warriors closed on her, pointing their spears at her chest, but she was unafraid. She felt something moving within her, buoying her heart as she looked at the door. She kept walking.

The warriors looked over their shoulders at the High Mage, unsure what to do. Ixiltical nodded and two of them closed on Canowic. She heard Gila barking somewhere behind her, but she did not shift her gaze from the stones, not even to look at her enemies. When the warriors' hands touched her skin, Canowic felt a surge of light welling within her. The men flung their hands away, gasping in pain as if they had been burned. Ixiltical's eyes ignited.

"Ah!" he exclaimed, strangely delighted. "So you have learned something after all!"

The subordinate magi were still arrayed at the bottom of the mound. When Canowic was ten feet from their hooded picket she stopped and fixed her gaze on Ixiltical. He looked out of place in the midday sun, like a dark creature emerged from its lair to hunt at an unnatural time. Canowic felt his power covering the grove like a viscous film. She pushed her revulsion away.

"Soon the time for shedding innocent blood will be ended," she said.

The crowd remained silent. Were they so afraid? So resigned to their fate?

Ixiltical croaked his dragon laugh. "Innocent? No one here is innocent, including those who will be sacrificed. From the day we first saw the stars that would lead us west across the desert and into this land, we have known the Ancagua for what they are. A bloodthirsty people. They are complicit in their own fate. This is what they wanted. You cannot save them from that which they have freely chosen."

Canowic held the mage's gaze, though doing so felt like gripping a blade. His eyes cut her, willing her to buckle, but something resolute had solidified within her, something strong and brimming with light. She felt its fortifying power quiet the part of her that demanded to know why she should intervene on behalf of these people who had done nothing but reject and persecute her.

"It is not only a question of what they want, but of who you are," Canowic rejoined. "And who I am. I shall not stand by while evil runs rampant. I shall not close my eyes and let the darkness eat the light."

Her words came out loud and clear, piercing the thick air of the grove. Now all false humor fled from Ixiltical's face. His lips twisted with annihilating hate, and the dark skin around his eyes seemed to sag, as if his physical body could not contain his loathing.

"You hold no power over me," Canowic said, "for I do not fear you."

"It does not matter whether you fear me!" the mage spit. "Whatever cheap tricks your master taught you will not avail you now. I claim you as an offering to Teulanic!"

Still grasping his knife, he raised his hands towards Canowic.

"I will show you what your belief has bought you. Your blood will break these stones!"

Two of the lesser magi stepped forward, reaching for Canowic's arms like the warriors before them. She felt the presence that had been building in her burst forth, igniting her fingers like the wicks of ten lamps. The magi hissed and fell back as Canowic started up the slope of the mound.

Ixiltical opened his mouth and uttered a word of pure darkness. A horn of green fire leapt from his hands and sped towards Canowic. She found herself raising a hand and deflecting it easily. Now she was a third of the way up the mound. A violent wind arose, flogging the grove and blasting the deerskin hood from her head. Canowic felt sparks in the air a moment before a bolt of lighting sheared the sky and plunged into the ground directly in front of her, sending up a great fountain of earth. She staggered but did not fall, shielded from the worst of the shock wave by an invisible cocoon.

Now she was only a dozen paces from the High Mage. He closed his eyes, held out his hands as if to receive a stream of water, and roared like a wild beast. A wave of sulfurous fire exploded downslope, engulfing Canowic in brimstone and lapping flame. Yet somehow, when the wave had passed, she found herself still standing, her cloak singed but her face unharmed and shining with light.

The wall of fire continued into the grove, igniting many of the trees. As flaming leaves and cinders rained down from above, the people began to scatter, trampling one another in their haste to escape. The chaos barely registered in Canowic's ears. She continued climbing until she reached the High Mage and stopped before him.

Ixiltical's eyes were churning whirlpools. Even now there was no fear in them, only hatred gilded with malevolent curiosity. In that moment Canowic knew the power inside her was strong enough to defeat him. It was this same power that had scarred Yengwa's face and later birthed the phoenix on the night she rescued Leokita. The master had been right. She was but a vessel.

Somewhere in the distance thunder cracked, boulders rumbling down the slopes of heaven. Canowic's eyes were drawn beyond Ixiltical, back to the stones. Her eyes traced the runes carved into them. What golden fields lay beyond the doorway's lintel? She had only to step through and find out. She looked at the High Mage again. She could overcome him, best his fire with greater fire. But there was another way. She felt the knowledge suddenly prick her, piercing her heart like a thorn.

The mage's lips twitched and a vein bulged in his forehead. Sweat stood out on his face. He said something in a tongue Canowic did not understand. She raised her hands and he flinched. But no fire came forth. No devouring sword. Instead, she widened her arms like a supplicant, opening herself.

"Strike true," she said.

For a moment Ixiltical stared at her, not comprehending. Then he lunged forward. His knife passed through her chest and came out her back. Canowic looked down at the blade, blood already starting to leak from her mouth. She heard Leokita scream her name but the sound was dim, as if coming through a thick curtain. The High Mage ruthlessly pulled his knife out as Canowic sank to her knees.

Looking up she saw Ixiltical towering over her, his eyes flooded with malice. He raised his knife high for the killing stroke. And then something shifted. The High Mage's eyes widened and his arm stiffened. At the base of the mound the other magi began turning in hasty circles, swatting at themselves as if beset by hornets. Ixiltical's eyes rolled back in his head. His skin began to smoke. Moments later it started peeling off in layers, great strips falling to the ground like pieces of dead bark. An inhuman scream tore from his mouth as he clawed the air. He tripped and fell, tumbling down the mound toward his brethren whose robes were bursting into flame, white light illumining their skulls as they were undone by a power greater than any they had ever availed themselves of.

. . .

Canowic could feel the sun through her eyelids. She kept them closed for a long time, letting the warmth wash over her like the memory of a dream she could not recall but which comforted her nonetheless. She was lying on something soft. Someone was saying her name. She opened her eyes and found Leokita kneeling beside her.

"Get up," Leokita begged. There were tears on her cheeks.

Gila stood next to her sister, her limpid green eyes full of terrible knowledge. Canowic only smiled. She could feel the drying blood on her chin crack as she did. Behind Leokita the stones towered in the sun, their cool shadows angling away down the back of the mound. A bee droned lazily through the small white flowers dotting the grass. Bits of ash from the burning trees still floated through the air. Canowic tried to rise and failed, sinking back onto the grass with a wet laugh. She could hear voices.

Most of the crowd had run when the grove caught fire but a handful remained, including several of the captives who had been consigned to death. Four or five of these were huddled together now, whispering. Soon one of them broke off and began walking up the mound. It was the tattooed thief Ixiltical had been about to sacrifice. Canowic raised a hand toward him. He flinched and stopped, but she was only pointing.

"You are free," she said, gesturing weakly towards the doorway. The man looked at the stones, confused. The blood was hot and bitter in her mouth.

"Lie back," Leokita said, a tremor in her voice. "Just rest now."

Canowic obeyed, but kept her eyes on the man. He looked down at the other prisoners, seeking guidance. One of them called to him in a musical tongue. Canowic tried to point to the door again, but her arm was too heavy. She managed to turn her head and find Gila.

"Old friend," she said softly. "Faithful friend."

Gila put her muzzle against Canowic's cheek and let out a low, mournful sound. Canowic reached up and took hold of the fur at the nape of her neck. She closed her eyes and breathed deeply. When she opened them again the man with the stars on his feet stood directly in front of the door, looking over at her with a mixture of concern and uncertainty. Leokita wept openly, holding Canowic's hand in both of her own. Canowic nodded at the man and tried to motion for him to step forward, but her strength was nearly gone.

The man looked back at his companions a final time and murmured something in their beautiful tongue. Then he stepped underneath the lintel and vanished momentarily behind the door's near pillar. Canowic drew a ragged breath and waited for him to reappear on the other side. She exhaled slowly and drew another painful breath. Then another. Then still another, and now her heart began to swell with wonder, and still the man had not reappeared. The sky was bright above her, the warmth of the sun perfect on her cheeks. A light breeze tousled her hair. She let her head fall back and closed her eyes, one hand still full of Gila's fur. Something inside of her was dimming. She felt her wick flickering gently as she listened for a sound from the man who had passed through the door, for his shout of exclamation or the whisper of his feet in the grass. But though she strained, nothing came to her ears save silence.

Slowly her hand unclenched from Gila's fur and fell to the grass. Leokita, who had not ceased watching her sister intently, saw something pass across Canowic's face. The stillness spread out around them, a portion of eternity catching in the tops of the trees.

the sight of the wolves' bared teeth. Her wide face was illuminated by the crimson glow of the phoenix stars. The shaman raised a hand to silence the wolves and began walking towards her, retying his breechcloth around his waist as he went. The stranger bowed low at his approach.

"Her majesty Kulkas requests your presence and that of your acolyte in her chamber. She asks that you would come with great speed, returning with me even now."

So soon, the shaman thought. *Scarcely have I returned and already the wheels of fate begin moving.*

"What does the queen require?" he asked in his deep drum voice.

"Alas, my lord," the handmaiden said, sounding genuinely forlorn, "she has given me no further instruction." She looked at the sky as she spoke. The reason for the queen's request was evident enough. And yet if that was the case, why did he feel the prick of a familiar doubt?

· · ·

There had been a handful of times over the years, almost always near dusk, when the shaman had sensed a watching presence near the cave. It was always when Canowic was nearby, plaiting rope beside the fire or playing in the surf with the wolves. It had not been difficult for him to determine where the watcher sat, though she thought herself well hidden. It was always the queen.

She had summoned the shaman and his acolyte to the castle on several occasions, ostensibly to get the shaman's opinion on the princesses' health. She seemed to value his opinion above the king's physicians. Yet no matter what she asked him about, or how clearly he discerned her true concern for her daughters, the shaman sometimes had the sense during these visits that the queen was not fully listening to him. It was not the feeling of being mocked or merely humored. He would not have continued to answer her summons if that had been the case. No, it was something else entirely. She seemed distracted. There was no one else in the room during their meetings besides the princesses, the handmaidens, and Canowic.

For years he had entertained various theories about what was going on, but he had always refused to sate his curiosity through the use of his stone. Then one day in the autumn of Canowic's thirteenth year something had happened. Master and acolyte had been standing in the king's throne room listening to the elders discuss the harvest, when the shaman happened to look over at the queen. A loose piece of hair had fallen across her face and she tucked it behind her ear using only one finger. Though the shaman had never seen her do this, the motion was instantly familiar. He had seen it a thousand times somewhere else. In that moment, understanding had bloomed in him like a rose.

. . .

"As you see, my acolyte is not here," the shaman said, gesturing to the empty cave. "I await her return."

He looked toward the cliff at the end of the beach where a small figure could be seen picking a path down its flank. He left the queen's messenger staring at the sky and stepped into his cave. When he re-emerged his cloak of black feathers was gathered about him like night itself. He looked at the wolves and uttered a phrase in a tongue the handmaiden did not know. The wolves became agitated and started barking. The shaman shook his head and repeated the phrase, but it did not seem to help. The pack began to howl.

Chapter Twenty

SENECWO

. . .

Senecwo was disoriented, falling down into her body out of the oily clouds of a dream so real the world had seemed to be breaking into flame. She sat up too abruptly, her forehead slick with sweat, limbs tangled in the silken sheets. *The palace was catching fire! The babies were next door!*

But... wait. She felt her heart thudding as she struggled to catch her breath. There was nothing but silence coming from the children's room next door.

Only shadows.

Pieces of light danced around the room, mottled liquid shapes sliding across the floor and walls. As Senecwo looked around she saw Wiwoka awake and standing by the door to the balcony. Fear floated in her eyes like ashes from a funeral pyre. The queen stood and walked over to her friend, pulling on her robe as she went. The two of them walked out to the balcony together, and discovered the source of the strange red light.

Within minutes Senecwo dispatched three of her handmaidens.

Their eyes had widened as she named the various oracles they were to bring back with them, but they had not protested. She expected their greatest obstacle would be getting out of the castle. If her suspicions were correct the guards had been instructed to keep them locked in, prisoners on the pretext of safety. Instead, when Senecwo opened the door, steely-eyed and ready to talk her way past anyone, she found the hall empty. The guards had vanished, leaving nothing but the torrid light of the falling stars pouring over the flagstones. It was worse than she had thought.

She sent her handmaidens off with a kiss on the cheek and barred the doors tight behind them before returning to the balcony. A carved screen shielded the balcony from the street below. Great beasts copulated on its wide panels, rolling heavily amidst the wooden waves. Hankasi had commanded the panels be set up soon after their wedding day and ordered his young wife to remain hidden behind them, citing the dangers of the street and the prying eyes of his enemies. She would be shielded from the arrows of assassins and her honor protected at the same time. Senecwo wondered why he bothered pretending to consider her to be anything more than a piece of property, a fetish to be fondled in private and kept hidden from other men.

The screen made her feel even more like a prisoner, its violently mating beasts serving as a constant reminder of the demands her captor made of her. But he was gone now, and for one night at least she would be free. The screen was lighter than she had expected. She slid it aside with ease and stood at the railing, exposed at last to the street and a royal view. The city spread out below her, but she ignored its dark grandeur. Her eyes were fixed on the dragon tails shearing the sky.

The stars were falling in even greater numbers now, burning through the atmosphere in eerie silence. There was nothing to do but wait, and so she stood at the railing for the next several hours, watching the brilliant wakes phosphoresce in the black kettle above her. At last